MARIE ANTOINETTE
DAUPHINE

Marie Antoinette.
Presented to The Comte de Mercy-Argenteau.

Allen & Co. Ph. Sc.

THE GUARDIAN OF MARIE ANTOINETTE

LETTERS FROM THE COMTE DE MERCY-
ARGENTEAU, AUSTRIAN AMBASSADOR
TO THE COURT OF VERSAILLES, TO
MARIE THÉRÈSE, EMPRESS OF AUSTRIA
1770—1780

BY

LILLIAN C. SMYTHE

ILLUSTRATED WITH NUMEROUS PORTRAITS,
PHOTOGRAPHS, FACSIMILE LETTERS, ETC.

VOLUME I

WILDSIDE PRESS

PRINTED IN GREAT BRITAIN.

Dedicated

TO

THE COMTESSE DE MERCY-ARGENTEAU

PRINCESSE DE MONTGLYON

PREFACE

THE letters of the Comte de Mercy-Argenteau
are well known to French and Austrian students
of history, as the majority of them have been published
by the Keeper of the Austrian Imperial Archives.
But to readers in this country they will present much
that is new and interesting.

The relative values of the coins mentioned in the
accounts have given much trouble to define, as there
is no authoritative work on the subject ; and opinions
differ.   This ambiguity is disturbing, as without a clear
comprehension of the relative values of these coins
the very interesting details of Marie Antoinette's
expenditure fail to convey much information.   I
have, therefore, embodied in Appendix I. the results
of the investigations of friends—Mr. Archibald Con-
stable, Mr. Philip Somers-Cocks, and the Vicomte
de Manneville—who have kindly aided me, and to
whom I here express my thanks for their valuable
help.

Another point is the Stewart descent of Louis;
and as the intermarriages between the Bourbons and
Stewarts are always of interest, I have traced the
descent of Louis XVI., by the help of Mr. Charles
Stewart, Colonel Duncan Stewart, and Mr. J. K.
Stewart of the Stewart Society, Edinburgh. An
account of the double line of Stewart blood in
Louis XVI. will be found in Appendix II.

The illustrations must be mentioned with special
reference to the beautiful portraits that, presented
by their Imperial and Royal owners to the Comte
Florimond de Mercy-Argenteau, are still among the
treasures of the family, and in the possession of
the present Comtesse de Mercy-Argenteau. They
have never before been reproduced; and the permission given me to include them in my book
is one for which I make grateful acknowledgment
to the Comtesse de Mercy-Argenteau. The very
charming portrait of Marie Antoinette, with her
bright, innocent child-face; that of Louis XVI., a
fine work of art; the shrewd, humorous face of the
old Empress Marie Thérèse and its contrast, that of
her son the Emperor Joseph II.; the refined, thoughtful, brilliant diplomatist, Comte Florimond de Mercy-
Argenteau, are all of the greatest historical as well as
artistic value. The old picture that gives the Château
d'Argenteau as it existed before the army of Louis XIV.
destroyed its fortifications, hangs still in that part or

the ancient barracks which is the *château* of to-day. The charters that are reproduced include the Letters Patent, conferring the Governorship of the Netherlands upon the Comte de Mercy-Argenteau, signed by Leopold II. of Austria ; and also the very interesting document that empowers the Comte de Mercy-Argenteau, as Minister Plenipotentiary, to conclude a treaty of commerce with the United States. This charter, which is of special interest to American readers, forms Appendix III.

Its translation has given rise to many questions, owing to the difficulty of identifying the places indicated in the Latin original. My very grateful thanks are due to Professor Larpent and to Mr. Ashton-Cross for their invaluable assistance.

LILLIAN C. SMYTHE.

March, 1902.

CONTENTS

VOL. I

Contents

Contents

PEDIGREES.

LIST OF ILLUSTRATIONS

VOL. I

xvi   # List of Illustrations

THE GUARDIAN OF
MARIE ANTOINETTE

CHAPTER I

Secret Correspondence—Sealed Letters and *Lettres de Cachet*—The House of Mercy-Argenteau

IT is for some to admire the pretty historical puppets that play their parts and fill their stage, and for others to look behind for the string-pullers. No prettier period of history exists than that which lies between the years 1770 and 1780, nor one more artificial ; and no stage could better subserve their acting than the Court of Versailles. But the real interest of the time lies in observing the strings to whose pulling danced all the princes of Europe till they wound themselves in that network of intrigue which it took a revolution to cut. Many men and more women had their hands on the strings, but few kept them there ; for the appearance of being guided was more annoying than the knowledge of betrayal, and when Catherine of Russia called the Duc de Choiseul *le cocher de l'Europe*, the phrase worked his exile more effectually than did the hatred of the Du Barry.

One man alone kept his power for all and more than all that time, and he kept it because his diplomacy was so consummate that its full influence was never known during his lifetime ; what was not suspected by his contemporaries remains for us to see, for time has shown the dry bones of history, and we have made the skeleton articulate. This was Florimond, Comte de Mercy-Argenteau, who was Austrian Ambassador to the Court of Versailles, and remained there from 1766 till 1790—to the world an acute diplomatist : to the Empress of Austria her privately appointed guardian of Marie Antoinette's manners, mind, and morals : to Madame Elizabeth (the young sister of the Dauphin), who spoke her mind quite frankly, always "*le vieux renard.*"

It is in the second of these capacities that he most interests us, for he fulfilled his guardianship with the utmost exactitude, watching over the little Dauphine with all the care that an anxious mother—certain that her daughter was going into the most immoral of Courts and extremely uncertain as to her capacity for shining in it—could enjoin. The Comte de Mercy-Argenteau had a difficult part to play. He had to retain the confidence of Louis XV.—no easy matter ; he had to be on friendly terms with all the various cliques at Court, each at bitterest enmity with all the others ; he had to advise, watch over, and warn Marie Antoinette, see to her expenditure, her education, her manners, her Court etiquette, her daily exercise, her clothes, and even—in so old and trusted a friend it may be pardoned—her underclothes. We find him much concerned about her figure, because she would not wear a *corps de baleines* ; he had to acquaint her mother with these and all other small details of Court life, with the movements in politics and the intrigues that seethed round the little child-figure of the Dauphine.

He had to carry on this correspondence with the Empress of Austria by daily reports for the ten years that ended with her death in 1780; and he had to do it in inviolable secrecy at a time when the easiest method of publishing any matter was to post it. The extent of this system of espionage is almost incredible. *All* letters entrusted to the post were opened, read, and their contents utilised before the addressees could receive them. By his spies Louis XV. maintained touch with every personage of importance in Europe; obtaining extracts from their correspondence, he was enabled to forestall and defeat their intentions. But the natural development of this system was that the Court of Vienna adopted Louis's own tactics, read his own " secret " correspondence, which he did not communicate even to his own ministers, and was as well acquainted with his " secret " cipher as if it had made no pretensions to this mystery.

Yet neither Louis nor any of the spies in his royal pay had any inkling of the long series of letters passing between Mercy-Argenteau and Marie Thérèse,

which commenced soon after the marriage of Marie
Antoinette and the Dauphin, and closed only with the
death of the aged Empress in 1780. The extreme
confidence that Marie Thérèse reposed in the Comte
de Mercy-Argenteau and her reliance upon his judgment are shown throughout the letters, in which
the Empress discusses with him vital questions that
affect her government and that of France, the policies
of all Europe and their united means of confronting
them ; but more interesting than the weaving of
political intrigues are the small details of Marie
Antoinette's daily life that are laid before us, which
put the breath of life into the pictured personages
of that time.

The Comte de Mercy-Argenteau wrote almost daily ;
his labours extended over many years ; and yet this
long-continued correspondence was unsuspected because
it was sent entirely by special and trusted couriers,
only the ordinary letters being sent by that vehicle
of transmission of news, the post, the tapping of which
was such a matter of course that in the national
archives were preserved the letters of Louis XVI. to his
Minister of Foreign Affairs, M. de Vergennes, which
the young King commenced by stating that he enclosed him *les interceptions ordinaires*. The letters of
the long correspondence between Marie Thérèse and
Mercy-Argenteau have been published by M. le
Chevalier Alfred d'Arneth, Director of the Imperial
Archives of Austria, where they have been preserved,
in three ponderous tomes, to which the reader, intent

THE ANCIENT CHÂTEAU D'ARGENTEAU.

(*From a contemporary painting now at the Château d'Argenteau.*)

[*Page* 5

on deeper excavations in their mines than those of this book, is referred.

Comte Florimond de Mercy-Argenteau, the trusted friend of Marie Thérèse, the guardian of Marie Antoinette, was a link in a long chain of famous men, the line of which reaches back for over eight hundred years. The first charter of the family of Argenteau, dated 1070, is signed by Henri IV., King of the Romans ; but as it confirms yet earlier rights granted by his father, the Emperor Henri III., it does not limit the date at which commenced the connection of the Seigneurs d'Argenteau with their old rock castle over-looking the Meuse, which served as a stronghold throughout the centuries, and was defended more or less successfully by the warlike ancestors of Count Florimond. It had its times of splendour, and also of evil fate ; it was burnt by the Liegeois in 1347, taken by the troops of the Prince of Orange Nassau, besieged and taken by the Spanish troops of Philip II., and taken, for the last time, by Louis XIV., who destroyed its fortifications so effectually that great trees grow on the ruined ramparts, and the rock is still black with his powder. But the barracks were left standing and serve to this day as the château of the living representative of the House of Mercy-Argenteau, who is Comtesse de Mercy-Argenteau and Princesse de Montglyon in her own right, and Duchesse d'Avaray by her marriage.

The history, therefore, of the ancient family of Argenteau is interwoven with that of the castle on the great rock, the cradle of the race, and throughout these hundreds of years the names of the famous men of the race are connected with their old castle; and even the most cosmopolitan of the long line, the Comte Florimond of these letters, writes his thankfulness, even in the throes of the Revolution, that his lands of Argenteau were saved from devastation.   These ancestors of Argenteau were all born fighters, and held their sovereign rights by their sword, for they were seigneurs of *terres libres*, holding their land direct from the Emperor, and subject to no other.

There was Renaud I. in 1235, who first bore the gold cross on the azure field—still the arms of Argenteau—and his son Henri I., the crusader ; Renaud III. in 1347, in whose reign came the first destruction of the castle ; Guillaume I. in 1417, to whom was given the title of the Prince de Montglion, and the privilege of possessing his own mint and coining gold ducats stamped with his head on the obverse and coat-of-arms on the reverse ; Jacques I. in 1451, Renaud V. and his son Jacques II., whose lives were filled with wars ; and Jean II. in 1566, whose greatest act was that of signing the famous petition to the Duchess of Parma against the religious persecutions of Philip II., and who risked in consequence life and lands.   Then after a broken and troublous interval came Charles Antoine, the adopted son of the Maréchal de Mercy and the first to bear the name of de Mercy-Argenteau, whose wife, Henriette de Rouvroy, was the descendant of Jean de Rouvroy, friend in the crusades of Godefroy de Bouillon ; and these two were the father and mother of Comte Florimond de Mercy-Argenteau, Vicomte de Looz, Comte de Noville, Baron de Moermael, Knight of the Golden Fleece, etc., etc.

It was to this Comte Florimond de Mercy-Argenteau, Ambassador to the French Court, that the guardianship of Marie Antoinette was confided upon her marriage with the Dauphin. The anxiety of Marie Thérèse for her young daughter's future was justified. Marie Antoinette at the time of her marriage was only fourteen and a half years old, she was simply a child, scarcely knowing how to write, reading very little, speaking French incorrectly, playing the harpsichord with as much mastery as is usual in unwilling little girls of fourteen (even if they had played with Weber and met Mozart) ; thin, badly formed, badly dressed, and sufficiently careless with regard to such matters as the brushing of her teeth that several of the letters of Marie Thérèse to the little Dauphine are taken up with maternal instructions for her better education in these things.

She was childishly idle, pleasure-loving, fond of babies and dogs, of riding donkeys and of playing games, swayed by a kind word, and heedless of ceremony. She was truthful, sincere, and proudly honest,—virtues that handicapped her even more heavily than her failings in her endeavours to win the liking of the corrupt Court of France. The upright, lonely little child Princess is a strange figure in the history of that Court, surrounded by eager and malicious enemies, married to a heavy, half-dazed youth, scarcely more than an imbecile (who needed seven years of patience and the straight counsels of his brother-in-law, Joseph II., before he awoke to the fact that he was a husband), cut off even from corresponding with her own family, and balanced between her duty of being pleasing to the unspeakable Louis XV.—with Madame du Barry barring her approach to that fountain of all honour in France—and her desire to live in friendliness with those narrow, withered old souls, " Mesdames."

In all her difficulties she had but one real friend and counsellor near her, the Comte de Mercy-Argenteau, and to his faithful guardianship was due much of the success that crowned her later as Queen of France. His guiding hand might perhaps have averted the most terrible of royal shipwrecks, the terror of which he foresaw, but at the very time of danger to his beloved Queen Marie Antoinette the apparently even greater danger to the Imperial House of Austria, from the menacing Netherlands, forced the Emperor Leopold to withdraw the Comte de Mercy-Argenteau from Paris and entrust him with the important Governorship of the Austrian Netherlands. He was appointed Minister Plenipotentiary, with powers extended beyond even those of Governor-General ; and his letters patent, signed by the Emperor, made out to *notre cousin le Comte Florimond de Mercy-*

Argenteau, gave him practically unlimited power over the Low Countries, *faire par soi-même tout ce qui conviendrait à notre royal service*. Keenly alive to the first threatenings of the Revolution, fully realising the approaching storm that swept over Europe and blotted out in blood the royalty of France, he yet obeyed the call of Austria and flung himself into the pacification of the Netherlands, driven into revolt by the tempestuous reforms of Joseph II.

But though absent from France, his warnings of the imminent danger to his beloved Queen Marie Antoinette did not cease ; he it was who approached Mirabeau with the hope of reattaching him to the royal cause, and his influence prevailed upon the King and Queen (at first adverse to Mirabeau) to adopt this same course. But Mirabeau died too soon ("*La reine est le seul homme que le roi ait près de lui*"), Mercy-Argenteau was far away and could not avert the approaching ruin ; and as the Revolution broke over France, the aged statesman's whole thoughts were bent on saving the lives of the unfortunate royal prisoners from the fury of the revolutionaries.

His letters, written in the years of 1792-3, are still in existence in the possession of the present Comtesse de Mercy-Argenteau, and breathe through their faded ink stained paper and tremulous, almost illegible writing, the indomitable spirit which, stronger than the frail old body, swept the aged Comte across Europe, stirring up the nations as he passed, that their armies might possibly save alive the poor Queen and her children. He writes of his hopes of Spain ; of the part that the Swiss cantons will take ; he stirs up the Duke of Brunswick to rapid (but futile) action ; he rouses Prussia, and the King sends twelve thousand men at his appeal ; England is neutral but awaking slowly : "*L'Angleterre arme, elle paraît reconnaître la profondeur du mal présent et l'urgence du remède, elle tarde à se prononcer, mais il paraît infallible qu'elle se decidera très incessamment ; ses apprêts sont immenses : d'après les nouvelles publiques la guerre est bien resolue en Angleterre.*" Hanover is moved to send four thousand men ; the Elector Palatine is urged to renounce neutrality. Mercy-Argenteau crosses the Continent in the depth of winter, his coach dragged through the deep snow by many horses, but despite despairing endeavour writes : "*Tout va mal, mais très mal, même honteusement mal,*" as his efforts are frustrated by folly and worse.

The French emigrant ladies at Spa, who had competed for the favours of Madame du Barry, refused to recognise or associate with Madame de Ritz, Comtesse de Lichtenau, the lady who governed King Frederick William of Prussia ; and their ostentatious virtue so irritated the King that he withdrew his troops. Quarrels broke out between the other Powers and their respective generals, which even the diplomacy of Mercy-Argenteau could not smooth. Then came the horror of the execution of King Louis ; and the one hope for the life of Marie Antoinette lay in the slowly awakening indignation of England with her great forces and resistless power. To win this aid de Mercy-Argenteau resolved to hasten himself to London and rouse public feeling there ; with the despairing knowledge in his heart that he was playing his last card for the life of Marie Antoinette.

But the blow fell before England was stirred, and though it is said that the whole nobility of England, with the one exception of Lord Grey, went into mourning for the royal victims, their grief was too late ; and the only thing left for Mercy-Argenteau to do in England was to raise subsidies in London for the preparation of a coalition against France. He was entrusted with that mission by his Government, embarked at Helvoetsluys in August 1794, had a stormy and terrible crossing, arrived in London ill and worn out with the dread of what the future would bring to Europe, and died, without seeing any one, on 26 August, 1794, at the age of seventy-two.

CHAPTER II

The Child Dauphine—*La petite rousse*—The Suppers
at St. Hubert

THE marriage-day of Marie Antoinette was on
16 May, 1770, and was the culmination of
years of the policy of Marie Thérèse, who, recognising
that the Bourbons were the most ancient enemies of
Austria, sought by this alliance to give check to
Prussia. To the ever-encroaching Frederick II. she
had been forced to give up Silesia and the Comté de
Glatz; but with her daughter as future Queen of
France she held Prussia safe, and, notwithstanding
maternal alarms, was probably the personage rendered
happiest by the marriage. No one else rejoiced;
the half-alive Dauphin was quite indifferent, the Du
Barry was angry and suspicious, "Mesdames" the
aunts were jealous and prepared to be insolent to
"the Austrian," and Louis XV. was doubtful whether
it would not have been wiser if he himself had
married instead.

But Marie Thérèse was reaping the reward of ceaseless work for twenty years; from 1750 she had
striven for this, and France might have had the
choice of any of her series of daughters during that
time. To attain this alliance she had sought the

friendship of Madame de Pompadour with the gift of her own miniature set in Brazilian diamonds; to maintain it she directed her daughter to seek that of Madame du Barry. When the proof of her mother's intercourse with Madame de Pompadour, the miniature with the inscription, was presented to Marie Antoinette after the sale of the Marquis de Marigny's effects, she said: " Hide quickly this proof of my mother's policy. Perhaps I owe to it the honour of being Queen of France, but really sovereigns are sometimes forced to stoop too low " (*à trop de bassesses*).

The policy of Marie Thérèse, though it crept through tortuous paths, arrived at its goal; and Marie Antoinette was destined soon after her birth in 1755 (the year of the great earthquakes) to cement the alliance; and was brought up accordingly. She had French modistes and *couturières*, French fashion books given her to study by Marie Thérèse, and a French hairdresser; and Ducreux, the French artist, came to Vienna in February 1769 to paint the portrait of the future Dauphine, then just over thirteen years old, for Louis XV. Rehearsals of the etiquette at Versailles were arranged, by the forethought of the Comte de Mercy-Argenteau, at Vienna, receptions, called at Versailles *le jeu de la reine*, wherein the most minute details of etiquette were rigorously observed, even playing the tedious game *Cavagnol*, of which Voltaire said: "*Et l'ennui vint à pas comptés. S'asseoir entre des Majestés, à la table de Cavagnol.*"

As the time of the wedding approached there was keen interest among the ladies of Paris to hear what was thought of their future Queen; and de Rohan, who was considered an experienced judge, was sent as an Ambassador to Vienna. This was the Cardinal of the *collier* episode, and he duly fulfilled his mission of inspection and wrote that the Archduchess "is of a height proportioned to her age, such as is seen in a young person not yet fully formed. . . . Her hair is of a pure and clear blonde, *qui n'a pas le moindre reflet de hasardé*; it grows well, the seven points being visible, and they dress it according to the prevailing mode, which may appear to you to make her forehead look rather unfurnished. This is, I suppose, in accordance with the wishes of her governess, who liked her to appear to have a high forehead and tied her brows with a woollen band that has dragged out the hair. . . . The form of her face is a perfect oval . . . the eyebrows as well furnished as a blonde can have, and a shade darker than her hair, the eyelashes of a charming length. . . . She has a little mouth, scarlet as a cherry, the lips are thick, particularly the lower one, which is, one knows, the distinctive trace of the House of Burgundy. . . . The fineness of her skin is marvellous, and its whiteness astonishing, and she has natural colour well placed, which loses a good deal by being covered with rouge that is of no use. . . . Her natural dignity is softened by her sweetness, also natural, and by the simplicity of her education."

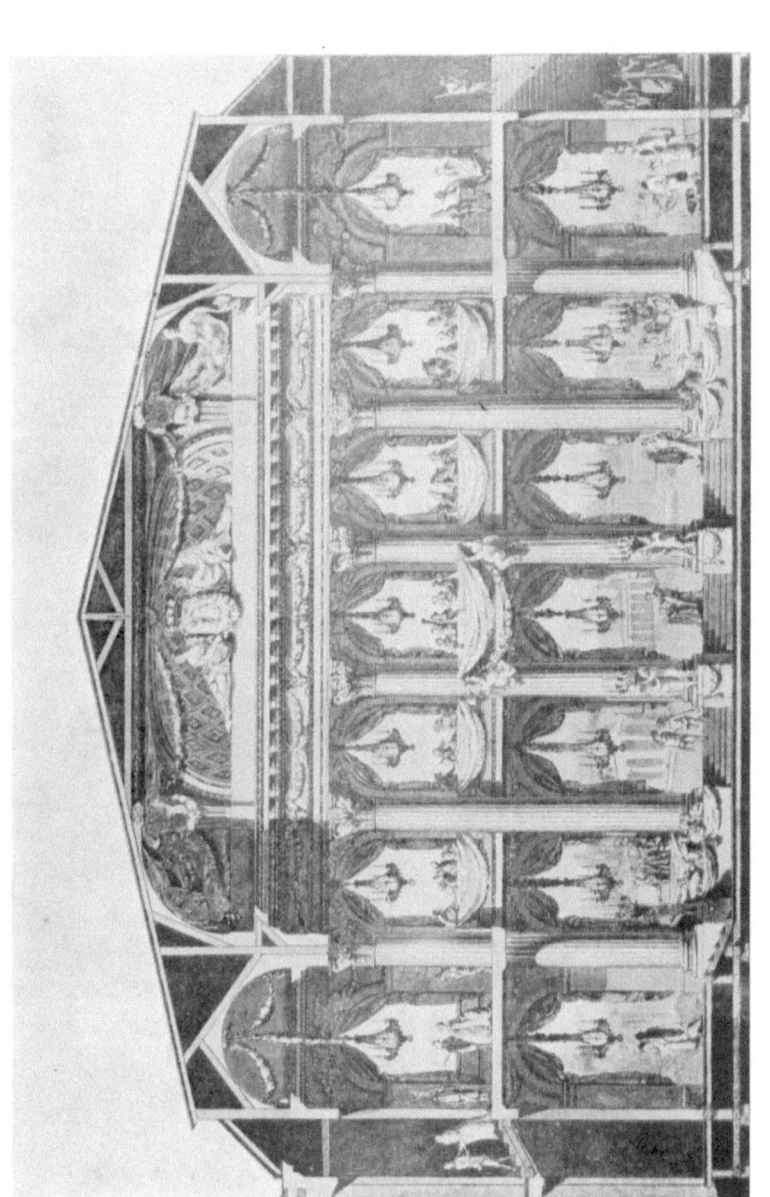

FÊTE GIVEN BY THE COMTE DE MERCY-ARGENTEAU,

On the occasion of the Marriage of Marie Antoinette and the Dauphin.

(*From the original drawing at the Château d'Argenteau.*)

[*Page* 15.

Madame du Barry says : " I see nothing attractive in red hair, thick lips, sandy complexion, and eyes without eyelashes. Had she who is thus beautiful not sprung from the House of Austria, such attractions would never have been the subject of admiration ; " and further mentions her as *la petite rousse*. But this feeling was very natural on the part of Madame du Barry.

Louis XV. was favourably impressed, gave to Marie Antoinette all the diamonds and pearls of the late Dauphine, who had died three years before, and in addition the famous pearl necklace left as an heirloom by Anne of Austria, mother of Louis XIV., to the queens and dauphines of France, and of which the smallest pearl was as large as a filbert. But he qualified this affection for the wife of his grandson by insisting she should have Madame du Barry at her table at supper that night, she having prevailed upon the *lâche amour* to ask of Marie Antoinette what she could not refuse.

The little Dauphine had a cheerless entry into her future Court. There were to be ceremonies at Versailles, but the fountains did not play as they were out of repair, and the basins were dry, the canal dirty and full of mud, the statues broken and lying on the ground, the streets were not lighted, no lamps nor lanterns were there, and all was dark —no music, no food, and no welcome.

Still this negligence was better than the dreadful scenes that marked the first public entertainment.

The Champs Elysées were not then planted, nor the Bridge Louis XVI. built, nor the Quai des Tuileries constructed, and the street from the Porte St. Honoré was not completed, but lay with half-demolished houses and deep ditches blocking its course.

Down this dark and dangerous place the multitudes poured to see the *feu d'artifice* in the Place Louis XV. There was an accident with the fire, a panic, deaths and injuries to more than four thousand persons, and instead of the Dauphine and Mesdames seeing an entertainment, the whole of the next day was occupied in removing the heaped corpses from the Place Louis XV. and the Rue Royale. The first news to be sent to the Austrian home was that of a horror-striking catastrophe.

30 May, 1770.

The correspondence that commenced immediately between the three personages of interest, Marie Thérèse, Marie Antoinette, and de Mercy-Argenteau, opens with a letter from the Empress to her daughter. It is dated 21 April, 1770, and was thus intended to be a sort of manual of maxims for the perpetual use of the Dauphine ; they are an interesting mixture of advice as to serving God and Mammon. She enjoins a reverence in passing a church—if others are accustomed to do so.

" In the churches remember all eyes will be upon you . . . so remain as long as possible on your knees, to give a good example." " Do not permit yourself any contortion [in praying]; it might savour of hypocrisy—above all to be avoided in that country." " Listen to

FÊTE GIVEN BY THE COMTE DE MERCY-ARGENTEAU,

On the occasion of the marriage of Marie Antoinette and the Dauphin.

(*From the original drawing at the Château d'Argenteau*)

[*Page* 16.

no one if you wish to be happy." " Have no curiosity ;
it is on this point that I fear for you." " Have no
familiarity with inferiors." " Reply agreeably to all
the world, with grace and dignity ; you can if you
wish." These are excellent maternal hints, and Marie
Thérèse marks her wish that the little Dauphine should
become entirely a Frenchwoman by telling her she had
better not write to any of her family except to
her brother, Joseph II., her uncle and aunt, Prince
Charles and Princess Charlotte of Lorraine, and Prince
Albert (who had married her elder sister, Marie
Christine). She adds : " The Queen of Naples will
wish you to write to her. I do not see any objection."

The Queen in question was her daughter Marie
Caroline, who had married the King of Naples in 1768,
and was as great a trouble to her mother as another
daughter, Marie Amélie, Duchess of Parma. The
Duchess of Parma had heard that to govern it was
necessary to have knowledge of men. She took that
so literally that she sought to know them all, had her
bodyguard to sit at play with the princes, and her
ushers and valets to dance at the balls. The Queen
of Naples, on the other hand, wished to rule without
any men at all, and defied her minister, Tanucci.

Marie Thérèse evidently thought that neither sister's
correspondence was likely to benefit Marie **24 May,**
Antoinette. On May 24 Marie Thérèse **1770.**
wrote to Mercy-Argenteau giving him full description
of the way she wished their private correspondence
carried on. The letters were to be sent by private

courier, under cover, to the Baron Nenÿ, who was chief confidential secretary to the Empress, and handed them unopened to her Majesty. Mercy was to send unimportant communications at regular intervals, which could be read aloud if need be.

Mercy begins his confidential despatches on 15 June, just about a month after the marriage, and promises to send a daily diary when he was at Fontainebleau or Compiègne, as there he would be with the Court all the time ; but with the Court at Versailles or Marly he could not do it so readily, as only the Ambassadors representing the Courts of the Bourbon family (Spain, Naples, Parma) were allowed there.   He mentions an interview that the Comtesse de Noailles had with the King, when the Duc de la Vauguyon had already insinuated that the little Dauphine had shown a lack of enthusiasm in regard to accompanying the old King on his weekly journeys to some country house, with the object of irritating the monarch by suggesting a childish slight.   The Comtesse de Noailles reassured his Majesty, who then turned his wrath on to the Dauphin, and said that he was extremely *timide et sauvage*, and not a man as others were.

This was the first of many acts of malice from the Duc de la Vauguyon, who formed an anti-Austrian clique against the Dauphine, listened at her keyhole whenever the Dauphin visited her (where he was once discovered, planted there, listening, to her vast indignation), read her letters, and even tore pages out

(margin note:) Paris, 15 June, 1770.

of her copy-books to study and imitate her hand-writing. When he died, Louis XV. dismissed his memory with the epitaph, "Well! there is one intriguer the less for the next vacant post."

Mercy continues that he had had to scold the Dauphine for neglecting her lessons ; she had promised to read daily, the Abbé de Vermond was there for the purpose of her instruction, and her idleness was giving opportunities to her enemies. The result of his lecture was that the poor, contrite little Dauphine, much embarrassed, said she would begin reading that very day, and did so that afternoon. She told Mercy that she liked the Dauphin, whose timidity and coldness were due to his bringing-up ; but he seemed to be of good character, and she thought he was afraid of the Duc de la Vauguyon ; but although she had put out many little feelers to find his opinion of people around him, he was so reserved she could never get a word out of him. Others were anxious to extract opinions from the silent Dauphin, and among them Madame Adélaïde, the eldest daughter of the old King, who asked him (says Mercy) his opinion of his wife, but only extracted " *qu'il en était bien content.*"

But he did not show even that tepid affection to his wife.

Mercy writes that the Dauphine must learn more outward control—she showed her feelings at table or when playing at the wearisome *Cavagnol*—a game with little pictures in five cases, figures and numbers—which apparently bored hardened players,

much more so the lively little Marie Antoinette;
that she makes jokes upon people whom she considers
ludicrous, and puts enough salt in her remarks to
make them dangerous; but "her chief fault is her
extreme repugnance to reading." Mercy mentions
that Madame du Barry had thought fit to pay her
court to the Dauphine, who received her one morning
without affectation, and there was no incident.

The maternal injunctions as to the policy of civil
endurance of the du Barry bore fruit, and
Marie Antoinette wrote to her mother on
9 July, 1770: "I wrote yesterday for the first time
to the King, and was in a great fright, knowing
Madame du Barry reads everything, but you may
feel sure I shall make no mistake for or against
her"—very diplomatic for a child of fourteen.

Another letter of Marie Antoinette's, of 12 July,
says: "Our journey to Choisy was delayed
a day, as my husband had a feverish cold,
but he slept for twelve and a half hours
straight off and found himself much better." Choisy
life was very tiring to the little Dauphine: "We are
away from home from one o'clock, when we dine,
till one at night, which wearies me very much, for
after dinner we play for six hours, then go to some
entertainment which lasts till half-past nine, then
supper, and play again till one or even half-past.
But the King, seeing last night that I was exhausted,
very kindly sent me home at eleven, which was
delightful, and I slept well till half-past ten, although

[margin note: 9 July, 1770.]

[margin note: Choisy, 12 July, 1770.]

alone, my husband coming home and going to bed immediately before supper, in his own room."

She tells her mother the usual routine of her day : " I rise about nine or half-past, dress, and say my morning prayers, then I breakfast and go to see my aunts, where I usually find the King. That lasts till about half-past ten, then at eleven I have my hair dressed, at twelve is my reception, and all may enter who are not common people. I put on my rouge and wash my hands before them all, and then the men go and the ladies remain, and I finish my dressing before them. At midday is mass ; if the King is at Versailles I go with him and my husband and my aunts ; if he is not there I go alone with the Dauphin, but always at the same hour. After mass we dine, just the two of us, before all the company, but that is over in an hour and a half, for we both eat very fast. After that I go to the Dauphin [she tried hard to interest herself in his employments and blacked her pretty hands with his forge], and if he has business I come back to my own rooms ; I read, I write, or I work, for ·I am making a vest for the King, which does not get on a bit, but which I hope, will be finished by the grace of God, after a few years. At three o'clock I go to call upon my aunts, where the King generally comes about that time ; at four o'clock the Abbé [de Vermond] comes to me, at five every day the music master for the harpsichord (*clavecin*), or singing till six. At half-past six I go nearly always to my aunts, when I do not go out for a walk. From seven we play until nine, but when the weather is fine I go for a walk, and then there is no play in my rooms, but in my aunts'. At nine we sup, and when the King is not there my aunts come to sup with me, but when he is there, we go to sup with him and await the King, who usually comes about a quarter to eleven, and when waiting for him I lie down on a large couch and sleep till his arrival; but when he is not there we go to bed at eleven." She ends by begging her very dear mother to pardon the letter being soiled: she had to write it in the only moments not duly marked out for her—those of her toilette—and it had taken her the toilettes of two days to write.

On 14 July, Mercy-Argenteau writes that the Duc de la Vauguyon was intriguing against the happiness of the Dauphine. As he had been averse to the marriage, his plan was now to induce a divorce, and, as a first step towards it, to create ill-feeling between the Dauphin and his wife. An easy means lay to his hand— Madame du Barry. Mercy writes that "The Dauphin had the desire to be admitted to the suppers at St. Hubert [a hunting-lodge at Versailles], where the King entertained his guests after hunting." The Comtesse du Barry was informed of the Dauphin's wish, asked and obtained the King's consent, and from that time the Dauphin had always been in the little hunting expeditions and joined the little hunting

*Paris,
14 July,
1770.*

suppers, where, as Mercy-Argenteau says, "*la décence n'est pas toujours bien scrupuleusement observée.*" But the Mesdames of France, alarmed at the danger to the innocence of the Dauphin, felt it their duty to give him an extremely detailed account of the favourite, and a few striking episodes of her life, which discourse so impressed the Dauphin that from that moment he gave open marks of his aversion.

It seems difficult to realise that the Dauphin's brain was so sluggish that it took the plain speaking of the elderly spinsters, Mesdames, to inform him of the position of Madame du Barry at the Court, when that position was so well recognised that delegates from the *fermiers-généraux* of France came on New Year's Day to present Madame du Barry with a complimentary address as now recognised *maîtresse en titre.*

Mercy continues that at Marly it was a very difficult and delicate situation for the Dauphine, as she had to play lansquenet each night, with the Comtesse du Barry sitting by her side, "but she manages so discreetly that no one can say she has treated the favourite either well or ill." And he imparts to Marie Thérèse his dread lest the influence of Mesdames, "whose intimacy has its advantages, but also many little inconveniences," may make the Dauphine timid with the King—a mistake, as Mercy lays stress on the fact that a very caressing manner is quite certain to captivate him. But "Mesdames love to mix themselves up in little intrigues, and it will be dangerous if they drag in the Dauphine. . . . As for Madame de Noailles, I cannot persuade her to drop her tone of flattery, by which she thinks she is pleasing the Dauphine, whereas she is not succeeding at all.   The Dauphine treats her very well, but has lost all confidence in her, and believes her incapable of giving true counsel."   He adds: "The Dauphine is winning her way to the Dauphin, and is so gay and so graceful that the sombre, reserved, young Prince, impenetrable to all, has yielded to her charm."   Louis had actually confided an opinion—his dislike of Vauguyon!

CHAPTER III

IN July matters reached a climax, and Mercy wrote
a description of what must have been a lively
scene.

During the stay of the Court at Choisy Louis had
some entertainments given in a theatre too **Compiègne,**
small to hold comfortably all the ladies who **4 August,**
followed the Court. On one occasion the **1770.**
ladies of the palace took possession of all the front
seats, and refused to give them up to Madame du Barry
and the two ladies who were content to be of her
suite—the Duchesse de Mirepoix and the Comtesse
de Valentinois. The most piquant remarks were
made by the Comtesse de Gramont, who was the
leader on the other side ; and Madame du Barry and
her two ladies went to the King and laid the matter
before his Majesty, who exiled the Comtesse de
Gramont fifteen leagues from the Court as a punishment. The sensation caused by this edict was
immense. The Comtesse de Gramont was not only
a relative of the Duchesse de Gramont (sister of the

Duc de Choiseul, the *cocher de l'Europe*), but a *dame du palais* of the Dauphine, who was asked to intercede for her.   Mercy's acuteness here was invaluable, and the little Dauphine went to her interview with the King armed with the only point which could be felt by one to whom etiquette had long taken the place of conscience.

Marie Antoinette did not enter into the rights or wrongs of any one ; she regretted that a lady of her Court should have incurred the displeasure of his Majesty ; she did not seek to inquire into his Majesty's motives for punishing her ; but she felt deeply that a person attached to her service should have been exiled without his Majesty first conveying to her the expression of his will.   As Mercy-Argenteau had foreseen, these tactics were successful.   The King, etiquette-stricken, was actually embarrassed, and murmured excuses while laying the blame upon the Duc de la Vrillière, who ought to have informed the Dauphine in due course ; and said, amid many affectionate remarks, that a similar breach of etiquette should not occur again, which greatly gratified Mercy.

The chief danger to the Dauphine lay, however, in the home circle of Marie Antoinette.   Mesdames were the great bugbear of Mercy-Argenteau, who wrote to Marie Thérèse : "These Princesses, although they are quite respectable, have never had the talent of behaving suitably . . . they permit themselves a licence in conversation which is, to say the least of it, indiscreet, sometimes even too broad ; then the Dauphine

repeats these things, and I know for a fact that they
then tell the King."

These curious old sisters had a large influence over
the early life of Marie Antoinette, and incidentally
over the whole Court, for although their withered little
minds were incapable of large intrigue, they had in
full the love of petty inter-meddling. They lived in
the chills of etiquette, the *culte* of their rank ; they had
never married because their *dot* would have been too
expensive. All they thought about were little *chatteries
de boire et de manger* ; all their opinions of others were
regulated by the measure of their own stunted wishes.
Mesdames were between the two millstones of the
Court ; the du Barry and her chosen tool d'Aiguillon
on one side, with de Rohan representing religion : and
the de Choiseul set, detested by the *dévots* on account
of the expulsion of the Jesuits, on the other. They
were as bitter and malicious to each party as they
dared be, and were utilised and despised by both.
They led pitifully dwarfed lives ; they lived in little
dark rooms ; they loved flowers, but a garden was far
too great a luxury for poor Mesdames, and they had
to content themselves with growing a few pots on
their window-sills like workgirls.

One of the first acts of Louis XVI. upon his
accession was to give his old aunts the splendid château
of Bellevue, where they could hold their little court
and have their beloved flowers ; but their father,
Louis XV., gave them nothing—but nicknames. They
were four sisters, these Mesdames de France : Adélaïde

(Loque), born in 1732; Victoire (Coche), born in 1733; Sophie (Graille), in 1734; and Louise (Chiffe), in 1735; and the mind of the four was centred in Adélaïde. She was ungraceful, masculine in voice and manner, brusque and deliberate, she had a taste for music, and played all instruments from the horn to the Jew's harp. She had all the essential qualities, she lacked only the superficial: but for Louis XV. the superficial were the essential.

She measured influences once with the Duc d'Aiguillon, with Louis XV. for the object, but she was worsted, as the Duc purchased Louis by presenting him with a new luxury—Jeanne Vaubarnier, afterwards Comtesse du Barry—and Adélaïde withdrew from open participation in Court matters, in pique, not outraged morality, for though aggressively religious, she had truckled to Madame de Pompadour, who had chosen her father confessor for her. She it was whose intriguing spirit was so feared for the Dauphine, the rest of the sisters were merged as nonentities.

Sophie was of a rare hideousness and many eccentricities. She was so scared that she looked at people from the sides of her eyes like a hare, she walked extremely fast, and was so lacking in courtesy that she would meet a person every day for years without speaking. She became of gracious manner only in thunderstorms, which terrified her into civility.

Louise—Chiffe ("rubbish") in her father's contemptuous tongue—was a middle-aged Christian whose Christianity belonged to the Middle Ages. She also was unbeautiful, rather invalidish, of simple faith, and was lost in the boundless imagination of ignorance.

Chiffe was the happiest in her fate of all the old sisters ; she left *Cavagnol* and similar luxuries of life for the convent of the Carmelites (after begging her father for permission for eighteen years), where she grew very fat and was quite content. She, as the weakest and most amiable, was always employed as the go-between to gain concessions from the Pope in such religious acts as the annulling of the marriage of Madame du Barry in order to facilitate Louis XV. marrying his *maîtresse en titre*.

Mesdames' education was the study of English, Italian, mathematics, clock-making, and the use of the turner's lathe ; their employments, cards, needle-work, and religion, the last-named of the type which would be expected from the daughters of the pious *bourgeoise* Marie Leczinska, who was always accompanied by a skull, that she called her *gentil mignon*. These were now the nearest relatives of little Marie Antoinette, to whom she had to look for advice, guidance, and example ; her other relatives were the brothers-in-law, the Comte de Provence (who hoped much from her husband's neglect) and the Comte d'Artois (who hoped more from his own compromising attentions).

On 2 August, 1770, Mercy-Argenteau wrote, there was stag-hunting. This was the real business of life to Louis XV., the one occupation he took so seriously that on the days when he

Compiègne
4 August,
1770.

did not hunt it was announced : " *Le roi ne fait rien aujourd'hui.*"   Marie Antoinette went with Mesdames, who followed the hunt in coaches, and the King interested himself in pointing out to the Dauphine the direction of the hunt, so that eventually she found herself in at the death. "The Dauphin rode as violently as usual." He took all exercise as he took food, immoderately ; would descend from his horse to chop down a tree if riding seemed insufficiently exhausting, and on returning from hunting reeled and staggered as if intoxicated.

"This Prince had given himself indigestion a few days before by eating too much pastry ; at supper-time to-night the Dauphine ordered away all the dishes of this kind which were on the table, and forbade that any more should be served until further orders. The Dauphin smiled and took this mark of attention very well." The Bourbon voracity was increased and encouraged by the custom of dining in public, for the populace watched with the admiration of respect the immense capacity of their monarchs, who, stimulated by these spectators, performed feats of assimilation.

The Dauphin kept up the traditions of his house and ate until he was torpid, but he drank very little. Mercy-Argenteau continues in his letter : "The same evening I had a long conversation with the Comtesse de Noailles . . . this lady asked me if there was no means of inducing the Dauphine to wear a whale-boned bodice, as the result of going without one was that the figure of the Princesse was becoming visibly deformed, and that her right shoulder was growing out, which is really true and necessitates prompt precautions. The Comtesse de Noailles added that she had spoken to the King, but had said and would say no word to the Dauphine, and she begged me instantly to communicate with your Majesty that a command to this effect should be laid upon the Dauphine. Every one knows that the King has never been able to take upon himself to reprove or correct his children upon any subject whatever, and it will be the same with the Dauphine."

Madame de Noailles' course of procedure in this matter was very characteristic of "Madame l'Etiquette," as she was called by Marie Antoinette; it would have been so simple, as *dame d'honneur*, to have mentioned to the shrewd, quick-witted little Dauphine the desirability of a corset; but it was said that etiquette was for her a sort of atmosphere, and any omission of its grave inutilities suffocated her, so Madame de Noailles pursued the correct course of informing the Austrian Ambassador that he might duly acquaint his sovereign, Marie Thérèse, of the danger that attended the right shoulder of the Archduchess Marie Antoinette.

It will be seen that the Empress Marie Thérèse wrote in reply, in November, and impressed upon her daughter that she was to maintain both her figure and her rank, and she sent boned bodices for the one and advice for the other. The mother, the woman of the world, and the Empress appear by turns in the letters of Marie Thérèse.

The next time Mercy writes he sends a sort of diary of notes relative to Marie Antoinette. He remarks that the King always receives the Dauphine far more tenderly when she goes to him alone than when accompanied by Mesdames, and adds his conversation with the Duc de Noailles (brother-in-law of the *dame d'honneur*), who is "the most intelligent man in France, and the best acquainted with his King and the Court. He said that he was assured one day the Dauphine would govern the mind of the King, whose ephemeral passions were weakening with age, and he would come back to seek happiness in the bosom of his family; then the charms of the Dauphine would bring her that empire that was their right. On August 6 the Dauphine was passing through the rooms of the Dauphin when he held out his arms to her and evinced a desire to talk. He suggested that they should go into the rooms of the Dauphine to be less exposed to the importunities of his gentlemen-in-waiting, who came in every moment to bother him. The Dauphine had much to say, and said it without any attempt at contradiction. Amongst other things she said that the Duc de la Vauguyon and his son, the Duc de St. Mégrin, were a couple of knaves (*deux fripons*) of whom they should beware, and she mentioned several new intrigues as proof. The Dauphin bowed his head without replying, but appears to have had his eyes opened to the character of his governor."

Compiègne, 20 August, 1770.

The Duc de la Vauguyon had been governor to the Dauphin and his brothers, a post for which he was pre-eminently unfitted ; and Louis, when King, remained always conscious of that neglected education that made him appear even less capable than he was. Almost the only records of his training which have survived are the copies which were set the Dauphin in his youth and which are still preserved among the MSS. of the Public Library of Petersburg, such as, "*Les rois sont des dieux sur la terre, ils peuvent ce qu'ils veulent.*" Louis XV. said of his grandson, at the time of his marriage : "The Dauphin possesses all the obstinacy of persons of confined understanding ; he has but slender judgment and will see with no eyes but his own." Poor, bright, little Marie Antoinette trying to light up the human intelligence in this clod !

"On 7 August," continued Mercy, "the Dauphine had supper with the King and asked his consent that the wife of the Dauphin's chief valet, Thierry, should be appointed one of her women of the bedchamber, which was granted at once." Mercy disapproved, as the Thierrys were creatures of the Duc de la Vauguyon, but the Dauphine persisted, for two reasons, one she told Mercy and the other he guessed ; firstly, that Mesdames had made a great point of it ; secondly (though this did not appear), that the Thierrys had a pretty enough little boy of four, whom, as the Dauphine was passionately fond of children, she had in her rooms to play with. Unfortunately (as Mercy says), there was another little boy there already, aged five, the son of the first woman of the bedchamber, and as the children were always in the rooms, they caused so much disorder and distracted the Dauphine so greatly from her lessons and serious occupations that Mercy and the Abbé de Vermond were concerned. " But neither of us has been able to prevail, or to reform this, and we greatly fear that Monsieur le Dauphin may be annoyed." The poor little Dauphine, only a child herself, would not be fifteen until November.

On 8 August there was a great hunt, at which the Dauphine was present with Mesdames. Although they had begged the Dauphin to moderate this excessive exercise, he fatigued himself so extremely by his exertion that he could not stand for exhaustion.

" On 9 August was a violent quarrel between the Duc de Choiseul and the Duc de Richelieu, because the latter had accused the Duchesse de Gramont [de Choiseul's sister], when she was going to the waters at Barrège and passing through Provence and Languedoc, of having endeavoured to raise the Parliament of these two provinces against the decision of the Court in the business of the Duc d'Aiguillon."

This was one of the first ripples of the Revolution, although none of those against whom it broke realised it. The Duc d'Aiguillon was impeached for gross misconduct by the Provincial Parliament of Bretagne, and the affair was brought before the Parliament of Paris. Louis XV. quashed all procedures, forbade investigation, inquiries, or complaints, and imposed absolute silence upon every one connected. The Parliament of Paris, supported by the Parliaments of Toulouse, Bordeaux, Rennes, and others, continued the impeachment of the Duc d'Aiguillon, and the whole nation watched the struggle, for they held that the Parliaments were the only barriers left against the royal despotism. Louis laid his commands of silence upon the Parliament of Paris : its members had " illegally tried to impeach and deprive a peer of the realm of his privileges, a peer whom it was the King's pleasure to consider irreproachable." Bretagne was less peaceable than ever ; Rennes, the province where the chief malpractices of the Duc d'Aiguillon had been carried on, sent back *unopened* the *lettres de cachet*, and this arbitrary act of the King's, stopping by his will alone all proceedings against the Duc d'Aiguillon (the friend of Madame du Barry), was resented all over France, and led directly to the scenes of the year following and the revolt of the Parliaments.

Mercy says in his letter that the Dauphine appeared to have heard unfavourable rumours against the Duchesse de Gramont, and he endeavoured to persuade her that probably the Duchesse was innocent of everything of which they accused her ; but the Dauphine would not let herself be persuaded that the whole thing was merely got up by the enemies of de Choiseul, wherein she showed judgment beyond her years. But the forcing atmosphere of the Court of Versailles was fast ripening the brain of the little

Dauphine, and she told Mercy she would give him her reasons at some more suitable time—the moments of the discussion being broken by her play.

The next point was the discussion of that poor incapable, her husband. That night he was to sup at the Hermitage, a little château at the gate of the city, to which the King invited his intimates, including Madame du Barry. The Dauphine expressed her growing uneasiness at the way the Dauphin was being led into these suppers, and feared it meant a scheme to draw him into this unsuitable society. The Comtesse de Noailles had given the advice that Marie Antoinette should demand to be invited also, and the matter was discussed between the Duc de Choiseul, Mercy-Argenteau, and the Dauphine. The result at which they arrived was that it would not be judicious to *ask* for an invitation to the Hermitage, but that if the King proposed her presence, she should go with appearance of pleasure. This day the King was besieged by requests from all the ladies of the Court. Madame du Barry demanded the *entrée* to the chamber for the Comtesse de Valentinois, her friend ; Mesdames immediately demanded the *grandes entrées* for their ladies-in-waiting, the Comtesse de Narbonne and the Marquise de Durfort ; and the Dauphine then demanded that the privilege of the *grande entrée* to the Dauphin should be given back to those who had been deprived of it by the Duc de la Vauguyon. The King consented all round, and commanded the Duc de la Vrillière to communicate this grace to all

concerned. After which, it is expressly mentioned by
Mercy-Argenteau, the Dauphine took a bath.

The patience and friendliness of Marie Antoinette
towards the Dauphin were winning their way, and on
one occasion Mercy wrote to the Empress respecting
her letter to the Dauphine, that he delivered just
as the young couple was sitting down to supper.
Marie Antoinette was so impatient to read her mother's
letter that she finished her supper in ten minutes,
sending the dishes away almost as soon as they were
placed on the table, while the Dauphin, who had
been hunting and was extremely hungry, had scarcely
time to eat at all ; but instead of being impatient he
only laughed.

A letter from Mercy-Argenteau to Marie Thérèse
marked " Private " was upon the subject of Compiègne
the Dauphin's health. He says : " The 20 August,
Dauphin's natural development is very late ; 1770.
probably his physique has been weakened by his
sudden growth. But there is nothing to make one
doubt that his constitution will in time become sound
and robust, if only he will avoid these too violent
exercises, which may have grave consequences. He
seems charmed with the Dauphine, and shows a
sweetness and complaisance towards her that he was
not believed to possess. [She spoke of him to Mercy
as the best of boys—*le meilleur enfant*.] She governs
him in all trifles, to which he offers no opposition.
So with a little patience all may be well . . . in this
country they wish to hurry everything . . . the King

and Mesdames make suggestions which only serve to agitate the Dauphine." But the late development of Louis was answerable for many things, and if instead of a lethargic, slow-witted, irresolute, silent boy, feeble in mind and in body, Marie Antoinette had married a manly Dauphin with sound judgment to balance her brilliant wit, a mind capable of receiving impressions, and will to carry them out, the history of France would have included no such chapters as those of the Revolution.

CHAPTER IV

The Donkeys of the Dauphine—Her |Pug—Gambling
at Court—The Amusements of the Dauphin—The
Forge at Versailles—Marie Antoinette's Revenues.

IN September Marie Thérèse writes that she wishes
send a present to the King : " If I knew whether
the life-size bust of the Dauphine, in porcelain
that they call biscuit, would please the King, **Schönbrunn,**
1.
I would send it to you to present to him. If **September,**
1770.
you think it would not have a good effect I
will keep it myself. You might let me know also if
we ought to send Tokay, and to whom ; it is the right
time now, but I wish that they would send us some
champagne." Mercy duly replied that the King had
long been suggesting that he would like some Tokay
sent by Marie Thérèse. He thought if an *antal* of it
(seventy-three litres) were sent, it would make a good
impression : and that it was quite certain the King
would offer *un provision* of champagne.

In the same month at Compiègne there was a great,
new interest in the circle of the Dauphine : she had
expressed a strong desire to ride. Mercy wrote that
he had tried every possible means of dissuading her,
spoken to the Comtesse de Noailles and the Duc de

Choiseul, represented her tender age, violent exercise, possible contingencies, etc., but in vain; so at his suggestion the Duc de Choiseul laid the matter before the King, who, being prepared for the Dauphine's petition, gave her permission to ride—but only on donkeys! The Dauphine was quite delighted; search was made everywhere for extremely sweet and quiet donkeys (*fort doux et tranquilles*), and Marie Antoinette rode her donkey and the ladies of her suite followed her on *soixante ou quatre-vingts destriers de son espèce*, as Touchard-Lafosse says, in the forest without any danger.

On 21 August there was a great promenade on donkeys; Mesdames wished to be also of the party (a great concession of etiquette), also the Comte de Provence and the Comte d'Artois. All the world crowded to the forest to see them pass, and the Dauphine stopped her donkey whenever she perceived any distinguished persons, to greet them with grace and kindness. From this time the Dauphine had a new sport : she rode her donkeys gaily three or four times a week (which unaccustomed exercise nearly exhausted the ladies of her suite, who were not of an age under fifteen), she rode all about the vast park of Fontainebleau, observing and inquiring into the historical interests of the ancient buildings, she took her donkeys for a promenade *fort longue et pénible parmi les rochers*, and grew visibly better and stronger for the long excursions. She asked Mercy one evening to procure her a pug dog from Vienna, "*un chien mops, le couleur jaune fade, avec un museau noir, et retroussé,*" and he replied that doubtless one could be brought by the courier. He says: "Madame la Dauphine loves dogs very much ; she has two already, which are unfortunately extremely unclean, and if their number is to be augmented, this amusement, very innocent in itself, will not be altogether without inconvenience."

The affairs of the Court could not permit the Dauphine to play in peace with her dogs and donkeys, and the guidance of Mercy-Argenteau was needed through the bristling intrigues that surrounded her, arising from the petty jealousies of the rival little Courts, and not only from the spite of Mesdames. There was no difficulty at this time that could not be traced to the injudicious interference of Madame Adélaïde ; but Mercy always detected the malice and pointed out the evils for which she was answerable, directly or indirectly. It was Madame Adélaïde who had pressed upon the Dauphine to take into her service Madame Thierry ; it was the same fruitful source of discord who inspired her to omit the necessary waiting for the appointment to be duly made out, and to give Madame Thierry at once authority in her household as woman of the bed-chamber ; and again it was Madame Adélaïde who suggested to the Dauphine that the best way to announce her wishes to the lady-in-waiting, the Comtesse de Noailles, was to send Madame Thierry herself to convey them. For once "Madame l'Etiquette " forgot her policy (quite ineffective with Marie Antoinette but she did not know that) of speaking only smooth things ; she told the Dauphine, with the courage of deep mortification, that she was not there to receive orders from a *femme de chambre*, and one, moreover, who had no right to convey them before her appointment was confirmed, and retired into seclusion with the intention of resigning her duties in a royal household that so forgot Court correctness.

Mercy came to the rescue at once, found the piqued and mortified Comtesse de Noailles, and listened to *de longues plaintes* patiently. He told her if she had shown more sincerity and less adulation she would have won more respect from the Dauphine, revealed the person to whose acid mischief-making all these irregularities were due, mentioned that if she retired she would only be making way for some one of the du Barry coterie, and *enfin je parvins à calmer entièrement la Comtesse de Noailles*. Mercy then waited on the Dauphine and found her at her toilette, from which she arose "with precipitation " to greet him, said she would converse with him directly after her dinner, which waited. She sat down to table alone, says Mercy, as the Dauphin had gone with the King to Choisy, and the dinner did not last longer at the outside than ten minutes.

Then Mercy laid before the Dauphine the mischief that had been done by Mesdames her aunts, said that if the Comtesse de Noailles retired it would give the impression that the Dauphine was difficult to serve, and further (again the clinching argument) that her place would be given to the Maréchale de Mirepoix or the Duchesse d'Aiguillon, both creatures of Madame du Barry. Madame de Mirepoix was duenna to Madame du Barry, and the first lady of the Court to receive her. In return she was given the privilege of *entrée* to the Court—a privilege granted equally to Mesdames de Maillebois and de Souvré, who held the posts of keepers of the wardrobe—a salary of 100,000 francs [£4,000] a year, and a yearly " gratification " of 12,000 livres [£480]. Mercy says he laid all possible weight upon his arguments, and the Dauphine acknowledged without hesitation that she had been misled, and promised to repair all that she had done amiss.

Mercy then took the opportunity of pointing out another little bit of treachery which Mesdames had in train. Etiquette demanded that a reception should be held each night by the chief royal lady, and that at it the solemn hours should be passed in gambling, if such a word could be applied to the wearisome games of *Cavagnol*, etc. The little Dauphine was so exhausted with boredom at these games that in order to avoid playing she had given up holding her Court of an evening. The keen scent of Mesdames for exploiting an error induced them to impress upon Marie Antoinette that they would hold their Court nightly to save her the tedium. Mercy pointed out the full meaning of their complaisance, for as custom demanded the reception to be held by the lady of highest royal rank, it was placing the Dauphine in a position second to that of Madame Adélaïde ; and further, that when the Comte de Provence (Louis's younger brother) married the Princesse Josèphe-Louise of Savoy, the Comtesse de Provence would hold the receptions if the Dauphine did not, and thus she would again be in a second place.

Marie Antoinette promised to take up the wearisome duty of play, and if in after years her accounts show the pecuniary result of this duty, it is not to be blamed to her own gambling spirit. In the Court records of the reigns of Louis XIV. and XV. there are frequent mentions of high play, a loss of 700,000 ecus (£84,000) on one Christmas Day, setting 150,000 pistoles (£27,000) on three cards, and a frequent loss of as much as 100,000 ecus (£12,000) at a time being ascribed to Madame de Montespan. But the dreary nature of these games is shown by an anecdote told by Madame de Créquy. The Court was in mourning (October 4) at Versailles, and the Queen (Marie Antoinette) wished to play *Loto* to distract herself. It was asked whether etiquette permitted *Loto* to be played as the Court was in mourning, and Madame de Créquy, to whom the point was referred, said " Yes, because to play *Loto* is mourning."

Mercy adds at the end of his long letter that the Dauphine had all the gazettes brought to her, in which she only read the news of Vienna, and that she had confided to him a thought of which she had repented. She had read that the plague was increasing in Poland, without afflicting herself that it was approaching the frontiers of her native land, because if the disease did come dangerously near the Empress, she would be obliged to take refuge in Flanders, and there perhaps there might be some hope of seeing her mother again.

On 2 October, Marie Thérèse wrote to Mercy : " I preach to my daughter patience, and to redouble her caresses. I spoke very strongly to her in favour of the corset, and about her figure, telling her, what is true besides, that I have seen a letter from some one in Brussels, who considered she was not well dressed and that her figure was not good. I told her that I had commanded you to see after that and to write to me about it. . . . I send you her letter, which you can burn and pretend you have not seen. I send it to you that you may see how much it leaves to be desired that she should apply herself to better writing and orthography. I also mentioned that if she had asked my permission to ride I should not have granted it, but I see that the King spoils her. . . . *Pour les 5,000 florins de plus pour votre fête* [which Mercy had given in honour of the marriage] *d'abord que la chancellerie fera la proposition, je le resoudrai, de même le placet de vos sujets en Hongrie qui se plaignent pour le libre exercice de leur religion. Je l'ai envoyé tout de suite à la chancellerie de Hongrie pour voir combiner la chose.* . . I will send the Tokay, and the bust of my daughter ; say nothing until the King receives them."

Mercy wrote in the middle of October : " The Dauphine's figure improves daily. Her **Fontaine-** health is perfect, and she is getting a little **bleau,** **20 October,** plump : this is attributed to the continual **1770.** exercise that she takes either walking or riding her donkeys. . . . She has now determined to wear a corset, and if only she will continue it there will be no more fear for her figure. [When Catherine de Medicis first introduced corsets into France she did not realise what a weight of responsibility she was laying on future generations. Her corsets of steel and whalebone have been long preserved in the Cluny museum—among the instruments of torture.] The King is increasing his attentions and marks of tender friendship for the Dauphine. . . . She lives now in the apartments of the late Queen, adjoining those of the King ; if only his Majesty would form the habit of going in to see the Dauphine in the day, very good effects might be produced, resulting in distracting the King from his irregular associates. I do not despair that the Dauphine may one day succeed in rendering this important service to France, but to succeed she must adopt the entire opposite to the conduct and manners of Mesdames her aunts. . . . On the 12th the Dauphine spent the evening at play, at Mesdames', and then had supper with the King, where she ate so abundantly of sucking pig that she gave herself indigestion ; but this light accident had no serious consequences, and she was up at eight the next morning to see the Comte de Provence and the Comte d'Artois start for their ride. In the evening there was an entertainment ; they played an Italian piece, the only kind that amuses the Dauphin, who has a decided aversion from music, and little liking for French comedy."

The amusements of the Dauphin, even for years after he had become King, were such as to drive Marie Antoinette into despair, for his hands were always black, and all her reproaches could not induce him to keep himself clean or his hair in order. It was a taste as unhappy in its choice as in its results, and " *le gros enfant mal élevé*," as Madame du Barry called Louis, with his inappropriate passion for the career and appearance of a blacksmith, was as ludicrous a husband for Marie Antoinette as the Duke of Parma was for her sister, Marie Amélie. The Empress of Austria must have wondered at the dispensations of Providence in providing her with one royal son-in-law forging keys at Versailles and another spending his days either "ringing the bells in all the belfries of Parma or else in roasting chestnuts."

" The Abbé de Vermond discussed with me the matter of the bad writing and orthography of the Dauphine, and he told me that the Dauphine never writes so badly as she does to your Majesty [the Empress]. The reason is that the Dauphine is con-vinced that her writings are not safe from spies, therefore she awaits the moment of the departure of the courier before writing, and in consequence the letters are filled with the errors of haste."

Mercy tried to reassure the Dauphine; said her suspicions were unjust; that he had examined the surroundings and was convinced that no one would open her bureau, provided she always took the precaution of carrying the key on her person. Marie Antoinette was in this suspicion more accurate than Mercy-Argenteau, as was shown when the royal notepaper, stolen from the bureau, served as a circumstantial link in the necklace episode.

On 14 October the Dauphine confided to Mercy that she was much hurt at many things her mother had written to her, and mentioned the subject of her figure. Mercy seized the opportunity to inculcate corsets, also "I mentioned several other articles of dress and recommended cleanliness as a very useful means of pleasing the King and the Dauphin;" and then warned the Dauphine of further intrigues on the part of Mesdames, Madame Adélaïde and Madame Sophie. Loque and Graille had been endeavouring for some time to set the Dauphin against their sister, Madame Victoire, who was, as Mercy said, "without doubt the best of the three sisters and the one with the most character."

Madame Victoire was called by her father Coche as she was the fattest. Louis XV. knew, as his household remarked, many strange epithets: his daughters thought he learnt them from dictionaries: those better informed knew that he picked them up from less orthodox sources. Coche, who was the victim of her sisters' animosity, had suffered all her life from fits of nervous panic, impossible to control, due to terror when a child, for she had been forced to do penance in the Abbey of Fontevrault by praying alone in the vault where they buried the nuns. She was better looking than the other sisters, and had a pleasant, gracious smile. She had a full appreciation of the comforts of life, and was prevented by thoughts of her favourite lounge chair from embracing a convent life. "*Voici un fauteuil qui me perd*," she said from its depths, when asked whether she intended to follow Madame Louise to the Carmelites.

The revenues of the Dauphine were scandalously mismanaged. She asked Mercy to give her 40 ducats (40 Austrian ducats = £27 13s. 4d.) which she had promised to two persons of her suite in Vienna ; and although the royal treasury ought to pay her 6,000 francs (£240) a month, she had not a single écu (3 francs) she could call her own and spend as she wished. "The revenues of the Dauphine are received as by right by her treasurer, named Pomeri : he deducts 2,500 livres (£100) of this for the long standing pensions bestowed by the late Queen, which are charged upon the Dauphine without her knowing why. Her grooms of the chamber receive 100 louis (£96) a month for the expenses at play of her Royal Highness, and whether she wins or whether she loses, nothing is ever seen of that again ; the *femmes de chambre* take possession of the rest, which is for the most part distributed in charities suggested by the Comtesse de Noailles, and for which she extracts the consent of the Dauphine, who by this means retains nothing at her own disposal. Happily she is very far from being inclined to squandering or to extravagance: the little money she has at her command is employed in well-bestowed alms."

Nothing is more astonishing in that astonishing period than the greed of all, however highly placed, for what Mercy-Argenteau called *les graces utiles*. They all accepted—in fact, demanded—gifts of money upon every possible occasion, and their readiness in demanding was only equalled by their facility in forgetting, or the deftness with which they diverted the current of any available golden stream to which they had access.   M. de Calonne once said to the Archbishop of Narbonne: "*Mais, monseigneur, tout le monde a des dettes; vous même vous en avez !*" Monseigneur replied: "*Et vous, M. de Calonne, vous en aviez.*"   M. de Calonne was then Minister of the Treasury.

Mercy-Argenteau continues to give little intimate details of the Court; he says: "It is true that the Dauphine is not advantageously dressed, but it is entirely the fault of her *dame d'atours* (Mistress of the Robes), who understands very little about it and pays very little attention;" and then he describes a petty little intrigue of influences.   The Empress Marie Thérèse had desired that the Dauphine should procure some little mark of favour for the Marquis de Durfort—say a dukedom—as he had assisted at her marriage with the Dauphin, and had been sent by Louis to ask her hand for that alliance. But Marie Antoinette found Mesdames and their *dame d'atours* (Madame de Narbonne) in the way of this, simply because if the Marquise de Durfort, who was in attendance upon Madame Victoire, were made a duchess, it would be very annoying to Mesdames the other sisters, and incidentally to Madame de Narbonne, who was merely a comtesse. As for the Marquise de Durfort herself, Mercy describes her as "witty, with knowledge of the Court, more honesty and less intrigue than the other women of this country"— an interesting distinction.

The education of Marie Antoinette, which had been greatly neglected, was now confided to the Abbé de Vermond, who, being an obscure *bourgeois*, was one of the most discussed men at the Court. He had been selected by the Duc de Choiseul, approved by Marie Thérèse, and supported by Mercy-Argenteau ; he was considered by some to be a prudent, devoted, and invaluable counsellor to the young Dauphine ; by others he was called vain, babbling, arrogant, ill-mannered, a chattering fool who despised what he did not comprehend, an ignorant instructor and an extremely ugly man. All these descriptions are culled from memoirs of the period, and the last was by no means the least count against the Abbé.

The course of instruction for the child Dauphine

that was laid down by the Abbé de Vermond is enclosed in a letter from Mercy-Argenteau to Marie Thérèse on October 20: " The subject of study that appeared to be most pressing was that of French synonyms. . . . I read to the Dauphine two or three pages a day. Her French improves, and she speaks with more vivacity and less strain, expressing herself easily, agreeably, and very nobly upon occasion. Sometimes she uses phrases that are not quite French, but she gives them an energy and meaning far preferable to grammatical exactitude. When I see that she is bored with her French lesson, I read to her the letters of the Comte de Tessin to the Prince of Sweden, his pupil [published in 1755], or some old pamphlets called *Bagatelles morales.*" These last were pieces by the Abbé Coyer, whose wearisome observations, published in London and in Frankfort in 1765, could never have been of educational benefit to any one.

Yet Mesdames endeavoured to convince Marie Antoinette that her education was over severe. Their point is better understood when it is known that Madame Louise at the age of twelve had never learnt the whole of the alphabet, and did not know how to read when she first took up her residence at Versailles ; and this in a century when taste and judgment in literature were more necessary than morals, and the polishing of a poem or the tasteful turning of a phrase the accomplishments of every drawing-room !

Mercy-Argenteau wrote a private letter to the

interested mother on the delicate subject of the relations between the Dauphine and her husband. The Dauphin had promised his wife he would sleep in her apartment on September 20. The Dauphine, full of excitement, confided this to Mesdames, who confided it to all the world, till it became the topic of the day. Madame Adélaïde then increased her indiscretion by adding that of exhortations to the Dauphin, who was so scared (*effarouché*) that he entirely failed to keep his word to the Dauphine. He renewed his promise for October 10, but the Dauphine told her aunts, and all happened as before ; and Mercy then felt it behoved him to do something. He therefore said to the Dauphine, very diplomatically, that a ridiculous rumour of misunderstandings between her and her husband was spreading in the Court, and that he should have been uneasy only that it was obviously fabricated, for it was impossible that any one who knew the circumstances could have imparted them. The Dauphine, embarrassed, confessed her confidences to Mesdames, adding : " Who would have thought they were such indiscreet babblers? " The King reproached the Dauphin for his coldness (all these little matters were published on the house-tops) ; and the Dauphin replied that he found his wife charming, that he loved her, but he must have more time to conquer his shyness—and Mercy ends with " Patience, all will arrange itself " !

CHAPTER V

MARIE THÉRÈSE wrote to her daughter :
" Madame, *ma chère fille*, at last this everlasting
courier has arrived at nine last night. Thanks
to God your health remains good, according to the
courier who was one of your suite : he
finds you grown and fatter. If you did
not assure me you wear corsets, this account
would have made me uneasy. I beg of you not to
let yourself get careless ; at your age it is unsuitable,
and in your rank even more so : carelessness brings
in its train uncleanness, negligence, and indifference
in all other respects, and that would be your downfall.
This is the reason why I bother you, for I cannot
sufficiently warn you against the little failings that
would let you slip into the faults wherein all the
Royal family of France have fallen for long years ;
they are good (*vertueux pour eux-mêmes*), but not

**Schönbrunn,
1 November,
1770.**

in any way calculated to make a good appearance,
set an example, or amuse themselves straightforwardly,
and this has been the natural reason of the deviations
of their lords, who, finding not a single resource at
home, have felt themselves justified in seeking them
in other places and other ways. One can be virtuous
and yet gay."

"La Marie-Anne [her eldest daughter, the Abbess
at Prague] has entirely recovered from her fever
and goes to all the hunts and promenades, everywhere
except the theatre. La Windischgraetz has arrived,
safely but *bien défaite*." [It is of this Comtesse
Windischgraetz that Joseph II. said, "She can listen,
is intelligent, and can understand reason. There
are not many of her sex of whom one can say
that"]. "She tells me that you neglect your person
too much, particularly about brushing your teeth. . . .
She added you were badly dressed and she had
dared say so to your ladies. You say you have
still kept some of your trousseau dresses ; which
have you kept? I intend, if you will send me a
good pattern, having some bodices or corsets made
here—they say those of Paris are too tight ; I will
send them to you by courier. I hope that a certain
bust has arrived ; it grieved me to part with it,
but I hope that they will send me back a good
portrait, and especially that it may be by Liotard,
who is going to Paris expressly for the purpose. I
beg you will give him time to do it well." Liotard,
a famous painter of the day, in miniature and pastel,

was in great favour at the Courts of England, Holland, Austria, and France. He always wore Turkish dress, for inspiration.

Writing on 16 November, Mercy sent a long diary to Marie Thérèse, in which occurs : " The King held a review of his regiment, and the Dauphin went to the camp with Mesdames. In the evening the Comte du Châtelet, colonel of the said regiment, gave a supper, to which the King and the Dauphin went. The Comtesse du Barry and the women of her society were admitted to this fête." These two ladies were the Comtesse de Valentinois, granddaughter of that Duc de St. Simon who enshrined himself and his time in memoirs of endless volumes, and Madame de Mirepoix (who quarrelled with her brother, the Maréchal de Beauvau and all the de Choiseul friends by becoming intimate with the du Barry) the lady of whom Madame du Deffand wrote : " *Une grande dame, une très belle conduite, beaucoup d'esprit, beaucoup d'agrément, toutes ces choses réunies, ce qui en résulte, c'est d'être l'esclave d'un infâme.*"

Fontaine-bleau, 16 November, 1770.

The affair of the Comtesse de Gramont, who had been exiled from Court at the instance of the offended Madame du Barry, now came up again. To the Court lady of that time, exile from Paris and its " rose-pink vapour of sentimentalism " meant banishment from all the ameliorations of life ; and two months of country existence had reduced the Comtesse de Gramont to despair. She therefore wrote to the Dauphine that her health was in a condition likely to need the promptest medical attendance, and praying her to intercede for her with the King. The Dauphine took the opportunity, when having supper with his Majesty, to ask the favour of the return of the Comtesse, one of her ladies of the palace. The King, rather embarrassed, but charmed with the graceful little manner of the Dauphine, replied that he would think about it.

The Dauphine, next morning, sent for the Duc de la Vrillière (to whose department such affairs of State belonged) and instructed him to wait upon the King and take from his Majesty his orders, saying that it was by the desire of the Dauphine he did so. The Duc de la Vrillière duly carried out Marie Antoinette's injunction ; the King said it was necessary first of all to ascertain if the Comtesse de Gramont were really ill (a courier was sent to that lady's doctor to find out), and secondly to obtain the consent of Madame du Barry, before she could return. Then the Duc de la Vrillière informed Madame du Barry, who prepared to resist the wish of the Dauphine. In the evening, at supper, Marie Antoinette returned to the point, which she pressed. " Madame," said the King severely, " I told . you I would give you an answer in due time." But the Dauphine, without the least embarrassment, replied : " But, papa, apart from all questions of humanity or justice, consider what a grief it would be to me if a woman attached to my service were to die in your displeasure."

The clouds rolled away, the monarch smiled, assured

Marie Antoinette she would be satisfied ; and the next

23 October, 1770. day, upon the return of the courier with the doctor's certificate, and before departing to the entertainment, the King ordered the Duc de la Vrillière to send instant permission to the Comtesse de Gramont to return to Paris. This was done without the knowledge of Madame du Barry. When the Dauphine next saw the King, she thanked him for the permission ; the King replied smiling : " Madame, I have executed your orders." All this caused a great impression at Court ; the Duc and Duchesse de Choiseul rendered their humblest acknowledgments of the favour to their relative ; and Mesdames complimented Marie Antoinette on conduct they could never emulate, saying : " It is easy to see that you are not of our blood."

For some time the diary of Mercy-Argenteau con-

30 October, 1770. tained only such entries as : " The Dauphine this day went for a ride on her donkey ; nothing remarkable happened," which occur with great frequency until, on 30 October, a deep scheme was carried out. This was that the Dauphine should give up her donkey and ride a horse, and Madame Adélaïde undertook all the necessary negotiations to obtain the King's permission, which was gained, rather by surprise. The riding party left the palace very mysteriously, all riding donkeys as usual, until they arrived at a certain rendezvous in the forest, where a horse was in charge of a groom, the only person to whom the plot had been confided.

The Dauphine mounted the horse, to her intense delight; it was led by the rein of the groom, and other persons walked by the side, and when she returned home all the Court crowded to her reception to take part in her pleasure—except Mercy. He stayed away, partly because *tout ce qui est le moins convenable à Madame l'Archiduchesse* was always due to the machinations of Mesdames, and partly because on alighting the Dauphine hàd said to the Duchesse de Chaulnes that she wondered what sort of a face he (Mercy) would make!

This riding aroused the most diverse feelings : the Empress Marie Thérèse looked upon it as simply disastrous, but could say nothing, as it had so pleased the King ; he had made an order the next day for 24,000 livres (£960), to buy riding horses for the Dauphine's own particular stable, and given directions for the necessary extra grooms. The Dauphin was understood to be pleased ; and henceforward the items follow almost daily : " The Dauphine rode on horseback," " The Dauphine again rode on horseback, and cannot endure the idea of riding a donkey, and there is every appearance that these animals will be put down at once."

The letters do not say what description of horses Louis ordered for the young Dauphine, but his own hunters were all imported from England, for he would only ride *des courtaults du Suffolk*, and they had to be chosen for colour as well as make, the colours preferred being *soupe de lait* (a yellowish white), *tigrée* (white marked black) or *porcelainé* (white spotted black). Every one rode at the Court. Mesdames rode, Madame Adélaïde well and boldly, and although Mercy regarded their interference on behalf of the Dauphine's riding as highly culpable, it does not appear this time to have been actuated by malice. One reason which Marie Antoinette begged might be represented to her mother in extenuation of her desire to ride was the good influence that her presence might exercise on the Dauphin, for she laboured daily upon his civilisation, and attained it by very slow steps.

On 6 November the Dauphine made a great point to her husband that he should not stay out so late hunting, but return at a reasonable hour, be dressed in time, and not keep the entertainment waiting. The Dauphin came home late, long after the King, as was his habit. He found the Dauphine with the King, approached her awkwardly, and said : " You see I am back to time." To which the Dauphine replied, very dryly : " Oh, remarkably good time ! " Then they went to the entertainment, and the Dauphin sulked through the whole performance. On coming out of the theatre he tried to explain, and then the Dauphine administered a little but extremely energetic sermon. She represented to him, with vivacity, all the inconveniences of his " life of a savage " ; she pointed out that none of his suite could stand that existence, especially as his uncouth manners and ways were not calculated to counterbalance it in the minds of those attending upon him, and that if he continued he would end by ruining his health and getting himself detested. The Dauphin received this lesson with sweetness and submission, acknowledged his faults, promised to amend, and formally begged pardon from the Dauphine. It was noticed next day that he paid her far more attention than usual.

Mercy described, in a letter to Marie Thérèse, how it was that he was enabled to send such full accounts of the hourly doings of Marie Antoinette: "I have assured myself of three persons of the inferior service of the Dauphine, **Fontaine-bleau, 16 November.** one of her women and two *garçons de chambre*, who give me an exact account of what passes indoors. I am informed day by day of the conversations that her Royal Highness has with the Abbé de Vermond from whom she hides nothing; I learn from the Marquise de Durfort all that passes *chez Mesdames*, down to the smallest subject that is mentioned, and I have even more people and more means of knowing what passes when the Dauphine is with the King. In addition there are my own observations, so that there is not an hour in the day upon which I am not in a position to know everything that the Dauphine may have said, or done, or heard." All this Mercy does, reporting upon his "faith and fidelity" all details of Marie Antoinette's daily life, "for the repose of your Majesty." And the **Vienna, 1 December, 1770.** Empress writes to Mercy on 1 December, her thanks for the watchful guardianship, for "I know my daughter well ; she will carry through all she wishes, and will dare much."

Marie Thérèse wrote to the Dauphine a letter in **Vienna,** which (as she told Mercy) she maintained **2 December, 1770.** her influence by mingling much tenderness with remonstrances. "You were quite right in thinking I should not approve your riding at fifteen ; Mesdames, whom you quote, did not ride till thirty, but you tell me the King approves, and the Dauphin, and that suffices for me ; it is they who have the ordering of your life, it is in their hands I have placed my charming Antoinette. Riding on horseback ruins the complexion and ultimately the figure. I consider that if you ride like a man (which I do not doubt you will) it is very dangerous . . . if you ride, as I did, as a woman, there is less to be said. . . . Accidents cannot be prevented ; the mishaps of the Queen of Portugal and of many others are not reassuring. Having said all this I shall now try to forget it, provided that the *Gazette* does not arrive full of the horse-racing of the Dauphine—which would never do. . . . One thing more, a great Princess never breaks her word, and if you promise, ' I will never hunt on horseback,' I will try and reassure myself. . . . I await eagerly the picture by Liotard, but it is to be of you in full dress, not in *negligé* or in anything mannish."

The instructions of Marie Thérèse as to the costume of the portrait were not unnecessary, for there was a great vogue to be depicted as spurious classics or anything else if sufficiently incongruous. It sounds strange to think of Mesdames Rag, Snip, Pig (as the elderly withered daughters of Louis XV. were called by their royal father) being painted by Nattier, for the greater adornment of the palace of Choisy, as Flora, Diana and Hebe; and the famous picture of Madame de Pompadour, who was painted by Vanloo as Ste. Clotilde, for an *altar-piece*! The selection of Madame du Barry, who had herself painted by Doyen as Phryne, does not seem so surprising, especially as the lady described her famous prototype as "that fair Thessalian who removed her veil when before some Roman emperor on a charge of witchcraft."

Mercy wrote a detailed account of an adventure that had befallen the Dauphine and Mesdames, and resulted in some fright for Mesdames and a sore throat for the Dauphine. On the day when the King and his Court commenced to move from Choisy to Versailles, his Majesty went hunting. The Dauphine and Mesdames wished to accompany the King as far as a place where it was necessary to cross the river on a ferry-boat. But coming back, the timid Mesdames were convinced the coach would upset, and insisted on getting out "in an extremely boggy place." The Dauphine, after vainly endeavouring to persuade Mesdames to retain their composure and their seats in the carriage, had to alight also and follow them: she lost one of her shoes in the mud, and came back

Paris, 17 December, 1770.

to Choisy very wet and so cold that in trying to dry herself at the fire at Choisy she burnt her garments.

They continued their journey to Versailles, for when the King once marked his dates of arrival and departure on his calendar (always done on January 1 for the year), by those dates the Court abided, whatever accident intervened. There no preparation had been made : the Dauphine found her rooms not heated, and caught a fresh cold ; but it passed away in three days, which is of interest in view of the fact that handkerchiefs were not in use in France until the Revolution twenty years after this date.

" Lately the Comtesse de Noailles has been again in a bad temper, because the Dauphine too often gave her leave of absence from the hunting parties, and appeared to prefer to be accompanied by the younger and livelier ladies of the palace. When the lady-in-waiting bemoaned herself to me [says Mercy], I told her it was for her to decline the dispensation from duty when offered it by the Dauphine, and that she should invariably accompany her Royal Highness on these hunting parties." The reason for this insistence of Mercy, with the special mention of the hunting parties, is explained. Two or three times a week the Dauphine accompanied the King out hunting, and then it was her pleasure to have her carriages filled with cold meats and other refreshments and hold little picnic parties, giving hospitality to all those of the Court who followed the hunt.

In this the keen eye of Mercy detected possibilities.

"These Frenchmen have such a tendency to become too easy and too familiar"; and the gathering round her carriage of all the young men of the King's suite would probably include some feather-pates, who might not observe that circumspect and respectful bearing due to the presence of a young Princess. Mercy, still anxious, warned the Dauphine to be on her guard against these airs *d'aisance et de familiarité* that would certainly greet her, and he recommended the Comtesse de Noailles as a fit and proper person to repress them.

This Comtesse de Noailles, so easily mortified, so futile in her assumptions, was the wife of Philippe Comte de Noailles, Marquis and Maréchal de Mouchy. He had his claims to attention : had fought at the battle of Fontenoy ; was in great favour with Louis XV., was made Governor of Guyenne and afterwards of Versailles ; a good officer, he impressed his individuality upon his soldiers even to the soles of their shoes, upon which he ordered to be written "Monseigneur le Maréchal de Mouchy," so that the title should be visible in rows when his men were on their knees in church. Both "Madame l'Etiquette" and her husband, the ingenious Maréchal of the shoes, died on the scaffold in the "Terror," faithful to their duties till the end, coming out of their retirement at Mouchy to offer the services of devotion to their doomed King and Queen at the Tuileries, and perishing at the hands of the Revolutionaries on June 27, 1794.

A little incident served to rouse feelings of much interest in the Dauphine, who, regarded

29 November, 1770.

merely as a child, and, further, as an Austrian, had to convince her world that she was a French-woman. Marie Antoinette was returning from the hunt in the neighbourhood of Versailles, when the postillion of her coach fell as they crossed a bridge, the four horses passing over his body. The Dauphine was instant in sympathy, sent on all sides to seek surgeons and stretchers for the unfortunate man, drawn bleeding and insensible from under the coach, and for over an hour stayed on the spot superintending the dressing of his injuries, which was undertaken by one of the officers of her guards. They wished to carry him away in a chaise ; the Dauphine " most judiciously " forbade this, pointing out the impropriety of jolting about an unfortunate man who was a mass of bruises. Eventually a stretcher was discovered and the invalid carried to Versailles, escorted by two surgeons and many persons of the *cortège* of the Dauphine, who told the story with the greatest vivacity : " I said to all the world that they were my friends— pages, grooms, postillions ! I said to them, ' My friend, run and find a surgeon; my friend, run quickly for a stretcher ; see if he can speak, if he is conscious.' "

And at this recital all present dissolved in tenderness and admiration, saying : " By this is known the daughter of Marie Thérèse and the heiress of Henri VI." Truly " light mortals walking their light life minuet" touched to the heart by the facile humanity that had casually hoped that every peasant might have a fowl in his pot, and, amazed, recognising the same Royal quality in a sensitiveness towards a crushed groom. The opinion of the fleeced populace as to the heirs of the chicken-wishing King is shown in the following verse :

Enfin la poule au pot sera donc bientôt mise,
On doit du moins le présumer ;
Car depuis deux cents ans qu'on nous l'avait promise
On n'a cessé de la plumer.

The coachman who had driven her was the father-in-law of the fallen man ; his brother was driving one of the King's carriages and had to pass by the postillion carried on a stretcher. Marie Antoinette's tender heart was hurt afresh at each revelation, but they consoled her at Court by saying " all stable people have hard hearts " and felt nothing. But de Vermond assured the Dauphine that quite poor people had been known to love each other. It was not only in the Court that this episode wrought the impressionable into enthusiasm ; and when the price of bread was lowered in Paris, the whisper ran through the streets and markets : "It is surely the Dauphine who has begged for us this abatement for the poor."

"The Dauphine is gaining in influence," wrote Mercy ; " she pleases the King by her wit and gaiety ; he grows fond of her in spite of all that has been done to prevent him. . . . The Dauphin redoubles his friendship and attentions ; he lends himself to all that pleases her." The Dauphine showed she enjoyed dancing ; the Dauphin, who disliked it extremely, was the first to suggest there should be balls, and "there is one held every Monday in the rooms of the Dauphine"—unceremonious, the ladies in white dominos, the gentlemen in ordinary dress. This action, by "a Prince so taciturn and secret" as the Dauphin, was impressive. Mercy says that it was hoped that the daily meeting with the Abbé de Vermond would be of benefit to the Dauphin's

17 December, 1770. mind, "but up to this day he has never addressed a single word to him [although de Vermond had now been met daily for seven months], and this, not from any active prejudice, but simply from embarrassment and supineness."

Mercy ends with the details that the Dauphine's health is stronger, that she grows prettier, that her figure is improving thanks to the corset, that she rides on a woman's saddle, that she devotes much more attention to cleanliness, and that Liotard is painting her portrait, which may be finished next month.

CHAPTER VI

The Fall of de Choiseul—*Le Cocher de l'Europe*—The
First Meeting of Louis XV. and Madame du Barry
—Morality *v*. Religion—The *Lettre de Cachet*—
The Indiscretions of Mesdames—Arrival of Dr.
Ingenhouse—Intrigues of the Ladies-in-Waiting—
Causes of the Fall of de Choiseul

THE year 1771 opened with dire premonitions
of evil. The news had just reached Marie
Thérèse of the disgrace of the Duc de Choiseul
and his fall from power, which had occurred with
great suddenness on 24 December; and the Vienna,
Empress was filled with dread at what this 4 January,
downfall implied—for the Dauphine herself, 1771.
in this triumph of the du Barry; for the alliance,
in the accession to power of the Duc d'Aiguillon,
the two heads of the anti-Austrian cabal. She wrote
to Mercy: " I confess the fall of Choiseul appals
me. I fear we shall feel his loss only too much. The
dismissal of Vermond is as certain [he was selected
by de Choiseul] as is the fall of my daughter. You
will no longer have facilities for approaching her, and
no one will dare to keep you informed of everything.
This abominable clique will ruin my daughter and
make her either suspect or find irksome all those who

could give her good advice. I confess to you I fear
that this blow is decisive for my daughter's fate, but
not for the alliance, which belongs as much to France
as to us. I beg that you will let me know all the
particulars, but above all, the comments and bearing
of the Dauphin, whom I do not think so much foolish
as swayed and led by this false and hypocritical clique.
If you learn from time to time anything of the des
Choiseul and the cause of their disgrace (for their
inconsistencies and impertinencies, tolerated for so
many years, cannot be the cause of their fall) I
beg you will let me know. . . . I pity them, and
if I can be of use to them it will be a pleasure
to me ; they can rely on that. Our situation
becomes even more delicate ; it is fortunate for us
that we have you. Believe in my confidence and
acknowledgment."

The Duc de Choiseul was so long the pilot of
France that his dismissal, at the requirement of
Madame du Barry, shook every Court of Europe with
amazement. To trace the causes of his fall it is necessary to see clearly the man himself, his family and its
branches, and the policy that broke into dust before
the charms of Madame du Barry. The Duc de
Choiseul has been the subject of many descriptions.
In Madame du Barry's memoirs she wrote of him :
" He was witty and gallant, and gifted with manners
so elegant and fascinating that they never failed to
remove the first unfavourable impression caused by
his excessive plainness," and if the memoirs are of

doubtful truth, the character is not. Another description is that of M. Vatel, who said : " He was as deficient in dignity as he was in gratitude, and succeeded in proving that there is a creature infinitely more loathesome than a courtesan, and that is a courtier." Yet a third description is that of Carlyle, who calls him " stout Choiseul," and the " last substantial man " of " Louis the royal valet." And the three are mutually destructive criticisms.

He had been minister of Louis XV. from 1758, and had during that time directed the foreign affairs of France as he willed, the King never opposing his advice, and yielding to him upon every course. But his political influence dates from 1753, when he first astonished the quiet Court of Pope Benedict XIV. with the state of a French Ambassador, and won Rome by the irresistible grace with which he employed all parties for his own ends. He then was transferred to Vienna, where the Franco-Austrian alliance, matrimonial and political, was planned; and finally he gathered up the reins of Louis' Government, and showed a nation not yet ripe for revolution how exquisitely a polished gentleman could unite a certain capacity for business with the courtly accomplishments more necessary in an elegant statesman. The countenance of Madame de Pompadour raised him to highest favour : the charms of Madame du Barry overthrew him.

The morality that led the de Choiseuls to shudder at the proximity of Madame du Barry was merely

relative, for the Duchesse de Choiseul had the abhor-
rence of all virtuous women for vice—not in their
own rank—and the Duc de Choiseul possessed that
well-regulated moral standard which merely desired
a *substitute* for the du Barry, and sought to provide
one in the wife of his nephew. During the period
in which Madame de Pompadour ruled in Europe,
de Choiseul was at the height of his power ; he
arranged the famous Family Compact in 1761
which bound in alliance the Bourbon crowns of
France, Spain, Parma, and Naples ; he reorganised
the army, he created a fleet, and he established
schools ; and in the year of her death (1764),
he concluded the expulsion of the Jesuits from
France, in spite of the strenuous opposition to
that measure by the Dauphin, the eldest son of
Louis XV.

The judgment of the Duc de Choiseul was assisted
by good luck ; he weighed the chances of father
and son, stirred up the hatred that lies in the heart
of every ruler for his successor, played on the distrust of the King for the Dauphin, and, flinging
away the future Louis in favour of the present, won
the game, for next year the Dauphin died. But in
1764 Madame de Pompadour died, as a Queen should
die, in rouged and royal state at Versailles, distributing honours to her clustering courtiers with her
dying breath while Louis confirmed her demands ; and
she was wheeled to her grave in a hand-barrow, which
Louis watched as it trundled past in the rain, saying

indifferently : " La Marquise has a wet journey."
De Choiseul lost his powerful ally; but there was an
interregnum of *maîtresse en titre*, and, undisturbed,
he completed the Franco-Austrian alliances.

In July, 1768, Louis first met Madame du Barry,
and thus she became his mistress three weeks after
the death of his wife, Marie Leczinska, who had died
on 25 June; but the proximity of dates implies nothing.
De Choiseul tried every means in his power to break
off the connection. There was a young and wonderfully beautiful Creole *née* Raby (or de Rubi), wife of
the Comte de Choiseul ; there was a beautiful lady the
wife of a Paris doctor, Madame Millin de la Courvault,
both of whom were quite willing to assist in so
important a service, but neither was successful. Then
de Choiseul endeavoured to arrange holy matrimony
for the King, and selected a consort of royal rank
for that honourable state ; but Louis's reply was
given in the following letter to the Duc de Choiseul,
written at Versailles in June, 1770, which runs,
rather breathlessly and entirely without stops, as
follows : " She [Madame du Barry] is very pretty
she pleases me that ought to suffice you do you want
me to marry a lady of rank if the Archduchess
were such as I should desire her to be I would
take her to wife with great pleasure for there must
be an end of this and the fair sex otherwise would
always trouble me for very surely you will not see
on my part a Dame de Maintenon."

Jeanne Bécu, now Madame du Barry, was not of a

nature to sit idle while de Choiseul worked thus hard to oust her.   Madame du Deffand writes in November, 1769 : "'La Dame' does not conceal her hate of the Duc de Choiseul any longer. . . . He receives every day little annoyances, such as not being nominated or invited for the *souper de cabinet* ; and at her house grimaces when he is her partner at whist, mockeries, the raising of shoulders, etc." To punish the Duc de Choiseul she refused any longer to invite the Duc de Gontaut (who had married a sister of the Duchesse de Choiseul), which, as Madame du Deffand remarks, was making a *hussard* of him. A *hussard* was the little whipping-boy who was whipped whenever Louis XV., in his youth, refused to say his lessons.

The whole Court took sides : "morality" on the one, with the shocked de Choiseuls, the Duchesse de Gramont (who had failed in obtaining the succession to her friend Madame de Pompadour : *D'aspect viril, osseuse et sans grâce, elle avait su qu'on chansonnait les leçons d'ostéologie qu'elle voulait donner à Louis XV.*"), the Prince and Princesse de Beauvau, and all their friends and relatives ; and "religion" on the other, as embodied in the du Barry, friend and champion of the Jesuits, the Duc d'Aiguillon, the *collier* Cardinal de Rohan, Maupeou ("*Ce noir vizir despote*") the Duc de la Vauguyon (who had fomented the quarrel between de Choiseul and the late Dauphin), and a crowd of paid newsmongers.   Mesdames hovered, hesitating between religion and morality,

and embracing neither : against Choiseul by sympathy with their dead brother, the Dauphin, yet
scandalised at the success of his enemies. Louis himself hovered likewise, but embracing both, until—the
final triumph of Madame du Barry—he sent the Duc
de Choiseul the *lettre de cachet* exiling him to his
estate at Chanteloup, on 24 December, 1770. In the
twenty-four hours that were permitted de Choiseul
before departure, nearly every personage of importance
in Paris came to inscribe his name upon the books.
He drove off to Chanteloup escorted by a double row
of carriages of endless number, more powerful than
the Louis who had exiled him.   " They could not
have made more of him if he had been a celebrated
criminal ! " said the Duc d'Ayen.

Marie Thérèse's counsels to the Dauphine were
coloured by the fall of de Choiseul : " Never
forget that your position is due to the des January,
Choiseul ; never forget it is your duty to
prove you recognise this. You have more need
than ever, my daughter, of the counsels of Mercy-
Argenteau. . . . Do not be led into any faction ; remain
neutral in everything ; ensure your safeguards—the
approval of the King, the good-will of your husband.
Try to line your head a little (*tapissez un peu votre
tête*) with good reading ; this is more necessary to
you than to any one else. I have been waiting two
months for that list [of studies] from the Abbé . . .
but the donkeys and the horses have taken up all
the time you should have been reading. Reading is

the more necessary to you in that you have no other accomplishments, neither music, nor drawing, nor dancing, nor painting, nor any other pleasing form of knowledge. Be always reticent ; give no confidences and have no curiosity, if you wish to preserve your peace and general approval. . . . I am sorry to have to say it : do not confide in those aunts whom I esteem so greatly ; I speak from experience. Perhaps even Mercy does not know, but I do not speak without cause. I am delighted to hear you are giving balls ; it will do much good to the Dauphin."

Mercy detailed to Mary Thérèse all the arrangements that, on the fall of the minister, he had made on behalf of the Dauphine. Within an hour of hearing of the disgrace of de Choiseul, he had despatched de Vermond to tell her what bearing would be most befitting. He could not have gone himself : it would have been remarked. She was advised to preserve a deportment combining natural grief at his disgrace, with regret that he had displeased the King his master ; and to show no knowledge of his enemies nor of the means they had taken to ruin him. She was perfectly discreet—until she met Mesdames. " I have the unhappy certainty that of all the ideas that Madame Adélaïde instils into the mind of the Dauphine, there is not one that is not radically false and injurious to her Royal Highness. Madame Adélaïde has no mental coherence or consistency. She openly declared herself the protectress of the Duc

[margin note: Paris, 23 January, 1771.]

de Choiseul and the Duchesse de Gramont, but the morrow of the exile of the Minister, she was the first to aggravate his conduct and inculpate his sister, to the public scandal."

Madame de Narbonne governed Madame Adélaïde entirely, and sought through her to govern the Dauphine, but the invariable presence of de Vermond prevented this. Mercy lays great stress upon the fact that if this clique succeeded in dismissing de Vermond there would be no confidential channel to convey information to or from the Dauphine. Mesdames, on their side, took measures to prevent the Dauphine from having sufficient leisure ever to see Mercy.

The arrival of Dr. Ingenhouse was an event of importance to the Court. He was a celebrated doctor born in Breda in 1730, who had been living for years in London studying the Suttonian method of inoculation for the small-pox, and had been elected Fellow of the Royal Society in 1769. The President of the Royal Society, Sir John Pringle, recommended him to the Empress Marie Thérèse. He had inoculated all the members of the Austrian Royal Family, and the Empress had sent him to Paris to report on the health of Marie Antoinette, of the Dauphin, and of the other members of the Royal Family. Mercy occupied himself with making the necessary arrangements, but found an objection raised by the Dauphine, that she could not receive a man who had not the privilege of *entrée* to Court. This stumbling block of etiquette, of course due to Madame Adélaïde, was swept aside by Mercy, who represented to Marie Antoinette that a doctor sent to her by her mother was exempt from all such regulations of etiquette, and Dr. Ingenhouse was accordingly admitted to see the Dauphine, who was very gracious to him. It will be remembered that one of the accusations levelled in later years against Marie Antoinette was that she had advised the inoculation against small-pox of the King and his brothers, "which was an Austrian practice."

Mercy then describes the success of the Dauphine when unhampered by Mesdames : balls every Monday, the Dauphine's manner to all quite charming, no one forgotten or overlooked, every one enchanted. " The King shows his pleasure at her success, and wishes her to enjoy herself. His Majesty has commanded that two comedies shall be played each week at Versailles, simply because it has been suggested to him that it would please the Dauphine. The Dauphine increases her influence over the mind of the Dauphin in everything, and this young Prince changes, to his visible improvement. . . . He once observed : 'She is so graceful, she succeeds in everything ; one must admit that she is charming' "—amazing words from the timid and taciturn Dauphin.

Now occurred a little intrigue in which the play is amusing. The Empress desired that the Marquis de Durfort should be rewarded by the Dauphine for the services in connection with her marriage. Madame Adélaïde, moved by the Comtesse de Narbonne, prevented this, but did not reckon on the ready wit of the Marquise de Durfort, who held the same position with Madame Victoire as Madame de Narbonne in the household of Madame Adélaïde. The brother-in-law of Madame de Narbonne now desired preferment : he was the Bishop of Gap and wished to be chief almoner to Madame Victoire. But the Marquise de Durfort, exerting her influence, put as effectual a stop to the Bishop's ambitions as Madame de Narbonne had done to those of the Marquis de Durfort. Both ladies discovered that reciprocity was the only means of success, both capitulated, both exploited their respective royal ladies ; and Madame Adélaïde was henceforth in favour of the Marquise de Durfort and Madame Victoire of the Bishop of Gap. The Dauphine, finding this change of front, presented her request to the King, who granted immediately to de Durfort the dignity of a dukedom and peer of France. Marie Thérèse had recommended her daughter to do this on 4 May, 1770.

In this letter of January 23 is the first mention of the *parties de traîneau* which afterwards became so celebrated. Mercy went to Versailles. " I found preparations for a sleigh party at mid-day, which left the Dauphine neither time nor opportunity to speak to me." Mercy, at a very inappropriate moment, embarrassed her by speaking about her studies ; and she replied that it was impossible to do lessons regularly in the Carnival, but she would make up in Lent. Mercy says : " The Dauphin shows neither pain nor pleasure at the disgrace of the Duc de Choiseul. . . .   He seems to take no interest in any one at the Court, not even in those who have served him from infancy. . . . With a little management the Dauphine will certainly govern the Prince, her husband, whose apathetic condition seems to arise more from a bad education and excessive timidity than from a vicious character."

Mercy, in his letter of 23 January, summed up the causes of the fall of de Choiseul: "These are the chief: the arrogant temper and indiscreet language of the Duchesse de Gramont [Beatrix de Choiseul Stainville, his sister] and of the Princesse de Beauvau, her intimate friend ; the facility with which the Duc de Choiseul yielded to all their impulses ; the open war against the favourite into which they dragged him ; the bold remarks that he permitted himself to make to his master about this woman, and even more the public and piquant jokes that he made about her ; the embittering of the King by false witnesses that de Choiseul had excited the Parliament to disobedience against him ; the pressure of the chancellor and the Prince de Condé ; and incessant prayers from the favourite."

The disgraced Duc received the news with the greatest coolness. He started at once for Paris, and found the Duchesse just sitting down to dinner. "You look like an exiled man," she said, "but sit down ; our dinner will not taste the worse for that." They dined perfectly calmly while an enormous crowd gathered to inscribe the chief names of France in

the book at the gate ; then he arranged his domestic
matters and left in the morning for Chanteloup,
followed by his wife and sister. " They are there
now with a number of their relatives, leading a life
of great comfort to all appearance. . . . The King
has shown no sign of resentment against the Duc
de Choiseul since his departure ; there are even
moments when he appears to doubt whether he has
been deceived about his minister, and to regret him.
We assume from this that he will be permitted to
keep the appointment of colonel-general of the
Suisses and his governorship, which are the more
necessary to him as he has left office with debts of
over three millions, although he has had revenues of
50,000 livres from the King's bounty alone."

The question of money grew serious to the Duc
de Choiseul after his fall. His patrimony was small,
as his inheritance was one of nobility merely, but his
marriage with the sister of the Duchesse de Gontaut
made him rich ; offices and revenues were heaped
upon him, but with an income of three-quarters of
a million per annum he was always swamped in debts.
His graceful adaptability to circumstances made him
support the loss of political power with perfect
philosophy, but the loss of revenues touched him
more nearly. This appointment of colonel of the
Suisses was worth 100,000 francs (£4,000) a year ;
but he forfeited it by encouraging further publications
of those scurrilous libels against Madame du Barry
that he had promoted before his fall.

He then petitioned (or rather demanded) from the King the settlement of all his debts, amounting to 6,000,000 francs, a revenue of 40,000 francs to be charged on the Forest of Hagenau, forest rights amounting to about 800,000 francs, and an annuity of 50,000 francs, to be continued to his wife if he died first, also a valuable military command and liberty to travel. These demands, translated into modern equivalents, are much the same as if a disgraced minister were to ask for the settlement of £240,000 of debts, and an income of £35,000 in addition. In contrast with these exorbitant demands it is said that he received a "gratification" of 100,000 écus (£12,000) and a pension of 60,000 livres (£2,400), with remainder to the Duchesse de Choiseul—all through the intercession of Madame du Barry. But nevertheless his debts amounted at his death in 1785 to 3,000,000 livres (£120,000) although he had sold his pictures, diamonds, and plate for nearly 1,700,000 francs (£68,000).

CHAPTER VII

Dissatisfaction of Marie Thérèse—Mental Development
of the Dauphin—Wages of Servants at Court—At
Chanteloup—The Princesse de Lamballe—The
King of Sweden and Madame du Barry—Her Dog
—Tributes to her—The *Lit de Justice*—The Comtesse de Provence—Confusion at Court—The Duc
de St. Mégrin

M ARIE THÈRÉSE wrote to the Dauphine:
"I hope sincerely that your complexion
and your figure are not suffering from so
much horse-exercise; the gazettes say that February,
during the cold weather you take it in the ¹⁰ 1771.
riding-school. I beg that you will tell me truthfully
if you dance any better than you did, particularly in
the *contredanse*. I fear that the future Comtesse
de Provence will cut you out; they say a great deal
about her and her excellent character, that she is
sweet without being pretty, with *beaucoup de physio-
nomie et très bien prise dans sa taille*. You seem
to be doing nothing but amuse yourself—nothing
solid or useful, only killing time by promenades and
visits. I must tell you that the style of your letters
is every day worse and more incorrect; in ten months
you ought to have improved." And to Mercy she

wrote her uneasiness more fully respecting the apathy of the Dauphin, and her fear for her daughter, in these stormy times at the Court of France. "Her carelessness, lack of taste for serious application, indiscreetness, *liaison* with the aunts, particularly Madame Adélaïde, the most intriguing of them all, are all causes of uneasiness in the circumstances ; and as to the Durfort affair, I am thankful there are no such examples of *manigances* at my Court."

Mercy, in his report, recounts a great sensation caused at a ball given by the Comtesse de Noailles, by the entrance of the Dauphin and Dauphine arm in arm. He not only said to his hostess, "I hope, madame, that you will receive both husband and wife ; we have come to share your amusements," but even danced, and spoke to all those presented to him. "This conduct has raised hopes for which we have never before had justification." Louis, under the inspiriting influence of the Dauphine, had summoned words to address the Duc de la Vauguyon with contempt, and had complained of the bad education he had given him ; this mental activity had astonished all at Court.

"I have begged the Dauphine to put her accounts a little in order, and set down her expenditure from time to time. This has been done this month and the treasurer of her Royal Highness, a person named Pommery, has sent in his statement, which accounts for a sum received of 80,000 livres (£3,200)." Of this sum 7,000 francs (£280) remained, and the Dauphine ordered it to be divided amongst her lower servants, who, not having been paid their wages, were "in that state of embarrassment and misery common to all who constitute the domestic service of this Court." Mercy pointed out that although the Dauphine ostensibly had a revenue of 92,000 livres (£3,680) at her disposal, she really had the spending of only a quarter of that sum, because the greater portion of the money was "converted to the uses" of those who regulated it, which is a very delicate phrase for peculation.

" The Dauphine is on better terms than ever with the King, who very often kisses her hands; and when she is at her ease and forgets the lessons in timidity given her by Mesdames, the King is enchanted, and shows a gaiety never revealed to any of his own children. The Duc and Duchesse de Choiseul, the Duchesse de Gramont, and many of their relatives are at Chanteloup, quite peacefully, and *assez gais et contents*. The enemies of the Duc do not cease to work furiously against him with the intention of taking from him the command of the Suisses and Grisons; but at present they have not succeeded, because the chief persecutor [the Duc de la Vauguyon] is ill of a mortal malady that may deliver France from one of the most dangerous subjects she has produced. Paris continues, with a sort of enthusiasm, to give marks of the public esteem and regret to the fallen minister."

This much-coveted colonelcy of the Suisses, that

meant a revenue of £4,000 a year, was only held during the King's good pleasure, as was, in fact, everything else in France, for the Crown disposed of persons by *lettres de cachet*, of property by confiscation, and of the public revenues by imposts. There was nothing in France to withstand the King's desire : the nobility had lost their powers, though retaining the shells—their titles and distinctions ; the people had no rights, royalty felt no limitations except from the wits. A "despotism tempered by epigram" sought vainly to suppress that tempering, and from Chanteloup came a series of biting verses and *jeux d'esprit* directed against the favourite, for the Duc de Choiseul kept open house there to any man of letters who would write something scurrilous about Madame du Barry. Louis acknowledged the wounding by taking away the regiment of Suisses ; but this did not stop the shafts. A vast mushroom growth of anti-du Barry literature sprang up all over France, beyond the power even of Louis to suppress. Books multiplied in spite of the searchings of entire districts. A story is told *à propos* of these suppressions that a magistrate of Berne, instructed to search his district for copies of the *Esprit* of Helvetius and Voltaire's *Pucelle*, wrote in his report to headquarters : "That after a most scrupulous search, *Nous n'avons trouvé dans tout le canton ni Esprit ni Pucelle.*"

The strange supineness and mental indolence of the Dauphin caused great anxiety to Marie Thérèse,

who, knowing how strong a party was working to
bring about a divorce between Marie Antoinette and her husband, begged Mercy to keep   **Vienna**
                                              15 March,
her fully informed as to any improvement   **1771.**
in the Dauphin, whose conduct was, as Mercy said,
grievously inexplicable.   Marie Thérèse's anxieties
grew and increase ; in her letter of March 15 she
writes : " I am not satisfied with the Dauphine, but
these things are difficult to remedy.   I will pull a
little on this cord again, but I shall have to touch
it delicately.   I know my children ; preach to them
too much and it spoils everything and does not
correct them.   I am afraid that on the arrival of the
Comtesse de Provence jealousies will break out ; French
lightness and Court intrigues will do the rest. . . . I
am glad to hear the Dauphin improves, but I cannot
understand his conduct to his wife; is it the result
of bad principles ? "   And she ends with : " Is it
true the King has taken to drink ? "—truly a gathering cloud of evils.

In March of this year is the first mention of the
charming Princesse de Lamballe who was
so closely connected with Marie Antoinette   **Paris,**
                                              17 March,
in life and in death.   Mercy writes to   **1771.**
the Empress : " For some time past the Dauphine
has shown a great affection for the Princesse de
Lamballe, who was born a Princesse de Carignan and
is widow of the Prince de Lamballe, son of the Duc
de Penthièvre.   This young Princesse is sweet and
amiable, and, enjoying the privileges of Princesse of

the blood royal, is in a position to avail herself of her Royal Highness's favour." This privilege of the blood royal was widely diffused by Louis XIV., for the *roi soleil* was the source of more than honours, and recognised many of his descendants by the simple course of legitimation and dukedoms. The inter-weaving of relationship and the intermarriages of all these claimants to royal privileges form an intricate study, not unamusing for those who like to disentangle the lines of Madame de Montespan's descendants from those of Louise de la Vallière and both from the legitimate members of the Royal family ; to dis-tinguish for example between the daughters of la Vallière and de Montespan, both entitled "Made-moiselle de Blois," of whom the one married a Prince de Conti and the other Philippe, Duc d'Orléans ; and to trace the origin of the alliances, temporary or permanent, that ensured the privileges of royal blood.

The Princesse de Lamballe owed her position at Court and the opportunities it gave for intimacy with Marie Antoinette to the fact that her husband's grand-father was the third son of Madame de Montespan. She had been married while still a child to the young Prince de Lamballe ; at eighteen she became a widow on the death of her husband, a youth with the vices and without the constitution of the Duc de Chartres —that de Chartres (afterwards d'Orléans) of whom Carlyle wrote that he lived "in dull smoke and ashes of outburnt sensualities," within whom "confusion of confusions sits bottled." Her father-in-law, the Duc de Penthièvre, was growing old, and Marie Antoinette, who pitied both the sad little widow and her own lonely self, took her into her household for friendship, and to give her the pleasures she had not yet enjoyed ; for from the time that she had married the Prince de Lamballe, she "had nothing but tears to shed."

Round the pretty widowed Princesse de Lamballe intrigues gathered, and Mercy continues to the Empress : "The Comtesse de Brionne, always keen about what would benefit her family, has formed the project of marrying the Princesse de Lamballe to her son, the Prince de Lambesc, and has made the Dauphine promise to consent and give her approval." Mercy went immediately to Versailles to point out to the Dauphine that the Princesse de Lamballe would, by marrying de Lambesc, forfeit her rank as a Princess of "the blood," and that if the Dauphine interested herself in the matter she would have to indemnify the Princess for that loss, and would find in addition that she had charged herself with all the pretensions of the Comtesse de Brionne's entire family.

The Comtesse de Brionne was a de Rohan-Rochefort, and had married into that Lorraine family to which was allied the Austrian Royal House. She was very ambitious for her children, and demanded that precedence should be given to her daughter, Mademoiselle de Lorraine, at the minuet danced at the wedding of the Dauphine. This caused such wrath amongst the nobles present that an immensely long remonstrance was drawn up and presented to the King against this breach of their privileges. The only amusing thing in connection with this solemn remonstrance is in Louis's reply. He said that the choice in such matters was merely one of his will, especially as the ball was given in honour of an advantageous alliance, that tended to the happiness of his family and, addressing directly the bearer of the remonstrance, the Bishop of Noyon, "*la felicité de vos enfants.*"

The Prince de Lambesc did not marry the Princesse de Lamballe, distinguished himself greatly in the time of the Revolution, and fought at the head of his regiment in the garden of the Tuileries. He was Master of the Horse to the King, and at the Restoration the office was not filled up, on the assumption that it was still occupied by de Lambesc, who was living in Austria in 1827. The error into which the Dauphine might have fallen, in promoting the marriage of the Princesse de Lamballe with the Prince de Lambesc, was very clear to the Empress, who wrote to Mercy-Argenteau her thankfulness that his advice had guided the Dauphine.

Marie Thérèse adds, of her daughter's letters : "Here is her letter, still very badly written, which tells me nothing interesting. The confusion that reigns amongst you makes me shudder, although our own situation is not smiling. Starhemberg [formerly Austrian Ambassador to Versailles, now Minister Plenipotentiary of the Netherlands under Charles, Prince of Lorraine] will

Vienna 1 April, 1771.

have told you the movements of troops in the
Netherlands and in Italy. I have no opinion of
these demonstrations, so costly and so ruinous, but
I should have even greater difficulties to encounter
in war. We are not in a position to carry on at the
same time two wars against the Russians, and probably
one against the Prussians. . . . I have received the
gauzes, which are very nice ; also the bureau, which is
beautiful and richly ornamented with good taste . . .
it will be placed at Schönbrunn, in my cabinet near
the garden ; I should like to find out what it cost. . . .
I confess I should not like to see St. Mégrin here,
the son of that contemptible Vauguyon, an ambassador sent by *that woman*. They talk here of
the unworthy acts of the King of Sweden towards
that woman ; what a disgrace ! "

The Crown Prince of Sweden, afterwards Gustavus
III., had been on a visit to Paris, and had paid that
amount of court to Madame du Barry which her
position as virtual ruler of France justified. He had
travelled *incognito* as the Comte de Haga, but his
person was as well known as his attentions, and the
presents that he had given Madame du Barry were
widely advertised. He sent her every year afterwards
a handsome box filled with Swedish gloves, as an
annual tribute to her sovereignty, and gave her a
collar and chain for her little dog, the collar of
red morocco with a clasp and ring of diamonds,
and the chain, more than a yard long, composed
entirely of rubies. Madame du Barry's little dog

was a Blenheim spaniel, to judge by the description, and was a personage of importance ; her name was "Dorine" ; she generally wore a rich gold collar bearing the Du Barry arms, and clasped with a large sapphire surrounded by diamonds ; she drank her coffee from a golden saucer and had a slave-boy, Zamor (the same slave to whom Louis gave the governorship of Louveciennes), to wait upon her.

A less successful, but equally historical, act of tribute to Madame du Barry was the embassy sent to her by Tippoo Sahib when he desired to make war against England. Six bejewelled ambassadors bore offerings of finest muslins to her, and entreated that she would, in return, give the alliance of France. But Tippoo Sahib was the victim of a miscalculation of time ; his embassy arrived in 1788, when Louis XV. had been dead for years and Louis XVI. reigned. Madame du Barry kept the muslins—as homage—but the ambassadors lost their heads on their return to India.

On 16 April Marie Antoinette wrote to her mother (who had impressed upon her "to avoid all French lightness and remain a good German and glory in that") : "I should be very sorry if the Germans disapproved of me. I confess I should have spoken more to the Marquis de Paar [nephew of Marie Thérèse's ancient Grand Mistress of the Court], and the little Starhemberg if they had had a better reputation here. But I did summon the Marquis de Lamberg. and Starhemberg to balls, and after

16 April.

seeing that they could dance I let them dance with me. There is much going on here now ; on Saturday there was the *lit de justice*, to confirm the abolishing of the ancient Parliament and putting a new one in its place ; the Princes of the blood refused to come to it and have protested against the King's decree. They wrote to him a very impertinent letter, signed by all of them except the Comte de la Marche, who behaved very well on this occasion. [He was the son of the Prince de Conti, afterwards Duc de Conti, and was cast off by his father for this.] What is the most astonishing thing of all in the conduct of the Princes is that the Prince de Condé has made his son [father of the Duc d'Enghien shot by Napoleon, 1804] sign, though he is not yet fifteen years old and has always been brought up here. The King has sent him away and also all the other Princes who are forbidden to appear before him or before us. All the Dukes have protested, and from what I hear there will be quite a dozen exiles."

Thus casually does Marie Antoinette mention the first grapple between the people and the despotism of royalty : the first surge of the *déluge après moi*— her only feeling being shocked surprise at any one disputing the King's decree ! This was the disorganisation of the ancient Parliament, engineered and carried through by Maupeou, to *retirer la couronne du greffe*, with endeavour to renew that absolutism whose mainspring Louis XIV. wore out by too protracted tension and Louis XV. snapped.

Marie Antoinette's letter continued : " In a month's time I shall be able to give your Majesty news of the Comtesse de Provence, for the marriage is fixed for May 14th : they had prepared many fêtes for this marriage but now they are economising in them for want of money." [It was estimated that the fêtes at Versailles in honour of the Dauphin's marriage the previous year had cost 20,000,000 livres (£800,000) ; even the Abbé Terray, the financier, could not arrange for similar expenditure merely for a Dauphin's younger brother.] " Your Majesty may rest assured about my conduct towards the Comtesse de Provence ; I will certainly try and gain her friendship and confidence, without going too far. But I am much afraid that, unless she has wits and is warned, she will go over to the side of Madame du Barry. They are doing all they can to gain her, for her lady-in-waiting, who is Madame de Valentinois, is altogether of that party ; there is also Madame de Caumont, who goes to meet her ; she it was who embroiled the late Dauphine with everybody ; and there is M. de St. Mégrin, son of Madame de la Vauguyon, who is even more intriguing and malicious than his father ; he wanted very much to go to Vienna in place of the Baron de Breteuil : I knew what an annoyance that would be to your Majesty, and, thank God, that affair is broken off." This letter shows the Dauphine developed and with sharpened wits, observing the Court intrigues with much amusement and that " salt " with which she was credited.

The expected arrival of the Comtesse de Provence
exercised all members of the Court, each of
whom saw in her either a *pantin* whose strings   Paris,
16 April,
could be worked to advantage, or a rival   1771.
against whose encroachments a guard was to be raised.
Mercy-Argenteau, with his keen scent for anything
likely to weaken the position of the Dauphine as
leading royal lady at the Court, employed every means
of awakening her to a sense of the danger, and wrote
to Marie Thérèse his efforts and his anxieties :

"The moment of arrival approaches, and I recall
to the Dauphine the essentials of the situation. . . .
I think if your Majesty will also write on this subject
it will be useful. Madame de Provence will be
assuredly well tutored and she will strive to attract
the King to her house ; the Dauphine in giving herself
over to Mesdames, her aunts, has neglected this
advantage. . . . From October last I have not ceased
speaking to the Dauphine about this. . . . Contrary
to all hope the Duc de la Vauguyon has recovered
from his recent dangerous illness. . . . The existence
of this dangerous man is a great misfortune, and his
intrigues are the more to be feared because he is
so entirely unscrupulous as to his means. . . . This
day was a very remarkable one : the *lit de justice*
was held in the morning, and the new Parliament
created. All minds are seething with excitement. . . .
I begged the Dauphine, in so critical a moment, to have
no opinion at all ; neither praise nor blame."

Mercy adds in another letter that the reason why

Marie Antoinette's writing was so invariably bad, in
her letters to her mother, is that she writes
them in the greatest possible secrecy and
haste, through dread of being caught by
the Dauphin or by Mesdames, as her correspondence
with her mother was quite unknown to them. He
says : " Notwithstanding what I write in my ministerial
despatches, it is almost impossible for your Majesty
to form any adequate idea of the horrible confusion
which reigns here in everything.   The throne is
degraded by the shamelessness and the unlimited power
of the favourite, and by the unscrupulousness of her
partisans.   The nation breathes sedition in indecent
writings, which do not even spare the person of the
King ; Versailles has become the abode of treachery,
hatred, and revenge ; everything is worked by intrigues
and inspired by personal ambitions, and it seems as
if the world had renounced even the semblance of
uprightness. . . . I have represented to the Dauphine
that her only safeguard in these critical times is pro-
found silence on matters and on men."   Thus Mercy
described that France of which Carlyle afterwards
wrote : " A powder-tower, where fire unquenched and
now unquenchable is smoking and smouldering all
round."

Mercy-Argenteau gives Marie Thérèse details of
the cost of the bureau that Marie Antoinette had
sent her ; its price was 1776 livres (£71 0s. 9d.) and
the frame for the portrait cost 228 livres, (£9 2s.),
all of which would be paid out of the Dauphine's

*Paris
16 April,
1771.*

money. He continues : " I feel that the choice of
the Duc de St. Mégrin as Ambassador of France
would be disagreeable to your Majesty. This young
man, of an emotionless bearing, is believed to be
one of the most vicious persons living, far exceeding
his father. It is terrible to think that the King now
is entirely surrounded by people of this stamp, who
succeed in removing all those in whom they suspect
any virtue. It is true that the King of Sweden
[who arrived on February 4 in Paris ; and heard of
the death of his father and his own accession on
March 1] has stretched his political complaisance
toward the favourite rather overmuch ; . . . but it
is nevertheless true that he was deceived, and when
the King of Sweden went to sup with Madame du
Barry he was led to believe that the most Christian
King would be there also, which did not happen. . . .
Your Majesty commands me to say whether the King
has taken to drink. The report is not well founded,
and arises from the fact that one may often observe
in this monarch attacks of vacuity (*absences d'esprit*)
which resemble the effect of drunkenness. It is
obvious that the mind of the King weakens daily,
and to the failing is added the apathy caused by
the universal disorder that surrounds him."

CHAPTER VIII

The Portrait of Marie Antoinette—The Jesuits in France
—Presentation at Court of Madame du Barry—
Madame du Barry and Marie Antoinette—The
Duchesse de St. Mégrin—Arrival of the Comtesse
de Provence—The Archduchess Marie Amélie of
Parma—The Playthings of the Dauphine

THE much heralded portrait of Marie Antoinette
arrived in Schönbrunn, and Marie Thérèse
writes thus to Mercy of her present : " I am
enchanted with my bureau ; even more so with the
frame ; less with the picture. She was
prettier when I saw her last. Does she hold
herself so stiffly ? And does she dress her
hair like that ? I await the large portrait by Liotard
impatiently, and I hope that they will not forget the
one on horseback. In the meantime, if you can,
send me a little sketch of her, painted on horseback,
hat on head, a miniature if possible, even if the
likeness is not good. They say that the Jesuits will
come back, and that they are all in the ascendant
from this time forward. I shall be curious to see
if it is so."

*Schönbrunn,
7 May,
1771.*

The fall of de Choiseul from power was the signal
of the reversal of his policy ; his action in the ex-

pulsion of the Jesuits from France had concentrated against him all the forces of the Church—their centre of attraction was Madame du Barry ; their hope of returning influence in France, her influence over the King. The *Cabale des dévots*, the " Aiguillonistes," and the " Barrins " as they were termed from their titled figureheads, utilised to the full the sway of Madame du Barry over the failing senses of Louis XV., *le fils aîné de l'Eglise*, and rewarded her for her success with the *roi très chrétien* by giving her, in 1772, the diploma of the order of the Society of Jesus and the sacred scapulary. Even as early as 1769 the whole hope of the Church lay in the charms of the *maîtresse en titre*, and their prayers were for " the presentation [at Court] of the modern Esther, who is to throw down Haman [Choiseul] and deliver the Jews [the clerical party] from oppression."

This presentation at Court had been productive of the liveliest scenes : without it Madame du Barry could not be admitted to royal suppers, or reside in the palace, or flit unvirtuously with the King from one palace to another. But it was essential to etiquette to have had a father, and, although " maternity is a matter of fact, paternity a matter of opinion," Madame du Barry could produce only a mother. Louis proposed to get over this difficulty by purchasing for her the principality of Lus-en-Bigarre for 700,000 livres, and letting her pass herself in as a foreign princess to whose existence, apparently,

a father was not needful.   It is not known how the
matter was settled, but "the modern Esther" was
duly presented on April 22.   No wonder, in view
of these religious complications, that Marie Thérèse
straitly enjoined her daughter : "Never discuss Jesuits."

The next letter of Marie Thérèse to the Dauphine
Schönbrunn, gives throughout evidence of Mercy-
8 May, Argenteau's skilful suggestions, which, coming
1771. from her mother, were not suspected by
Marie Antoinette to have been inspired by Mercy's
knowledge of her surroundings.   She touches lightly
on the portrait's deficiencies : "I do not find that air
of youth that my dear daughter had eleven months
ago," and then goes on diplomatically with regard
to the Comtesse de Provence : "You will give
me pleasure by letting me know what you think
of your sister-in-law ; according to Rosenberg's
accounts you will have no cause to be jealous of
her, but rather to pity and care for her ; it will
do you honour and be befitting her place if you
try to save her from her embarrassments, but not
to lead her, for that would be as uncalled-for as
jealousy.   They say she has not a good figure, is
very shy, has no manner, but is, after all, very well
brought up" [which is a masterpiece of suggestion
for the maintenance of the Dauphine's superiority].
"What you tell me about the two ladies appointed
to the household of the Comtesse de Provence
should prove to you how fortunate you are to have
Madame de Noailles. . . . She is a woman who

appears to be straightforward and attached to you, this is a great point; and among the chief families, where could you find one perfect? All are either intriguing or else wearisome." [Mercy said of her: "This Comtesse has so few wits and so little character, that it is impossible to make her listen to reason on the best method adequately to fulfil her duties."] "Take care not to lose what you have gained by neglect of the means that gained it; it was not your beauty (which candidly is insufficient), or your talents, or your knowledge (you know quite well that all these do not exist), but your goodness of heart, unrestraint, attentions well bestowed. . . . They say you neglect to single out and talk to distinguished persons, that at table or when at play you only chatter to your young ladies, whispering in their ears and laughing with them. . . . Never turn others into ridicule; you were always inclined that way. . . . Do not imagine that Mercy has written to me about it, but I must tell you that it is astonishing how much people know here. . . . Follow the advice of Mercy, who only thinks of your welfare, and mix yourself up with no party; if you could even ignore all of them it would be better. It is in times like these that I prefer to hear of those rides on horseback, coach drives, ball, entertainments, and everything that is called pleasure, even if the amusements are childish."

By this time, a year since the Dauphine had first arrived at the Court of France, it had become evident that it was no longer possible for Marie Antoinette

Paris,
22 May,
1771. to play the pretence of ignorance—or rather of passive ignoring—of the favourite. At first it had been assumed that Louis's fickle, exhausted senses could not remain enslaved by one ; it was believed—and no efforts were spared to convert the belief into a reality—that the light of Madame du Barry would soon be eclipsed by the rising of some other star, but, although a galaxy was available, none succeeded in outshining the favourite. Each month seemed to make the power of Madame du Barry more assured, and the abject submission of her royal " valet " more complete. Exile and disgrace awaited all that spoke lightly of the sovereign lady ; nor were the members of the Royal family spared, if any lack of enthusiasm towards her was noticed by the senile autocrat, for, to do justice to the lady, she seldom took the trouble to resent such matters herself. It is recorded of her once that, when the lieutenant of police caught a writer of libels against her, and waited upon her to learn her wishes as to how he was to be dealt with, saying : " Madame, we have caught a rascal, who writes scurrilous songs about you, what shall we do with him ? " she merely replied : " Make him say them, and then give him something to eat."

Mercy-Argenteau, recognising the necessity of conforming to surroundings, took an opportunity of explaining the matter to the Dauphine, and wrote to Marie Thérèse that he had drawn a picture, a very circumstantial one, to the Dauphine of her actual position, and represented the expediency " of establishing a course of conduct, by means of which, without dissimulation or falseness, she could attain to an appreciation of the qualities of any one." Which is an entirely delightful and diplomatic cloak of words. He pointed out that it was beneath the dignity of a great princess not to accept what she could not alter, and that she should not show her powerlessness by useless opposition, nor flatter the partisans of Madame du Barry by being aware that they were partisans ; that their greatest punishment would be her easy indifference to them, and that, in short, she would show " elevation of soul " by condescending to speak to Madame du Barry.

The Dauphine, quite ingenuously, replied that only the fear of Mesdames prevented her from speaking a word to the favourite, but that she would commence with the Comtesse de Valentinois and the Duc d'Aiguillon, and she did so speak next day to the open amazement of the *cabale*.

Mercy continues in his diary that the Dauphine is as fond of riding as ever, and records a little accident, " of which I was informed, in spite of all the precautions taken to hide it from me." · The Dauphine was out riding in the neighbourhood of Versailles ; the horse of one of the grooms kicked and injured the foot of Marie Antoinette, who gave not the slightest sign of pain, continued her ride, and returned with her foot greatly swollen. When her ladies reproached her for not having declared the injury at once she replied she had hidden it to spare the groom the grief of having caused her an injury.   Mercy has to report that the Dauphine has slightly (*un peu*) broken her word never to hunt on horseback ; she had followed the hounds boar-hunting, under the pretext that she had come upon them by accident.   The Dauphine had strongly impressed secrecy upon every one, lest Mercy should find out ; but he had discovered it, and suggested that if the Empress reproached her for this breach of faith the surprise would doubtless be great.

The next endeavour on the part of the du Barry coterie was to instal the Duchesse de St. Mégrin in the household of the Dauphine as a lady-in-waiting, in the place of the Duchesse de Villars, who wished to resign in favour of this daughter-in-law of the detested de la Vauguyon.

The Dauphine wrote instantly to the King to implore her "*cher papa*" that he would spare her this annoyance, and Mesdames insisted upon inserting (very injudiciously) a few choice phrases.   The King, ever anxious to grant everything to everybody— refusal being a greater strain to the mind—replied the same day, that he was not surprised that Madame de St. Mégrin did not please the Dauphine ; she was " too young and much too stupid."

On 11 May the Court went to Fontainebleau, and 11 May, on the 12 arrived the much anticipated 1771.   Comtesse de Provence.   All the Royal family went out two leagues to meet her, the King embraced her affectionately (saying behind her back that he found her very ugly, a sentiment in which the public all agreed); her husband received her with "transports of joy"; the Dauphin considered her "*pas trop bien*" according to rumour, and the Dauphine greeted her sister-in-law " with an easy air, with friendship, and with all the grace possible and without affectation," showing every little consideration, and joining therewith " a continuation of cajoleries for the King, which will produce a great effect."

Altogether Mercy was quite satisfied with the position the Dauphine had taken and her evident intention to retain it. He tells Marie Thérèse, with enthusiasm and a glow of satisfaction, that, although it might have been expected on such an occasion that the Comtesse de Provence would be the central figure, yet the King was much less interested in her than in the Dauphine, who had never looked so charming or had so complete a success. The King had even invited himself to breakfast with her the next day, and actually came, in "*robe de chambre*" into the bedroom of the Dauphine, and had his coffee with her there, making it himself (his invariable habit) and remaining with her for about two hours while all the Royal family arrived in succession and took coffee.

To Mercy, who had so dreaded the advent of the Comtesse de Provence, this was a triumph. The King had even commanded that a door of communication between his apartments and the Dauphine's (those of the late Queen), long closed, should be opened, which gave every prospect of a continuance of the coffee-drinking honour.

Louis had many minor accomplishments, and especially the skill with which he removed the top of an egg with a single blow from the back of a fork ; but another was the perfection with which he made his own coffee, the berries for which he roasted, ground, and prepared with his own royal hands. Madame Campan relates how this coffee-making was performed daily, to the filial admiration of Mesdames, in the room of Madame Adélaïde, whither the other old sisters, summoned by a bell, ran *à toutes jambes*, lest haply His Majesty might be gone before they could be embraced.

The appearance of the young bride also was soothing to the mind of Mercy. He says : " Her figure is not at all good, and her deportment not attractive, She has no graces at all ; she speaks little and dis-agreeably," and he adds that the Dauphine was not filled with pride at her manifest superiority, although she recognised it.

In another letter, written on the same day, Mercy reassures the Empress on the point of the portrait, saying that it was so bad he had hesitated to send it ; that the Dauphine does not hold herself so stiffly, or dress her hair like that—in short, " there is no resemblance at all " (although Marie Thérèse had to pay Liotard 1,800 livres [£72] for it) ; that the Dauphine is so much taller and more beautiful than

LES BERGÈRES D'ARCADIE.

Fêtes at Parma, on occasion of the Marriage of the Archduchess Marie Amélie and the Duke of Parma.

(*From an engraving, 1769, after Petitot.*)

[*Page 107.*]

before that her mother would be surprised to see her. " I do not cease to press forward the finishing of the great picture of the Dauphine mounted on horseback ; the death of the painter Vanloo, who commenced this work, has stayed its execution. I will send your Majesty a little portrait of the Dauphine, as she looks in her riding habit and with her hat on."

The exquisite portrait of the Dauphine that forms the frontispiece to this volume was painted at the Court about a year later than this date, and presented by Marie Antoinette to the Comte de Mercy-Argenteau. It has never before been reproduced.

To her faithful friend Mercy the Empress reveals her thoughts on the subject of her daughter Marie Amélie, who had married the Duke of Parma the year before Marie Antoinette had become the Dauphine.

Schönbrunn, 6 June, 1771.

This alliance had been heralded with great rejoicings, as it had bound the House of Austria to one of the Bourbon sovereigns of the Family Compact. Don Ferdinand, Duke of Parma and of Plaisance and of Guastalla, was the grandson of Phillip V., King of Spain (the grandson of Louis XIV.), and as his father had married Louise Elizabeth, the eldest daughter of Louis XV., he stood in the same relationship to the King of France also. The festivities at Parma were lavish : there was a tournament with all heraldic circumstance of golden armour, emblazoned arms, and knightly jousts, *fêtes* of noble *bergères d'Arcadie* (where the bride and bridegroom took the names of Phillis and Daphnis), and many other diversions.

But that was in 1769, and by 1771 the last shred of illusion had long been lost. Ferdinand of Parma was little better than an idiot, with a stupefied brain in a brutal body; without education save what had drifted from the teaching of so inappropriate an instructor (for eighteenth century Parma) as *Lycurgus*; with a mind attuned to the roasting of chestnuts and pervaded by superstition, and with just enough intelligence to leave all Government affairs entirely in the hands of the minister chosen by his two guardians, the Kings of France and of Spain—du Tillot, Marquis de Felino.

Marie Amélie, who was nine years older than Marie Antoinette, and had that preponderance of importance at the time of the marriage, that is given when the wife is an alert, vain, and impetuous woman of twenty-three, and the husband a boy of eighteen, at once timid and stupid. She commenced ruling by breaking down all the safeguards of etiquette, and then flightily set herself in opposition to du Tillot, and thus ranged the little state of Parma against the kingdoms of France and Spain and even the Empire of Austria, for Marie Thérèse (as will be seen) spared no endeavour to convince her daughter of the folly of her way.

The Empress said to Mercy: " The Infanta, my daughter, has written to me of her fresh attempts against du Tillot, but I have answered her that I remember quite well the promise she and her husband gave to the two great Kings, that they would let du Tillot act for four years without interference, and that she ought to respect me more than to speak to me of such a thing. . . . I fear that the disorders of Parma are such that they no longer admit of remedy ; I believe that France and Spain recognise this, and wish to draw me into the turmoil.   I can tell you that I do not want to associate myself with it, for many reasons ; you must, therefore, drop any such proposal, for it can never be.   They have another idea, as bad as the first, to send the Infant travelling and return me my daughter. I declare that I will never stand that ; the young people must remain together.   It would be shameful for the Bourbons to desert thus a Prince of their house.   I should be very sorry to have to give a plump refusal to my daughter's return ; either she must come with her husband (which would be the more natural arrangement), or she stays in Parma or Plaisance. . . . They are all right together just at present : let them remain so.   Rather than have them in my house, I can tell you, I would rather they went to Venice."

The next letter of Marie Antoinette to her mother was very bright and cheerful.   She says : 21 June, "I am glad to hear that your Majesty is well, 1771. as for me I am marvellously well ; my dear husband is taking medicine to-day, as he has had indigestion [a penalty of the Bourbon temperament] and been very sick.   But he is better now, and promises me that it will not be long before he returns to my room.   We are all very happy together, my sister, my brother [the Comtesse and Comte de Provence] and me ; I hope it may last.   My sister is very sweet, very agreeable, and very gay.   She likes me very much and has much confidence in me.   She is not at all on the side of Madame du Barry (as they feared), nor for M. de la Vauguyon ; she spoke to me about them very reasonably and behaved very well that day at Marly, when she had to sit beside her. . . . We came back here yesterday from Marly. . . . I am very sorry to find myself back at Versailles ; it was much more amusing at Marly. There were so many people, and we played before and after supper : when the King was away we danced one night, which was very delightful ; my sister seemed enchanted with it."

This marriage, so interesting to the Dauphine, brought for the first time a girl friend into the circle of her relatives.   The Comtesse de Provence was a little older than her husband, who, born in 1755, was the same age as Marie Antoinette, so that the united ages of all the four young husbands and wives was only about sixty-four years.   Marie Antoinette had little to fear on the score of looks from the swarthy little Comtesse de Provence, with her heavy black eyebrows—"capillary hedges" as they were called—and the little dark down upon her thick lips, that "would be more appreciated in a guard-room."   Marie Antoinette's proud carriage

THE COMTESSE DE PROVENCE.

From an engraving.)

[*Page* 110.

of head was the greater distinction, now that the rather thick-set figure, *un peu Savoyarde*, of Madame de Provence was beside her at Court. Mercy duly reports all these points to the Empress :

" The Dauphine treats her sister-in-law marvellously well, with friendship and perfect grace, feeling that in all she has the advantage both by the charms of her person and her wit. The Comtesse de Provence has none of these advantages ; she gives sign of no talent that might make up for the lack of them ; her countenance is cold and embarrassed ; she speaks little and awkwardly ; she has nothing necessary to please this nation. . . . I am surprised and distressed to find that the Dauphine has developed a liking for that Comtesse de Narbonne, who with neither wit nor understanding has succeeded in subjugating Madame Adélaïde until her conduct is at times quite pitiable."

Paris, 22 June, 1771.

What most excited the jealousy of Mesdames, and served also to annoy the Dauphine, was the extreme ostentation of the households of the Comte and Comtesse de Provence. To vex the Dauphin and Dauphine, please the Comte de Provence and his wife, irritate Mesdames, and fill his own pockets by one stroke was success in intrigue to the Duc de la Vauguyon, who invented appointments for the new households, and filled them with the representatives of the noblest families of France, taking a good commission for his share in distributing these lucrative sinecures. To the household of the Comte de Provence were appointed no less than thirty-six gentlemen of rank, their offices including such as a "first falconer, *chef des oiseaux du cabinet*," and a "*capitaine des levrettes de la chambre*" ; and the household of the Comtesse de Provence was almost as numerous, so that this young couple lived as nearly as possible in sovereign state.

On the other hand, the Dauphine had no taste for ostentation, and when it was proposed that, as she so much loved dancing, balls should be given to please her during the time the Court was in residence in Fontainebleau, she replied, that much as she would like that, it meant more expense, and she would not wish people to say that money could be found for her amusements, but not to pay the wages of her servants ; an answer that greatly astonished the Duc de Duras, who, as lord-in-waiting, had made what he thought was a proposal certain to please. Mercy had one point of regret to record :

"During the last few weeks the Dauphine has again taken to the habit of playing with children, and unfortunately her first *femme de chambre* has two, a boy of six or seven years and a girl of twelve, both of them very noisy, dirty, and plaguy. The Dauphine passes the greater part of the day playing with these children, who spoil her clothes, tear and break the furniture, and put the whole of the apartments into the utmost disorder. And what is worse is, this amusement leaves the Dauphine no time to do any lessons, and they have been so neglected for some time past that, unless your Majesty deigns to write very sharply, they will cease altogether. The extreme vivacity of the Dauphine renders serious occupation even more necessary to her than to others ; when she has given herself up for some hours to dissipation it is impossible for her to fix her attention upon anything. When one speaks to her directly after her studies she is disposed to listen, and can reason with perfect justice on all points under discussion. . . . The stay at Marly produced no ill effects, although such occasions are dangerous, because the Royal Family there is in a position to meet the members of the different parties. When the Duc d'Aiguillon was presented to the Royal Family as the new minister I observed to my great regret that the Dauphine would not speak a single word to him, while Mesdames, and above all the Comte and Comtesse de Provence, greeted him with much affability. I must try to repair this breach, as it will be injurious."

CHAPTER IX

THE icy reception of the Duc d'Aiguillon by
Marie Antoinette, upon his presentation to her
as minister and supplanter of de Choiseul,
brought its instant penalty, as foreseen by Mercy.
To the Dauphine he was not only the bitter
enemy of her friend, but the representative
of du Barryism, with all which that implied ;
and it is improbable that she should have been
unaware of that yet wider reputation of all evil,
that had spread from Bretagne, of embezzlement,
of tyranny, and worse ; for de la Chalotais had
already spread his accusations broadcast, and the
Marquis Duzel had been imprisoned for his pamphlet against *le Pacha d'Aiguillon*. The Parliament
of Rennes, which was the province wherein the
chief malpractices of the Duc had been carried on,
had dared greatly, and sent back *unopened* the King's
lettres de cachet, sent to them as punishment for their

Paris,
22 June,
1771.

impeachment of one supported by the du Barry; and the Parliaments of Toulouse and Bordeaux had gone further, and deprived the duchy d'Aiguillon of all rights and privileges, until the Duc had been duly acquitted by law of all the charges brought against him.

Louis XV. could suppress all Acts relative to these complaints of the Parliaments, and all petitions, but he could not suppress the gossip that flew through his own Court. Marie Antoinette had shown her disfavour towards d'Aiguillon, and in return it was that same man who was selected by Louis to convey his displeasure at such contumacy.

On June 22 Mercy writes to the Empress that he had an interview with the Duc d'Aiguillon. He had commenced by asking whether it was true that the Empress Marie Thérèse had planned to marry the Emperor Joseph II., her son, to Madame Marie, the sister of the Dauphin. Mercy replied that, if Madame Marie had been of an age more nearly approaching that of the Emperor, doubtless the Empress would have regarded the alliance as in every way advantageous, by forming another link with the Royal Family of France. " To which the minister answered nothing, and I suspect that this question arose from an old proposal to that effect made to me by the Duc de Choiseul, which he had discovered among his papers."

The Emperor Joseph II. had already been twice a widower. His first experience of married life (which lasted three years) was with Marie Isabelle, daughter of Philippe of Parma ; his second was with Marie Josèphe, daughter of the Emperor Charles VII. of Bavaria, and continued only from 1765 to 1767. He was now, in 1771, a man of thirty, and Madame Marie Adélaïde Clotilde was a child of twelve. Even at that age she was so enormously fat that she was called by the irreverent people the *Gros Madame* ; but she had "a fine wit in a thick body," and eventually married the Prince of Piedmont, King of Sardinia. This marriage greatly pleased the French people, who saw in it a return of one Princess of equal value to the two Princesses of Savoy (by that time married to the Comte de Provence and the Comte d'Artois), and this verse states their view :

> *Le bon Savoyard qui réclame*
> *Le prix de son double présent,*
> *En échange reçoit madame ;*
> *C'est le payer bien grassement.*

The Emperor Joseph remained a widower until his death, without carrying out this plan of the Duc de Choiseul.

Mercy continues that the Duc d'Aiguillon, after praising the character, grace, and wit of the Dauphine, arrived at the real point of the interview, by saying that the King was much displeased at certain transgressions in her conduct. He had commanded the Duc to confer with Mercy upon the facts that his Majesty had observed with annoyance "signs of an aversion, too strongly marked, towards the people who

formed the society of the King," and that she did not
merely refuse them the recognition due to members
of the Court, but added remarks full of " satire and
hate " ; that she was much too lively and too childish ;
that all these accumulated misdeeds were quenching the
King's tenderness towards her, and that it was necessary
to remedy immediately such improprieties.

Mercy says that such remarks, at the second time
of meeting the Duc d'Aiguillon, astonished him, " for,
knowing the character of this personage, I realised
the risks I ran of being compromised." But he had
explained that *les impulsions étrangères* had been given ;
that persons had dared to speak to the Dauphine of
things she ought never to know, or to see [fraud,
flagrant immorality, and the like !], hinted at *des
conseils pernicieux* ; and d'Aiguillon, understanding the
reference to Mesdames, named them without cir-
cumlocution, and added " rather cutting remarks "
concerning them. The Duc touched lightly upon his
own chilly reception by the Dauphine, expressing his
very respectful attachment for her Royal Highness
and his desire to win her favour, and left Mercy
wondering how much mischief he intended to make
out of the interview.

" It was clear," said Mercy, "that the whole proceeding has been planned with the advice of Madame
du Barry, and is intended to make Marie Antoinette
treat the favourite better. The same design has
governed the choice of the Prince de Rohan, Coadjutor
of Strasburg, as Ambassador to Vienna. This ecclesiastic

has yielded himself up entirely to the *cabale*, and I fear this is not the only impropriety that renders him unfit for the post for which he is destined. . . . As to the embroilments of Parma, it is resolved to send the Marquis de Cevallos and the Comte de Durfort as conciliatory Ambassadors, to employ only the method of moderate and respectful persuasion to induce the Infant to favour his minister. . . . Fortunately here they believe that the Archduchess-Infanta counts for nothing in the actual disorders, and I have been at great pains to impress this opinion more deeply.

Marie Thérèse informed Mercy that there was not the slightest indication of the Emperor con-

Schönbrunn, 8 July, 1771. templating a marriage with the Dauphin's sister. " Apart from her youth, the portrait painted of her, that shows how very much too fat she is, is quite sufficient to prevent such an alliance. The fact of her being French would be another obstacle. But I shall never propose a third marriage to the Emperor. He must choose a bride for himself, if he ever intends re-marrying, of which there is not, at present, the least indication, and I do not think I shall live to see it. I am very much dissatisfied with the choice which France has made for her Ambassador here in sending me such a bad lot (*aussi mauvais sujet*) as the Coadjutor of Strasburg. I might have refused, but for the consideration of the disagreeables that might have recoiled upon my daughter ; but you might suggest to the Court of

France, that they would do well to recommend to this Ambassador to behave himself decently, in accordance with his state and the post that he will occupy. Say further, that I am not in the humour to connive at any of the transgressions and scandals to which he will probably abandon himself. I confess to you that I am afraid what our women here may do."

This too-famous Coadjutor of Strasburg, the "collier" Cardinal de Rohan, had as many vices as were customary in a man of rank, joined to a vanity unusual even in a high ecclesiastic. Marie Thérèse, prepared to overlook immorality, if it were accompanied by outward decorum—the tribute vice renders to virtue —had thrust upon her a man who found it possible to retain a pre-eminence, even at the Court of Louis XV.

There were few amusements that did not find ready condonation in those days; but de Rohan overpassed even the extensive bounds permitted. "*Les serviteurs de Dieu conduisent la piété bon train quand ils sont mitrés*," said a contemporary; and to keep up the state he deemed necessary, the Cardinal adopted many methods, including smuggling. He took advantage of his position at Vienna to smuggle such quantities of silk, that it was said more was sold in his household than in all Lyons and Paris; and this commercialism was felt to be more degrading to a Prince of the Church than even the notorious establishment at Bergzabern, with its constant replenishment.

Marie Thérèse wrote to Marie Antoinette in

Schönbrunn, 9 July, 1771. July : " You are now in Compiègne, with all its pleasures and amusements ; I trust you still have enough tenderness for me to keep your word and not hunt on horseback. . . . I am still waiting in vain for a list of your studies and occupations ; is the Abbé Vermond no longer with you ?   I should be sorry if he were gone, but still more sorry if he were with you without your deriving any benefit.   At your age one may easily overlook some few trifles and puerilities, but in the end they will bore you and every one besides . . . In your position you need to read, and to take to any occupations likely to be of use to you in attracting esteem and consideration, especially in a country where every one is so accomplished. . . . I cannot hide from you that people are already beginning to gossip about you, and that will shatter the great ideal they have raised of you : an essential point for us— who are on the stage of the great world—to consider. A life continuously wasted in occupations without serious importance will have its influence, even upon your conscience.   I am much pleased to hear of your friendship with your sister-in-law. . . . God guard you from jealousies and mischief-making. . . . You delight me by the appointment of M. d'Aiguillon and the destination of de Rohan, even although the latter is not as estimable as he should be, con- sidering he is in the Church. . . . They tell me you did not receive this new minister well and, in general, you hold yourself too much aloof from all this party : no unworthiness, no familiarity, nor cajolery ; but they are of the King's Court as well as you, and you should submit to his will with the respect and submission of a child, without endorsing their merits or picking holes in their characters. It ought to suffice for your favour that the King distinguishes such or such an one ; but do not truckle. Up to this present time they say you are swayed by Mesdames ; in time the King will weary of that ; and you ought to know that these Princesses, filled with virtue as they are, and possessing real merits, have never learnt how to make themselves liked or respected, either by their father or by the public. . . . One knows everything that is done or said in their house, and in the long run all will be put down to you, and you will bear the blame alone."

Thus vigorously did the Empress expose the characteristics of those ladies of whom Walpole wrote : "The four Mesdames, who are clumsy, plump, old wenches with a bad likeness to their father, stand in a bed-chamber in a row, with black cloaks and knotting-bags, looking good-humoured, and not knowing what to say."

Her words bore fruit. Mercy wrote to Marie Thérèse that, upon receipt of this letter and after Mercy's own regret at her be-haviour towards the Duc d'Aiguillon, the Dauphine became very grave and thoughtful ; and

Compiègne, 24 July, 1771.

that evening, when she was playing Lansquenet with the King and all the Royal Family, she showed the result of her meditations. She found herself seated beside Madame du Barry at this game; and with perfect ease, showing neither disgust nor temper, she spoke to the favourite, when the rules of the game enjoined it, gracefully and with no affectation, saying neither too much nor too little.

The next day the Duc d'Aiguillon presented himself when the Dauphine was at play, and was extremely well treated, Mercy saying that " the Dauphine spoke to him continually with a charming air of gaiety; the Duc appeared rather embarrassed, and only replied in monosyllables." That same day the Dauphine was returning from Marly (to Versailles) and wished to do so on foot. As Marly was eight kilomètres from Versailles that meant a walk of nearly five miles. Mercy writes : " The people who had assembled to watch her pass were transported with joy. When she arrived at the entrance to the park of Versailles, the Dauphine perceived a great crowd, and dis- appeared like a flash (*s'échappa comme un éclair*), and still on foot." (Apparently the little Dauphine took to her heels and bolted.) " When her Royal Highness did me the honour, a few days afterwards, of con- fiding this, I took the liberty of asking her why she had fled, and she said : ' Because there were so many people,' an answer in which I saw clearly the influence of Mesdames, and I ventured therefore several reflections on the desirableness of conciliating the affection and

THE CASCADE AT MARLY.

(From an Engraving by Rigaud.)

[Page 123.

attachment of the people, by showing herself to them
with goodwill and without any marks of repugnance."

The Dauphine was particularly fond of Marly,
and often mentions her preference for that palace,
where most of all the strain of etiquette was relaxed.
Marly was created by Louis XIV., who designed it
as a peaceful little country spot, where the Court
could repose in sylvan simplicity. It developed into
one of the most magnificent royal palaces in France.
The plan of its building was in compliment to the
roi soleil, for it had a centre royal pavilion, representing the sun, and round it were twelve lesser
pavilions in allusion to the signs of the Zodiac. The
park was formed by the transplanting of trees from
Compiègne, and one of its chief features was the
celebrated cascade, supplied by a feat of engineering,
with water from the Seine which flowed in forty
waterfalls and nine fountains, and was called the
Cascade Champêtre. A group of gilded metal Tritons
nine feet high supported a basin at the head of the
cascade, and from it shot up a grand jet of water,
that fell, rushing down the forty torrents, between
white marble statues and great vases of beautiful metal
work. The whole of Marly, with its park and
buildings, was utterly destroyed during the Revolution.

Mercy continued, in his diary of 24 July, to record
further proof of the influence of the Empress's letter,
with its reference to the Duc d'Aiguillon : when
the review of the King's household took place, the
Dauphine had offered a place in her coach to the

Duchesse d'Aiguillon : when the Duc d'Aiguillon brought the Coadjutor of Strasburg, to present him to her in his capacity as Ambassador to Vienna, she was gracious to the minister and civil to that de Rohan, whose diamonds, in later life, were the first stones thrown at her reputation.

On 25 June, the Dauphine had fever and a severe cold, from taking too hot a bath and then going out riding. . . . During her little illness **25 June.** the Dauphin showed anxiety, and the King went to see her several times in the day, remaining a long time and talking with perfect friendliness and cordiality. . . . " The influence of this Princess upon the mind of the Dauphin grows daily more remarkable. On Monday, in the presence of the Comte and Comtesse de Provence, the Dauphine gave the Dauphin a lecture on his immoderate hunting, which injured his health and led him into habits of negligence and rudeness. The Dauphin tried to cut the reproof short by retiring into his own apartment, but the Dauphine followed him and continued forcibly to represent the annoy-ances caused by his manner of living. This language caused the Dauphin so much emotion that he began to cry." Whereupon the Dauphine, weeping also, was reconciled, and forgave him, and remembering that the quarrel had begun in the presence of the Comte and Comtesse de Provence, shrewdly brought the conquered and weeping Dauphin back with her. They said : " Is peace made ? " and the Dauphin replied that lovers' quarrels do not last long, which was sufficiently remarkable coming from the "*jeune cyclope de Versailles.*"

Mercy notes that the tone of Madame du Barry in reference to the Dauphine is changing ; she even praises her, speaks of her charming face, of her natural grace, making comparisons to the disadvantage of the Comtesse de Provence, who has shown a lack of enthusiasm for the favourite that is rather disconcerting. Mercy says : " The Dauphine is supposed to know nothing of the position that this person, Madame du Barry, holds ; and in consequence she can only regard her as a woman who has been presented at Court, and therefore is to be treated similarly to all others who have the *entrée.*"

All the world repeated the little story of Marie Antoinette on her first arrival at Court. She inquired of Madame de Noailles what were the *duties* of Madame du Barry, and the Comtesse replied that Madame du Barry's duty was to please and amuse the King. Marie Antoinette replied : " Then, in that case, I will take her place," which was repeated as evidence of refreshing innocence, but showed an adroit little diplomate who took, with grace, the only position open to her, that of ignorance. Mercy begged the Empress, " if in her high wisdom she approves," to suggest to the Dauphine that a few words spoken to the favourite " about her dress, or perhaps about a fan, or something of similar nature," would put a stop to much of the mischief-making. He judged by the great effect produced by the two or three words spoken by the Dauphine to Madame du Barry at Marly, although they were merely words that the exigencies of the game required to be pronounced. Mercy also noticed that Mesdames, while impressing upon the Dauphine the necessity of preserving a silent and severe aspect, took good care themselves to have little judicious favours always in readiness for the Comtesse du Barry, so that it seemed as though they would like to make a stalking horse of the Dauphine, and from behind her shoot out that spite they dared not show openly. For they were " bad likenesses of their father " in moral cowardice also.

" As to the choice of the Coadjutor of Strasburg as Ambassador, the selection is as eccentric as it is misplaced, but I shall know how to make them feel at this Court that your Majesty is waiting to judge his conduct ; and I believe that this ecclesiastic will manage to remain within the bounds that his appointment prescribes. He is adroit enough to restrain himself, and he will see the necessity. I am sending by this courier a portrait of the Dauphine, it is a speaking likeness, but it is in pastel, and I am afraid that will not stand travelling. But they tell me there is an artist in Paris who understands fixing pastel ; I shall go and consult with the people of that trade."

Mercy ended his report of 24 July by saying he considered the service of the Empress required him to resume the threads of his acquaintance with the Comte de Broglie (" sort of minister of occult foreign affairs "—*i.e.*, chief spy upon correspondence), "and I have, I believe, obtained some credit with him. He stands in as cordial relations with the Duc d'Aiguillon as two persons can be who watch each other incessantly, each believing he hoodwinks the other. If the Comte de Broglie remains in possession of the secret correspondence, we can measure the amount of confidence the King places in the Duc d'Aiguillon. I know that, when the Comte de Broglie is away, they take to his house every week a locked box containing letters. This box is sent to his estate at Ruffec by an express messenger, whom the Count sends back the same week with his answers. This fact is certain, but I have not yet been able to find out anything more about this mystery." When de Choiseul had been minister there had been no difficulty about *les interceptions ordinaires*, because he was superintendent of the Royal mails, which yielded a good income as well as information.

CHAPTER X

Advice from Marie Thérèse—Marie Antoinette's Ridicule of French Absurdities—At Compiègne—Mercy-Argenteau's First Meeting with Madame du Barry—His curious Interview with Her—The King confides in Him—The Dauphine goes Stag-hunting—Engineered Interview between Marie Antoinette and Madame du Barry; Mercy's moves; Mesdames the Marplots

MARIE THÉRÈSE often testified her gratitude to Mercy-Argenteau for his vigilant watch and the unwearied reports that enabled the Empress to keep her finger on the pulse of the Court at Versailles; and in her letter in August *Schönbrunn, 10 August, 1771.* she repeats that no one in the world, not even the Prince von Kaunitz (Prime Minister and chief of her Privy Council), suspects their correspondence, "which is secret and for me alone." She tells him the pleasure it is to her to read every detail of the Court life of her daughter, and assures him of her appreciation of the benefit his guardianship is to Marie Antoinette.

"Your accounts make me forget how curt her style is; she has answered me in nothing; this time again

my letter contains nothing of interest. Truly this is
not the moment to press the marriage of the Emperor
with Madame Marie ; I shall be glad to see him defer
for some years his trip to France. Perhaps Madame
Marie might get thinner in that time ; then there
would be some chance that he might look at her, but
it is a very doubtful event, and I have not the slightest
faith in its success. There is not even the smallest
appearance of it, but I embrace this faint hope lest I
should become more discouraged even than I am. . . .
I am very glad my daughter has begun to treat the
Duc d'Aiguillon better. Without entering into their
personality she ought to be the same to all the persons
of the ruling party, even to the Comtesse du Barry,
and speak to her on any unimportant subject, as she
would to every other lady whom the King admits to
his Court ; she should even distinguish her. She
ought to ignore what this woman is, and treat her
well, without descending to anything unworthy.
Perhaps by this course of conduct she will annoy her
aunts and thus weaken the bonds, at present too
intimate, between them ; but, above all, the Dauphin
must approve of this ; if his judgment disapprove, I
would rather my daughter continued to avoid Madame
du Barry."

What an arbiter for Marie Antoinette ! This
Dauphin of whom, when in after life he had attained
to such ripeness of wits as was his at his best, his
brother-in-law, Joseph II., said : " This man is a
little weak, but not imbecile ; he has ideas and some

judgment, but is as apathetic of mind as of body. He can hold a reasonable conversation, but has no desire to learn anything, or curiosity. In short, 'Let there be light' has not been spoken."

Marie Thérèse reiterated to Marie Antoinette her warnings against conduct likely to endanger her position, giving her maternal advice with the pleading little preface to disarm the pride of a rebuked Dauphine : " The messenger starts late this time, but I have been so full of hindrances, and I begin to grow very old (*furieusement à vieillir*) ; even when I work it takes me twice as long as it did [born in 1717, the Empress was now fifty-four].   I have received your portrait in pastel ; it is very like you and is my delight and the pleasure of all the family ; it is in the cabinet where I work, and the picture [by Liotard] in my bedroom, where I work at night, so that I have you always before my eyes, as I have you always within my heart. . . . Mercy tells me that you have, at his suggestion, commenced to treat the ruling party politely, and have even addressed a few vague remarks in that direction, which have had a marvellous effect. . . . I am always convinced of your success when you undertake anything, as *le bon Dieu* has given you charm, and a pretty figure, and you have goodness in addition, so that all hearts are yours whatever you do. . . .

" But they tell me you neglect to make just distinctions between persons, and they say this is all

Schönbrunn,
17 August,
1771.

due to Mesdames, who have never known how to win confidence or regard ; and, what is worse than all, they say you are beginning to hold up people to ridicule, to burst out laughing in their faces ; this will do you infinite harm. . . . To please five or six young ladies or gentlemen you annoy the rest . . . and the result will be, that to curry favour with you your example will be followed by all the courtiers—always useless people, and the most worthless in the kingdom —and you will drive away those who are upright and sincere, for they will not stay to be ridiculed, and will leave you at last with only bad companions. . . . They repeat widely how you neglect the Germans : be just to the true merit of this nation. They may be laughable in appearance, or in pronunciation, or in their hairdressing, but they have real talents and merits all the same."

There was, without doubt, ample subject of laughter in the ludicrous personalities of the Court, that mixture of parade and poverty, of dirt and diamonds, concerning which Walpole wrote so vividly ; and Marie Antoinette's sense of fun had grown instead of diminishing, by contact with a nation that illustrated so convincingly the difference between wit and humour. Sense of humour was practically non-existent in France ; but wit of the brightest and keenest edge, polished by custom, pointed with slander, was the weapon of daily encounter, and so much was it regarded as a tool that a recognised wit was bought up by every gentleman of rank, who regarded this as essential an accessory as a *chef* to a good establishment.

The Princes of Conti and Condé, the Duc d'Orléans, the Duc de Choiseul, each kept a salaried wit in the household, a paid purveyor of epigrams. Conti had Pont de Veyle, Condé had Laujon, d'Orléans had Collé, and Choiseul had every one else who would compose a poem, turn out a du Barry scurrility, or invent a charade with neatness and despatch. But humour, that salt of life, would have preserved the French Court from the follies of its decay ; and to its entire absence were due the solemn absurdities that so amused Marie Antoinette.

Walpole said of this period : " I cannot think how the French came by the character of a lively people . . . they are more lifeless than Germans " ; and the twinkle of fun in the little Dauphine, when she contemplated some edifice of absurdity bowing before her, was remembered as a crime by a people who saw nothing remarkable in Madame de Matignon's *coiffure à la jardinière*, that included a red-checked dish-cloth upon her head, in which Léonard, the great hairdresser, had entwined artistically a little artichoke, a head of green broccoli, a pretty carrot, and some little radishes. It was merely found *si simple, des légumes*! so much more natural than flowers ! And these touchy *esprits* pointed the limitations of their amusement and their bitter annoyance at a laugh from Marie Antoinette in after years by a song whose refrain was:

Petite reine de vingt ans,
Vous qui traitez si mal les gens,
Vous repasserez la barrière. . . .

A long and very interesting letter, or rather diary, from Mercy to Marie Thérèse was written in September, and deals with the life at **Paris, 2** Compiègne.   Louis XV. was very fond of **September, 1771.** this royal palace, which had been a favourite residence of the Kings of France from the days of Clovis, who built the first castle, enlarged by Charlemagne, rebuilt by Charles the Bald, and added to by St. Louis and Louis XI. ; the present *château*, however, dates from the time of Louis XV., and was built under his own royal supervision, aided by that of the architect Gabriel.

Every year Louis XV. went to Compiègne for the hunting, the serious employment of his old age, and here gathered all those members of the Royal family adroit enough to retain favour.   This year, owing to the marriage of the Comte de Provence, the assembly was so enlarged that the King had to command that the Dauphine and the Comtesse de Provence were to go hunting on days alternating with those upon which Mesdames took that diversion, as the immense number of vast, unwieldy coaches, dragged at full speed after the hunt, had resulted in the chaos that might have been expected.

Mercy writes that the Dauphine had sent for him to discuss her plan of action with regard to Madame du Barry, for it had become necessary to formulate a distinct course. Mercy impressed upon her the views of the Empress Marie Thérèse, detailed his interview, so curious and so ominous, with the Duc d'Aiguillon, read to her a letter of the Prince de Kaunitz on the subject, and insisted that the Dauphine ought to go to the King and speak frankly to him. The Dauphine was extremely reluctant, said it would be no use speaking to the King, it would only embarrass and annoy him without leading to any explanations, but that she would consider the matter, and be so careful in her conduct, that assuredly no one could find anything further of which to complain.

One proof she gave ; on the first opportunity she invited the Duchesse d'Aiguillon to drive with her out hunting, which greatly pleased the Duc d'Aiguillon, that " mask of very smooth varnish." 28 July was a date of importance to Mercy. He says that this, being a Sunday, was observed with all the usual rites of gambling, and the *grand couvert*, or dinner in public, which being a spectacle without charge was thronged by all conditions of spectators—" Princes of the blood, *cordons bleus*, *abbés*, housemaids, and the Lord knows who "—who rushed in, in a mob, upon the opening of the doors. " I went to supper upon the invitation of the Comtesse de Valentinois, with the Nuncio and the Ambassador of Sardinia, who were also invited. We found there the Duc and Duchesse d'Aiguillon, the Duc de la Vrillière, a lady of the palace, some other ladies of the suite of the

Comtesse de Provence and—the Comtesse du Barry;
it was the first time I had met this woman."

(If this statement is true it reveals remarkable
diplomatic powers on the part of Mercy, for Madame
du Barry had been the King's mistress since July 1768,
and to have successfully avoided seeing the chief
personage in Paris, the true centre of the Court, for
full four years, is a fact worthy of *le vieux renard*.)

"The Ambassador of Sardinia spoke to her, as to
a person with whom he was well acquainted. The
Nuncio showed much eagerness to enter into their
conversation; I considered it fitting that I should show
more reserve, and it was not until the favourite addressed
me directly that I lent myself to ordinary conversation
with her. She showed me much more favour than
to the others; I did not sit down to table, and the
Comtesse du Barry, under the excuse that she ought
to be home before eleven o'clock, did not sup either.
Conversation was carried on upon unimportant subjects,
until it was interrupted by the Duc d'Aiguillon, who,
taking me aside, informed me that the King wished
particularly to talk to me, and that he had been
commanded to suggest to me that I should await him,
at the house of Madame du Barry, the next day after
hunting. I replied, without hesitation, that I would
go wherever the King required me. I added, smiling,
that having promised the Duc d'Aiguillon I would
speak to him with perfect candour, I assured him
that I realised quite clearly that the only reason the
King could possibly have for this plan was to make

me call upon the favourite. Without entering in
the least into the great or small reasons that had
prevented all the other Ambassadors from calling,
one thing was certain that they had all refused up to
the present moment ; and I was at a loss to know why
I had been selected to be the bridge upon this occasion."

The Duc d'Aiguillon had endeavoured to explain,
said his conclusions were wrong, that the King wished
to see him, but his Majesty's own apartments were
not arranged so that he could receive in comfort, and
therefore he proposed the house of Madame du Barry ;
and he ended by suggesting that, if Mercy told all the
other Ambassadors that he only went to that house
upon the direct command of the King, his character
would not be compromised. Which Mercy fully
resolved to do, until he discovered that the so-friendly
Ambassador of Sardinia had already told the Duc
d'Aiguillon how much he wished to see the favourite
at her own house, and that the Ambassadors of
England, of Venice, and of Holland had all determined
to make the same diplomatic sacrifice.

On the morning of the 30th, the Dauphine came up
to Mercy, and whispered to him that she congratulated
him upon the good company which, to her knowledge,
he had kept at supper on Sunday. To which Mercy
could only reply that there were still more interesting
events arranged, and he would tell her all about them
the next day. The Duc d'Aiguillon made an appointment with Mercy at the *château* at seven o'clock. On
arrival the Duc told him that the King had returned

from hunting and was dressing, and conducted Mercy
to the Comtesse du Barry, " who received me with the
most marked attentions, and begged me to sit down
beside her."

The Duc d'Aiguillon then swept off the three other
personages present, on pretence of showing them a
picture in the next room, and the favourite seized the
opportunity.   She told Mercy what pleasure the
King's idea had given her ; for, by appointing her house
for the interview with his Majesty, she had been enabled
to make Mercy's better acquaintance.   She wished to
confide in him ; she had a grief that greatly affected
her.   She knew that for a long time past enemies had
been trying to lower her in the estimation of the
Dauphine, and to attain that they had even recourse
to *scandal* ; they had dared to attribute to *her*, du
Barry, disrespectful remarks on the person of the
Dauphine, although she, far from having so enormous
a fault with which to reproach herself, had never
permitted herself a word of complaint against the
Dauphine, in spite of her Royal Highness having
treated her with severity and a species of contempt.
She had always united with those who were loud in
their just praises of the charms of the Dauphine, and
she had only complained against those scandal-mongers
who inspired the Dauphine with feelings of aversion.
She said, further, that when there had been a question
of certain objects which the Dauphine appeared to
desire (for instance, her recent wish that the wages
of her household should be paid), she, du Barry, had

eagerly pressed it, and had even represented to the King that he could not help yielding to such reasonable desires as these of the Dauphine ; and, finally, that the King would be there directly, and then Mercy could ask his Majesty himself, if all she said was not true.

The point of view of Madame du Barry, and the entire absence of consciousness that her position was not one of the most acceptable, is shown delightfully in this speech to Mercy, which reveals her as not so much im-moral as un-moral : unconscious of the very existence of those social barriers termed morality by "a purely geographical expression " : unable to comprehend that the Dauphine could have any other cause of aversion from her than resentment at some stray gossip that she had slightingly referred to the Dauphine's eyelashes ; and really convinced that she, du Barry, had deserved well enough of her to have earned her friendship by the generosity with which she had forwarded her desires, by employing her— surely unobjectionable—influence over the Royal grandpapa.

This incapacity for understanding in what she could have given offence explains much of her attitude in later years. As she considered, she had merely attained to that for which she saw all others striving, and had used generously and without rancour her position on that " sunlit height," upon whose slopes the less successful were stumbling. Virtue to her was merely un-success ; any other translation of that word would have been unintelligible ; and the perfect simplicity of her outlook upon the things of life was shown in later years, when, in the troubled times of Louis XVI., she wrote to Queen Marie Antoinette, and offered to place at her disposal all the wealth "gained in the service of the King," saying she was but rendering to Cæsar the things that were Cæsar's.

Mercy, unable to reply adequately to the ingenuous pleadings of Madame du Barry, explained that the Dauphine was by nature incapable of hating any one, and fortunately for his embarrassment, the King entered the room at that moment, by a little staircase which opened just where Mercy was standing. The Comtesse retired ; and the King commenced his interview with Mercy by a prepared speech : " Up to this moment you have been the ambassador of the Empress, but I beg of you to become my ambassador, at least for some little time " ; and then he was at a loss to continue. He told Mercy he wished to speak to him about the Dauphine, that he loved that Princesse with all his heart, that he found her charming, but that, being young and lively, and " having a husband who was not in a condition to guide her," it was impossible that she should be able to avoid the snares which were spread for her by intrigue. " Knowing the confidence that your Majesty has deigned to bestow upon me," writes Mercy, "the King has determined to bestow upon me his own, and to give into my charge those cares that I alone could undertake, to watch over an object that involved his happiness and that of his Royal family."

Mercy had replied that the instructions laid down by the Empress for the guidance of her daughter were under two heads : firstly, to love and respect the King, obeying him in everything, the Empress relying on the friendship of the King that he would use his authority over the Archduchess ; secondly, to seek to obtain the tenderness, esteem, and confidence of the Dauphin, to live in good friendship with the Royal family, and to unite with them in endeavours to contribute to the happiness of the King.   If, therefore, the Dauphine had in any way strayed from these rules, it was not from any ill-will on her part ; and he knew with certainty that, if the King would explain his wishes to the Dauphine, he would find her prepared in all things to obey and please him with ready tenderness.

But a personal explanation, involving a moment of possible embarrassment, was the last thing the King desired with any one.   He begged Mercy to take that duty upon himself.   He said that he observed with displeasure, that the Dauphine yielded to prejudices, to dislikes, which were not her own but "were suggested ; " that she treated badly persons [a term of useful vagueness] whom the King admitted to his own particular society ; that all he required was she should accord to such persons the treatment that every one who had been " presented " had a right to expect, and that any other course of conduct would occasion " scenes " at Court.   He said : "Some one gives bad advice to the Dauphine ; it must not be followed; " adding, "you see what confidence I place in you, by telling you what I think of the members of my own family."

Mercy tried, respectfully, but quite vainly, to induce the King to speak himself to the Dauphine, 30 July, and then said that he would convey his 1771. Majesty's own words, "neither extending nor interpreting them," so that the King should not imagine he would take upon himself to mention the *name* of the du Barry, which even the King had found himself unable to mention. And the extraordinary interview (as Mercy rightly calls it) ended, by Louis calling the favourite and the Duc d'Aiguillon (who had been waiting in a sort of little passage leading to a dressing-room) into the conversation. This then passed into such general matters as the King's desire to meet the Emperor Joseph II. (Marie Antoinette's brother and his own grandson by his first marriage with the Infanta Isabella), his satisfaction that both the Emperor and the Empress Marie Thérèse had friendly feelings towards him, some vague sentiments upon the Turkish war, a suspicion that the King of Prussia would turn those troubles to his own account —"he turns everything to his own account, even false coining "—ending with : " It is late ; I must go and have supper with my children," and plentiful compliments to all. Mercy remained, "seeing clearly the aims of this little scheme, against which I shall be attentively on my guard."

The next day the Dauphine listened to the whole **31 July, 1771.** account, and commanded Mercy to give her his opinion. This was that the Dauphine had only two courses before her : either to announce publicly that she was aware of the position of Madame du Barry—in which case her dignity demanded she should require from the King that he forbade this woman to appear henceforth in the family circle: or to pretend to be ignorant of it, and treat the favourite as she would any other woman who had been presented ; it would suffice if she once addressed Madame du Barry when passing her. But in either case she must have the approval of the Dauphin, and she must speak directly to the King. And the Dauphine was left to reflect upon her selection between these two courses.

This day the Dauphine went stag-hunting, following **1 August, 1771.** in a coach. The stag took to the river, and in order to be in at the death it would have been necessary for the Dauphine and her suite to have driven their coaches across a field of standing corn. This she refused, saying she would rather lose the hunt than destroy the crops of the poor farmers, " who are almost always ruined on similar occasions " ; and this self-denial was the talk of all Compiègne.

Fully to appreciate this consideration for the livelihood of a mere peasant, it is necessary to remember the hunting laws of France, of which the following will serve as an example :—That for six miles round Paris, within the circumference of the Warren

of the Louvre, no grass nor green food might be cut
while the King's partridges were hatching, nor vine-
props left standing in vineyards, lest they hamper the
Royal chase.

"The King on this day came up many times to
the Dauphine ; he mounted up into her coach, took
her upon his knees and caressed her a thousand
times," and on her return she told Mercy she had
made up her mind and would speak, just once, to
Madame du Barry. The Dauphin had approved,
but Madame Adélaïde advised her not to speak to
the King, it would only be useless and embarrassing.
Mercy pointed out the futility of this argument, and
the Dauphine promised to speak to the King, after
Mercy had held forth for three-quarters of an hour,
with the strongest possible remarks upon Mesdames.
He said their system of weakness had lost them all
consideration, both with the King and with the public ;
and that the King, repelled by their lack of sweetness
and consideration, and by their stiffness and constraint,
had been forced to find his compensations in a manner
very injurious to the State and more so to the Royal
Family.

The next day she told Mercy she would speak to
him—but that her courage failed her entirely ! 8 August,
Mercy again encouraged her, begged her to 1771.
consider to what evils any cowardice at such a moment
would lead, dwelt upon the kind heart of the King,
his timidity towards his children, and his natural
preference for her, exposed the unreasonable and

pernicious counsels of Mesdames, and again she promised ; and went off hunting in her coach, in such a storm that the rain and mud streamed into the coach. "But her Royal Highness enjoyed it none the less, and came in extremely wet."

On August 11 was arranged the all-important occasion upon which the Dauphine was to speak to Madame du Barry in public. The day before, Mercy learnt that the Comtesse du Barry intended to join their assembly and had proposed to the Comtesse de Valentinois to accompany her ; he warned the Dauphine, who had expressly charged him to watch for this moment, and she assured him that she would speak to the favourite, but she wished that he should be present. It was planned that at the close of play Mercy was to approach the favourite and speak to her, and that the Dauphine, in walking round, should stop to speak to him, and then, as if taking an opportunity, speak a few words to Madame du Barry. Marie Antoinette said to Mercy that this was the only way to reassure herself as she felt so afraid ; and Mercy hoped that she would be firm, as if, after all, she shrank back, then he would obviously have failed and be covered with ridicule. Marie Antoinette was hurt that he should doubt her resolution. Mercy's last injunction was that she should mention nothing of this little arrangement to Mesdames, which the Dauphine promised—but told them.

"In the evening," says Mercy, "I went to the

rooms ; there was the Comtesse du Barry and there were her ladies. The Dauphine called me aside and told me she was frightened, but meant to carry it through ; the game was nearly at an end. I placed myself beside the favourite and entered into conversation with her. All eyes were turned upon me. The Dauphine commenced to speak to the ladies present ; she arrived at my side, not two steps away, when Madame Adélaïde, who had not lost sight of her for one moment, raised her voice and said : ' Let us go ; it is time to await the King at my sister Victoire's ; ' and at these words the Dauphine went, and all the plan failed."

That evening there was a stormy scene at Mesdames', they blaming Mercy for his advice ; the Dauphine defending him faithfully, and the Dauphin actually observing : "In my opinion, M. de Mercy is right, and you are all wrong." The same evening all the Ambassadors, including the Nuncio, had supper at Madame du Barry's ; the King came, and pushing Mercy, as it were, into a corner, said in a very confused way : "Your advice bears no fruits ; I shall have to come to your help," and left him without time to reply. And Mercy could only draw the attention of the Dauphine to the conduct of the Comte and Comtesse de Provence (who were so very prudent as to be almost underhand, pretending to follow the guidance of Mesdames, and yet taking great care to be upon friendly terms with the favourite), and mention that the Comtesse de Provence had even entertained the du Barry at dinner. While the regretful Marie Antoinette could only plead that, although she knew his advice was good, she was too much afraid of Madame Adélaïde to carry it out ; and she was grieved above all that she should have compromised him by failing.

CHAPTER XI

TWO letters were sent from Paris on 2 September,
one from Mercy, and one from Marie Antoinette.
Mercy is still troubled about the " fat Madame," the
young sister of the Dauphin, in case the Emperor
Joseph should seek her in marriage and find
more than he anticipated. He says : " This   Paris,
                                               2
young Princess grows, but gets no thinner, September,
                                              1771.
which is very deplorable, for otherwise she
is of an agreeable appearance, polite, very amiable, and
extremely well brought up, a sufficiently remarkable
fact in the midst of a Court where education is at
such a disadvantage." The poor *gros Madame*
in after life, found Piedmont and matrimony
sufficiently wearing to prevent her retaining this
distinctive embonpoint for very long ; and when
those Royal fugitives from the Revolutionaries, the
Comte and Comtesse d'Artois, arrived for refuge in
Turin in 1789, on September 27, her thirtieth birth-
day, they found her aged, thin, unrecognisable, and

having lost her teeth.   Joseph's aversion to avoirdupois was unusual in this century, which was an epoch of eating.   His own younger brother, the Elector of Cologne, at the age of thirty-two years, weighed thirty-two stone ; and his colossal appetite never diminished, nor was even affected, by the horrors of the Revolution and the tragedy of Marie Antoinette.

Marie Antoinette wrote to her mother a little letter full of resolves to amend.   She said : "I will try to treat le Broglie better, although he has personally offended me [he had shown a private letter of Marie Antoinette's to his immediate circle].   I am in despair that you should believe it when people tell you that I do not speak to them ; you must have very little confidence in me, to think that I should be so unreasonable as to amuse myself with five or six young people, and fail in attentions to those whom I should honour. . . . I pity my brother Ferdinand [on his marriage with Béatrix d'Este, heiress of Modena.   He also had to leave his home and country, and take up his residence in the country to which his marriage called him], knowing by my own feelings how sad a thing it is to live apart from one's family.   I hope that he will soon have fruits of his marriage : for me, I live always in hope, and the growing tenderness of the Dauphin does not permit me to doubt, though I should like better that all were settled. . . ."

Marie Thérèse had been greatly vexed by Mercy's account of the failure of his efforts for peace and

toleration, and she wrote a letter to Marie Antoinette,
that she sent to Mercy, for inspection,
saying : " It is a little strong ; but, after
she has failed you so utterly, it is necessary
to wake her from the lethargy into which
she is sinking. If you find it too strong, you can
keep it and tell my daughter that I was unable to
write to her this time."

She wrote : " Every one tells me that you only
act as your aunts direct you. I esteem them, I like
them, although they have never known how to make
themselves either esteemed or liked by their own
family or by the public ; and you wish to follow on
the same road. This fear, this embarrassment about
speaking to the King—the best of fathers—about
addressing people whom you are requested to address !
This reluctance, this fear of saying a simple ' good
morning,' a word about a dress or any other trifle,
costs you so many grimaces, actual grimaces or worse.
You have let yourself be dragged into such bondage
that your reason, and even your duty, have no longer
power to rule you. I cannot longer be silent ; after
the conversation of Mercy and all he impressed upon
you that the King wished and your duty demanded,
that you should have dared to fail him ; and for what
good reason ? None. You ought not to consider
the du Barry in any other light than as a lady
admitted to the Court and to the society of the
King. You are his Majesty's first subject ; you owe
him submission and obedience ; you owe an example

to the Court, to the courtiers, who execute the will of
your master.   If they required of you anything degrading, any familiarities, neither I nor any one else would
counsel you to that, but an indifferent word, a certain
attitude, not for the sake of the lady but for your
grandfather, your master, your benefactor !   And you
fail him so entirely on the first occasion upon which
you could oblige him and show him your attachment !
And what is your reason ?   A shameful compliance with
the wishes of people, who have reduced you to dependence by treating you as a child, giving you amusements
with horses, with donkeys, with children, with dogs :
see the great causes for your preference for them over
your master, which will, in the end, make you
ridiculous, unloved and despised.   You began so well.
Your judgment is always true and just when not over-
borne by others.   Let yourself be guided by Mercy ;
what interest could either he or I have in anything
but your own happiness and the good of the State ?
Shake off these false notions ; it is for you, after the
King, to lead, not to be led away like a child when
you wish to speak.   You are afraid to speak to the
King, but not afraid to disobey and disoblige him. . . .
I have detained the courier a day late, because I was so
overwhelmed with the news that I needed time
to recover. . . . Do not think I am merely scolding
with such energy ; I see you sunk in a subjection from
which you must be plucked as quickly as possible and
by force. . . . I do not demand a total break with
the company you frequent, God forbid ! but that

you tell them nothing, and learn to act for yourself. Too much compliance is degrading; you must play your own part, if you wish to be valued. If you do not, I foresee great trouble before you; nothing but mischief-making and plots, which will make your life unhappy. Believe the advice of a mother, who knows the world and idolises her children, and desires only to pass her sad days in being useful to them."

The letter of Marie Antoinette to her mother, in reply to this, shows the Dauphine anxious 13 October, to prove herself no longer childish, docile, 1771. uncomprehending. The intrigues that surrounded her are deftly touched upon, and relegated to their just place amid the disorders of the Court. She says, with a shrewdness that sits oddly on her fifteen years:

"I have many reasons for believing that it is not the King's own wish that I speak to the du Barry, besides the fact that he has never spoken to me about it. He has shown me much more favour since he knew that I had refused, and if you were in a position to judge, as I am, all that passes here, you would be convinced that this woman and her clique would never be satisfied with merely a word; there would be perpetual encroachments. . . . I was very sorry not to have been able to arrange the matter of Madame du Bussy, but it was impossible on account of M. du Bussy's birth, although her own is good enough."

[Madame du Bussy had wished to be presented

at Court, but her husband was not of sufficiently
noble family for that.   He had distinguished himself
in India under Dupleix, fought in the Deccan struggles,
and been taken prisoner by the British troops ; he had
returned from India with such booty, that it gained
him the name of Bussey-*butin*, but neither his laurels
nor his loot could gain admittance for his wife—a de
Messey, and a relation of the Duc de Choiseul—to
a Court so exclusive, that it reserved its chief honours
for the daughter of Anne Bécu, the cook.]

"The death of Madame de Villars has given rise
to a great deal of scheming.   M. de la Vauguyon
has persecuted me to the extent of inducing the
Dauphin (who at heart cares nothing at all about it)
to write to the Duc d'Aiguillon, to make him speak
to me in favour of Madame de St. Mégrin.   Although
you say I am afraid to speak to the King, I told
him about this consent of the Dauphin, and he
authorised me to refuse their request.   I also asked
him to let me nominate one of my own ladies for
the place of lady-in-waiting, which he has refused
at the instigation of Madame du Barry.   They have
given me the Duchesse de Cossé, daughter of M.
de Nivernais and daughter-in-law of the Maréchal
de Brissac.   Her reputation is good. . . ."   [The
Duc de Nivernais, "the cream of the mediocre,
manqué partout," Louis de Mancini Mazarin, was
that nobleman regarded as the perfect type of his
order by Lord Chesterfield in the well-known letters
to his son ; and his daughter, this Duchesse de Cossé,

is she, who, with her mother, is included in Walpole's phrase, " two ecclesiastic fagots."]

" I have taken the Duchesse de Luxembourg, daughter of M. de Paulmy, in place of Madame de Boufflers ; she is young and appears good-natured ; but at this moment there is really not much to choose between all these ladies, on account of their intrigues and the schemes of the favourite." [Again Marie Antoinette gently reveals her entire acquaintance with the relative values of " *these ladies.*" Of the particular lady who is thus quietly superseded, there are many stories. Madame de Boufflers, from his Majesty's age, could not occupy *all* the places in the Court formerly filled by her mother, Madame de Craon, so indemnified herself with his Majesty's Chancellor. One day the King exclaimed, *à propos* of Madame de Boufflers : " *Regardez, quel joli petit pied ! Et la belle jambe ! Mon chancelier vous dira le reste,*" which is the official formula in which a King of France, addressing his Parliament, refers them to his Chancellor for further details.]

" You have doubtless heard, my dear mother, the misfortune of Madame de Chartres, whose child is born dead. But I would rather have even that, terrible as it is, than be as I am without hope of any children. They say that the Abbé de Langeac is at Vienna with the Coadjutor [de Rohan] ; he is a very bad lot, and is the son of la Sabatin, the mistress of the Duc de la Vrillière [who had imprisoned her husband by *lettre de cachet*]. The mistress of the *contrôleur général* has been sent packing, accused and convicted of having sold offices ; I should be glad to see all the others sent packing as well. To convince you of the injustice of the du Barry's friends, I must tell you that I did speak to her at Marly ; I do not say that I will never speak to her, but only that I cannot consent to speak to her upon a given day, at a given hour, that she may tell every one beforehand, and have a triumph. I ask your pardon for saying all this so strongly ; if you had only seen the grief your dear letter gave me, you would excuse the terms in which I write." And she ends with " the most respectful submission to my dear mamma."

Mercy's acquaintance with Madame du Barry ripened rapidly, considering its recent com-
Fontaine-
bleau,
15 October,
1771. mencement. He wrote in September to Marie Thérèse that he was beginning to understand her very well, that she seemed to have " little intelligence and much levity and vanity, but to be neither spiteful nor revengeful." He found her always ready to chatter, and generally to be indiscreet in doing so, whereby, he says, he gained many advantages. In October he had a very curious experience. The favourite sent Mercy a message by the Duc d'Aiguillon to ask him to go and see her the first time he was in Versailles. Accordingly on October 10 he went to her house. He had always adopted a truthful and candid attitude in talking to this lady, neither anxious to please nor to flatter her, and whether her confidences to him were in con-

sequence of this very unusual treatment, or the result
of mere natural levity, Mercy could not decide. But
the confidences were made, and they were " *assez
extraordinaires*," as he observes.

She began by speaking of her extreme desire to
stand well with the Dauphine, and her wish that her
Royal Highness should no longer look upon her
with the eye of aversion ; this she knew was not
due to Marie Antoinette's own feelings, but to the
instigation of Mesdames. She told Mercy that she
had explained all this clearly to the King, and had
begged him to consent to her wish, that the Dauphine
should never appear in the company of Mesdames,
either at Versailles or upon any of the little journeys
to which these Princesses were usually admitted ; but
the King, having made no reply to this speech of hers,
Madame du Barry had sent him her request in writing,
and had had a very satisfactory letter from his
Majesty in return, in which he suggested various
plans to please her. Mercy was so amazed at this
incredible relation, that he decided he must see the
King's own letter before he could believe it. He
therefore tells Marie Thérèse how he had affected
total misapprehension, and carefully misunderstood all
her quotations from his Majesty's letter, and succeeded
in making her produce it, for she gave him, reluctantly,
Louis' own note, which was very careless alike in
composition and in handwriting.

It is to be regretted, for the sake of comparison,
that her own letter of request is not still in existence,

for her writings are untrammelled by education, and therefore more amusing than those compositions of her secretary, that she signed, and "*je n'est point darjan je n'en est pas prie le mois passé*," is a good example of her spelling.   Louis's letter commences : "You are wrong to believe I love you less because I did not answer you at once ; I love you always very much and always the same."   And the Most Christian King then entered into explanations.   He could command Mesdames to be more civil to her, and he believed they would obey him, but with a very bad grace.   He said their distant manner was less political than religious, not due to the Duc de Choiseul but to their own devout scruples, and remarked that the late Queen—although extremely pious—had never behaved like this in similar cases.   [A regretful tribute to the tolerance of Marie Leczinska, whose matrimonial experiences included memories of Mesdames de Mailly, de Vintimille, de Lauragais, de Châteauroux (the four sisters successively successful), and de Pompadour.] The King wrote that he was wearied of the dulness and awkwardness that Mesdames caused whenever they were present on the little journeys, or they found themselves in the social circle of the King ; that he thought the best plan was to exclude these Princesses from all similar gatherings, and only to admit the Dauphine and the Comtesse de Provence ; and that the favourite had better think it over, and let his Majesty know what he had to do.

In case Marie Thérèse should find it impossible to

believe, that the King would say in writing to the
favourite what should obviously only be mentioned
in a conversation, Mercy explains that it has always
been the King's habit to make his wishes known in
writing to his children, his ministers, or his mistresses,
lest speaking might occasion him a moment's embarrassment.   He was incapable of refusing anything
asked him in conversation, but majestically resolute
in writing.   Mercy begged Madame du Barry to let
him have some time to form an opinion on what she
had confided to him, and to say nothing to the King
until he had put it into shape ; and in the meantime
he told the favourite, in plain words, how she should
bear herself towards the Dauphine, hinting present
and future considerations, which she understood perfectly.   Mercy then had the task of convincing the
Dauphine that he knew the King's intention to exclude
Mesdames from his society, without revealing to her
that he had actually seen the singular letter ; and of
impressing upon her the delicacy of her position and
the impossibility of refusing the King, should he make
these or any other arrangements.

Mercy described to the Empress the effect of her
very severe letter of 30 September upon the Dauphine.
She had been at her toilette when Mercy arrived
with her correspondence, and she opened her mother's
letter first, read it quickly, and seemed startled by
it.   But Mercy wrote : " I have learnt to know
so well what her manner indicates, that I was not
at all satisfied with what I observed.   Her Royal

Highness spoke but few words to me, and those in a tone more of impatience than of docility or obedience." He gave a forecast of what he imagined would be Marie Antoinette's reply, from his knowledge of Madame Adélaïde's views, and this was exact in its judgment.

Marie Thérèse's reply is filled with thankful recognition of Mercy's devotion. She says **Vienna, 31 October, 1771.** that she encloses him a copy of the letter she is sending to Marie Antoinette, which she hopes may have effect in the end. "But I notice in her last letter more temper than edification. . . . You have done very well in your last interview with Madame du Barry, and, to speak candidly, it seems to me not a bad thing, if the King sometimes makes his little expeditions in the sole company of his young daughters-in-law and without Mesdames. Perhaps such a demonstration would embarrass them, and make them more yielding and circumspect. . . . I should regret infinitely if the Comtesse de Noailles has to leave. Tell me if you think she would be flattered, and whether it would be judicious if I sent her some jewel, my portrait, or some of the treasures of this country, porcelain for instance."

CHAPTER XII

NOTWITHSTANDING the brave show of the
Dauphine, she was at heart much perturbed
by her position, and by the vigorous and emphatic
letter of her mother. Mercy remarked that she had
received a severe shock, which rendered her grave,
thoughtful, and amazingly little interested in hunting,
this last indicating a high degree of preoccupation.
She endeavoured to set herself right in Mercy's eyes
and to explain that some one had been exaggerating
the defects of Mesdames ; but Mercy gave her yet
another lecture upon the false policy of estranging the
King, to which she listened in an impressed silence,
by which Mercy, who knew her way, saw he had
spoken with effect. She appealed to the Abbé de
Vermond to convince Mercy that she was not to blame,
and he replied with so much "freedom and zeal"
that she was again reduced to silence.

But the position was in fact one of the most difficult.

Horace Walpole wrote from Paris in this very summer of 1771 : " The distress here is incredible, especially at Court.   The King's tradesmen are ruined, his servants starving, and even angels and archangels cannot get their pensions and salaries, but sing, Woe ! Woe ! Woe ! instead of Hosannahs.   Compiègne is abandoned [where were the King and his chosen], Villars Coterets [the Duc d'Orléans] is crowded, and Chantilly [the Prince de Condé], and Chanteloup [de Choiseul] is still more in fashion. . . . You never saw a great nation in so disgraceful a position.   Their next prospect is not better : it rests on an *imbécile*, both in mind and body."   Walpole spoke often of this poor creature, Marie Antoinette's husband, and compared him with his younger brothers ; the Dauphin " weak and weak-eyed, with a sickly air and without grace," the Comte de Provence " a fine boy," the Comte d'Artois " very fat, and most like his grand-father of all."

And one of the greatest of Mercy's anxieties, rendered keener as month passed month without natural action of mind or body in the feeble-witted Louis, was the growing prestige of the two younger brothers.   This was leading to the formation of a political party, that saw in the Comte de Provence and his wife the successors to Louis XV. and hoped for the nullification of the marriage of the Dauphin, his blotting out in imbecility or death, and the return of the Archduchess Marie Antoinette to her own country.

Mercy wrote to Marie Thérèse that on 17 October the Comte de Provence had held the review of his regiment : " this ceremony taking place with all the magnificence they always try to give to those occasions upon which this young Prince appears ; which is calculated to make him respected." On the 18th the King went hunting, and on his way passed before the regiment of the Comte de Provence, who placed himself at its head for that honour. But the King drove by, not alighting from his carriage, or even glancing at the troops : " which greatly mortified all the officers." And in the evening the Comtesse de Provence sickened of the smallpox.

Fontaine-
bleau,
16
November,
1771.

The horror of this widely diffused disease was increased in France by the absence of cleanliness, ventilation, and elementary medical knowledge. In that country, in the year 1754, the death-rate from smallpox was one in ten, no doubt due to the custom for all the friends of a patient to visit him during the early stages of the disease. Inoculation was in its infancy ; and its unpopularity was increased by it being considered merely an Austrian fad. Even when Louis XV.'s pestilential ending had filled all Paris with horror, when the malignance of infection from that one sick-room had resulted in death to those who passed near its passages, and all recognised that their only safety lay in flight from the Œil-de-bœuf, yet the inoculation of the Dauphin, the Comte de Provence, and the Comte d'Artois, which followed immediately that horrible death of their grandfather, was regarded by the generality of Frenchmen as a wicked and rash action, due merely to the desire of Marie Antoinette to enforce an Austrian whim. Louis XV. himself had, however, long been interested in inoculation, and a letter of Joseph II. to his Majesty is extant, in which the Emperor dwells upon its manifest advantages, saying : " Why was this not discovered before ? I should still have a wife, the happiness of my existence " ; and another, a little childish letter from Louis's great-grandchild, Joseph's only daughter, the little Archduchess Thérèse, whose inoculation had been cause of great anxiety to Louis XV.   The child writes : " Knowing that you love me, dear grandpapa, I assure you that I am marvellously well. *Je n'ai eu que cinquante boutons qui me font grand plaisir.*"

The Comtesse de Provence had the disease lightly ; and Marie Antoinette showed her every **15 November, 1771.** possible attention.   There is a mention, in one of her letters to her mother, that she had seen the Comtesse before she started for change of air to La Muette, and " it has passed marvellously ; she is scarcely marked at all."   Out of sympathy, rather than as a sanitary precaution, the Dauphine refused to go to the hunting parties, or to take part in any of the Court amusements, until the illness of her sister-in-law had run its course, and she had been pronounced better.

Mercy tells with great enjoyment a false step made

by Madame Adélaïde, her defeat on a matter of
Court routine being specially pleasing to him. Madame
Adélaïde had, as *chevalier d'honneur*, the Baron de
Montmorency, whom she disliked because the Comtesse
de Narbonne did, the moral feelings of the lady-in-
waiting being stirred by the Baron's prudent civility
to Madame du Barry.   The Baron had been given
the appointment of Lieutenant-General of Aunis, which
necessitated six months' residence in that place ; and
Madame Adélaïde, seizing her opportunity, told the
Baron he must, in consequence, send in his resignation
of the office connected with her household.   The
Baron replied that, having taken his oath of allegiance
to the King as *chevalier d'honneur*, it was only the
King who could dismiss him.   Madame Adélaïde, in
anger, plunged deeper into the wrong, by sending for
the Duc de la Vrillière and enjoining him to get rid
of the Baron.   There was the usual furious storm
at Court.   The Baron was supported by the favourite,
to whom he had behaved diplomatically (*s'est comporté
sagement*) ; the King decided in favour of the Baron,
and Madame Adélaïde lost her cause and her credit,
and retained her *chevalier d'honneur*.   Mercy pointed
this out so convincingly to the Dauphine, that for
once she had no excuse to offer for her aunt.

"On 28 October," says Mercy, " the balls re-
commenced which had been stopped during the illness
of the Comtesse de Provence.   They are given every
Monday in the theatre of the *château* ; they are
held only to amuse the Dauphine, who refused at

first to have them, for fear of the increase of expense. But that has been arranged ; there are to be no operas, and this retrenchment will defray the cost of the balls. These occasions show the Dauphine in her most charming light, she is so gay, so amiable, and so grace-ful, that all the world is enchanted. The King never comes to these balls, probably because the favourite dare not present herself, and I know it is the presence of Mesdames that serves most to keep her away. But this Monday I spied her up high in one of the boxes, where she was with the King, and both of them were trying not to be seen." These were the little Monday balls, at which all present had to be dressed in white, the ladies in white dominos, and the gentlemen all in white except their coats, which were of blue velvet.

Mercy speaks of the Comtesse de Provence, who had
11 October, safely departed into quarantine at la Muette
1771.   after her attack of smallpox, and describes
the interview between her and the Dauphine, men-tioned by Marie Antoinette. It was held under the supervision of the King and the Dauphin, who had a wholesome dread of infection, although it did not reach the mania of that of the Duc d'Orléans who forbade the mention of death, and to whom the words "*feu roi*" had to be explained as merely a title that Kings take. The Dauphine was at one end of a gallery, and the Comtesse de Provence at the other, and they spoke from a distance, the Dauphine paying this mark of attention with the most graceful friendship possible.

Mercy adds, not too reluctantly, that the Comtesse de Provence has many red spots, "but they tell me she will not be pitted with the smallpox."

Both Royal families had reason to dread the disease; and in Marie Antoinette's remembrance still clear and vivid was the death of the second wife of her brother Joseph II. carried off in a few days by smallpox; and the last embrace of her own sister Josèphe, who, on the eve of her departure for her marriage to the King of Naples, was commanded by Marie Thérèse to pray first beside the coffin of her dead sister-in-law. The young Archduchess, feeling this command her death-warrant, said good-bye to her little sister Antoinette with tears, saying their parting was not for Naples but for ever, went down into the fatal vault and prayed as she was bidden; and died in a few days from the disease. Her younger sister, Marie Caroline, took her place upon the throne of Naples in 1768.

Mercy's answers to the questions contained in the Empress's letters were always despatched on the same date as the diary that chronicled such daily items as: "The Dauphine rode to-day, but did not follow the hunt, standing *Fontaine-bleau, 16 November, 1771.* on a mountain to watch it half a league away." Or, "To-day the Dauphine had a slight cold, and the Dauphin paid her the attention of suggesting she should drive in a closed coach rather than in a *calèche*." He now writes: "For the last few weeks the Dauphin has been scarcely recognisable; his manners have so much improved towards the

Dauphine, he is almost gallant in his attentions and cares. There are always little caresses, a desire to be as much as possible with the Dauphine, and to please her in everything. . . . In short, his tenderness grows day by day. The King was recently with his family, and said jokingly that the only heirs he expected would be those provided by the Comte d'Artois [then a boy of fourteen and unmarried]. The Dauphin, turning to Madame Victoire, said, laughing : ' My father has no great opinion of me ; but he will change that some time.'   In the meantime, the Dauphine is tranquil and calm about this subject, and has ceased to make confidences about it, which is what I have long been trying to arrange.''

Mercy adds that the Duc d'Aiguillon is unable to work any great mischief, as he is so embarrassed and tied down by the circumstances of France, the critical situation of the monarchy, the dearth of resources, etc. . . . " He is at the feet of the favourite because the King cannot yet get used to him, and everything he does offends. And now he is afraid of the Coadjutor at Strasbourg, and has set as spy over him a young man named Nayac, who is a creature of the family of Aiguillon, whom the Prince de Rohan has been obliged to employ in his own despite.''   The chaos of France, the hopelessness of any remedy, the appalling evils, were pressing heavily upon Louis XV. and his minister ; for the King had annihilated his Parliaments and ruined public credit, and the minister's idea of government was one of balance, by setting a spy to watch a spy, and by mistrusting both.

Marie Antoinette wrote her good wishes for the new year, and her joy that her mother was no longer angry with her: "If you had only seen what pleasure it gave me to receive your last letter, you would feel assured that I shall never be happy, my dear mother, without the knowledge that I have pleased you. I send you the measure of my height and that of the Dauphin; mine was taken without shoes or headdress; his includes shoes, but they are very flat ones, and his hair counts for nothing, being very flat also. Although I am so much grown, I am not any thinner; as for the Dauphin, although he is much sunburnt, his complexion is getting clearer and his health better. He is more amiable each day; and nothing is wanting to my happiness but to be in the condition of the Queen [of Naples]; I hope it may be soon. . . . The Comtesse de Provence has been back a week with us; she is not marked at all, and hardly even red. People say all sorts of horrors about her husband and the Duc de Choiseul; but I do not believe them, and we continue to live very happily together." [Marie Antoinette alludes to the intrigues of the Comte de Provence to oust de Choiseul from the rich command of the Suisse regiment.] "I have been to-day to see the Dauphin shoot; he shoots really well, and with judgment; he killed forty head of

18 December, 1771.

game, which proves that his sight is not as bad as every one believed it to be."

On 19 November the Court had left Fontainebleau, and Mercy records in his letter of the following month the signal favours shown by the King to the Dauphine ; he had come to her room to breakfast, had stayed there quite a long time [in distinction to the cursory parental blessing administered to the breathlessly hastening Mesdames, " while the dogs were uncoupling for the hunt "], and had appeared very gay and happy. " The monarch then took the Dauphine in his carriage with him, and also the Dauphin and Mesdames, and drove them all half way to the meet ; for it is the King's custom to follow the hunt always on his return from one of these journeys." These great vehicles were of a vast capacity, similar to that of our own Royal State coach, built in 1762 ; and upon hunting occasions they carried an entire household. The coaches of Louis XIV. carried ten or twelve persons ; and thus three coaches could convey out hunting the thirty ladies who usually accompanied that monarch.

Paris, 19 December, 1771.

Mercy continued in detail to Marie Thérèse the result of his endeavours to undermine the influence of Mesdames. The Dauphine had summoned him upon her return to Versailles, and had herself commenced the discussion. She confessed her many faults of levity and vivacity ; but, said she : " If the Empress could but see all that goes on here, she would pardon me ; nobody's patience could stand it." She continued that she was not blind to the defects of Mesdames, and knew well how petty was their character; but nevertheless they were her only resource for society, and she had to put up with many little disagreeables in consequence.

She told Mercy an anecdote of Madame Adélaïde, whose discourtesy was more surprising to the Dauphine than to the expectant Mercy. She had been telling the aunts how much pleasure had been given her by the marriage of her brother Ferdinand to the Princess of Modena. Madame Adélaïde had snapped: " We are very much annoyed at it, as this marriage would have been very suitable for the Infant of Parma." This affronted Marie Antoinette doubly; for Mesdames' wish that their nephew of Parma [son of their elder sister, Marie Louise Elizabeth] should have won the rich heiress of Modena, not only conveyed the regret that the Archduke Ferdinand was her husband, but also the insinuation that this Infant of Parma would have done better for himself, if the Archduchess Marie Amélie had not been his wife; and Marie Antoinette was thus insulted in the persons of both her brother and her sister.

Mercy was delighted: "I perceive that her Royal Highness commences to have her eyes opened, and to make sound and just reflections upon her surroundings." He tried to influence Marie Antoinette, in reference to the all-powerful Madame du Barry, but found her less amenable to his persuasions. " The power of the Comtesse du Barry over the mind of the King has scarcely any limits ; it is visible in everything that concerns the Royal family, and the more the favourite is mortified by rude treatment the more she tries to use her present advantages to show her resentment. The result is that every favour asked by Mesdames is refused ; that they experience countless annoyances of every description, and that the King's breach with his children widens until it has now reached the point of a grievous scandal. Up to the present I have succeeded in separating the cause of the Dauphine from that of Mesdames, and in letting all the blame fall upon them . . . but in the end it is impossible that the Dauphine should avoid being entangled . . . and if the ruling parties have reason to fear that the Dauphine's present dislike of them may lead to a prospect of evil in the future, these people would not hesitate to take proceedings, which might bring about the most serious and significant results. Though this conclusion may seem strange, it is justified by the disorders of this Court, and the suspicious characters who have the greatest authority in it."

Mercy here hints that, if the du Barry and her set had reason to imagine that when Marie Antoinette's day of power dawned, their own of reckoning would come, then they would make use of their almost limitless influence at the present moment to take steps that would prevent her ever being Queen of France. Mercy continues : "Few days go by without mischief brewing in the Royal family ; but for some time past the Dauphine has shown such prudence and moderation, that they have not succeeded in embroiling her with those against whom they endeavour to irritate her. The other day the Comte d'Artois confided to the Dauphine that he had been praising her in the presence of the Duc de la Vauguyon, who had contradicted him bitterly, and mentioned the Dauphine with great disrespect: and that the Comtesse de Marsan [the governess of Mesdames Clotilde and Elizabeth, the Dauphin's sisters] went even beyond him, instancing the Dauphine's ill-will towards her family, and putting in a malevolent word against Marie Antoinette whenever she had the opportunity. The Dauphine spoke to me with some emotion, and I had no difficulty in making her feel that it was beneath her to take any notice of the enmity of such people. . . . It has not been so easy to guide the Dauphine in her relations with the Comte de Provence, whom she mistrusts, and, I must say, with good reason. The whole tendency of this young Prince is towards deceit, and his little political schemes seem extending far beyond the aims one would expect from his age [now sixteen]. He shows in everything a far-reaching ambition: he seeks to attach the dominant party to himself by all sorts of means, and is trying to make himself the rallying point of this party; this shocks the Dauphine greatly, and, notwithstanding the strongest representations possible, it is not always in my power to prevent her showing signs of her resentment."

The resentment was not only for herself, it was on behalf of the poor, feeble "*cyclope de Versailles*"— incapable, inefficient, but her husband—that Marie Antoinette's wrath flamed on the sly, plotting, younger brother, who, smoothing his way to the throne of Louis XV., by servile truckling to the *maîtresse en titre*, could only attain his aim by removing from his path the dim-witted Dauphin. Mercy tells how once the storm broke. While the Comtesse de Provence was at la Muette, recovering from her smallpox, the Comtesse de Valentinois gave a *fête* at her country-house, which was very near the Royal *château*. This was attended by the Dauphine, the Comtesse de Provence, and Madame du Barry, who tells in her own Memoirs that her dress upon this occasion was of green satin with finest Flemish lace, with wreaths of roses looped up with pearls, that she wore earrings valued at 100,000 écus (£12,000), a string of pearls round her forehead from which hung a diamond star, and on her head a garland of full-blown roses, all of gold work, besides other jewels. The entertainment consisted of a theatrical performance and the verses were composed expressly to do honour to Madame du Barry, with a refrain :

> *C'est la beauté*
> *Qui nous mène à la verité,*

and allusions to :

> *Ce que n 'a pu faire*
> *La raison sévère*
> *L'amour seul l'opère*
> *Et rien n'a coûté,*

MADAME DU BARRY.

(From the miniature at the Château d'Argenteau.)   [*Page* 172.

MADAME DE POMPADOUR.

(From the miniature at the Château d'Argenteau.)   [*Page* 335.

which displeased the Royal family extremely. To
add to their disgust the Comtesse de Provence greeted
the du Barry with distinguished honours, coming
down to receive her upon her arrival, in her own apartment, before her appearance at the assembly. There
was an interview and exchange of sentiments between
the Dauphine and the Comtesse de Provence after
this affair, whereat the Comtesse, discomfited, excused
herself by saying she acted upon her husband's orders ;
and the Dauphine, returning to Versailles, found the
Comte de Provence opportunely paying his court to
Mesdames ! She made a spirited attack upon him,
for the double game he was playing, and pointed out
the defects of his character with a bitter mockery that
entirely disconcerted the Comte de Provence.

However, this moment of lightning wrath passed
without further incident until a second act of duplicity
renewed the electric storm. The Dauphine returned to
see Mesdames alone [their first gift to her had been
a private key to their apartments], and passed the room
of the Comte de Provence ; he was there, with open
door, loudly commanding the Duc d'Aiguillon to
propose to the King an arrangement by which one of
the ladies-in-waiting of the du Barry was to be transferred to the service of the Comtesse de Provence.
The Dauphine, horrified at hearing another proof of
the baseness of the Comte de Provence, ran to find the
Dauphin, threw herself on his neck, and embraced him
tenderly, saying :

" My dear husband, I love you more each day.

You are honest and straightforward ; the more I compare you with the others, the better I know that you are worth more than all of them." And then she told him all the story, and in the recoil of her frank, proud nature from the degrading traffic of the Comte de Provence, she was farther than ever from Mercy's counsels of toleration.

In a private and separate letter to the Empress Mercy permits himself to speak plainly on the position of affairs at Court. He says : "In regard to the character of the people who govern the King, it is impossible to carry too far our suspicions of the possible effects of their malevolence. The King without being old in years [he was then sixty-one] is worn out by the life he leads ; he grows weaker, he may fail altogether in a short time. The ruling party cannot regard that prospect without trembling ; above all, as they suppose the Dauphine is filled with a spirit of hatred and vengeance, for people of this sort measure others by their own standards of thinking and acting. They see, besides, that the Dauphine is gaining a paramount sway over the Dauphin. They feel, in consequence, that their fate will one day lie in her hands. These reflections, based upon the dread due to a bad conscience, may result in strange deeds by villainous people, who see no other means of saving themselves, and believe they have nothing left to gain by intrigue."

"I have tried to show this significant truth to the Dauphine, and induce her to take the only method

of preserving herself from these malignant people, by
letting them understand that her pardon might possibly
be obtained by better conduct ; which would calm their
minds and prevent them from proceeding to extremes.
But her Royal Highness, from her high spirit and
extreme repugnance to think for one instant of things
that do not please her, has not felt in the least the
force of my representation. . . . The Duchesse de
Brancas, *dame d'honneur* of the Comtesse de Provence,
has lost her appointment, on account of some too
marked opposition to the favourite " [she was dismissed
by the time-serving young Comte de Provence].

"Similar events happen here with ever greater
frequency ; they cannot take place without scandal, or
without causing great trouble to the Royal family. . . .
Having weighed and examined the Duc d'Aiguillon, I
think it probable that he will let himself follow all the
impulses of a character inclined to intrigue, to little
schemes and underhand manœuvres, and will adopt
no decided policy. Having no deep knowledge of
affairs of state, he meanders in their shadows, and as
he cannot fail to run against obstacles everywhere, he
is bound to retrace his steps. . . . But whatever he
does, he can never be more than an inferior minister."

[With such leaders, France felt the speech of the
Pope, Benedict XIV., who said : " Does the existence
of Providence need any other proof than the fact that
the Kingdom of France prospered under Louis XV. ? "]

Mercy ends his letter and his report of the year of
1771 with excuses for the Dauphine's short letters to

her mother : " Her intention is always to tell your Majesty a thousand things ; but, when it comes to the point of sitting still at a desk, she is so full of life that this seems to her very difficult. And to this quickness is due the fact that the Dauphine often intends by a short phrase to convey a much wider meaning. She observes sometimes the same method in talking, and it is only by force of habit and by thinking that I succeed in understanding all that her Royal Highness wishes to convey to me." Bright, vehement, agile-witted little Dauphine, with thoughts crowding too thick for a pen, or even for a quick tongue ; with flashing temper and a pride disdaining unworthy stepping-stones or even safeguards ; passionately longing for affection, and reaping, as its return, from all but the stupid, sincere clod, her husband, treachery and baseness that made the most of her hasty impulses.

CHAPTER XIII

The Command of the Suisses—Provence sows, the
Dauphin harrows, d'Artois reaps—The Dauphine
speaks to Madame du Barry—The Dauphin dances
—Illness of the Empress—Revenues, regular and
irregular—Marie Antoinette's Shoes—Death of de la
Vauguyon—*La petite* Carmelite

MARIE THÉRÈSE commenced this year with
a letter to Mercy-Argenteau, in which she
showed her clear recognition of the invaluable aid he
is rendering to Marie Antoinette : " I see, with grief,
the dangers that threaten my child . . . I
put my trust in your discernment and zeal
alone. Your task is, in truth, arduous, in
view of the indifference and levity of my daughter
(with a little obstinacy besides), who is accustomed to
content herself with passing amusements, without
reflection upon their consequences ; but that is one
motive the more to encourage you to redouble your
efforts, and not to let yourself be thwarted by the
difficulties that you have to encounter in your task."
Her letter to her daughter, however, had veiled so
skilfully her disapproval, that Marie Antoinette had
said joyfully on reading it : " For this once I am
not scolded ! "

Vienna
4 January,
1772.

Mercy conveys this relief of the Dauphine in
his first letter to Marie Thérèse in 1772.
Paris 23 January, 1772. Intrigues thicken at the Court, for now a new
and indefatigable schemer is adding his quota
to the net-work ; the Comte de Provence is entering
actively into the life of machinations. His manœuvres
are laid bare in the affair of the Duc de Choiseul and
the command of the Suisse regiment, and the exposure
is considered so unseemly, that even he dare not
profit by the successful plot. When de Choiseul
fell from power, Louis retained sufficient judgment to
regret his loss and to doubt his successors, during those
flashes of comparative intelligence that shed a fitful
light upon his consciousness. It was certain that he
would have pursued the fallen minister with no penalty
but that of disgrace, but for the manœuvres of the
vindictive " *dévots*," whose vengeance seemed incom-
plete while de Choiseul still enjoyed the revenues of
the colonelcy of his regiment.

To despoil the popular Duc de Choiseul of the
command, it was necessary to find some such excuse
as that a Royal prince should supersede him, and the
Comte de Provence, with great alacrity, commenced
to play the game. The King was induced to demand
de Choiseul's resignation, in order that Provence might
receive it ; and the Comte was on the point of reaping
the spoils of victory when all was upset by the surprising
intervention of the ignored Dauphin, who (how inspired
they could not imagine) showed positive symptoms
of anger, and spoke quite plain words as to the under-

hand trickery and meanness of his brother. The *cabale*, in unexpected discomfiture, found that for the reputation's sake of the Comte de Provence his share had better be hushed up. The Comte took the simple course of denying everything, even his own words, and had to see the command given to his younger brother, the Comte d'Artois, a boy of sixteen. But, as it was found out and widely spread that the Comte de Provence had been the prime mover, and had himself written to the King to ask for the appointment, he had the discredit of his intrigue, together with the dishonour of having lied unsuccessfully.

Mercy relates all this, and adds that this defeated roguery, together with the dismissal of the Duchesse de Brancas from the household of the Comtesse de Provence and innumerable other little servilities, show that the Comte has entirely gone over to the favourite ; and this has resulted in a family split. " Lately I have been solely occupied in trying to restrain the Dauphine from any too rigorous demonstration against this young Prince, her brother-in-law, and I have induced a certain moderation up to the present. But the occasions are so frequent, and they produce so much fermentation and acidity, that it is almost impossible to prevent the outcome of so critical a situation. The Comtesse de Provence is playing a very suspicious part. She complains of being obliged to conform to the requirements of her husband, of which she wishes to appear to disapprove ; but, after carefully verifying the facts, I am perfectly certain that this young Princess is a humbug; and, without enlightening the Dauphine too much in this matter, I have implored her not to give too unreserved confidence to the Comtesse de Provence."

As for Mesdames, Mercy is easier in mind, for the Dauphine has given proof of her independence, and he rejoices that the yoke of Madame Adélaïde has been thrown off, at least for once. On New Year's Day it was the custom for all ladies that had been presented to pay their court to the Royal family. "I was informed that the Comtesse du Barry had decided to perform that duty, and on New Year's Eve I had an interview with the Dauphine, and persuaded her Royal Highness, by every means in my power, not to treat the favourite badly. . . . The essential point was that Mesdames should not be informed, which happily was obtained. On the morning of New Year's Day Madame du Barry appeared, to pay her respects to the Dauphine; she was accompanied by the Duchesse d'Aiguillon and the Maréchale de Mirepoix. The Dauphine spoke first to the Duchesse; then passing before the favourite, and looking at her without constraint or affectation, she said to her: "There are very many people at Versailles to-day"; after this her Royal Highness spoke immediately to the Maréchale de Mirepoix."

At last Mercy's counsels had borne fruit. The proud little Austrian mouth, " scarlet as a cherry," so firmly closed against a suspicion of servility, whose silence had perturbed the King and discomposed the whole *cabale*, had uttered a sentence to the mistress.

Mercy went that evening to the Dauphine to hear the
pregnant sentence ; directly he appeared the Dauphine
exclaimed : " I have done what you told me ! there
is the Dauphin who will bear me witness ! " Whereat
that heavy Prince smiled, but spoke no word (as was
usual) : and the Dauphine had to tell her own story,
which she did quite willingly, ending with : " I have
spoken this once, but I am quite decided to stop there,
and this woman shall not hear the sound of my voice
again." Mercy says that this was the first opportunity
he had of speaking in the presence of the Dauphin,
and he made the best use of it. " I perceived that
the Dauphin understood what I was saying ; he
seemed to approve by certain gestures and movements
of the head, but he did not utter a single word. . . . I
noticed after this interview that the Dauphin seemed
well disposed towards me, and I am the only one of
the foreign Ambassadors to whom he has ever spoken."

The King was overjoyed at the success of Mercy's
long endeavours ; the Dauphine had addressed one
entire sentence to the favourite, beyond the mere adjunct
of Lansquenet. All was therefore well, and his Majesty
welcomed the Dauphine with every demonstration of
tenderness at her happy inauguration of the New Year.
But " chez Mesdames " there were reproaches and
regrets, pointed by the Comtesse de Narbonne, to urge
on the Royal aunts, and " I saw the moment in which
her Royal Highness was almost repenting what she had
done." This winter the amusements were two
theatrical performances and one ball a week, " the

Dauphine dances better than ever, she has inspired the Dauphin with the desire for this exercise," and he was endeavouring to learn laboriously : alone with locked doors, to the sound of a little fiddle, and "sweating great drops," as the memoirs of Touchard Lafosse bear witness.

Mercy's next letter related an alarm that had been given to the Dauphine on account of **Paris, 29 February.** the health of her mother. The newly appointed Cardinal, de la Roche-Aymon (who had been Grand Almoner to the Court, and whose signature is scrawled under those of the Royal family in the marriage contract of Marie Antoinette) came on the day he received the hat, as was the custom, to pay a State visit to the Dauphine. But before the Cardinal arrived, the Duc d'Aiguillon entered, asking very impressively if the Dauphine had had news of the Empress. At her surprised look, he added she was not to be uneasy, but the Empress had been ill and been bled twice. The Duc d'Aiguillon pretended afterwards that he had continued with reassuring words ; but the Dauphine, too much agitated to listen, retired in floods of tears to her room, and sent a message to the Cardinal that she was unable to give him an audience.

The Comtesse de Noailles, on her own responsibility, went to the Duc d'Aiguillon to demand the letters upon which was based his disquieting announcement. The little Dauphine, in terrible distress, asked for a chaplet of beads her mother had given her, and betook herself to her prayers, with the sympathetic

Dauphin beside her, equally distressed. Mercy was sent for hurriedly, but news he had none to give, so he despatched a courier in the night to the Duc d'Aiguillon ; at last it was found that anxiety was entirely superfluous, and that the Empress had recovered from her temporary indisposition. The Duc d'Aiguillon, conscious of an indiscretion, blamed Marie Antoinette for not having listened to his later explanations ; she believed that his conduct was due to malicious intentions ; and Mercy had difficulty in restoring peace, or its semblance. The result of this grief was Marie Antoinette's resolution to obey her mother's wishes, whatever her own scruples, and she said to Mercy : "I will try to conquer my repugnance to the favourite, for my heart is always with my family, and, if I quarrel with them, I feel that my duties here would be too heavy for me to bear." Mercy approved the wise decision, and added, if the Dauphin succeeded suddenly to the throne in the midst of these disturbances [the King's health weakened daily and visibly], what renewed scheming and resulting dangers might not ensue. To which Marie Antoinette answered briskly : "I will answer for the fact that, when the Dauphin is master, all these bickerings will cease."

The financial affairs of Marie Antoinette were in such chaos by this time that Mercy felt compelled to describe them to Marie Thérèse : February, "to give an idea of the abuses that flourish 1772. here in everything." There was an annual sum of 120,000 livres (£4,800) assigned solely for the wardrobe of Marie Antoinette. This sum was paid to the order of the Mistress of the Robes, " who at the end of the year produces an account, of which one can understand nothing at all, and that has, nevertheless, to be approved and signed by the Dauphine. When the Duchesse de Villars held the appointment she was rendered so incapable by her age and infirmities that her department became an immense system of pillage, and instead of 120,000 livres, the expenditure of the wardrobe, for eighteen months, amounted to over 350,000 francs [£14,000]."

It is of interest here to compare the revenues of Madame du Barry at the same period. The Abbé Terray, Comptroller-General of Finance (and adroit juggler with funds), curried favour with the favourite by honouring all that lady's drafts, which in eight months amounted to 1,500,000 livres (£60,000). In addition she had her " appointment," as " mistress in form," at first of £2,000 sterling a month, afterwards raised to £4,000 a month ; and when the Comte de Clermont died, his annuity of 300,000 livres (£12,000) was divided, and she reaped one third (£4,000). Thus, without including the incalculable sums that Madame du Barry received as commissions, from the sale of monopolies to the *fermiers-généraux* (whose "farming" was of the national revenues), from the sale of regimental appointments, etc., etc., she had an annual income of not less than £142,000, and the much higher purchasing power of money in that century must be remembered.

" When the Duchesse de Cossé took up the duties
of her office, she was frightened at the extravagance,
that she appeared to think was due to the whims
and fancies of the Dauphine.   Then I felt it my
duty to intervene . . . and I proved that her Royal
Highness (who has never chosen, or asked for, a
dress or any ornament whatsoever, and whose wardrobe has been entirely controlled by the Mistress
of the Robes) has had no part in these wasteful
proceedings."

Mercy described how he had gone through the
accounts, and what crying evils he had found in their
records of robbery.   He mentioned a few of the most
absurdly outrageous ; that the *femmes de chambre* had
put down in the expenses, three ells of ribbon each day
to tie the peignoir of the Dauphine, two ells of taffetas
each day to cover over the basket in which were placed
the gloves and fan ; and, amid an infinity of similar
items, the purchase of four new pairs of shoes a week.
The question of the shoes seemed particularly pre-
posterous at a Court in which it was mentioned as
proof of extravagance in the *charmante et opulente*
Madame Leblanc, *dame de l'élégance et de la prodigalité*,
that she changed her shoes twice a day ! Madame
Leblanc was the heroine of many stories, not always
connected with shoes, nor even with " *talons rouges*,"
one of which arose from her friendship with the
Procureur du Roi, a Monsieur Lenoir.   But although
they were seen about together, and even went thus to
the Opera, there was no scandal : " *attendu que Monsieur*

Lenoir et Madame Leblanc ne sauraient faire que des œuvres pies."

Mercy continued his details of the Dauphine's money matters. She had 96,000 livres [£3,840] a year for her privy purse ; but from this was deducted 20,000 livres [£800] for pensions that the late Queen had bestowed at different times. " I have expostulated against this injustice, for not only did the Queen leave by will, payable from her own property, sufficient sums to defray these pensions, but it is absurd to burden the Dauphine with charges that she did not bestow and do not concern her in the least. If her Royal Highness would only listen to me, it would be easy to free her from these engagements, but in her easy good nature she wished to make no change in the established order."

In these eighteen months the Dauphine had lost 1,235 louis [£1,185 12*s*. 0*d*.] at play, but in spite of that at the end of the first year there was a sum saved of seven thousand and some hundred livres. In the rare event of there being any savings at all in the accounts of a member of the Royal family—an event that, as has been observed, it was the endeavour of the household thriftily to prevent—the sum was distributed among the most deserving of the servants ; and this "gratification" was the more welcome as it represented the chief part of, if not the only, wages they received. The treasurer, Pommery, had been in the habit of apportioning this " gratification " ; but Mercy impressed upon the Dauphine that it was for her to observe her servants and reward them herself; and he added that Marie Antoinette was neither parsimonious nor extravagant, and that she had spent but very little of the sum of 1000 louis [£960], the amount Marie Thérèse had authorised Mercy to hold at her order.

"One of the events most favourable to the Dauphine is the fact of the death of the Duc de la Vauguyon. This old Governor of the Dauphin was despised by him, yet imposed upon him, and preserved an ascendency over him sufficient to be very dangerous from such a wicked man. . . . The world has shown such universal joy at his decease that it has been almost indecent. The Dauphin refused to go even once to see him, although the Dauphine asked him to perform this act of consideration. . . . The King has shown equal indifference at the death of this old courtier." Mercy speaks with pride of the wonderful memory of the Dauphine, and says that now she is acquainted with nearly all the families of France and remembers the name of each individual who has been presented to her. The last paragraph of his letter refers to Madame Louise, who, sheltered in the covent of the Carmelites, gathered a great accession of power by the very act with which she had openly laid it aside. While simply one of the four Mesdames she was a negligible quantity : when she adopted a religious vocation she was to be reckoned with. She could then write boldly to the King (from the washhouse where she superintended the preparation of the lye), "*de la part de Dieu*," and reprove him for his manner of life, indicating herself as the sacrifice for his sins.   [This sacrifice was otherwise explained by the Court, as her one opportunity for self-advertisement.]

Louis, appreciating this abnegation of what gave her no pleasure, felt the value of a daughter who could be a go-between with God ; and he employed her as a means to try and obtain from the Pope the divorce of Madame du Barry from her husband, as a preliminary to his marrying her.   Mercy says : " There is now a question of transferring the convent of Carmelites to Versailles, but there seem great difficulties in the way ; and the project is pressed only when the health of the King indicates a possible return to a more regular and more Christian life.   As this Prince is better in health, and the return of milder weather suits him, it is evident that things will drag on upon their old lines at present." Madame Louise was called by Marie Antoinette (who had always a happy knack of *le mot juste*) : " *La petite Carmelite, la plus intrigante qui existe dans le royaume.*" She was exploited, for their own ends, by the Archbishop of Paris (a reasonably honest man as the times considered), and by the Chancellor Maupeou (" who had not a grain of religion, or honour, or honesty, but affected a vast deal of all "), who used to write sermons, intended for the edification of his vassals in the country, and submit them, with delicate flattery, to the holy revision of the Royal nun at St. Denis.

CHAPTER XIV

The Ambassador de Rohan and the Cardinal Sins—
Madame de Marsan—Uniform Edicts—Division of
Poland—The Dauphin quarrels

THE Empress Marie Thérèse was not long discovering the character of the man Louis XV. had sent to her as his Ambassador. The Coadjutor of Strasburg, afterwards Cardinal de Rohan, had already shown his nature. Marie Thérèse wrote : " I cannot approve of the Ambassador de Rohan ; it is a large volume stuffed with evil suggestions, as little suited to an ecclesiastic as to a minister, which he reveals imprudently upon every occasion ; without knowledge of affairs and without adequate talents and fundamentally frivolous, presumptuous and trivial. One cannot rely either upon his explanations or his reports. His suite is similarly compounded of people, with neither merits nor manners." It is as if the great Empress recognised in this man the evil genius of Marie Antoinette : her instant recoil from his vicious and puerile character was as much from instinct as from experience.

The state in which this prelate deemed it necessary to live was flagrantly extravagant and immoral ; he

Vienna, 1 March, 1772.

kept a stable of fifty horses, and when hunting galloped
with his followers through the midst of a religious
procession rather than deviate from his course. He
had state coaches that cost 40,000 livres [£1,600],
and four runners whose gold-laced coats cost 4,000
livres [£160] each ; fourteen footmen, seven noble
pages with their attendants, two noblemen, six valets,
aud other officials to do the honours of his establishment, a crowd of officers and ten musicians dressed
in scarlet.   All these in addition to the officials
necessary for the diplomatic service.   There were also
the expenses to be considered of the immense and
constantly replenished harem, that was situated near
Bergzabern. Obviously the resources of this prelate,
even when increased by profitable silk smuggling and
loans from his relatives, must be exhausted speedily.
De Rohan obtained permission from the Most Christian
King to borrow money upon his benefices, and raised
by that means some 600,000 livres [£24,000] ; but
his debts in Vienna soon exceeded a million, and Marie
Thérèse, finding his privilege of Ambassador was being
utilised for cheating the customs, was obliged to take
away the right to free entry of goods from all the
diplomatic representatives alike.

Mercy has also his de Rohan of whom to complain.
Madame de Marsan, sister of the head of
the house of Rohan, had been criticising,
with venomous tongue, the amusements of
the Dauphine, who, informed of the insolence, was
indignantly preparing a reply to Madame de Marsan,

Paris,
15 March,
1772.

when Mercy's soothing diplomacy intervened. He says : " I shall try every means to remove this intriguing, vindictive, and dangerous woman." Madame de Marsan, the Governess of the Royal children, had taken to the occupations of religion and intrigue when she found those of matrimony unobtainable. She was the aunt of Madame de Guéménée, who was appointed Royal Governess in reversion to her, and who proudly said of her bankrupt husband, " it takes a de Rohan to fail for twenty millions ! "

Mercy describes a charming ball given by the Comtesse de Noailles, where various masquerades added to the entertainment, and a wonderful dance, whose figures formed the letters of the name of Marie Antoinette. But he returns before the end of his letter to the burning subject of the de Rohans, as the Ambassador had so little reticence that he had actually dared to write with mockery of his first interview with Marie Thérèse ; and had sent the description to his aunt, Madame de Marsan.

Marie Thérèse, in her next letter, inveighed still more bitterly against the Ambassador : " The Prince de Rohan displeases me more and more ; he is a very bad character, without talents, or prudence, or manners. . . . The Emperor [Joseph II.] likes indeed to amuse himself with him, but it is that he may hear fooleries, babble, and gossip. . . . I should be very glad to see him dislodged from here."

And in her letter of 31 March the Empress still

Vienna, 18 March, 1772.

complained : " The Ambassador de Rohan is always
the same . . . but the Emperor and
Vienna,
31 March, Kaunitz endure him ; the one because he
1772. entertains him with trifles, the other because
he prefers a man of his small capacity."

One of the little details of etiquette, that were
as the breath of life to this Court, and
Paris,
15 April, increased in importance in exact ratio to
1772. their reference to clothes, is told in Mercy's
letter of 15 April. There was an order at Court,
that dated from the time of the King's marriage,
and was therefore of the sacred antiquity of nearly
fifty years, that the officers of the three regiments
of body-guards should not be admitted to the dinner
of the Queen, unless they exchanged their uniforms
for Court dress. But from the commencement of
this year there had been a fresh order that in no
circumstances should an officer of one of these regiments appear except in regimental uniform, which
obviously debarred them, according to the ancient
etiquette, from witnessing the dinner of the Dauphine.
The Colonels of these three regiments were the Duc
de Noailles, the Duc d'Aiguillon, and the Prince de
Soubise, and they addressed a request to the Comtesse
de Noailles that the old order should not stand, but
that uniforms should be admitted.

True to her name, " Madame l'Etiquette " rejected
this request, and all concerned instantly worked themselves into a frenzy ; and the three Colonels declared
they would appeal to the Dauphine. " As I know

from experience," says Mercy, " how trifles of this
nature give rise to agitation and effervescence in this
country, I thought it well to warn the Dauphine
what she had better reply." The Dauphine was quite
tranquil, and decided she would refer the agitated
officers to the King, as the sole arbiter of etiquette.
But the excitement spread, and Mesdames joined
in the turmoil so fraught with dire possibilities of
innovation ; their perturbation infected the Dauphine ;
suggestions flew, that added to the heat ; the Comtesse
de Noailles sought an audience with the King—
who entirely approved the old order ; the Colonels
sought an interview with the King—who was entirely in favour of the new regulation. The Comtesse de Noailles had triumphed, but prematurely ;
and then in woe and mortification she threatened to
quit the Court. Mercy, as usual, intervened, and
induced the Duc de la Vrillière, that mouthpiece of
etiquette, to write a letter saying that, although the
King had certainly told the Comtesse de Noailles,
he desired to maintain the old order, he had since
perceived inconveniences and changed his mind. This
expedient calmed every one, and the incident effaced
itself in peace, until the next trifle sent the " feather
pates " again spinning.

This was the project of the Duc d'Aiguillon to
reconcile the Princes of the blood with the Court.
They had all been filled with such patriotic motives
when they had signed the petition against the King
on behalf of the oppressed Parliament ; and all

were now so weary of the superfluous virtue that had sent them into exile for just one year. Condé and Conti and d'Orléans were ready for any servility that would restore them to Paris. The Comtesse de Marsan, the intriguer, exploited Mesdames successfully against this project, but failed to win the Dauphine to join them, for which Mercy rejoiced ; and the Princes languished yet many months in the shadow of disfavour, only returning in 1773.

As time passed, the Dauphine, now sixteen years of age and married for two years, grew out of the childish habits that rendered Mercy so anxious. He details with grave satisfaction that she is taking to more serious and more instructive books ; even reads to herself (an unusual mental effort in those days, which Mercy indicates by saying she "gives herself the trouble") ; takes the history of France for her subject, or important memoirs, and endures "without apparent effort" the Abbé de Vermond reading to her for full two or three hours, while she occupies herself with needlework. The children (so cordially disliked by Mercy) are scarcely ever admitted now ; and she is cultivating dancing with the greatest success. "The success is not quite so marked in music, but nevertheless this last occupation leaves her but few moments of idleness. Still, there are moments of boredom, that send the Dauphine to Mesdames, and these are the occasions I dread."

Paris 15 May, 1772.

The Dauphine has two Ministers, of whom she can make any use she wishes, and over whom she exercises

her influence for the benefit of petitioners, and always
with more charity than discretion.   These are the
Ministers of War, the Marquis de Monteynard, who
had succeeded the Duc de Choiseul in 1771, and
showed the greatest eagerness to carry out any wishes
of Marie Antoinette; and the Abbé Terray, Comptroller-
General, who found his advantage in being complaisant
to both leaders of the Court parties.   But for the Duc
d'Aiguillon she felt such invincible dislike that not
even in the cause of charity could she prevail upon
herself to ask anything that belonged to his department of State.   " As to the favourite, she has now
not the smallest complaint to make.   It is true she
has not shown herself since the New Year."   [The
favourite had won her game for the time, and would
risk no rebuff.   Louis' jealousy, also, guarded her,
with the Oriental suspicion that reaped its usual
return of successful deceit ; and the du Barry lived,
as a bird in a cage, in the exquisite rooms over the
King's, to whose windows, with their golden shutters,
among the sculptures of the Palace roof, high above
the marble court, Marie Antoinette is said to have
glanced up so often when stepping into her coach.]

Marie Thérèse in this letter to Mercy gives the
announcement of the proposed division of Schönbrunn
Poland, an act forced upon her reluctant 1 June,
acceptance by the trend of events in Eastern 1772.
Europe.   " I can well believe that the part we
are about to play in connection with Poland will
make a great sensation in France.   Although I

am well persuaded of the opinions of the King, I
cannot decide to write to him on the subject, but
I leave you entirely at liberty to say anything to
his Majesty you think suitable. . . . The mission
of Count Rosenberg to Parma has been quite useless ; my daughter has flatly refused all his proposals.
. . . In the meantime I have broken off all communication with my daughter, and have commanded
my family, here, in Florence and in Milan, to do the
same, and send back, unopened, all the letters she writes
to us . . . . we wait to see the result."

The division of Poland, to which Marie Thérèse
referred, was filling her political sky with as many
thunderclouds as the headstrong folly of her daughter
of Parma had called up on the family horizon. Of the
former, nothing at present reached Marie Antoinette ;
but in regard to the wholly unsuccessful mission of
the Comte de Rosenberg, to repair the credit and
reputation of Parma, she was quite well-informed,
and wrote to her mother :

"I cannot tell you how vexed I am with the
Infanta ; it is really astonishing that she
should not have profited by your good
counsel, and been influenced by all that you
told her of Rosenberg. But all the same, if I have
any opportunity of diminishing the bad impression
all this has made here, I shall seize it. . . . It seems
to me that if I were similarly unfortunate I should try
to improve, if only to save my dear mother from such
grief. I have just heard from la Böhme [lady-in-

**Versailles
13 June,
1772.**

waiting to her sister, Caroline of Naples] that the Queen is very happy at the birth of her child, although it is only a daughter ; but that will at least give hopes that she may one day have sons." Marie Antoinette always compares, in her letters to her mother, the happier fate of her sisters with her own childless condition, longing vainly for the time to come when she too should be a mother ; but this was not to be for many years to come.

The proud and yet affectionate character of the Dauphine proved very difficult for the Empress and the devoted Mercy to sway ; and, very diplomatically, Marie Thérèse, acting upon the advice of the watchful guardian, altered entirely her tactics. No more the " grumbling letters," that Marie Antoinette resented and obeyed reluctantly ; it was to her tenderness that appeals were to be made, and Mercy writes of the first fruits of the new policy. He had noted, with great care, the irritation caused by the lecturing letters, " in which the moral was presented rather severely," and now he describes the " delicious sight of the rising tenderness " that greeted the change of tone. " All the letters of your Majesty have been received with much respect, but, to say the least, with as much fear. The bad tone of her surroundings, the absence of all reprimand, or contradiction, or even advice, either from the King or from the Dauphin, added to the feeling that she is three hundred leagues away from you, are no doubt the causes why the severe letters have not

always produced a good effect. . . . Besides, the
Dauphine always imagined she was not loved, and
that she would always be treated sharply ; but the last
letters have swept away that fallacy. The Dauphine
has such great powers of mind and character, that
there cannot be the least doubt that we may rely
upon their effects."

The dancing continues actively, and the Dauphin
has even become emboldened to share her dancing
lessons, which therefore, as Mercy observes, become
a " useful amusement." Marie Antoinette exercises
ever greater ascendency over her husband, and points
out to him, quite naturally, all his defects, to which
he listens very well and pays attention ; with the
result that his bearing and manner are improving
daily, and all attribute it to the good influence of
the Dauphine. Music, which in after-life became
one of Marie Antoinette's passions, is also being taken
up, and Mercy mentions that he had induced her
to give little concerts, sometimes in her own apartments, sometimes in those of Madame (the sister
of the Dauphin), whereat she had even sung on one
occasion. Mercy's great preoccupation was to find
amusements for Marie Antoinette apart from Mesdames,
whom he regarded, balefully, as the root of all Court
evil ; and he wrote piteously how hard it was to
arrange any with such a dead weight of dullness against
him as the Comtesse de Noailles. " I made a plan to
attract the Dauphine to her house in the evenings ;
this plan succeeded sometimes and would become

a daily custom if the Comtesse de Noailles had
the wits to amuse the Dauphine and spare her the
wearisome discourses to which the said Comtesse is
only too prone. . . . But all I can do to sustain the
credit of Madame de Noailles is nullified by the extreme
ineptitude of this lady-in-waiting, who has sufficiently
straightforward ideas, but is without a single talent
to make them acceptable."

He gives an instance. Marie Antoinette, for a
long time, had been desirous of seeing Paris, which,
according to usual custom, she ought to have visited
directly after her marriage. She therefore planned to
send saddle horses to a certain point, drive there in
carriages, mount and ride along the boulevards without
entering the town itself; and all this could be done in
perfect *incognito*. The plan was approved, even the
obstinate Comtesse de Noailles had consented, when
Madame Adélaïde decided she would like to go too,
and insisted that her own lady-in-waiting should
attend instead of the Duchesse de Durfort, who,
being the daughter of the Comtesse de Noailles,
had greater claim to that honour. The Comtesse
then raised up so many obstacles, telling the Dauphine
she would meet crowds of people, that she would
certainly be recognised, that it would be very embarrassing and inconvenient, that finally the whole
project collapsed.

Mercy tells another little episode of the same time,
that had happened a few days previously, in which
the Dauphine's discretion had been so admirable

that Mercy would not have known the circumstance but that the Dauphine herself told him—with the strictest injunctions that he was not to mention it in his despatches to the Empress! There was a very beautiful piece of porcelain, that belonged to the Comte de Provence and stood upon his mantelshelf. Whenever the Dauphin found himself in this room, he was in the habit of taking down this precious porcelain and examining it, to the undisguised alarm of the Comte de Provence. The Dauphine was in the act of joking upon her brother-in-law's dread of accident, while the Dauphin held the porcelain in his hands, when the foreseen happened; the clumsy Dauphin let it slip, and it was smashed in pieces. In a moment the Comte de Provence had flung himself upon the Dauphin, collared him, and commenced to strike him, the Dauphin hitting back. For one moment the Dauphine thought of screaming for help; the next, she had thrown herself into the fray and separated the combatants, being, as Mercy says, scratched on the hand in the process; which looks as if the Royal Princes were not above using their nails. She then induced them to make up the quarrel, and as no one was present, no one knew of it, for which Mercy was thankful.

He unfolded to Marie Antoinette the culpability of the Comte de Provence in having raised his hand against the Dauphin of France, whose rank was distinguished by all the forms that etiquette could dictate from that of his younger brothers. But the

Dauphin himself recognised no such barrier, to judge
by the fact that his readiest repartee to his brothers'
nimbler wit was a kick ; this was considered by the
Court to be a form of humour very suitable to one
whose only vocation was that of a blacksmith.

The second portion of Mercy's letter had reference
to the division of Poland. This dismember-
ment had been arranged very comfortably,   **Paris
15 June,
1772.**
and without France having any inkling of the
events developing before her blind eyes. Catherine
of Russia, feeling Poland would make an excellent
buffer state if properly ruled, supplied it with her
own ruler—her lover, Poniatowski. Frederick II. of
Prussia, entirely in the interest of the balance of power,
made a treaty with Russia that she should leave Turkey
in peace (the war had lasted since 1768) and indemnify
herself with a slice of Poland, Prussia taking another
slice, as a guarantee of good faith ; and they signed
that agreement on 5 February, 1772. Marie Thérèse
could not see her enemy, Prussia, extending her borders
without *at least* an equal increase of her own territory ;
and took such steps to ensure that no injustice should
be done her, that in the final partition of Poland
there was not enough Kingdom left for Poniatowski
to rule at all. Marie Thérèse wept, but annexed two
thousand five hundred square leagues : Frederick got
only nine hundred square leagues ; and Catherine the
rest. Frederick the Great observed to Prince Charles
of Hesse : " She wept terribly, but her troops took
possession of her portions, she weeping the while.

All of a sudden we learned that she had seized much more than the part assigned to her, for the more she wept the more she grabbed, and we had a good deal of trouble to make her content herself with her share of the cake.   That's just like her ! "

However, Marie Thérèse did not get all that she expected, and her two griefs are shown in the one sentence :   " I have always been opposed to this iniquitous division—so *unequal* ! "   France's Ambassador to Vienna, de Rohan, was occupied in other matters than the business of his country, and quite heedless of it at the time these treaties were in progress ; and this accounts for much of his toleration by Kaunitz.   Mercy ended his letter with an interview he had here with the Comte de Fuentes (Spanish Ambassador), on the subject of the distracting family at Parma.   De Fuentes had given as his opinion, that it was not possible to reduce the disorders of Parma, the Infant was of such extreme feebleness and the Infanta did with him what she chose.   All the Courts had adopted the method of remedy by silence—as if insubordination fed upon correspondence—and neither the King of Spain nor the King of France had written to Parma for a long time, fully agreeing that the Empress had taken the wisest course possible.   This Comte de Fuentes, mentioned by Mercy, was he who had intervened with some effect in one of the many little intrigues of Madame Louise, the royal Carmelite. Maupeou, the adroit writer of sermons and Chancellor, was very ambitious of an honour not obtainable by

any but indirect means.   He wished to be made
Cardinal, and had every chance of gaining his hat,
as flattered Madame Louise was won to his cause,
and the chief objection—his wife—was conveniently
dead ; but the Comte de Fuentes dispelled that dream.

CHAPTER XV

MARIE ANTOINETTE was now considered old
enough to be of political importance to her
mother, in view of the influence she had obtained over the feeble heir to the throne of France:
the heir of whom Louis XV. wrote to
Versailles, 14 July, 1772. de Choiseul that he was *un bien petit secours,
vis-à-vis de la tourbe républicaine.* Mercy
had been instructed to tell the Dauphine of the division
of Poland and the exclusion of France from a share,
and to lay before her the possible resentment of Louis
and its effect upon the alliance. The Dauphine,
treated no longer as a child, wrote gravely : "Your
letter has touched me and given me subject of thought.
I will do my best to contribute towards the preserva-
tion of good friendship and alliance ; where should
I be if there were a rupture between my two families ?

I hope the good God will preserve me from this unhappiness, and will inspire me with right acts; I have prayed for this with all my heart."

She then gives the desired list of her readings: the "Mémoires de l'Estoile":—"it is a journal of the reigns of Charles IX., Henri III. and Henri IV., with an account day by day of all that happened in those times, the good and wicked acts, laws, and customs: I find in it the names, the offices, and sometimes the origins, of people now at this Court." Her confessor had given her the Book of Tobias, "with a very pious paraphrase," in which she read about two pages a day. "The Comtesse de Noailles has had a great fright. The Chevalier d'Arpajon, her youngest son, has just caught the smallpox; he had been inoculated by Gatti [the Florentine apostle of inoculation who formed part of the Duc de Choiseul's establishment at Chanteloup]; this is not the first victim after inoculation by this doctor, and now every one else who has been done by him is in a great fright. . . . There are not many people at Compiègne. The quarrellings of the Princes and the ministers have kept many away."

Quarrels and intrigues are the daily life, and Mercy's watch is incessant to try and save the Dauphine, who, from a certain idle facility of consent, is constantly led astray. There was a Comtesse de la Marck, a sister of the Duc and of the Comte de Noailles; her husband was grandfather of that Comte de la Marck, Mercy's great correspondent twenty years later—the champion of Marie Antoinette. This Comtesse de la Marck, audacious, decided, rather over-powering, swept the Dauphine into making the wildest demands from the King, for her own *protégées* ; and the refusal by his Majesty of these demands brought discredit upon the Dauphine. There were two Dutch sisters, "fallen from the clouds in this country," for one of whom Madame de la Marck extracted a pension of 1,000 écus (£150) from the Dauphine, simply because she had changed her religion and was now a Catholic. Mercy met this greed by a neat rebuff.

The Comtesse de la Marck, insatiable for her Dutch girl, obtained from the King (by other means than through the Dauphine) a pension of 4,000 francs (£160). Mercy went to Terray, the Comptroller-general of Finance, and arranged that this second pension should be paid into the account of the Dauphine, who, by paying that amount to this Mademoiselle de Nievenheim, could not be charged with any other pension. Mercy says there was "clamour," and we may rest assured that it was so. Another matter of deep anxiety is touched upon, the incomprehensible coldness of the Dauphin, who is gentle, affectionate, wishful to please his wife, but no nearer marriage union than at first, giving no hope of any change, devoid of any sentiment towards his charming young wife, save that of a dull docility.

Mercy says that for some weeks past he has noticed minutes of sadness, in which the Dauphine was reflecting upon her future, should this strange behaviour

18 July, 1772.

of the Dauphin not alter, and wondering how long this coldness and indifference would continue.

When the Court was at Compiègne there was a new outburst between the Dauphin and the Comte de Provence. The Dauphine was playing piquet in the afternoon with the Comte de Provence. The Dauphin, standing near with a little whip in his hand, amused himself by striking continually the arm of the Comte de Provence with it. There were warnings, repeated frequently and with irritation, but as the Dauphin would not heed or cease, the Comte de Provence sprang upon the whip and tried to wrest it from his brother. The dispute rose high, but the Dauphine possessed herself of the whip, broke it in pieces and ended the quarrel.

. When the Dauphine told Mercy of this friction between the Princes he implored her to lecture the Dauphin on the unsuitability of his jokes, and Marie Antoinette did so the next day. He received the scolding with sweetness and submission. "The Dauphin has nothing against him but the consequences of an excessively bad education : he shows many good qualities, he is honest, and can bear the truth, and there is not even the necessity of any beating about the bush." [The Comtesse de la Marck wrote of him to the King of Sweden in September of this year : " The Dauphin shows certain savage virtues, but he is without wits, without knowledge, without education, without even taste, and as severe in his principles as he is rude in his actions. . . . He is afraid of women, and as even his own wife has not cured him we can believe that none will."]   "This young Prince has spoken to me, and that is the more remarkable because there is scarcely any one to whom he speaks. . . .

"The Comtesse du Barry came to the Dauphine's reception to-day, after having attended mass with the King; she was accompanied by the Duchesse d'Aiguillon. The Dauphine addressed the Duchesse, and then turning toward the favourite made some general remarks upon the weather and the hunting, in such a way as to include the Comtesse du Barry without addressing her directly. The favourite was very well content. The King, informed of what had passed, was also well pleased and showed his approval by many little marks of attention that evening after the dinner *au grand couvert.* . . .

26 July, 1772.

"In case Mesdames should reproach the Dauphine, I suggested to her a suitable reply . . . but neither Madame Adélaïde nor Madame Sophie put any questions; they only sulked a little, which did not require any notice. . . . The King sups every Thursday in a pavilion detached from the palace. The favourite, in a manner, does the honours of this pavilion, therefore the Princesses of the Royal family never go there; the Dauphin has been there in previous years, but this year he would not go, which vexed the King. I asked the Dauphine to persuade him to reappear at these suppers; to this he consented with a good grace, and I found means of informing the King that this return of the Dauphin was due to the influence of the Dauphine, and the monarch was infinitely delighted. . . .

"The Dauphine spoke to me to-day of the Dauphin, his honest character, his sweet temper, his 30 July, good humour ; she said that upon all these 1772. points she felt happy. I saw, nevertheless, that her mind was troubled by other thoughts, upon which she could not express herself. . . .

"On the 31st the whole of the Royal family supped with the King, a ceremony that takes place 31 July. twice a week. Upon these occasions the King retires at eleven o'clock and goes up to the apartments of the favourite, where he plays piquet until one o'clock." (There was a little secret staircase that led from the King's rooms to those of the favourite, up which the King went to see her twenty times a day.)

The political anxiety of Marie Thérèse respecting Poland could not be allayed until the 16 King of France had shown either consent September, or indifference. Mercy had an interview 1772. with Louis—at the house of Madame du Barry—and the King drew him into the recess of a window to discuss the interesting subject. He asked, laughing, how the Emperor (Joseph II.) progressed—"with his friend, the King of Prussia?" Madame du Barry joined in, and said she was quite convinced that the Emperor had gauged the King of Prussia accurately, and it was therefore easy to imagine what degree of friendship would be his with a Prince accustomed "to deceive the whole world, and in whose good faith no one could ever trust!" "At this the King smiled," says Mercy.

Madame du Barry's politics were neither dangerous nor revengeful; too tolerant to plunge a minister into disgrace and a continent into war to avenge an epigram, as did her predecessor, Madame de Pompadour, her desire for intermeddling in diplomatic affairs was limited to insisting on attending one State Council; when she sat upon the arm of the King's chair and played all sorts of *petites singeries enfantines*, such as are customary diversions of senility. It was said that the Comte Wielhorsky appealed to her to save his country, Poland, from ruin. She replied : "Where is Poland?"

Mercy continues : " The combination of plans relative to Poland will certainly prove a new mortification for the French Minister [d'Aiguillon]; but I think I can state that the Most Christian King looks upon these arrangements with more reason and justice, and that they will not be regarded as any attack upon the *Status in quo*."

When Louis realised that his share of the kingdom of his father-in-law, Stanislas Leczinski, was only— epigrams, he cried out in the presence of the Duc d'Aiguillon : "Ah! if de Choiseul had been here this would never have happened." But Louis's inaction in the matter of Poland was not altogether due to the incapacity of his Ministers; it was the result of a tacit bargain between him and Marie Thérèse, in

which his abstention from all action was to be rewarded
by the acceptance of his favourite.

To gain even the amount of tolerance from Marie
Antoinette, that is represented by two sentences
per annum, the powers of Austria and France were
united ; and that Marie Thérèse was well aware that
her large slice of the *Gâteau des rois*—Poland—depended upon the greater or less familiarity of the
Dauphine with the *maîtresse en titre*, is shown by her
exhausting every means of severity and coaxing to
obtain the concession from Marie Antoinette.   And
the influence of Mercy ; and the words, " *il y a bien
du monde aujourd'hui à Versailles*," preserved the peace
of Europe.

"As to the Prince de Rohan, it is certain that the
death of his uncle [the Bishop of Strasburg] will oblige
him to return to this country.   There is, besides,
another event that might produce a similar effect—
a vacancy in the office of Grand Almoner of France.
This post is now filled by the Cardinal de la Roche
Aymon, an octogenarian, very much broken and infirm.
The Prince de Rohan has boasted of having received
the promise of this appointment, which is the object
of his ambition ; but, apart from these two reasons,
I cannot think that the Coadjutor will long remain
Ambassador, and I judge by the feelings of the
minister and the favourite towards him."   (Marie
Thérèse's desire to get rid of de Rohan with all speed
possible was waxing daily.   She wrote to Mercy, on
1 September, 1772 : "Rohan is still the same ; but

nearly all our women, young and old, beautiful and ugly, are bewitched by this model of extravagance and all follies. He seems to amuse himself so well that he declares he will stay here, even when his uncle dies!" And in her letter of 2 October, the worried Empress again wrote: "He is without manners, without character, without talents, without wits; he is a perfect sieve, but somehow makes all the women rave !")

"The health of the Comte de Provence is still very wavering. He is so feeble that he cannot take the exercises that would be advisable to strengthen his constitution. He is beginning to feel the inconveniences of humours in the blood. He has a skin disease upon his hands and he has lost his hair; all these symptoms, sufficiently disquieting, do not promise that the health of this young Prince will soon be restored."

Mercy's next letter had a new point of view, for in it he has to curb not the Dauphine's affection for her aunts but her indignation against them. This incessant adjustment to meet all emergencies, however various, that were caused by the quickly stirred and very human nature of Marie Antoinette, must have induced Mercy to wish that she had been given, when young, the sound advice that was administered to the Duchesse de Choiseul (and was, in fact, the only instruction she could remember ever having received from her mother) : "My child, have *no* tastes !" The incident was this:

Fontaine-bleau, 16 October, 1772.

The scaffolding and supports of the newly finished "magnificent bridge just built over the Seine, near the village of Neuilly," were to be removed in an exciting manner so as to afford a spectacle. The King was going to see them demolished and the whole of Paris intended to be present. There was a question in the Royal family whether the Dauphin and Dauphine should go ; and Mesdames decided not, because the Comtesse du Barry would certainly be there. The Dauphine did not think this at all a sufficient reason, and told the aunts that she intended to go wherever there was an opportunity of being with the King. The dispute grew warm, remarks " *assez piquants* " were bandied, " which were not forgotten for a long time in Versailles," and the affair promised to develop into an intrigue.

However, the emollient Mercy was at once on the spot, and found the Dauphine much irritated against Mesdames. She said to him : " If mamma could see me at this moment, she would know that I am not led by my aunts ! " Mercy replied that the Dauphine could never be led by anything but reason, which in this case was entirely on her side ; but he added that the dispute seemed to him rather premature, she had better wait until the King showed his wishes in the matter ; and in any case disunion in the Royal family was to be deprecated. The Dauphine saw the force of these remarks, and as the King gave no inviting sign she did not go ; but she took good care to tell the aunts that the King's silence was the only reason of her staying at home.   Mercy has a little pathetic plaint of his own.   " After having tried to make peace, I learned that I had toiled gratuitously in the service of Mesdames, because they were quite convinced that it was I who had put into the Dauphine's mind the idea of going to the bridge ; and they bore me a grudge in consequence.   This is what always happens."

Mercy's foresight was shown in another instance on the same day.   He learned that the Dauphin was to review his regiment of infantry on the following Monday ; it was important that on a public occasion such as this that the Dauphin should behave himself with reasonably good manners ; so Mercy said it would be well if the Dauphine accompanied her husband to the review, and coached him well beforehand " that he should behave in a way to annoy no one."

The continuation of the story is in Mercy's next letter ; he made an appointment with the Dauphine and asked her how much she proposed giving to the regiment of the Dauphin upon the review day.   It was customary upon such ceremonies for the chief performers to distribute largesses, and Mercy was well aware that, from disgust at the wicked extravagance of her surroundings, Marie Antoinette's mental pendulum was swinging far too much toward parsimony.   She would give—when importuned ; she would not spend, even when this would be judicious.

Fontaine-bleau, 14 November, 1772.

Mercy told the Empress that of the 1,000 louis she had placed to her daughter's credit only one quarter had been drawn ; and when he reminded the Dauphine of this fund, she always replied it was better to save it for some necessity.   He was therefore as much afraid that the Dauphine would show herself a niggard on the occasion of the review as that the Dauphin would reveal himself a lout, as he was when not judiciously pushed on the path of civility.   To Mercy's question as to the amount of expected generosity, Marie Antoinette replied that the Comtesse de Provence had given her husband's regiment 50 louis (£48), and she intended to give the same.   Mercy pointed out that as there was no comparison between a Dauphine and a Comtesse de Provence so there should be none between their acts of liberality.   "The Dauphine did not seem at all pleased with my remark : she leans too much towards rigid economy."

On the important day the Dauphin started at midday to join his regiment ; the Dauphine, full of 19 October, Mercy's last appeals to be gracious to the   1772. Duchesse d'Aiguillon and the Duchesse de Mirepoix, followed soon after, and all awaited the King.   His Majesty came, and the Dauphin himself put the troops through their evolutions, inspected all ranks, spoke to all the officers, presented them to the Dauphine, and covered himself with success finally, when a cuirassier fell from his horse and the Dauphin ran to pick him up, and gave him three louis with his own royal hand. (Mercy's conscience compels him to add that the soldier had only one slight bruise.)   Then the Dauphine presented cockades to all, first to the Dauphin, who fastened it at once in his hat, and then to each officer ; and after the departure of the King they both remained talking for nearly an hour with the officers, with great graciousness ; and then went, the Dauphin distributing 200 louis (£160), and the Dauphine 100 louis. " This was better throughout than I had dared to hope," says Mercy, " and I had the satisfaction that evening of hearing every one attribute the marvellous improvement, both in bearing and actions, of the Dauphin to the influence of the Dauphine."

Three days after this Mercy has an interview with the Dauphine and finds her in a passion, that even Mercy has to admit was justified. Madame du Barry had caused a new pavilion to be built beside her own apartments ; and not only did she seize for this purpose a piece of the garden that ran level to the apartments of Mesdames upon which to build it, but she also arranged the new building so that the garden, once the private promenade reserved for the Royal Family, was now commanded by it. Marie Antoinette considered this act to be intolerably impertinent, and, in fact, as Mercy admits, it is impossible to regard it otherwise ; and these aggressions on the part of Madame du Barry embittered their relations yet more, for the building fad continued, and always with intent to annoy. On 7 December, Madame du Barry purchased from M. Réné Bidet (the principal valet of the Dauphin) a small house near Versailles, and commenced rebuilding it upon a large scale under the superintendence of Ledoux, her architect. The Dauphin

was, this time, the sufferer, but his annoyance could
find no remedy ; and Le Roi, the librarian at Versailles,
records that the more he objected, the more ostentatiously she pressed on the work.

Mercy's task in these days was no light one, as
may be gathered.   On 26 October he called
upon Madame du Barry, and learnt that **26 October.**
she intended going the next day to pay her court to
the Dauphine, and that she relied on Mercy to ensure
her the best reception possible.   Mercy, answering
that it was neither necessary nor correct to open such
negotiations, and that obviously none were needed,
since the favourite had been satisfied with her reception
at Compiègne, hurried off to open them.   " The
Dauphine seemed to me rather startled ; but assured
me all would be well.   But on the 27th, I was so
uneasy, remembering the indecision of the previous
night, that I proceeded to the house of the Dauphine.
She had just returned from mass, and said immediately : ' I have been praying earnestly ; I prayed,
" Oh, God ! if Thou wishest me to speak, make
me speak : I will act as Thy inspiration guideth
me." ' "

Mercy did not hesitate when diplomacy required
the assigning of a convenient Divine mouthpiece ;
and he assured Marie Antoinette that there was but
one voice in the world that could be regarded as
a correct transmitter of the will of God *en matière
de conduite*, and this was the voice of her august
mother.   He had no opportunity for more than these

words as the Dauphine had to leave him to go to the King ; but his interpretation of what was expedient as ordained by God for the benefit of persons of quality, was no new view to the Court of Versailles. When the slice of Austrian Poland was wavering in the balance was no time to await dilatory Divine inspiration, but to state boldly and clearly : " *Vox Mariæ Theresæ, Vox Dei.*" The moment came, and with it the Comtesse du Barry, accompanied by the Duchesse d'Aiguillon.   Marie Antoinette spoke first to the Duchesse, and then observed to the Comtesse du Barry : " The weather has been so bad that one has been unable to go out to-day."

But, whether due to memories of prayer, or of the newly built pavilion, the inspiration was a failure. Even this sentence, far from happy as it was, had not been addressed directly to the favourite ; and both the tone and the manner made the reception none of the best.   Says Mercy : " Happily the Dauphin was present on this occasion," and so without further scruple he told the favourite that to his presence must be attributed the Dauphine's coldness and embarrass-ment ; and even succeeded in making her believe that, on the whole, she had been rather well received than not, considering the presence of the Dauphin.   " On the 28th was a great fuss in which I was obliged to intervene.   The Duc de la Vrillière gave a supper that evening to the Comtesse du Barry, and invited to it the Duchesse de Cossé, lady-in-waiting of the Dauphine, who refused to go . . . although she owed her appointment to her [the du Barry] ; it was, to speak more accurately, accorded at the request of the Duc de Cossé, who is entirely at the command of the Comtesse du Barry. Therefore the refusal of the Duchesse de Cossé caused a great excitement, and bitter reproaches to the Duc de Cossé."

The favourite insisted that the Duc should use his authority over his wife ; and, not knowing how to extricate himself from the difficulty, he assured the du Barry that his wife had acted on the orders of the Dauphine. The Duc d'Aiguillon made searching enquiry of Mercy, who gave the lie to the Duc de Cossé, declaring roundly that he could prove the falseness of the insinuation. He spoke to the Dauphine, who, of course, had said no word respecting the favourite to the Duchesse de Cossé ; and then he proposed to the Duc d'Aiguillon that he should be confronted with the Duc de Cossé. " But they were already convinced of his lying, and he reaped all the confusion he merited." This Duchesse de Cossé, of whom Mercy writes, was one of the very few honest persons at Court, and probably the only one who at that time would have dared retain her own self-respect by refusing to meet the du Barry, especially when invited by that arbiter of etiquette, the Duc de la Vrillière, "*le grand congédieur ordinaire*," who had ruled as Secretary of State and Minister of Internal Affairs since 1725, and whose family had held the same office before him since 1621.

The Duc de la Vrillière was possessed, not merely

of power over the whole internal government of France, but of the deadliest weapon ever used against liberty : his department was that of the terrible *lettres de cachet*, against which no rank, or wealth, or honour could avail, and of which the Duc himself is said to have used over fifty thousand for his own purposes, selling them, in *blank*, to any man of fashion who chose to pay. The Duchesse de Cossé thus risked, not only her property, but her liberty, by defying the Chief of the Police, and her privileges by affronting the favourite. But she was the witty and charming daughter of Louis de Mancini Mazarin, Duc de Nivernais, self-reliant, straightforward, and without intrigue ; and she replied to her husband's baffled fury by declaring she would rather resign her appointment than mingle in the society of the favourite.

If anything could have opened Louis' eyes to the dangerous game he was playing, with his dynasty at stake, it would have been the alienation of all upright men and women from his Court ; for, even now, there were none left who would speak to the du Barry. Even at his Majesty's own table, at which they were obliged to attend, they sat in silence. The Comtesse de la Marck, in one of her letters, says : " I was at Marly yesterday. . . they played at Lansquenet. . . . Madame du Barry played at the King's table, surrounded by the Royal family. Nobody, either at table or in the salon, spoke to her the whole evening except the King and her nephew, *le petit du Barry*."

Marie Antoinette spent this, her seventeenth birth-

day, in devotion, remaining the whole day in retreat.
"This pious duty she fulfils each year 2 November,
upon this date," says Mercy; and in the 1772.
daily diary the entries alternate between accounts of
vespers and hunts attended.

"On 5 November the Dauphine mounted her
horse and went to the meet of the stag- 5 November,
hounds. Her Royal Highness was dressed 1772.
in the full hunt uniform, and this attire pleased the
King infinitely; he was much engaged with the
Dauphine, and seemed very well satisfied with this new
form of dress that she had devised." Dunoyer de
Noirmont tells us that Marie Antoinette hunted in a
dress of the royal blue velvet, and a hat with great
white feathers. Blue had been the colour of the
royal hunt since Louis XIV. introduced the ceremony
of presenting to members of the hunt a *justaucorps*
of turquoise blue, lined with red, and covered with
heavy *galons* of gold and silver, the members wearing
one braid of silver between two of gold to mark their
rank. Under Louis XVI. the novices had to wear
grey, with scarlet vest and breeches, great boots, and
gold-braided hat. The Orléans hunt was scarlet,
blue, and silver, until Anglomania overtook the Duc,
and he put his hunt in "pink," with black velvet caps;
but Mesdames, who had their own separate hunt
equipage, always rode in green, the colour in which
the hunting ghost of Francis I. rode about the Forest
of Fontainebleau.

A letter from Marie Antoinette to her mother gives

the capitulation of the Condés. " The Prince de Condé has written to the King tendering his own submission and that of his son. The letter was a very good one " [it was so grovelling that it could not be published], " although he did not mention the Parliament " [whose illegal oppression by Louis had been the peg upon which he had hung out his patriotic virtue] : " but they have agreed about it. The King permits him to return to-morrow, and he and his son have paid a visit to us, which has passed very pleasantly on both sides. I have invited the Duc, the Duchesse, and Mademoiselle de Bourbon to the ball which will be some days after [his reception by the King]. As for the Duc d'Orléans, and his son, and the Prince de Conti, they have not yet returned, but it is hoped they will not delay." The final arguments that had convinced the Prince de Condé (after two years) of the perfect legality of Louis' acts were : 1,000,000 livres [£960,000] to pay his debts ; the ground on which his old palace stood near the Luxembourg ; the blue riband of the Order of the Saint Esprit for his son, and a promise (quite valueless) of a marriage between his daughter " Mademoiselle," and the Comte d'Artois. Later on the d'Orléans house followed, the Duc being bribed by the suggestion that the King might recognise his private marriage with Madame de Montesson ; but the Prince de Conti (" my cousin, the wrangling attorney," said Louis), remained longest obstinate in his exile.

[Margin note:] Versailles, 15 December, 1772.

That these Princes' minds were so open to—reasons, brought them into much odium ; for none could boast of the youth that colours fickle changing of coats. Condé was now thirty-six, Conti was fifty-five, and d'Orléans forty-seven.   Madame du Deffand wrote of them :—" Their protests, their retractations, their recriminations, their contradictions, are to me mere *bouillie pour les chats*."

Mercy's last letter of 1772 is on the whole a report of advance made.   The chief gains in the year have been the amelioration of the 6 *sauvage* Dauphin, through the influence of the charming Marie Antoinette and her increase of self-reliance, improvement in health, in self-possession, and in accomplishments.   Especially in dancing is this improvement noticeable, for Mercy says she now dances with such perfect grace that she eclipses all others at the balls.   " The Dauphin has not, by a very long way, profited as much by his dancing lessons, although he has taken them assiduously, but there is much less awkwardness in his bearing : he holds himself better, and there is now nothing shocking in his gait and carriage."   Of her increased dignity, Mercy speaks highly, and tells the manner in which she rebuked the Cardinal de la Roche Aymon, who had presumed upon her youthful inexperience.

It was usual to provide a benefice for every ancient Almoner of the Royal family, upon superannuation, and this recompense for their duties was perfectly just, as they had scarcely any salary at all.   When the

Paris 6 December, 1772.

Abbé de Chastel, who had been Almoner to the late Queen, and for some time to Marie Antoinette herself, was to be given this reward, the Dauphine addressed herself to the Cardinal who had the control of such benefices. He let eight months pass, notwithstanding repeated reminders, and then appointed the Abbé du Chastel to an abbey, whose revenues were beneath those that custom prescribed for these ex-members of royal households. When the Cardinal came to inform Marie Antoinette that he had carried out her wishes, she said to him gravely :—" I am much obliged to you ; I hope that another time you will not keep me waiting so long."

The Cardinal, irritated at this very mild reprimand, went to the Comtesse de Noailles, his good friend, and charged her to tell the Dauphine that he should not appear again at her house until she commanded him ; which very improper message was, also improperly, given in due course by " Madame l'Etiquette," who ought to have known better. Marie Antoinette replied that the Cardinal's absence was a matter of perfect indifference to her ; and that when next she had some ecclesiastical preferment to ask, she should address herself to the King. The apprehensive Cardinal and Comtesse, *très-consternés*, applied to Mercy, " as always happens when they wish to make up for some slip " ; who rated them both for neglect of duty and lack of respect, and then obtained a sufficiently humiliating grace for the Cardinal de la Roche Aymon, that he might present himself in the Dauphine's apartment, but would not have a word spoken to him.

Mercy rejoices over the dignified Dauphine, whose firm stand is due to his ceaseless tuition. He adds that the respect in which she is held casts its radiance even upon that dolt, the Dauphin, towards whom the Court has in consequence shown less contempt. She is more regarded by the favourite ; Mesdames, in losing their slave, have increased the King's affection for his grand-daughter ; and all would be well, but for the false and malicious Comte de Provence, who already shows indifference to, and almost disgust with, his wife. The Dauphin has been prevailed upon to *read* something, " so that I hope this young prince may yet turn out well."

Louis, afterwards the XVI., kept a diary for twenty-five of his life of thirty-nine years ; it was therefore commenced in 1768, before his marriage. Throughout the whole of these periods of storm, excitement, and fury, of complex intrigues, of political passion, of the whirlwind approaching to sweep away his dynasty, even in the days of the Revolution itself, Louis found nothing to enter in this diary but the hours of mass and vespers, cures by whey and accounts of heads of game. His marriage day itself is marked by an entry of but one word: *Rien*. Years after this date, the feeble mind was as insensible to its surroundings. There is an autograph letter of Marie Antoinette's to the Princesse de Lamballe, preserved in the British Museum, that was written when the menace of instant murder was thrilling all Europe. The Queen writes of her husband : " His health is re-established, thanks to his good constitution. The calm with which he takes things has something providential about it, and the good Elizabeth is as touched by that, as if it had been an inspiration coming from on high." What wonder that Marie Antoinette, quick to her finger-tips, spoke of the sluggish incapable by the term that roused the severe indignation of the Empress—" *le pauvre homme !* "

CHAPTER XVI.

The Return of the Duc d'Orleans—Mercy's Foreboding
of the Revolution—The Publication of *Letters
from the Provinces*—The Dauphin and Madame du
Barry—The Caricature by Rohan—The Masked
Ball at the Opera—The Palais Royal—Marie
Antoinette as Politician—Proposed Marriage of the
Comte d'Artois

MARIE ANTOINETTE'S letter to her mother
is the first of the correspondence with which
commences the new year. She has just learned
that both her sisters, the Infanta of Parma and the
Queen of Naples, are awaiting the birth of
children. "When shall I be able to say the
like?" The Infant of Parma, still in
deepest disgrace, had written the important news to
the King, the Dauphin, and his brothers ; but the King
had not permitted any one to reply, and Marie
Antoinette followed the example of both her families.
" It is to be hoped, that when the Infanta sees herself
with many children about her, she will learn her duty
and try to please her relatives. . . . The miniatures of
my young brothers, that you have sent to me, give
me very much pleasure. I have had them set in rings,
and wear them every day. . . . The favourite came

Versailles,
13 January,
1773.

to see me on New Year's Day ; there were many people present, and I addressed them generally. . . . You will have heard of the return of the Duc d'Orléans and the Duc de Chartres " [now twenty-six years old, later in life the notorious " Egalité "]. " I am overjoyed at the prospect of peace, repose, and happiness for the King ; but I do not believe that my dear mother, had she been in the place of the King, would have accepted the letter they dared write, and had printed in the foreign newspapers. . . . I am still faithful to my beloved harp, and they say I improve. I sing also every week at the concerts of my sister Madame [de Provence] ; although there are very few people present, we amuse ourselves very well, and, besides, it gives pleasure to my sisters. I find time to read a little also. I have begun the *History of England*, by Mr. Hume ; it seems full of interest but one must remember that it was written by a Pro-testant. . . ."

The year of 1773 is opened by Mercy with a solemn admonition to the Dauphine and her husband, a warning and a forecast of evil to come, a prophecy of impending woe. With ominous conviction he draws their attention to that future, black with certain ruin, and in his strangely interesting letter of 16 January, he fore-shadows the fall of the dynasty ; and his prophecy is fulfilled in twenty years to the very month from the date of his letter. In January 1773 Mercy shows there is but one hope to avert the Revolution, and that

Paris,
16 January,
1773.

frail reed is the strength of the man who shall succeed to the throne of France. In January 1793 there was no longer any hope or saviour, the Dauphin had become King of France ; and in lieu of a virile ruler, the thirty-second monarch of a race that had given to Europe one hundred and eighty-nine sovereigns, Kings, Emperors, reigning Dukes, holding sway over France, Spain, Naples, Portugal, Parma, Hungary, Poland, Constantinople, and (by alliance) England, was an imbecile—a waddling, blinking, corpulent, bungling, incapable imbecile, defective in body, deficient in mind, with the low receding forehead of an idiot, and a monstrous double chin, that measured the third of his face. This clod was the husband of Mercy's secret ward, the protector of Marie Antoinette, this the King to rule a France of twenty-two millions of "frightful wild-animals," as Carlyle calls them, savages in torrents, ferocious, mad with starvation and injustice, destitute, disease-stricken, naked, despairing. And twenty years after the date of Mercy's January prophecy, in 1773, came the fulfilment in January 1793 : the guillotine lopped off the dazed head that yet "had studied some geography and Latin ; " and had the dim desire for honesty and justice in its dull brain.

The spur to Mercy's efforts was the publication in December 1772 of a book that had a wide sale for the boldness of its opinions, called *Letters from the Provinces : An Impartial Examination into the Origin, Constitution, and Revolutions of the French*

Monarchy. This work, supposed to be partly the work of the Chancellor Maupeou, dealt so freely with the abuses, scandals, and oppression rampant in France, that it was suppressed by an Order of Council. But Mercy had read it, and he felt the axe at the root of the State. He marked a copy, with all the warning passages and their danger signals, and took it to the Dauphine, begging her to read it herself, with deep attention, and to obtain the promise from the Dauphin that he also would read it.

" I was not sorry to seize an opportunity of stirring up a little the spirit of this young prince, and he was struck by the marked passages. I advised the Dauphine what observations she had better add ; she was quite prepared to do this, and to tell me what effect it had upon the mind of her husband. The importance of the matter was such that I impressed upon the Dauphine some great truths, that seemed to rivet her attention. I made her see that in a Government where authority and good order are set at naught by intrigue, by personal enmities and cabals, there is no sort of danger and trouble that may not be anticipated, and for which preparation must therefore be made. Human passions are intensified, rash and contentious spirits are daring to undertake everything ; thus the State nears its ruin and falls, unless the personal qualities of the virtues of the Prince, whom Providence calls to the leadership, remedy the evils and overawe those who seek to trouble it. I drew the conclusion that it would not suffice for the Dauphin to be merely an ordinary man; and that it was for the Dauphine to cultivate or excite in her husband all ideas that tend to elevate the soul, and that could give him the spirit of prudence and judgment necessary to remove present evils and avert those in the future. I perceived that my words astonished the Dauphine and made an impression upon her."

Truthtelling, of such uncompromising nature, had not been heard in Versailles, where the " rose-pink " glamour hid the corruption, starvation, and madness crouching without the gate. This prophecy of woe, albeit threaded on a delicate string of suggestion, carried the conviction of the shadow of death; for Mercy says that a greater than " an ordinary man," is necessary, and here is a dullard, far *less* than any man, half alive, ignorant, obstinate, obtuse, sullen, whose very absence of vices is against him in a country vice-tolerant, and even vice-approving. " Our best Kings have loved and have not been less great. . . . If the heart of Louis XVI. had been susceptible of love, I do not doubt that his crown would be intact," wrote the Comte d'Espinchal.

And one of the marked passages in the book, whose study is pressed by Mercy upon the Dauphine, is that which recommends the King to *choose* his successor. Marie Antoinette confides to Mercy her opinion of her husband, or such a one as she has formed. She " supposes " that he has a decided tendency for justice and for order and for truth, some good sense, and

some feeling of right in his manner of considering
things; but, "she fears the effect of his supineness,
his insensitiveness to all stimulus; in short, that
paralysis of perception that prevents him from
either thinking or feeling with keenness sufficient
to result in action." [Mercy is at his wits' end to
describe, in the language suitable from an ambassador to his Empress, the clouded faculties, the
poverty of mind and body that clogged the very
life of her son-in-law, the heir of France.] "But
I am convinced that he is susceptible to improvement, and I have explained to the Dauphine all the
methods that my imagination could suggest, to
direct her attention and care towards those things
most useful to this young prince." Mercy's forethought was for both far and near, he envisaged the
future of Louis XVI.; he also took measures for
the immediate moment, and impressed the essential
point of pleasing the King, by gracious acceptance
of his mistress. Marie Antoinette said that the
Dauphin held this woman "in horror," ever increasing;
but she influenced him so greatly by her eager
insistence upon such toleration that, when the favourite
was presented to him upon New Year's Day, he
received her very well, and even spoke a word to
her, to public amazement.

But to Mercy's despair the unexpected happened;
the Dauphine, thinking she had done enough duty
by persuading the Dauphin into civility, permitted
herself to give so frigid a reception to the favourite

that she did not speak at all, either to her, or to the Duchesse d'Aiguillon, or to the Maréchale de Mirepoix, and all was again undone and in turmoil. It needed all the practised suavity of Mercy to assure the favourite and her step-sister, Mademoiselle du Barry [sister of Comte Jean du Barry and familiarly known as " Chon," the chief adviser of the favourite], that, by inducing the Dauphin to speak, Marie Antoinette had done far more than if she had reserved her efforts for her own reception. But there were times when Marie Antoinette's clear vision recognised that Maria Thérèse was less mother than Empress, and that the price of political peace was her own exploitation as means of gratifying the mistress of Louis. She said to Mercy : " I love the Empress, but I fear her, even from far away ; even in writing I am not at my ease with her ; " and with tears in her eyes she had told him that she was afraid to render her mother uneasy by writing about " the things that go wrong," but that she did not mind the reproofs of the Emperor. " He is my brother ; I answer him when he annoys me, and I have always been accustomed to joke with him." And Mercy wrote his confidence that a character so full of truth, sincerity, and candour will preserve Marie Antoinette in " a whirlpool as dangerous as this is."

Marie Thérèse wrote sadly to Mercy on hearing that her rather severe tenderness had the result of making her daughter fear her. " In this century they only like the tones of jest and flattery ; and if, with the best intentions, one remonstrates a little seriously, here are our young people beside themselves, imagining themselves scolded, and, as they always think, wrongly blamed. I see my daughter is just the same. . . . I will write to her on the lines you indicate to me, dropping in some flattery, though I do not care much for that style. But I repeat to you that, until my daughter drops this levity and this facile consent, with which I am well acquainted, and applies herself to our counsels, I cannot count on their success. . . . The Infants of Parma still continue their gait ; nevertheless I admit that they ought to be reinstated in their pensions [Marie Amélie had been reduced to selling and pawning her diamonds] . . . and the arrears made up. . . . I still long for Rohan to be recalled, but not if it is to add to your troubles and difficulties, of which you have already enough. The disgraceful pamphlet that is published about the division of Poland has had a very bad effect, and will not be forgotten. In these petty spites France excels all the world." [Pamphlets, caricatures, and epigrams rained upon France, and all had the *Gâteau des Rois* as subject ; but the sting of none remained so sharp as that of the sketch sent by de Rohan from Vienna, that showed Marie Thérèse with a handkerchief in one hand and a sword in the other, wiping away the tears while she cut the more off Poland. This was said to have been the subject of great merriment when handed round at the supper table of the du Barry,

LETTERS PATENT CONFERRING THE ORDER OF THE GOLDEN FLEECE ON THE COMTE DE MERCY-ARGENTEAU.

(From the original document, signed by Joseph II., now at the Château d'Argenteau.)

[*Page* 235.

whereat were present the Ducs de la Vrillière, d'Aiguillon, de Duras, de Richelieu, and d'Ayen, the Marquis de Flammarens, and the Marquis de Chauvelin.]

The Empress refers in this letter to her great desire that Mercy should marry, "to secure for me the continuation of a family that has so many merits, and has done such services to my house;" and this recommendation had especial bearing upon the sale of his estates in Hungary, of which Mercy wished to dispose. Difficulties had been raised, because in the event of his dying unmarried the estates would revert to the Crown, and were therefore subject to a heavy payment in case of selling. But in spite of the persuasions of the Empress, the Comte Florimond de Mercy-Argenteau never married.

Marie Antoinette writes as brightly to her mother as if the foretold doom did not weigh heavily upon her. "Last Thursday we all went, **Versailles, 15** the Dauphin, the Comte and the Comtesse **February, 1773.** de Provence, and I, to Paris, to the ball at the Opera: it was the deepest secret. We were all masked, but they recognised us at the end of half an hour. The Duc de Chartres and the Duc de Bourbon, who were dancing at the Palais Royal, which is just near by, came in to find us, and begged us very much to go and dance at the house of the Duchesse de Chartres; but I excused myself, as I had permission from the King only to go to the Opera. We came home at seven o'clock, and heard mass before we went

ful. Before this clear, penetrating glance of Marie
Antoinette, no illusion of dignity and respect for the
unspeakable old Louis can be dangled ; she knows
him for the decrepid, and vicious, and worn-out
Seigneur of the Parc-aux-Cerfs, without morals,
conscience, or common honesty ; sunk in contemptible
senility, and rendered incapable, by "*l'ivresse du pouvoir
suprême*," of even recognising in others the decency,
sincerity, or uprightness he himself did not possess.

To this keen judgment, no longer that of a child,
Mercy appeals by argument, recognising that sentiment, such as is urged by Marie Thérèse in connection with "*ce bon père*," was most injudicious.
He points out that, for the sake of appearances, the
Royal family must not criticise too obviously the conduct of the King ; that, if this monarch is in the
paths of sin, it is not at all a thing his children should
notice ; and he ended—poor Mercy !—in despera-
tion, with an appeal to the Holy Scriptures, and an
apt quotation from the very appropriate case of Noah,
when he was also in a condition of "*ivresse* !" The
Dauphine permitted herself to be guided, but not
blinded ; gave fresh promises of conduct, but said
she should write out all her opinions upon people
that she had mentioned to Mercy, and should read
them again in one year's time, to note whether she
has changed her judgment.

Mercy objects to the Comte de Provence's habit
of telling the Dauphine all the satires, songs, and
epigrams, that are written against the favourite or

the ministers.   " He seems singularly well acquainted
with these things," and he must have found full
and congenial occupation, for their number was legion.
" The Dauphin continues to improve " (he was now
nearly nineteen) " both in hearing and in speech.   I
have opportunities of judging this on Mondays, for
then I am present at this Prince's supper.   On these
occasions he is in the habit of holding conversations
with me, and though they turn on subjects of very
little consequence, I notice that the Dauphin is
attaining more order in his ideas, and expresses them
more coherently.   He even has a little shrewdness
sometimes, as for instance on Monday last."   This
instance of " finesse " was connected with the return
of the King from hunting ; Mercy said it had been
at a quarter to six ; the Dauphin asked if he had
seen His Majesty, and if so whence he had seen
him.   Mercy realised that the Dauphin was trying
to find out if he had been in the house of the
favourite at the time, and he is thankful to be able
to record even such evidence of brain power.   " The
Dauphine neglects nothing that can coax her husband
to some sort of solid instruction ; she is taking a
personal pride in it."   Poor little Dauphine.

In the secret report that accompanies the fore-
going letter, Mercy writes of an incident
connected with the Sieur de Boynes.   De **February,**
Boynes was head of the Admiralty and   **1773.**
Secretary of State, in place of the superseded Duc
de Praslin (who had fallen with de Choiseul), but

was popularly supposed to have learnt whatever marine knowledge he possessed from theatrical representations of sea pieces. De Boynes had addressed himself to Madame Victoire, to confide to her that the marriage of the Comte d'Artois had been decided upon, and that it rested with him, de Boynes, "as master," whether the choice of the bride should fall upon a princess of Savoy, or on Mademoiselle de Bourbon, daughter of the Prince de Condé. (It will be recollected that this marriage had been the bait that Condé had swallowed, together with his own words.) "That, as the matter was one that might interest the Royal family, he, de Boynes, was resolved to do nothing but what the Dauphin and Dauphine were pleased to dictate; and that, in consequence, he prayed Madame Victoire to acquaint herself with their wishes, to which he would conform with as much zeal as respect." Coche, enchanted at being selected as a messenger of Hymen, rushed *sur-le-champ* to deliver herself of her mission. "The Dauphin appeared as if struck dumb" . . . (mute and gasping doubtless, as was usual whenever the brain was suddenly called upon); "but the Dauphine, with great presence of mind and prudence, made his answer for him, and also one for herself, saying that the subject was so delicate that they did not wish to mix themselves up with it in any way. Upon which Madame Victoire replied that they might take some days to think the matter over before giving a definite reply."

Marie Antoinette then sent for Mercy, whose advice was to avoid all appearance of any desire to intervene in this matter ; that the Sieur de Boynes was on such excellent terms with the favourite and with the Duc d'Aiguillon that his proposal had certainly emanated from them ; that she would inevitably offend one side or the other, if she took any step at all, and that her safest course was to take none. This advice was accepted by Marie Antoinette.

Mercy adds in a third report of the same date, an explanation of the matter respecting his estates in Hungary. The laws of that kingdom were so rigid and so unfavourable to foreigners, even if born in the country, that it was almost impossible for them to settle permanently in Hungary. "For thirty years my father defended his property with much trouble and expense ; and he was upon the spot and thus enabled to carry out his determination. But, after gaining all the lawsuits that were entered into, he died ; and I have seen all these same actions revive, and many others appear, which attack the whole of my possessions. I have felt for some time that it would be impossible for me to sustain this struggle. I see that my property in Hungary will be a present subject of uneasiness and expense, with a future prospect of poverty and ruin in my old age. Nevertheless, these estates form the chief part of my little fortune. . . and I have endeavoured to realise them even at a loss, that I may spend the remains in acquiring some ancient estates of my family ; for these at least I can enjoy with peace and leave in safety to my heirs. . . . These estates are a portion of the substance and the result of the industry of a family that has had the happiness for more than a century of serving the august house of Austria ; and I would rather present them to my Sovereign than have them dragged from me by the effort of individuals." The purchaser of these estates was the Comte d'Appony, and the duty that Mercy had to pay upon the transfer amounted to 160,000 florins.

CHAPTER XVII

The Failure of a *Fête*—The Disillusion of the Dauphine
—The Dauphin does His Accounts—*Parfilage*—
Defeat of Madame Adélaïde—*Gare l'eau*—The
Position of Madame du Barry

THE only distinction between the many *fêtes*,
that succeed each other so rapidly at Versailles,
is one of intrigues ; and Mercy records an entertainment of great splendour, given by Madame du
Barry, which, although sumptuous and ex-
travagant "to the point of indecency," as Paris,
17 March,
1773.
insulting the public misery and famine, was
nevertheless a failure so absolute, that all the memoirs
of the time take cognisance of the rebuff it dealt
to the favourite. The *fête* was given in the new
pavilion, the King was expected, and a great number
of invitations sent to all the chief ladies of the Court,
who, it was hoped, would be induced by curiosity
to attend.

There were more than a hundred singers and
dancers, amongst them the famous Mademoiselle
Raucourt ; and to amuse the guests a series of fantastic
devices arranged by Favart, of which one was the
following :—a large egg was placed in the centre of

the salon, and the Comtesse du Barry called upon to open it. But when she approached, it opened of itself; and out came Cupid armed, who let fall the bandage from his eyes before her. This was to symbolise that one glance of the lady could hatch love, and, it is stated, lest this pretty conceit should miss fire, there were hired interpreters of this impromptu, *complaisants à gages*, placed near. But despite the mad luxury of this *fête*, the comedians, singers and dancers had but a small audience for their efforts, for the King refused to go, and of all the expected concourse of the Court, there arrived but fifteen gentlemen and fourteen titled ladies.

Mercy notes that the *fête* had thus completely *manqué*, and the public had entertained itself upon this opportunity by songs and epigrams " sufficiently piquant." He touches on the difficulty he now experiences with the Dauphine, to whom has come all at once the knowledge of her surroundings. " She no longer shows carelessness or impatience when I speak to her of the favourite ; she listens to me with perfect coolness and reasons quite calmly ; . . . she is quite aware how important it is for her to please and captivate the King, but she believes, at the same time, that it will be impossible for her to succeed beyond a certain point, as she attributes to the monarch an entire indifference to his surroundings, and a general detachment from all subjects that are of interest to the mind, or tend to raise it. The Dauphine has, unfortunately, far too much perspicacity."

Mercy no longer glosses over the "horrible confusion of the interior of this Court." He knows that to attempt to deceive the Dauphine, and flutter before her any rags of respect for the Most Christian King, would be merely to render her suspicious of his own good faith and to wound her sense of justice; for "she has too much intelligence to be satisfied with bad reasons, and it is hard to find reasons good enough to efface impressions, that are often founded upon too solid facts." She has taken again to instructive reading, and has even stirred up a faint spirit of emulation in the Dauphin; "he is accustoming himself to read at least for some moments in each day, and seems pleased to show off the little bits of knowledge he has attained. . . . Many things go to prove that this young Prince begins to think and to have some coherence in his ideas."

Mercy then relates an instance. The late Duc de la Vauguyon had so overburdened the privy purse of the Dauphin with pensions of which the Dauphin was ignorant, that they actually exceeded the whole of that Prince's revenue by 15,000 livres (£600). Until this year the Dauphin had not sought to find out even the amount of his own revenue, or the method of its administration; but this time when the accounts of the year were given him he noticed the disorder and appeared shocked at the deficit. He then sent for the account of the pensions and cut them down to the level of the receipts. "He even changed the pensions themselves, selecting those persons who seemed most worthy; and he did this little work all by himself, consulting no one, and making his arrangements with justice. . . even writing, in his own hand, his reasons for changing them."

Mercy, for once, advises the Dauphine to imitate her husband, and examine into her own accounts. Marie Antoinette's generous carelessness in money matters was constantly exploited; and Mercy was in time this week to save her from the consequences of one such attempt. He had been at dinner with the Comptroller General, Abbé Terray, and that minister said that he wished in all things to please the Dauphine; but really her demands upon the treasury embarrassed him. In proof of his words he showed Mercy a memorandum, upon whose margin the Dauphine had written with her own hand : " I recommend earnestly to the Comptroller General the present matter, and desire that he carries it out." It was a demand for a pension of 16,000 livres (£640), made by one of her lowest rank *femmes de chambre*, to enable her to marry. Mercy assured the Comptroller General that this recommendation could only have been obtained from the Dauphine by a trick; and he took the paper to the Dauphine, and found out that, as he suggested, she knew nothing of the contents of the memorandum upon which she had made the recommendation.

" But what was most annoying of all, was to find that this business was only done upon the solicitation of the Comtesse de Noailles, who, probably, knew

nothing either of the exorbitance of the demand. . . .
I was very glad to notice that her Royal Highness was
rather annoyed by this discovery." The Dauphine
continued to improve in her music, which she loves ;
and "she has a particular taste for the harp, an
amusement that fills up much of her leisure." This
love of music was, in after years, one of the greatest
pleasures of Marie Antoinette and her diligent study
of it, and practice of her harp, gave her an occupation
noteworthy in a Court where "*parfilage*" was the
chief passion, having dethroned "*pantins*" (the in-
tellectual amusement of paper figures) in 1770.
This *parfilage* was one of the most amazing frenzies ;
every woman was absorbed in the unravelling of
gold threads from lace, or cords, etc. ; and it was said
its fascination lay in its similarity to the dissecting of
reputations :

> *Tandis que l'on déchire*
> *Et galons et rubans*
> *L'on peut encore médire*
> *Et déchirer les gens.*

Only the *parfilage* of reputations had not as its
aim the selection of their *gold* threads. So great a
vogue did this absurd occupation attain that all
gambling debts were paid in the gold thread ; and
lovers could give to their ladies no more acceptable
present than a gold thread animal, which they could
immediately unravel. The Duc de Lauzun gave
to Comtesse Amélie de Boufflers a 1,000-franc harp
of gold thread ; but Madame du Barry, as chief

parfileuse, received far more extensive offerings of material for damaging. Her memoirs say that upon one occasion the King presented her with a rosewood table, ornamented with medallions of Sèvres china and covered with three-fold cloth of gold; the Duc d'Aiguillon sent an enormous sheep, loaded with gold cords and threads and tassels; and Chancellor Maupeou sent a figure of Punch, life size, completely dressed in the richest gold laces. With regard to the last gift, the Duc d'Ayen remarked that the Chancellor of France suitably presented an image of folly.

In his secret report of this date, Mercy says that **17 March, 1773.** the Dauphine is now of age and of intellect sufficient to be initiated into affairs of State; and he has found her so advanced and ripe in understanding, that he proposes henceforth treating her as the future Queen should be treated. The Dauphine had been greatly stirred by the thought of what evils to her a rupture between the countries of France and Austria would mean. She told Mercy that she should have no dread of a possible break in the alliance, "if only the Dauphin had some authority or even access to State affairs, as she was certain of his opinion on the alliance between the two courts; besides, she would find it perfectly easy to direct the course of his ideas, and also she flattered herself that, in this respect, she had gained an influence over her husband, which he would never resist." She then told Mercy her well-thought-out plan of influencing the mind of the Dauphin, in which Mercy recognised his own suggestions, made at many different times, all of which had been remembered and woven into her scheme of his mental education ; for it was plainly seen, even now, that she was the " only man " Louis was likely to have at his side.

Marie Antoinette wrote to her mother that the marriage of the Comte d'Artois with the Princess of Savoy was fixed for 16 November. Louis was in haste to secure the succession

Versailles, 18 April, 1773.

to his throne ; with no heir, or prospect of one, to the Dauphin ; no child, and no present prospect either, to the Comte de Provence ; it was necessary to marry the third brother with all speed, although he was barely sixteen.

And Mercy wrote more fully upon the same important subject, for it had served like every other at this Court as the centre of a network of intrigue. It would have seemed

Paris, 20 April, 1773.

unlikely that dangers to the peace of the Dauphine could have been involved in the selection of members of the new household of the Comte d'Artois upon his marriage ; but Mercy bears witness that, upon few occasions have the quarrels reached so violent a pitch or been so menacing to Marie Antoinette.

Since the death of his old Governor, the Duc de la Vauguyon, the Comte d'Artois had been seized upon by Madame Adélaïde who had undertaken to superintend his education. She had here a fine chance for the intermeddling her soul loved; she had obliged the tutors to render account to her, and they had to receive from her what instructions she considered best to give. "The King seemed to approve" (he approved everything that kept the energetic, overpowering and imperious daughter occupied with other than his own concerns), "and in consequence Madame Adélaïde convinced herself firmly that she would have the appointments at her disposal when it was decided to give this young Prince a household of his own; and in this conviction Madame Adélaïde had already bestowed these appointments —in imagination."

" But the Comtesse du Barry, who intended quite differently, had no difficulty whatever in overturning all the arrangements of Madame, or in taking to herself the right of nominating her own creatures to the places in question." Result: a bitterness so mortal on the part of Madame Adélaïde, that she was ready for any action, however violent, that would spare her this deepest of mortifications. She endeavoured "with all the heat and effervescence possible," to drag the Dauphine into the matter, by making the question one that concerned the whole Royal family; and by insisting that she should go as the mouthpiece of complaint and lay the matter before the King. The Dauphine, always backed by Mercy, gave for answer that, as the point lay between promises made by the King to Madame Adélaïde, and by Madame Adélaïde to other people, she would not enter into the matter; and her aunt had better address herself directly to the King.

This simple course was not one that ever presented itself as possible to Mesdames, and the spleen of Madame Adélaïde could only vent itself in spite and impotence, which vexed and embittered all concerned without advancing anything. Mercy writes that the Dauphin is getting, very gradually, accustomed to occupations; he has shown curiosity about public events; he has had gazettes read to him, and some newspapers, and has even "spent some moments in reading historical works. This is undoubtedly the effect of the suggestion of the Dauphine, who plumes herself justly thereupon." As for Marie Antoinette herself, she is absorbed in the study of politics, "which finally I shall understand," said she.

The King himself had spoken to the Dauphine of matters of high political importance, concerning a rumoured alliance between Austria and Russia, to the detriment of Turkey, the ally of France; which is, as Mercy proudly notes, the third time his Majesty has addressed her upon serious and interesting matters. This accession of consideration is due, Mercy points out, to the excellent natural judgment and astonishing intelligence that develop daily in the Dauphine. "The only difficulty I have now is to induce her to conceal the impressions that she has formed. She estimates with remarkable justice the chief persons at the Court; she has conceived for the Duc d'Aiguillon a horror that passes

all bounds, and is founded on the wicked character of
this minister, unfortunately only too well deserved."
And Mercy strives to impress upon the Empress
that here is no longer a child to scold, but a
woman, developing into a stateswoman, "who will
one day govern this kingdom."

In response, Marie Thérèse takes up the tone of
Marie Antoinette's rising interest in public
affairs. The news had been received at
Vienna of the mobilisation of the French

Vienna
4 May,
1773.

fleet at Toulon and Brest, an important demonstration
in favour of Turkey, at war with Russia ; quenched,
without result, by the fear of England.   Marie Thérèse
writes : " I confess the news of the Toulon squadron,
(which has excited the ministers of all the Courts
except this one) grieves me on account of France.
France seems to play a part with respect to England
as humiliating, or even more so, as our own with respect
to the King of Prussia.   But there is a great difference:
France has the sea between [her and her enemy],
and all her frontier guarded by strongholds : we have
the King of Prussia at our door, without one single
protection but that of miserable Olmütz.   But enough
of politics ; Mercy is well pleased with the way you
grasp affairs. . . . Follow his counsels. . . . He
thinks in good French, like a good German."

To which Marie Antoinette replies that
" The King of Prussia is an ugly neighbour,
but the English will always be that for

Versailles
17 May,
1773.

France ; and from time immemorial the sea has not

prevented them doing a great deal of harm." And she records that the Dauphin has been ill with a sore throat and fever, and that Madame Victoire has had measles. Dirt and disease were ever present in the King's household; the neglect of the commonest sanitary precautions the condition of the stairs and the approaches to the palaces, the filth of person and dress, all served to point the plaint of Walpole about this period : "I shall never get over the dirt of this country. . . . Indeed, I wish I could wash it!"

The uncleanly habits of the time are shown in what Mercy calls a "sufficiently singular" episode, that he narrates to Marie Thérèse. "The Dauphine had gone one afternoon with the Comtesse de Provence to call upon Madame Victoire. On coming out of the house, the Dauphine and her sister-in-law stopped in the little court yard to look at a large sundial fixed on the outer wall. In that instant, from the second floor, and out of a window of the Comtesse du Barry's apartments, was flung a pail of water, of which a portion fell on the two Princesses.

To the inhabitants of Paris, there was nothing objectionable in making a common sink of their windows. "*Gare l'eau!*" was an ominous cry; but one so familiar for centuries, that it had become accepted as a normal condition of a life without drains. But Marie Antoinette was not a Parisienne to accept these liquid offerings without protest. In her instant

impatience, she ascended to the King, and said to
him : "See, papa, to what one is exposed in passing
under your windows ! You ought to keep better
order in your house !" The King, rather taken
aback, enquired as to the circumstances, and asked
from which window the water had been thrown. The
Dauphine pointed out the window (typically gold-
shuttered, but of unclean use) ; but contented herself
with saying : "It was from your house !" without
naming the favourite. The King understood perfectly ;
and to extricate himself from embarrassment gave
caresses to the Dauphine, and the promise of a
reprimand to the culprit. But although there were
many who wished to take advantage of this singular
adventure, and turn it into ground of quarrel, the
Dauphine, by treating it herself as a joke, prevented
any such development.

It was to be expected in a Court so peopled with
time-servers that the Duc de Choiseul should become
the scapegoat of all evils real or imaginary ; and the
most shameless of the time-servers was Madame
Adélaïde, who preferred to regard his exile as a direct
interposition of Providence for the benefit of the
religious orders, rather than as an intrigue of the
maîtresse en titre. That Louis XV. had no reason
to value the Order of Jesuits so highly as to dismiss
a minister on account of his lack of appreciation
of their influence, did not weigh with Madame
Adélaïde, who used religion as a stalking horse.
Louis himself did not pretend that religion had any

bearing upon this particular action; although he was so devout that he invariably prayed with his victims of the Parc-aux-Cerfs, and was quite interested in their souls. His opinion upon the dangerous influence of the Jesuits in his kingdom is shown in the retort he made to his son, the late Dauphin. Louis, the Dauphin, had been so entirely dominated by this Order that he said to his father, that if the Jesuits so advised him, he would renounce the throne. Louis answered: "And if they order you to ascend one ——?"

Mercy writes of a conversation that had been held in the apartments of Mesdames, and turned upon the Duc de Choiseul: "Madame Adélaïde permitted herself remarks respecting this minister, that were most rash in every way. She even declared that only his exile had saved religion in France, for it was quite obvious that the scheme of this minister had been to destroy all religion, root and branch. An imputation so grave and so false was the more surprising from the mouth of Madame Adélaïde, because this Princess had always ostentatiously vaunted her attachment to the Duc de Choiseul, who had reason to count upon her goodwill. The King appeared to pay very little attention to this outburst; the Dauphine heard it with an air of surprise and disgust, that was remarked by Madame Adélaïde, who challenged the Dauphine upon the matter." The Dauphine, in no way reluctant, replied vigorously, that she neither blamed nor justified the conduct of

ministers of which she was not in a position to judge ;
but that she could not hear a man slandered who
had at heart the alliance of the two nations, and in
whose ministry her own marriage had taken place.
Madame Adélaïde was mute at this rejoinder, and
Mercy only regretted that the King had gone before
the dignified reply of the Dauphine.

The Comtesse de Provence, always most subservient
to the favourite, had no scruples in prophesying the
speedy downfall of that lady ; and Mercy disapproved
the over-prudence that was already preparing for
the next mistress. He considered such forethought
very unseemly, and pointed out to the Dauphine
(no longer with any pretence of ignorance) that if
Madame du Barry were packed off, there would
certainly be the appearance of a new favourite
with whom to reckon ; and that this would be a
scandal.

The position of Madame du Barry had been weighed
and accepted by all the Courts of Europe, to whom
messengers had been duly despatched the very night
of her first presentation at Court ; as the personality of
the woman, who was virtual autocrat of France during
the six years of her reign, was of first importance in
its bearing upon the changed aspect of the Court of
Versailles, for the rest of the life of Louis, or the
duration of her own charms. All European govern-
ments were satisfied and content with what they knew
of Madame du Barry : tolerant, easy-going, good-
natured, unrevengeful, charitable to the poor, generous

to the arts (though somewhat prudish in her selection
of pictures, always covering studies of the nude with
curtains of taffetas), forgiving to her enemies—and
even to her friends. European Courts had summed
up Madame du Barry and accepted her. A new
favourite, therefore, would be distasteful to the states-
men who administered the affairs of nations.

Mercy pointed out to the Dauphine that her duty
was to prevent this calamity; for it depended upon her
to give the King pleasures of sweet entertainment,
which he had never been able to find in his own family,
and therefore had been obliged to procure in illicit and
grievous ways. He impressed upon her the importance of discussing matters with the Dauphin, and thus
accustoming him to think of them. Marie Antoinette
replied that she could answer for his intentions, which
she could always sway; but it was quite a different
thing to make him act or speak, because both were a
labour to him, in consequence of his timid, sluggish
nature. With great energy the Dauphine had taken
up the idea of educating herself, now that it was clear
to her that this was the only way of educating her
husband; and she drew up a table of intended
employments, filling up the hours of her day, and
showed it to Mercy. Prayers on rising, then music,
dancing, and one hour of " reasonable reading " ("that
is her own expression" says Mercy). Then her
toilette, a visit to the King, attending mass, and dinner,
complete the morning. Afternoons have one hour
and a half assigned for reasonable readings; walks

or hunting, conversations with the Dauphin and with other members of the Royal family, all in due order and in succession. I respectfully begged the Dauphine never to wander from so wise and well-arranged a plan. She replied to me with her usual frankness : " I do not know if I shall fulfil all that quite exactly, but I mean to try my best."

In the secret report Mercy treats of the state entry into Paris that had, from ancient times, been a ceremony immediately following the marriage of a Dauphin of France.

Paris,
18 May,
1773.

Three years had now passed and still there was no apparent intention of arranging this public entry of the Dauphin and Dauphine, and " whether this omission arises from simple neglect or from some other cause I do not know." This neglect of ancient ceremony vexed Mercy as impolitic ; for the Dauphine had already won a high reputation for her charms, although the French people had no opportunity of forming their judgment by seeing her ; and he thought that if the favourable impression were deepened by a sight of Marie Antoinette it " would be useful in many ways." He impressed upon the Dauphine to seize a favourable moment to recall to the King's mind the omission of the ceremony, and show curiosity and a desire to see the capital. The King replied warmly there was nothing he wished more, and that it was her prerogative to fix the date. Mercy writes that this state entry will make a great sensation in Paris, and one very favourable to both Dauphin and Dauphine ; and that he is coaching the Dauphine in all the little graceful ways and means of inspiring those sentiments of devoted attachment that are, " above all, important with such a nation as this."

CHAPTER XVIII

The State Entry into Paris—The King's Act of
Clemency—First and Last Salute—Madame du
Barry's Resource—Comte Jean du Barry—
Ambassador de Rohan—State Visits to the Theatres
—The Vicomtesse du Barry—The Dauphine's
Employments

THE state entry into Paris, from which Mercy
hoped so much, is at length to be accomplished.
On 8 June, 1773, the people of Paris, who have
built up for themselves an image of a radiant,
generous, beautiful, Heaven-sent Dauphine, out of the
flying descriptions of those who have already seen
her, are to see for themselves, and judge of their
future Queen with their own eyes. Mercy's desire,
that this favourable impression, " useful in so many
ways," shall be strengthened, has increased with the
increasing attractions of the Dauphine ; and it is with
the pride of guardianship that he weighs the influence
of her charms upon so impressionable a people. Marie
Antoinette is now seventeen and a half years old,
tall, slender, graceful, brilliant rather than absolutely
beautiful.

" No woman knew better how to carry her head ;
it was borne in a manner that lent grace and

nobleness to every movement," writes Sénac de Meilhan ; her walk has the dignity of her ancestresses of Austria, the bearing due to centuries of sovereignty, softened into perfect charm by the graceful personality that has so well profited by the continuous dancing lessons. Her complexion is dazzlingly white and rose, a marvel in a country where almost every face seems seamed and pitted with smallpox ; her great blue eyes, *à fleur de tête*, gleam with fun and sparkle upon *mes charmants vilains sujets*, as she calls her French people. The mouth "scarlet as a cherry," with the slight touch of the Hapsburg legacy in the lower lip, laughs as the surging, shouting thousands crush to catch a glimpse of her, filling the Tuileries, climbing the trees, swarming everywhere to roar to her their welcome ; to *her*, not to the lumpish, feeble, foolish Louis, sixteenth King of that name to be. Paris has gone mad with excitement at seeing Marie Antoinette, on this day of June 1773 ; Paris, of all the world most swayed by personality, has realised that here is a Dauphine, whom it can at last welcome with admiration, for a girl in the exquisite glow of grace, and not for some sullen constrained representative of Royalty.

It was so long since a beauty-loving nation had anything to admire ; it had endured, passively, a strangely unattractive Royal family for many years. There was Louis himself, now livid, deep-wrinkled, haggard, dim-eyed, and trembling of chin ; his daughters " Loque," clumsy, large-featured, plain ;

"Coche," corpulent, unwieldy, apathetic; "Graille," scared, dazed, surly, "of a rare hideousness," only civil in thunderstorms; "Chiffe," little, twisted, insignificant, and now shut peaceably away among the Carmelites. Memory was keen in Paris of the *bonne bourgeoise*, Queen Marie Leczinska, plain, dull, dreary, despised; of Louis, the late Dauphin, gloomy, sickly, consumptive. The most disagreeable of all, who died as unamiably as she had lived, was the late Dauphine, Marie Josèphe, of whom Walpole wrote: "She looks cross and is not civil, and has the true Westphalian grace and accent." She was entirely negligible, and with less claim to renown even than that achieved by her father, August der Starke of Poland and Saxony, who lives in history chiefly in virtue of having increased the population of his two kingdoms by no less than three hundred and sixty-five illegitimate children. Of living representatives of royalty there were besides *le gros Madame*, Clotilde, the immense sister-in-law of Marie Antoinette; the little Princess Elizabeth, "as fat as a pudding"; the Comtesse de Provence, dumpy, swarthy, bushy-browed, sly, and repelling; the Comte de Provence, bald and with skin disease; the Duc de Chartres, bald, copper-coloured, carbuncled. Louis, to be the sixteenth, is taken so little into the consideration of Paris, that not even on the day of this state entry is he more than just mentioned.

The wild enthusiasm of the surging throngs, "the crowds of your lovers, by permission of the Dauphin," as the Duc de Brissac phrased it with doubtful elegance, was for Marie Antoinette, and not for the heir of France, on the surface of whose stolidity came no ripple of intelligence, and from whom no more was gained by the wild emotion of his people than the facts (thankfully mentioned by Marie Antoinette to her mother) that he had behaved surprisingly well, had answered when speeches were made to him, had noticed when services were rendered him, and had shown graciousness to the people. No wonder that Marie Antoinette writes :

" I had a day last Tuesday that I shall not forget in all my life ; we made our entry into Paris. They received us with all the honours it is possible to imagine ; but it was not this **Versailles, 14 June, 1772.** that touched me most ; it was the tenderness and eagerness of these poor people, who, in spite of the oppressive taxes with which they are crushed, were in transports of joy at seeing us. When we went to walk in the Tuileries there was so great a crowd that for three-quarters of an hour we stood there, powerless to advance or to retreat. The Dauphin and I several times bade the guards refrain from striking any one, which made a very good impression." (Easy in such a country to win a name for humanity, where the memory was recent and living of such as that Comte de Charolais, born so few years before as in 1700, brother of the Duc de Bourbon, Louis XV.'s Prime Minister, who, in playful sport, had been used " to fire at tilers for the pleasure of seeing them roll from the roofs," as Lacretelle tells

264 The Guardian of Marie Antoinette

us.) "Such good order was preserved on this day that, in spite of the enormous crowd that followed us everywhere, there was no one hurt. On our return from the walk we went up on to an open terrace, and remained there for half an hour. I cannot describe to you, my dear mother, the enthusiasm of joy and affection that they showed us then. Before we retired we waved our hands to them, which pleased them very greatly. How fortunate it is to be in our rank, and thus gain the friendship of a whole people so very inexpensively!"

The love thus won so cheaply was as little durable as most bargains, although the King added the weight of a somewhat singular act of clemency to increase the joy of the day. He commanded that three hundred and twenty prisoners for debt should be released; and it is specially chronicled that this gaol delivery was to set free that number of prisoners, incarcerated for not having paid the wages of their children's wet-nurses; which gives rise to the reflection that, either there had been a wide-spread protest in 1773 against the charges of these purveyors of nature's supplies, or that the King considered such provision not worth paying for.

Mercy too bears witness to the complete success that had attended the Paris reception: "Nothing was wanting; the public was seized with a sort of delirium for the Dauphine . . . wherever she went she looked at the people with smiling glances; greeted personages of distinction

Paris,
16 June,
1773.

with courtesy ; walked in the garden of the Tuileries where there were, without exaggeration, over fifty thousand souls, and many persons had climbed into the trees ; her Royal Highness commanded the guards to let the people approach and not to drive them back. The suite of the Dauphine was often separated by the press, and on all sides were heard the clapping of hands and the cries of 'How beautiful she is ! how charming ! ' After the walk, and at the moment of departure, her Royal Highness ascended again to the great balcony along the front of the *château*, and to the right and the left she saluted the people, who raised a shout of universal joy and delight."

This, the first salute to her deliriously devoted people, was given in the grace of perfect and con-fiding happiness, from the balcony overlooking the gardens of the Tuileries. Her last was given as she looked over the same gardens (for that hour styled *Jardin National*) from the scaffold in the Place Louis XV., renamed " *de la Révolution*," where had been the fatal *fêtes* of her marriage ; with the same perfect courtesy, as she apologised to the executioner for having inadvertently stepped upon his foot, with the murmur " *Je vous demande pardon, monsieur.*"

" In the memory of man there has not been an entry that has made so much sensation or had so universal a success. . . . The public shows an enthusiasm truly extraordinary. . . . The King complimented her and appeared enchanted with the success of the ceremony.   It is, positively, still the subject of talk in Paris (eight days after), and all minds are as full of it as upon the first day."

Mercy has another point upon which to enlarge to Marie Thérèse, the ever fertile subject of Madame du Barry.   He says that, although the health of the King is no worse in the last month, it is remarked that he is more than ever subject to " the vapours " and to boredom.   His first flame for the favourite is quenched by time ; and "this woman having extremely few resources, either of mind or of character," the King now finds in her only an entertainment little diverting and filled with inconveniences that make themselves felt at every instant—" continual beggings for favours, often unjust, and nearly always for persons of no account who only exist by reason of intrigue.   All this annoys the King, who, with incredible indifference and weakness unites an excellent knowledge of his world, and appreciates its values with undoubted justice.   He sees himself eternally dragged into concessions, that only serve to increase hatreds, disputes, and disorder ; but habit has so invincible a hold upon the character of the King, that he is held in the bonds of custom, and it seems as if they will never be broken unless something very extraordinary and unforeseen occurs."

This dense indifference to everything, this all-absorbing apathy of the King's, alarmed those members of his intimate circle, whose power hung upon their more or less successful dissipation of this

boredom ; and, to Mercy's keen enjoyment, a proof
was given him by Madame du Barry. Hearing that
he was at Versailles, she sent for him and begged him
to visit her. " I found her very much embarrassed
with what she wished to tell me. After some very
much involved beginnings, she asked me to try and
induce the Dauphine to suggest to the King, that she
would like to be admitted by his Majesty into the
company that went with him upon his customary
excursions." This proposal was proof that the du
Barry party was at its wits' end for means of diverting
the King ; for, if its only resource was to beg for the
presence of the Dauphine, it was a confession that
without her there was inextinguishable indifference.
Madame du Barry ended her extraordinary request
with the tactless avowal, that the only obstacle seemed
the opposition of the Dauphin, which she did not
know how to remove ; and this gave Mercy his
opening.

He pointed out that Madame du Barry had promised
him nearly two years ago to do all in her power to
bring together the King and the Dauphine, but instead
of this she had apparently tried to widen the barriers
between them. If she had suggested that the Dauphine
should accompany the King on these journeys, when
Mercy had first proposed it, there could have been
no opposition from the Dauphin "as he was then
entirely passive and never formed a wish contrary to
arrangements already made." To which the favourite
found no word of reply, knowing that the mind of

the Dauphin, such as it was, was now emerging from imbecility, thanks to the ceaseless endeavours of the Dauphine to train it.

To the ever-present dread of Madame du Barry lest the bored King should find diversion elsewhere, there was now added the trouble of a quarrelling brother-in-law. This was the infamous Comte Jean du Barry, the founder of the fortunes of the Comtesse du Barry, of whom Mercy wrote, with a freedom he could not use to his Empress, in a letter to Kaunitz, the Chancellor : "He is a nobleman, as lacking in scruples as in money, who, obliged to live by his wits, carries on a trade that is worthy of them." He kept a gambling saloon, in fact, and Jeanne Vaubernier ruled his *salon de jeu*, and also his household, for the four years before she went through the ceremony of marriage with his brother Comte Guillaume du Barry, the necessary matrimonial preliminary to becoming a mistress of the King. While Jeanne Vaubernier was thus in his employ, as housekeeper and hostess of the salon in the Rue de la Jussienne, she followed the conventions prescribed by a "*mariage à la détrempe*" (diluted marriage : in water colours : would not wash) ; but he was neither a hard nor a jealous master, and to this most of the men at Court could bear witness, "*qu'il suffisait de payer son écot pour souper dans le ménage.*" This Comte Jean du Barry had a violent quarrel with the Duc d'Aiguillon and also with the Abbé Terray, who refused to pay his gambling debts ; Madame du Barry, with a keen sense of gratitude (a lively sense of favours to come), ranged herself on the side of the Comptroller-General.

Mercy adds his usual little secret report, which this time bears upon the changing opinion of the Dauphine for the King. Upon the **Paris, 16 June, 1773.** first day of the illness of Madame Victoire (it turned out to be only measles after all), the King was preparing to leave for St. Hubert, and the Dauphine observed : " Of course, papa, you will not go to St. Hubert while my aunt is in this state." On the King replying that the Princesse was not ill enough for him to put off his voyage, the Dauphine exclaimed : " Then, papa, it is very unfeeling." Mercy says that the Dauphine had shown him how shocked she had felt at his insensibility which " grieved her sweet nature," and that he had much difficulty in effacing this impression ; it was not the first time that Marie Antoinette had revolted from the cold-hearted cruelty of the King, and " I have noticed on more than one such occasion that her opinions of the King have taken a turn that appals me." There was no hiding from the quick, bright Dauphine, so instant in sympathy, so penetrating in her estimates, the cold cruelty and feebleness of Louis, that at times made of a man colossally selfish one quite inhuman ; and Mercy's task of glossing over what could not be hidden was daily more difficult.

Marie Thérèse wrote her overwhelming joy and relief at the success of her daughter's visit to Paris:

"I perceive more and more what good effect your *Schönbrunn,* counsels are having upon her; as her *July, 1773.* success is your work. I acknowledge it and render this justice to you. . . . As for the Parma affairs, I shall give them up, as I am convinced of the utter uselessness of all my efforts to recall my daughter, the Infanta, to her duty. If I had a Mercy at Parma, there would be some grounds for hope, but as things are there is nothing to do. . . . There is no prospect of any change in the behaviour of the Prince de Rohan. He is perfectly incorrigible, and his servants, all rascals, are exactly like their abominable master. They are ruining my people, in the same way as their master is ruining the nobility. Their insolence is carried to the utmost extreme and revolts my subjects, who find their ancient animosities against the French nation already reviving, and will probably come to blows over it. At an exhibition of fireworks at the Prater, they forced their way through the people there, who took up stones and pelted them; there was the greatest difficulty in suppressing the riot. Rohan had some of his servants imprisoned for ill-treating the secretary Gapp, but their fellow-servants were obliged to go to the prison in order to amuse them there. Then one of the prisoners fell ill; Rohan demanded the return of the prisoner to his house, offering to put in his place two others who should remain under arrest instead of the guilty one. All this accompanied by mockery, irony, and intolerable impertinence."

" The reply was made that it was not our custom in this country to make the innocent suffer for the guilty, and that the sick man would be well cared for where he was. . . . It is necessary for the sake of the Court of France itself to recall an Ambassador who is dishonouring it ; and, in order not to compromise Aiguillon, I think (if you approve) of writing myself to my daughter to find some favourable opportunity of speaking to the King about the recall of Rohan. It is quite indifferent to me who is his successor as long as it is a well-intentioned man, reasonable, and capable of controlling his own followers. At the same time, I should like to be quit of the Abbé Georgel and the whole of the suite of Rohan, and not keep one man of the whole of this villainous, shameless Embassy."

With such relations between Rohan and Georgel (his secretary) and the Empress, there is no wonder at the venomous spite with which these men revenged themselves, in the years after her death, upon their only available victim, the daughter of Marie Thérèse. It is upon the evidence of such a man as Georgel that the diamond necklace scandal is based : it was the immoral, contemptible rascal, Rohan, whose word outweighed the fair name of Marie Antoinette.

The brilliant entrance of the Dauphine into public life was followed by State visits to the Opera, the Comédie Française and the Comédie Italienne, of which Mercy writes that the King had commanded all ceremony should

be observed as if his Majesty had been present.   So
the Dauphine and her husband went to the theatre
with cannon firing from the Invalides and the Bastille,
two companies of the Swiss and French Guards on
parade with their colours before the entrance, two
men of the bodyguard on duty upon the stage, and
a detachment of the Swiss formed in square under
the box in which were the Royal guests ; which
accessories of state, instead of damping the general
enthusiasm, seemed to heighten it.   " And all this
was for the Dauphine . . . who did not omit the
smallest detail that could give pleasure to the people."

Mercy, full of forethought, and well acquainted
with the nature of "this nation," and the trifles
that swayed it, had watched at the Opera and
had noticed that people felt the pressure of
etiquette, which forbade them to applaud the actors
when Royalty was present.   He suggested to the
Dauphine a ready means of popularity, that she should
ask the King if he would consent to her breaking
this little formality.   The Dauphin, who was present,
approved so cordially that he actually undertook to
speak to the King himself, and immediate consent
was given.   The opportunity came at the Comédie
Française ; and at one point in the play the Dauphine ·
herself applauded, which mark of grace enchanted
the audience, who were now free to follow her example
and the custom to which they were attached.

The defeats of Madame Adélaïde in intrigue were
now not surprising ; but Mercy always chronicles

THE COMTESSE DE NARBONNE.

(From the miniature at the Château d'Argenteau.) [*Page* 273.

them with pleasure, as proof of the emancipation of the Dauphine ; and he unravelled and laid before her a very tangled little web. The Duc d'Aiguillon, tired of his absolute non-success with the Dauphine, and acquainted with no other motive than bribery, made terms of friendship with his old foe, the Comtesse de Narbonne. The terms were : for her son, the mayoralty of Bordeaux ; for herself, an interest in the approaching renewal of the lease of monopolies. But to obtain these advantages the Comtesse de Narbonne must secure better treatment of Madame du Barry by Madame Adélaïde, and, furthermore, undertake that this Princess should persuade the Dauphine to similar conduct towards the favourite. Mercy points out all these moves, with which he has become acquainted, and foretells what will happen, as Madame Adélaïde is of such feeble, illogical and frivolous character, that she will certainly allow herself to be exploited.

It all turned out as he foresaw ; and Madame Adélaïde held forth to the Dauphin and Dauphine, insinuating the wishes of an alteration in conduct to the prepared and awaiting Dauphine, who listened with perfect comprehension, saying nothing. " But the Dauphin spoke, frankly but rather roughly : ' My aunt, I advise you never to mix yourself up in the intrigues of M. d'Aiguillon, for he is a bad lot.' This energetic expression cut the words from Madame Adélaïde, and I do not think that she will dare again serve as a vehicle of insinuations from her lady-in-

waiting. . . . They have now advised the favourite
to present the woman that is to marry her nephew,
to the Royal family." This lady was Mademoiselle
Rose Marie Hélène de Tournon, who was related
to the noble house of Soubise ; and the Vicomte
Adolphe du Barry, then twenty-four years of age,
was the nephew of the husband of Madame du Barry ;
he was killed in a duel at Bath—years after, and
buried at Bathampton cemetery.

The joy at her successful entry into Paris still
filled the heart of the Dauphine nine days

17 July,
1773.
after the event. She refers to the warmth
of her greeting in her letter to her mother, and
describes the scene at the Comédie Italienne, when
the audience shouted in one chorus with the actors :
" *Vive le roi !* " and Clairval, the actor, added : " and
his dear children ! " and was immensely applauded.

Clairval was as noted a person in the memoirs of
the time as Mademoiselle Duthé (" she has been
twice employed in the Royal family, first in completing
the education of the Duc de Bourbon, and subse-
quently in perfecting that of the most amiable of
our grandsons "), or Mademoiselle Raucourt, or Mademoiselle Guimard. He was considered of so great
public importance that when, as a result of his success,
Madame de Stainville (sister-in-law of the Duc de
Choiseul) disappeared into the convent of the Filles
de Ste. Marie, by aid of a *lettre de cachet*, Clairval
was not arrested, in order that the public might not
be deprived of its favourite actor.

Marie Antoinette writes : "We have heard here of the birth of the Infanta's child ; the Infant, who has never written to me since his marriage, wrote to me on this occasion. True, he forgot that I was his sister-in-law ; he called me his cousin : it is, at all events, a near enough relationship, considering his behaviour."

Don Ferdinand of Parma and Plaisance was now twenty-two years of age, and his wife was twenty-seven ; but wisdom had not come with " the roasting of chestnuts," his chief occupation during the year of his marriage. Marie Antoinette ends her letter by the assurance that the worst intrigues against the Dauphin and herself were over, they had now nothing more to fear, and their party was by this time so firmly established that nothing would come between them. So loyal to her feeble husband, that not even to her mother will she hint at the causes for complaint she has against him ; and it is from Mercy that the Empress learns what grounds there were for disgust.

He wrote of the just irritation of the Dauphine with the Royal youth whose tastes were so hopelessly objectionable : "Although there is the most perfect harmony between the **Compiègne, 17 July, 1773.** Dauphin and Dauphine, there exist, nevertheless, little reasons for dissatisfaction. . . . All the influence that she has gained over the Dauphin does not suffice to turn this young Prince from his extraordinary taste for the building trade and everything connected with

it, bricklaying, carpentry, and the like.   There is
always something to be repaired in his apartments,
and he toils, himself, with the workmen, carrying
materials, beams, paving-stones, slaving for entire
hours at this exhausting work, and sometimes becoming more tired than any workman could be who
was obliged to do it for a living.   I have seen lately
that the Dauphine has been excessively irritated and
annoyed by this behaviour ; I can tell to what high
degree, by the bitterness of the complaints that she
has made to me, and by the dread she has of the
future consequences that such unsuitable labour may
entail upon the physical condition of her husband.
I have tried to calm the Dauphine, by representing
to her the only means in her power to win the
Dauphin gradually from such occupations.   It would
be dangerous to show any open opposition : it is only
by the bait of other amusements, more pleasant and
more suitable, that he can be induced to discard these.
I begged the Dauphine to avoid the least appearance
of bitterness or annoyance in her remonstrances :
sweet and continuous persuasion is the only way. . . .
I represented the considerable improvement that has
taken place lately in the Dauphin . . . and persuaded
her that she will succeed in time with ease and
certainty."

The only condition in life for which Louis was
fitted by nature was that of the son of a carpenter or
bricklayer ; had he been born a peasant, he might
have lived a happy dolt and died content ; but fortune

thrust a crown instead of a hod upon him, a sceptre instead of a saw. He had the preference for dirt often seen in those of weak intellect, happy when covered with soot and sweat, in greasy black apron, hammering a piece of metal; so miserable in his magnificent habit of the Order of the St. Esprit, gold-laced and adorned with diamonds, that his open discomfort was the subject of comment, even upon his wedding-day. Not only ridicule but a worse fate attended his tastes. When he became King of France, his ill-chosen present to Marie Antoinette was a spinning-wheel, which he had turned on his own lathe (and she promptly gave to her lady-in-waiting); but he might have lived his life out as King of France had he not meddled with the blacksmith's trade; the iron recess that he forged for his secret papers in the Tuileries, betrayed by his chosen associate in the forge—Gamin—was his ruin.

CHAPTER XIX

The Presentation of the Vicomtesse du Barry—The
Unravelling of a Plot—Madame de Narbonne's
Failure—*La Grande Chercheuse de Couronnes*—
The Dauphine drives a Cabriolet—The Abbé de
Vermond and his Abbaye—A Forty-Months' Silence
—At Fontainebleau—*Sic Transit Gloria Mundi*—
The Family of Rohan—Arrival of Nenÿ

MARIE ANTOINETTE had the experience,
and passed through it with discretion, of receiving the young Vicomtesse du Barry. There
had been much discussion upon the best
manner of receiving this young bride, for
although the Court resented the foisting of Du Barry
relatives upon them, the powerful family of Soubise,
to which the young Madame du Barry belonged, had
too much weight to be lightly affronted. The
Dauphine writes to her mother that the interview has
passed off well. " Just the moment before she came
to my apartments, they told me that the King had
not spoken one word to them, either to the aunt
[the Comtesse du Barry], or to the niece ; so I did
exactly the same. But in all other respects, I can
assure my dear mamma, that I received them very
politely ; everybody who was present agrees that I

13 August, 1773.

was neither embarrassed when they came nor eager to see them go ; the King has certainly been quite content with me, for he has been very good-humoured all the evening."

The Dauphin did not attempt the barest form of civility ; he was talking in the recess of the window when the Du Barrys arrived ; and, hardly turning his head, continued to talk and to "play the spinet on the window-panes." It was considered noteworthy that the King refused to speak a word, as the bride was reported to be very pretty, "very much like Madame de Châteauroux, only prettier," says Madame du Deffand ; and it may have been the memory of the beautiful Duchess, the third on the list of Louis' early loves, dead twenty-eight years ago, that induced the silence.

" Mercy has told me of the Prince Louis [Rohan] ; his evil conduct grieves me in many ways. It is a greater misfortune to this country, which he dishonours, than to Vienna, which he scandalises ; when Mercy considers the time has arrived I will do what he tells me, but I imagine that he will desire some little diplomacy, as much on account of Madame Marsan as of the power of M. de Soubise. . . . They are really painting my portrait ; it is true that the artists have not yet caught my likeness. I would willingly give all I possess to a painter who could express in my portrait the joy I should feel at seeing my dear mamma again ; it is very hard to be able only to embrace her in a letter. My husband is

touched with your kindness ; I hope that he will merit
it more in future," which dry remark has upon it
the remembrance of the bricklaying husband.

Mercy's next report has the promised clearing up
of the intrigues of which Madame Adélaïde
has made herself, so imprudently, the
mouthpiece.   It was a story so full of plots
and counterplots that Mercy had taken long to ferret
them out.   A visit to the Duc d'Aiguillon, "who was
filled with reserve and a kind of embarrassment,"
brought no light : then a call upon Madame du Barry,
" from whom I extracted nothing of importance ; "
then finally Mademoiselle du Barry, sister-in-law and
confidante of the favourite, was tried and found full
of information, and also of the spite that longed
for revenge upon D'Aiguillon, and took it by giving
what was desired—details.   Mercy heard all the
truth, and probably more than all, from Chon, the
sister-in-law, including the fact that Madame Adélaïde
had written to her father, stating her consuming desire
to oblige him in anything ; and that the King, thanking
her "for having saved him a verbal explanation,"
indicated that his cause of grief was that the Dauphin
"shows a marked aversion to the fair sex ; " and he
desired Madame Adélaïde to bring the Dauphin to
more sociable views and induce him to treat with
politeness the women whom the King saw habitually.

It seems incredible that Louis XV. should endeavour
to employ the elderly spinster, his daughter, to teach
his grandson and heir more enthusiasm for the King's

Compiègne,
14 August,
1773.

maîtresse en titre ; but it was so. These preliminaries had taken place on 17 July ; Mercy informed the Dauphine of all things on the 18th, and on the 19th the storm burst. "The Dauphin was in a temper ; Madame Victoire in revolt against the bargaining of the Comtesse de Narbonne ; the Comtesse de Provence, although generally reserved, expressed herself openly." Finally the whole family fell upon Madame Adélaïde, declaring "it was shocking to imagine her conduct should be bought by any bargain ; that as the King saw his children every day there was no need for any intermediary ; that his own expression of desire was a command to them, but that from no other than himself would they bear it." This union of sentiment taught Madame Adélaide two things : that she was on the verge of a serious quarrel with the whole of the family ; and that there was now no one who would be guided by her. She was frightened, retracted everything, promised she would never again take a commission to speak on this subject, and she would forbid the Comtesse de Narbonne to mention it to her. Nothing happened upon the next day, because the Dauphin had indigestion in the night. "This indisposition had been very slight ; but the young Prince stayed in bed, even against the advice of his doctors, who speak very strongly against the state of apprehension and depression into which the Dauphin throws himself upon the very slightest appearance of discomfort." The diligent Dauphine sat all day by the bedside of the sufferer from the slight indigestion, the penalty of his noble Bourbon voracity; so she did not serve to attract the brewing storm.

But on the 21st the Duc d'Aiguillon, suspecting that all was not well with his plan, paid a visit to the Comtesse de Narbonne. The next day the King was to sup at the little *château*; all the members of the Royal family were to be invited; he therefore called upon the Comtesse de Narbonne to carry out her part of the bargain, and make it certain that they should embarrass neither the King nor the favourite. No course was left open to Madame de Narbonne but to confess that she had overrated her influence with Madame Adélaïde; that she had failed entirely, and had no other resources left. The quarrel was intense, bitter and personal; d'Aiguillon rushed to Madame du Barry, "inflamed with rage, breathing accusations of others and justification of himself," and declaring that she was betrayed on all sides. Mercy knew all these details from Madame du Barry: all Paris knew them as well, which was wildly mortifying to the Duc d'Aiguillon, for even the foreign newspapers published his defeat, and the means by which he had hoped to attain success. Mercy notes that the King made no difference in his manner to the Dauphine; it was, if anything, even more caressing.

Mercy observes Louis, and the result of his observation is disquieting. "The King ages (he is now sixty-three), and he appears from time to time to repeat himself. He finds himself solitary, without help, without consolation from his children, without zeal, without devotion, without fidelity from the bizarre assemblage that forms his ministry, his society and his surroundings ; he has nothing to hope in his old age except from the Dauphine who joins the highest qualities of character to those of mind. I can see with certainty that this reflection is present in the mind of the King, from the way in which he treats the Dauphine. This is a point upon which I never cease to insist . . . the Dauphine understands the position of affairs perfectly ; and she fears her future too greatly. She will not permit herself to think that the power and the authority may one day be hers : the consequence is that her character inclines towards passiveness and dependence, towards a habit of timidity and fear, even upon minor occasions. Her Royal Highness dreads to speak to the King ; she fears the ministers ; even those in her own service influence her. It is of the highest importance that the Dauphine should learn to know her own importance better, and to value it more. I would stake my life upon this, that if she would take advantage of her ascendency over the King, there is neither favourite nor minister that could resist the influence and power that she would wield from that moment. Besides, the Dauphin, although with sense and with good qualities in his character, will probably never possess either the strength or the will to reign by himself. If the Dauphine does not rule him, he will be ruled by others ; and such deplorable consequences cannot be too clearly foreseen."

To Marie Thérèse, oppressed with the failures of
her two daughters, of Parma and of Naples, to govern
even themselves, the idea of Marie Antoinette as virtual
ruler of France did not present itself with any feature
of attraction.   To the Empress, the Dauphine was
still the little unformed child who had left her three
years before, to be scolded and flattered alternately,
and driven along the paths of duty like a reluctant
schoolgirl.   To Mercy, she was already the rising
hope, " sparkling like the star of the morning " as
Burke said, the one redemption hoped for France.
The gradual change, the sudden awakening of the
Dauphine's mind to her position, which shows itself
in the dread she has of the imminent future of
responsibility, is unnoted by the mother, to whom
the three years have brought no mark of the passing
of time.

She writes to Mercy : " I confess frankly to you
that I do not wish my daughter to gain too
Schönbrunn,
31 August, decided an influence in affairs.   I have
1773.
learned, only too well, by my own experience,
what a crushing burden is the government of a vast
monarchy.   Besides, I know the youth and levity of
my daughter, joined to her little taste for application
(and she really knows nothing), and this adds to my
fear for her non-success in the government of a
monarchy, so shattered as that of France is at present ;
and if my daughter could not sustain it, or the
condition of this kingdom changed more and more
for the worse, I should prefer that the people blame

some minister and not my daughter, and that it should be another's fault. I cannot make up my mind to speak to her of politics and affairs of state, at least not unless you think it necessary, and tell me *specifically* what I ought to write to her. My daughter ought to treat the favourite better, and like every other woman who comes to pay Court to her. I find this affectation of never speaking a single word to her, very strange ; but as I have told you many times, she does not like to make efforts to overcome her dislike for objects that are not pleasant to her ; and she can be very headstrong."

Always with expediency as her pilot, the Empress sees no reason why her daughter should shrink with " affectation " from a course that she herself had adopted with Madame de Pompadour without a qualm ; and she adds a very characteristic touch : " I am delighted with the proof of kindness my daughter evinced to the groom who was hurt by a fall. This sentiment ought to be evident upon all occasions . . . and it is important that *the public should hear of it.*" But the Empress, the *grande chercheuse de couronnes* as she was called by M. de Nolhac, was before her century in recognition of the uses of advertisement.

Marie Antoinette's views were clear, and her actions in accord with them ; and she differed—very respectfully—from the opinion of her mother 14 September, 1773. and told her so, in answer to the Empress's reproach of impolitic silence towards the Du Barrys. She writes : " As for the young Madame du Barry,

I am very sorry that my dear mamma is not pleased with me ; if she could see all that goes on here, she would judge that the good-humour of the King was sincere, and that it is only just when this cabal torments him that he desires one to pay them any attentions. As for my sister de Provence, I have never blamed her conduct ; but my dear mamma will permit me to tell her, in confidence, that there are certain small differences between her and me : (1) The Italian character gives her resources that I have not " [this periphrasis for a tendency to intrigue should of itself have convinced Marie Thérèse that her daughter was profiting by her studies in diplomacy] ; "(2) when she arrived here the Comte de Provence was already mixed up with these cabals, and enjoined the attitude that his wife was to take.   But in me, I am quite sure the Dauphin would have considered it base."   She describes the efforts she is making to remove from the Empress the incubus of the Ambassador de Rohan (whose conduct had become so unendurable that Marie Thérèse wrote that she would do anything to rid herself of this villainous priest, even consent to the Duc d'Aiguillon, " a thoroughly bad man," as his substitute).   Marie Antoinette, acting upon the advice of Mercy, had spoken to Madame de Marsan, the aunt of the reprehensible de Rohan.   " She appeared greatly distressed at the conduct of her relative ; " but there was no valuable result.

Mercy takes up his journal again in September,

and the first item of importance is chronicled on 12
August : " The Dauphine has given herself
a new amusement in her excursions in the   **Paris,**
forest [of Compiègne], she drives herself in **September,**
   16
   1773.
a little carriage with two wheels, and shafts,
which they call here a cabriolet. This method of
taking carriage exercise would not be without inconvenience, if the numbers of people on horseback who
surround the Dauphine did not obviate all danger."
Mercy always looks with a jaundiced eye upon any
new form of exercise ; and, as the Dauphine rode
on the day after she had driven her new little cabriolet,
he expostulated with her upon the amount of exercise
she was taking and the uneasiness her mother would
feel in consequence. To which the Dauphine replied
that she would give up riding the moment she had
any idea it might be injurious.

On 14 August, Mercy had a disagreeable surprise.
He opened his packet of letters, and found one from
the Abbé de Vermond, who, in common with all at
this strange Court, would rather write than speak,
upon any subject, to anybody. The Abbé de Vermond
wished to resign his post as reader to the Dauphine ;
and he tendered his resignation in a manner that
savoured more of the " vain, ill-mannered fool," as
one Court set considered him, than of the " devoted,
invaluable counsellor," that the other set held him
to be. Two causes he alleged as the reasons of his
resignation : first, that the Dauphin had never yet
spoken to him ; second, the Dauphine seemed bored in

his presence, and did not pay the slightest attention to observations that he deemed it his duty to address to her. He demanded finally three recompenses for his services (which he himself estimated so poorly in this letter of resignation, that he suggested they could be filled with equal value by any *femme de chambre*) (1) the permission to attend at the Dauphine's Court when he wished : (2) the gift of her portrait : (3) and most important, a better living than that bestowed upon him, for this was only worth 2000 livres (£80) after the pensions entailed upon it had been paid. Doubtless this was one of the " muddy sees " (*évêchés crottés*) that were given to the less popular younger sons, whom ambition or deformity took into the Church ; but the disinterestedness of the Abbé de Vermond and his devotion to his royal pupil do not seem very apparent in the manner of his resignation.

Mercy sent at once for the Abbé, but he had gone into the country for the day ; and therefore it was not until the second day that Mercy had the opportunity of upbraiding him for his omission of the courtesy of an explanation. De Vermond excused himself, and dilated upon the extraordinary sullenness and taciturnity of the Dauphin (he had met the Abbé every day for three years and four months and had never yet spoken one word to him). Mercy says : " This circumstance is very striking, and would give rise to all sorts of suggestions, if it were not proved that this habit of the Dauphin's was due, not so much to prejudice or ill-will, as to embarrassment and timidity with a man who was considered, justly, to have a well-informed mind, and who therefore over-awed the young Prince." But whatever excuse Mercy makes to the Empress, the chief thought is of the strange mental sluggishness of the husband of Marie Antoinette, that maintained silence for forty months of constant intercourse.

At length Mercy prevailed upon the Abbé to withdraw his resignation, and to promise to take 17 August, up again his duties as before, only with the 1773. difference that he was to spend one or two days each week in Paris. The reason for Mercy's maintenance of the Abbé de Vermond in this post was not discernible by the Court, to whom he appeared as the Malvolio of Marie Antoinette ; and he played the part, as Madame Campan tells us, even to " the trick of singularity," while the tongue " tanged arguments of State" with which he was made acquainted in the confidence that none but a gossiping fool would break. Stories were rife of the intolerable fatuity of the man, intoxicated with vanity, treating the highest in the land as his inferiors, receiving the ministers and bishops while in his bath, and inculcating the free manners of his own obscure class of the bourgeoisie upon a Bourbon Court. Mercy was once asked : " How can you endure this wearisome babbler ? " and answered : "Because I have need of him."

By his letters to Marie Thérèse we see that if de Vermond were gone, one great channel of communication and information would be closed, hence Mercy's endeavours to soothe the irritated vanity of the Abbé.

The Dauphine was next approached ; she was uneasy and anxious, but entirely for fear her mother should blame her for the Abbé's departure ; and Mercy so improved the occasion that, for her mother's sake, she promised everything that was desired. " She promised firmly to avoid her errors in the future and added with charming ingenuousness : " I will commit as few faults as I can ; and when one does happen I will always own it."

The whole efforts of the Du Barry set were now devoted to the acceptance by Marie Antoinette of the newly married Vicomtesse du Barry ; and the Dauphine, sensible of the motive, which was to smooth the future path of the aunt by the present reception of the niece, would have no tampering with first principles ; and was prepared to treat all connections of the favourite—by marriage regular or " *à la détrempe* "—with equal coldness. To Mercy, the invaluable, appeal was made by Madame du Barry, " who spoke to me very reasonably and without a single complaint as to her own position in respect to the Dauphine ; " and he, after an interview spent in lubrication—in what he called his " customary language, that tranquillises the minds "—had appealed on behalf of the young Vicomtesse. He told the Dauphine that, as she was a relative of the Maréchal de Soubise and had been duly presented at Court, it would be " an affectation " to exclude her from the privilege of forming one of the hunting company of her Royal Highness. But Marie Antoinette answered

all these reasons with one, her objection to everything
and everybody connected, either closely or remotely,
with the favourite. And Mercy says regretfully :
" I saw the moment was unfavourable."

On 25 August was the fête of St. Louis, the whole
of which day was passed by the King in grand receptions, the Dauphine going at ten o'clock to congratulate
his Majesty upon his *fête* day. These solemn receptions
by Louis of his family in state were among the few
occasions upon which the father and daughters were
together for more than a few moments. The hasty
embrace, that was bestowed upon each ancient
daughter daily at the *Débotter*, was a recognition of
duty done and a signal that now Majesty might have
its boots taken off ; but it was not a family reunion.
Mercy left the stately receptions in full swing on that
fête day ; and notes that he left Compiègne early for
Paris, as did all the other foreign ministers, who always
preceded the Court's exodus by several days, " to lessen
the difficulties of transport caused by the multitudes
of the King's servitors upon these journeys, which
resemble the march of an army."

These journeyings of Louis XV. from place to
place gave rise to the most amazing expenditure, as
his Majesty never travelled without a train of several
thousand persons ; and when the unwieldy coaches,
the masses of luggage, the vast preparations of stores
and food supplies and the condition of the roads are
considered, the mention, for instance, that "his Majesty
left Versailles for Fontainebleau " is an epitome of

colossal disorganisation.   Where Louis was, there was
the centre of the world, to certain people of the time ;
and no discomfort was so great but that it was
more willingly borne than the ignominy of being
excluded from Court circles.   When the Court went
to Fontainebleau, so large a part of the *château* was
uninhabitable from lack of repair, that the visitors
had to be quartered in the town, their names being
simply scrawled in chalk upon the doors, as was
customary at an inn.   Even for visitors to whom the
blessed privilege was extended of living under the
damaged roof of the Palace of Fontainebleau, no greater
preparation was made than that of the four bare walls
of a room ; and the guests, honoured by permission
to join the Court, had to find themselves in furniture
and linen, and even in food, for none was provided
for them.   But all the Princes kept a table for their
suite, and free meals somewhere were thus to be
obtained for the seeking.   As to the expenses of such
journeys, with an army of followers and an entire
outfit of furniture, plate, linen, household requisites,
clothes and food, fodder for many hundred horses, etc.,
etc., the accounts of the Comtesse de la Marche furnish
us with a criterion.   That lady took a little trip to
Barèges, and her expenses therefore were moderate, and
only touch the transport of herself and personal effects.
But it took six coaches and thirty-six horses to convey
them, and the expedition cost 100,000 écus (£12,000).

The King and Royal family returned to Versailles
and the Dauphine took the earliest opportunity of

revisiting Paris that had so warmly welcomed
her ; and showed its preference clearly by
giving a very different reception to the **30 August.**
Comte and Comtesse de Provence, when they made
their state entry on 10 September. The Dauphine
had taken her husband and " the two little Mesdames "
(that is to say, the young sisters of the Dauphin,
Clotilde now fourteen, and Elizabeth now nine) for a
walk in the Park of St. Cloud ; she had been to the fair
of St. Ovide, which was held in the Place Louis XV.
(now de la Concorde), and also to the biennial
exhibition of pictures and sculpture opened at the
Louvre. Each time of her appearance she had been
greeted with the liveliest enthusiasm ; and the public
had shown such eagerness to see the Dauphine that
it amounted to adoration.

The secret report bears on the recall of de Rohan.
Mercy had been so strongly urged by the
Empress, that he bethought himself of a **Paris, 16**
means whereby the powerful family to which **September, 1773.**
the Ambassador belonged should not be
affronted by the revelation of his baseness. The means
was the Dauphine's tact : she sent for the Comtesse
de Marsan, the intriguing aunt of this Rohan, and,
as a mark of special favour, told her the position
of affairs. She said that the Ambassador's offences
against decency were grave, that he had forgotten
his duty as a bishop, that his conduct was scanda-
lising Vienna; but that the Empress, in her particular
consideration for the family, had borne with him

until she felt that by longer endurance she was condoning insults to her religion. Marie Antoinette impressed upon the alarmed Comtesse de Marsan, that it was a tribute to the family that such means had been taken to avoid a public scandal as would result from any communication from the Empress to the King ; and that it was therefore for the Comtesse de Marsan to save her nephew and the reputation of her house, by contriving the recall of this Coadjutor with all possible celerity. The Comtesse de Marsan begged for details of the improprieties, for which the Dauphine referred her to Mercy. Her brother, the Prince de Soubise, was in the meantime being convinced by Mercy that nothing but instant recall could save the fortune, reputation, and existence of the Ambassador and of his family.

Both promised to do all in their power, only praying that the disgrace might be hushed up, and a public scandal averted ; and " I seasoned the whole with assurances of your Majesty's goodwill," adds Mercy. The Comtesse de Marsan had a long interview with Mercy on the subject, showed great grief at the conduct of the Coadjutor, shed tears, said she and her brother were now grown old and had looked upon this Prince de Rohan as the staff of the family, that she had sacrificed all other recompense for her twenty years of service than that of the office of Grand Almoner for him, that she had obtained the King's promise for this post ; but that, if the Empress showed her disapproval, he would be ruined without redress, and she begged the grace of her Majesty's silence in consideration of the fact, that she had brought up the Dauphin! Which, in view of her pupil's attainments, does not seem a fact upon which his governess could plume herself.

The arrival in Paris of Nenÿ, the secretary of the Empress Marie Thérèse, caused some interest, as the French Court, quite ignorant of the intimate knowledge which Marie Thérèse obtained through the medium of Mercy, concluded that Nenÿ had been sent by the Empress to report confidentially on the Dauphine and the Court. The Empress was far from entrusting him with any such mission, requiring perception and discretion ; she wrote to Mercy of Nenÿ that he was " honest, Christian, charitable. As his own nature is frank, he judges others by himself and has been frequently deceived. He talks readily, and for that reason he has never been permitted to see a despatch of yours . . . you will by no means let Nenÿ into our secret about my daughter [the secret correspondence]. He will bring a little present for my daughter, a diamond ornament ; and he will bring for you a snuff-box with our two monograms, the Emperor's and my own, all made in this country. The Abbé de Vermond will also receive one. . . . I owe to you my fullest gratitude for your services : you sustain me in my saddest days by your letters, but still more by your counsels and prudent conduct of affairs."

Nenÿ, therefore, was no spy, nor was one needed ; but the very suspicion shows the perfect secrecy in which the correspondence was carried on. Marie

Antoinette wrote, with the pleasure of a child, her delight at the diamond flower. " Just at the moment when Nenÿ arrived, I was receiving the wife of the Ambassador of Sardinia and all the diplomatic corps. What a joy and a glory it was to me to show such a charming proof of my mother's tenderness! And another great joy to me was the respect for my dear mother that the Dauphin showed to Nenÿ. . . . The Abbé is in transports of admiration and grati- tude. . . ." The Abbé had been won back to his loyalty by Mercy's arguments, the Dauphin's toleration of his presence, and the Empress's snuff-box.

CHAPTER XX

THE idea of the resignation of the Abbé de
Vermond had caused perturbation to Marie
Thérèse ; the loss of an excellent vehicle of information was to be feared, but also the effect upon
the mind of the Dauphine, of his letter, **Schönbrunn**
giving up his post in so questionable a **3 October,**
manner. "He will no longer have any **1773.**
control over her. . . . I know how much my
daughter likes to have her own way, and how
well she knows how to double and turn to arrive
at her goal. Only adaptable in matters that affect
her but little . . . her character is thoughtless, and
she is too much bent upon her own ideas. In spite
of her good qualities and of her wit, I always fear
the effects of her levity and headstrong ways. I
am relieved to hear that the Abbé Vermond remains
at his post, to have at least one trustworthy man near

her, capable of keeping you informed of everything, even if he no longer has sufficient influence to guide her decision.   I remain with confidence in your dexterity and watchfulness. . . . I approve highly what you have arranged with Madame de Marsan and the Prince de Soubise in regard to the recall of Rohan. I will keep to this, provided that Rohan leaves here by December at latest, and that his relatives and friends do not attempt to try to induce me to intervene for any especial favour from the King, his master.   I consider that I am doing enough, in withholding complaints against his conduct. . . . Here are three fresh proofs of irregularities.   Some of his suite, which included an ecclesiastic among the company, ill-treated some peasants in the neighbourhood of Vienna, and got well beaten for it.   His pages, when accompanying the Ambassador on his way to Schönbrunn, rode over the body of the sentinel on duty and injured him in the stomach.   Such is the insolence of his people that it is to be feared the public, already disgusted by their excesses, will proceed to some grievous action. The Ambassador himself, being on a visit to the Prince de Kaunitz at Austerlitz, formed the singular plan of going to Cracow ; and who knows whether he may not push on to Warsaw ! "

De Rohan, perhaps, had just become acquainted with the division of Poland, which had been diplomatically completed without his having any suspicion of it ; and had gone to find the answer to Madame du Barry's question : " Where is Poland ? "

The visit of Nenÿ, her mother's secretary, had been
of much interest to Marie Antoinette, whose strong
love for the members of her family was crushed, upon
principle, by their desire that she should live a life
independent even of the ties of family affection. Of
the Emperor Joseph, his mother said that, when once
his sisters or brothers had made fresh ties he ignored
their existence, or pretended to ignore them;
affected to think no more of them, and wished to hear
no news other than was contained in the newspapers.
He wrote occasionally to Marie Antoinette it was
true, but always with the superior air of his fourteen
additional years of knowledge; and the other members
of her family were constrained by the Empress to
write but seldom, so that Marie Antoinette herself
was reduced, for news of her family, to the meagre
gleanings of the gazettes.

But from Nenÿ, so recently from the Court of
Austria, there was much to hear, and Mercy
mentions the keen joy that the Dauphine Fontainebleau,
felt to have with her, for a stay of some 17 October,
1773.
days at Versailles, a man who could give
her news of such interest. He also tells of the
repeated visits to Paris, and their immense success
from the point of popularity. " She shows herself
to the highest possible advantage upon these occasions;
all is spontaneous and perfect; it is a replica of the
benevolence, the attention, the graces of her august
mother." Mercy is always deft in his similes. He
remarks further that the Dauphin does better on

these public occasions than would be anticipated from his moral and physical disadvantages.   Praise that recalls the tribute of the Duc de Choiseul (from his favourite occupation of worsted work) to Louis XV. : *" Il serait un si bon Roi, s'il n'avait tant de côtés d'un mauvais."*

The struggles of the various parties at Court were shown by their endeavours to win the public voice, a curious consideration of the popular sentiment which yet weighed as dust in the balance of their actions. Mercy watches jealously over the success of the Dauphine, and measures the values of the acclamations given to others ; and is much annoyed that the King consents to let the state entry of the Comte and Comtesse de Provence be on exactly similar lines to that of the Dauphin and Dauphine, even to the two sentinels on the stage, "which is never done except for the sovereign or the heir presumptive." He is quite gratified to find that Mesdames may come and go in Paris, may be seen on the promenades, may even go into shops !—"and all this receives not the slightest notice from the public ; the whole family is invariably and totally eclipsed by the Dauphine ; it is she of whom they speak, she whom they wish to see, and to her is attributed every sign of improvement in the Dauphin." Mercy also records that the long silence of the Dauphin towards the Abbé de Vermond has at length been broken ; he spoke to him at Versailles, for the first time in three and a half years.   He mentions that the Court

has been settled at Fontainebleau from 6 October, but
"by reason of domestic arrangements" (in fact
disarrangements), neither he nor any of the other
ministers could arrive there until the 11th.

Just before the departure from Versailles there
had been the presentation of a third Madame du
Barry, the three greatly confusing the memoirs of
the time. This third marriage was due to the natural
desire of the du Barry family to make hay while
the King shone, and the best method seemed to
" the Rake," Comte Jean, one of matrimonial alliance.
He could not marry, owing to the existence of a
wife, the superfluous and undesired Catherine Ursule
Dalmas de Vernongrese, whom he had married in
1748 ; but his brother Guillaume was the husband
of the favourite ; his nephew Adolphe the husband
of Mademoiselle de Tournon, and now his younger
brother Nicolas (sometimes called Elie) became the
husband of the rich and noble Mademoiselle de Fumel,
and created himself a Marquis, taking the title of
d'Hargicourt, while his wife kept that of du Barry.
Thus at Court at one time there were a Comtesse,
a Vicomtesse, and a Marquise du Barry. After the
extinction of the du Barry *feu d'artifice*, the Marquis
and Marquise (*née* Fumel) du Barry dropped this
name, that sufficed to recall memories inappropriate
to the reign of Louis XVI. ; and became d'Hargicourt
only, the title being that of the uncle of the Marquise.
The advent of yet another Madame du Barry at
Court was a great trial to the Dauphine, and she

received this third in perfect silence and with extreme coldness, her example being followed by Mesdames. Still, there were no complaints.

Mercy adds that the Rohan business is in train, and the Prince de Soubise, and the Comtesse de Marsan have already demanded his recall; which, to the surprise of the innocent Nenÿ, has been attributed to him.   Marie Thérèse writes of the complaints that de Rohan had made to Kaunitz about Nenÿ's pretended mission, " apparently made in order to put Kaunitz in a bad humour ; " and the Empress describes the lucky arrangement of Mercy's letters, which enabled her to show the chancellor a passage in one, describing Nenÿ at the Court and mentioning that he had not seen the Duc d'Aiguillon except in his [Mercy's] presence, and in another, the reference to the arrangement of the Prince de Soubise and the Comtesse de Marsan for de Rohan's recall.   " But I took out the last two pages, 5 and 6, of your letter, which mentioned Rohan . . . the paragraph ending at the bottom of the sheet without giving rise to any suspicion."   The Empress has just heard the good news of the birth of a daughter to her son, the Archduke Ferdinand and his wife Marie Beatrix d'Este : " There are three grand-children already this year, and a fourth I expect in December.   God be praised ! . . .   I hear my daughter of Parma is moving heaven and earth to come here.   The ministers of Spain and France wish it in order to be able to settle the country,

Vienna, 6 November, 1773.

and make the Infant travel in France and Spain. This does not suit me at all, and if she cannot follow her husband she will have to stay behind with her children at Parma. That is her place, and we are going to give a flat refusal to her request. . . . I am sorry for her with that fool for a husband but I cannot approve of these trips here : it would only increase my troubles of which I have enough. Here is another thing . . . this Rohan, having been at St. Hubert with the Emperor, prated to him for two hours about I do not know what, but it has resulted in the Emperor forming a great desire to go to Paris. The journey, the visits, the life to lead, all has been arranged, the people notified, and Lord knows what besides. You see by this sample what an audacious and plausible man can do with the Emperor: unfortunately a minister who knows his place would never take such an advantage, and that is what makes my position so disagreeable and intolerable : a wretch can overthrow with one word all the results of continued labour. He [the Emperor] despises Rohan, he even speaks too strongly against him ; but Rohan amuses him, and tells him things that no man of refinement says to him, and he can contrive to gain anything in such a moment." A contemporary manuscript attributed to the Earl of Holdernesse, and now in the British Museum, sums up this Ambassador de Rohan : " Of the Guimené branch, nephew of the Cardinal and his Coadjutor in the bishoprick of Strasburg . . . a titular bishop, himself of *Cesarea in partibus*, lively, some wit in conversation, graceful in manner, an agreeable person, ignorant, shamefully debauched and not remarkable for common honesty."

The journal of Mercy continues from 16 October, upon which date a series of events happened that greatly increased the popular admiration for the Dauphine. She was following the hunt in her coach when the stag, closely pursued by the hounds, leapt into an enclosure where a peasant was tilling. The stag, mad with fright, rushed upon the man, injured him with thrusts from its antlers, in thigh and body ; no one was near the hounds, the huntsmen nearly a mile away ; the wife, seeing her husband fall mortally wounded, fled shrieking in despair towards some riders : they were the King and his suite ; and the woman fainted. It was of course nothing to his Majesty, for the life of a peasant was of such absolute unimportance in the hunting-field —or elsewhere, in fact—that whipping and banishment for five years was a sentence considered humane for a poacher upon a second offence ; and Louis XV. was really playing quite the benevolent monarch when he commanded some one to see after the woman, as he went on hunting. Besides, his Majesty was engaged in the one serious occupation of his life, he was doing that which justified his sovereignty, the act of so great importance that the days when he did *not* hunt : " *Le Roi ne fera rien aujourd'hui* ; " and the affairs of State could not pause for a dying peasant.

[margin note: Paris, 12 November, 1773.]

Hence the hasty departing order to some one to look after things was chronicled as " *des marques de compassion et de bonté.*" But the Dauphine came up; rushed out of her coach to the fainting woman, administered " smelling-waters ; " and when by this means consciousness returned, gave every coin she had with her. Finally she was so touched, so moved with sympathy, that her tears fell; and Mercy notes that when the spectators saw the tears, they all wept simultaneously, "to the number of more than a hundred," and stood motionless, struck into fixity by their amazement and admiration. This paralysis of admiration seems to have deprived every one of common sense; for it was not until the Dauphine ordered up her own coach, and had the poor woman and her two friends placed in it, to be driven to their huts in a neighbouring hamlet, that any one betook himself to action. The Dauphine waited on the spot till the return of her coach, and inquired after the injured man, whose case was deemed almost hopeless. When all was over, the Dauphin, who had been present all the time, gave away all the money he possessed at the moment, thus following —at some distance—the example set by his wife; as the Duchesse de Beauvau remarked : " *Madame la Dauphine suivait la nature ; et M. le Dauphin suivait Madame la Dauphine.*"

When Mercy went shortly after this 18 October, day to congratulate the Dauphine upon 1773. having so dexterously won the applause of all Paris,

she replied that she knew people had praised her
for having shown goodness and compassion, but she
could not conceive how any one could have done
otherwise, and she had only acted upon the first
impulses of humanity ; and she changed the conversation immediately.

There was a great scandal at the Court at this time,
19 October, 1773. resulting from a proposed marriage. It is
one of the peculiarities of the period that
it was *only* when marriage was contemplated that any
scandal arose at all. There was a great lady at Court,
the dowager Duchesse de Chaulnes, formerly Duchesse
de Pecquiny, celebrated for her wit and her indiscretions, aged sixty years ; but, as Madame du Deffant
said of another sprightly sexagenarian, Madame de
Mirepoix, "Her mind grows backwards, she is not
above fifteen at this day." She was rich too, with
an income of 50,000 écus [£6,000], and a title that
placed her in the front rank at Court. But her
sixty years were halved by her quoted saying, that to
a bourgeois a duchess was never over thirty ; and her
ready wit condoned her entire lack of principles.

She had been first married to the Duc de Pecquiny
in 1734 ; and now in 1773, she selected a man
named Gyac, "*très mince personnage*, both in person
and in family," says Mercy, with neithèr money
nor prospects, aged thirty years, of mean extraction,
"*roturier de Gascogne*," only admitted into society
in his capacity as a man of law, who had been
foisted upon the household of the Dauphine as

superintendent of accounts, by the pressure of the Duchesse de Chaulnes, herself a "*dame du palais*." The whole Court was filled with mirth and wrath. The Duchesse de Chaulnes wrote for formal consent to her marriage with this Gyac, and the Dauphine, in accordance with Mercy's advice, made no reply; the custom of the Court being that a marriage so far beneath the rank of a duchess must first obtain consent from the King.

Not only the Court was indignant, but the gentlemen of the long robe also, who took prompt steps against the unworthy member of their profession. The announcement of the intended marriage was made on 19 October, and on 24 October a council met to strike Gyac off the rolls, on the grounds that he had entered into this alliance during the time that he was judge in a case of appeal, the action being brought by the Duchesse de Chaulnes against her son, who had—naturally—lost his case. The King heard his council and consented : Gyac, being thus declared suspected of connivance, was dismissed. But in spite of this scandal he remained superintendent of the Dauphine's household for two years longer ; and the Duchesse became to every one at Court simply "*la femme à Gyac*." In the same way a Royal duke, who had married a lady beneath him in rank, found he could not obtain for her the title of Duchesse d'Orléans but had made himself merely " M. de Montesson," the name of his deceased predecessor in the lady's affections.

The little balls given by the Dauphine continued weekly ; and at them " they observe no sort of ceremony, there are not even places set apart for the Royal family, all of whom sit down, any where, side by side with the ladies of the Court." The hours of these little balls were from five to ten o'clock ; and the absence of ceremony was marked by the adoption of a particular dress, the white dominos of the ladies, having to be made with a pleat in the back like a morning sacque, were worn over small hoops, and had long floating sleeves and trains. Similarly the *soupers* of the King, for which invitations were so eagerly sought, had to be attended in a special Court dress, old-fashioned and disused except for these occasions, a gown, a pleated sacque, and long lace lappets.

The usual evening ceremony, when Mesdames went to the King for the perfunctory paternal embrace, had also its special robes, without which they could not appear ; and when the hour approached, Mesdames dropped their reading, inserted themselves briskly into enormous hoops and skirts covered with gold lace and embroidery, tied a long train on round the waist, hid the rest of the neglected toilette under a great cloak of black taffetas up to the chin, and started in procession, with gentlemen-in-waiting, ladies, pages, equerries, and guards carrying great torches through the empty rooms of the palace. By dint of practice the whole business, from the first donning of the enormous hoop to its final dropping,

(margin note: 20 October, 1773.)

as Madame untied her train with relief and sat down
again to her work, took only about fifteen minutes.

The Dauphine again "took the diversion of stag-
hunting" in her coach, but happily there 12 October,
was no repetition of the misfortune of the   1773.
16th. The continued sympathy and interest of the
Dauphine had been shown by sending regularly
to inquire after the injured man ; and she had so
strictly commanded the Court surgeons to pay him
every care, that his recovery, at one time thought
hopeless, seemed now possible. Though the Dauphine
paid no attention at all to the effect that the account
of her kind action had made upon the public, Mercy
is not so casual ; and he mentions with considerable
acerbity to Marie Thérèse that a report had appeared
in the *Gazette de Paris*, which was misleading and
inaccurate, and tried to give some of the credit to the
Comtesse de Provence, "a very unjust assignment,"
says Mercy, who regards a pious act as invested capita
bearing, by way of interest, public regard.

The preparations for the marriage of the Comte
d'Artois are now going on ; and the Dauphine's
improving study will suffer, he says, until they are
over, and they will last a month. In the meantime,
singing and dancing are taking up all the time. On
27 October, Mercy says he had a very interesting
interview with the Comtesse du Barry. At first she
asked him about matters of political importance ; then
she turned to those of real importance, and confessed
that the object of her conversation was to obtain his

advice upon the delicate subject of her relations with the Dauphine. Mercy expected some complaint, some new demands ; but none came, only praises very respectful, very unreserved. There was but one thing she wished, a welcome from the Dauphine, and this had seemed to her quite possible of attainment, but was long in coming. Did Mercy think that a letter from the King would be of any use ?

The simplicity of the favourite in this proposition clearly shows that she was unable to realise that Marie Antoinette had any rooted objection to her profession ; she thought to arrange everything quite comfortably by dictating a letter to the King, that would make even an Austrian Archduchess overlook the only thing in which she differed from the majority of the other Court ladies, her low birth. This simplicity of hers served as a perpetual subject to the bitter wits of the Court ; and Madame du Deffant (herself not morally eligible for stone-throwing) wrote of her : " The du Barry herself is nothing, a mere stick that men may use as a prop, or as an offensive or defensive weapon. De Choiseul had it in his hands to make what he would of her : I cannot regard his conduct as kind or his pride as judicious." Mercy had it also in his hands, and could have done what the magic of Egypt did, turn the stick into a serpent at his will ; but he preferred the subtler feat of retaining it in balance. He therefore talked to the favourite so convincingly that things remained exactly as they were.

As his conversation with the favourite ended, the King entered, so overjoyed at having caught a glimpse of the Dauphine at her window that he could speak of nothing else ; and the favourite busied herself in adding her compliments to his Majesty's. Mercy informed the Dauphine of this proposal of the favourite's, and made plans with her as to the way she could best meet it by inspiring the Dauphin with certain lines of thought : " The Dauphine told me that the Dauphin sometimes mentioned to her that he knew there were intrigues ; but that he never gave any opinion clearly, and always asked what Mercy thought."

Louis gave no opinion because he had none to give ; the sole matter upon which he formed a sufficiently clear mental conception to enable him to speak definitely was the great Bourbon preoccupation—food ; though, even in that, the weakness of his digestion prevented his ever attaining the full perfection of Louis XIV. The *Grand Monarque's* usual supper was " four platefuls of different soups, a whole pheasant, a partridge, a great plate of *salade*, two great slices of ham, a plate of mutton seasoned with garlic, pastry, and after that fruit and hard-boiled eggs ; " and then he took a case of cold meats to be placed beside his bed at night. The Dauphin had the desire to excel in this family accomplishment ; but was hopelessly mediocre even in this, owing to constitutional weakness. Still the only occasions upon which he expressed himself clearly were when he spoke of eating ; and in this matter he sometimes acted without waiting for an extraneous impulse.

An anecdote shows to what mental briskness an adequate motive could inspire the Dauphin : at six in the morning he rang his bell to know what was preparing for his breakfast. "A fat fowl and some cutlets," was replied. "Extremely little ; tell them to cook some eggs !" And then the Duc de Lauzun records that the scanty meal, over the preparation of which the Prince presided himself, consisted of four cutlets, the fat chicken, six prepared eggs, and a slice of ham ; and the Dauphin returned to dinner "with an incredible appetite."

In the secret report Mercy writes with discreet allusions to the relations between the Dauphin and Dauphine. "I fear the happy time is not as near as one could wish. . . . I have no doubt the Dauphine has explained the position to your Majesty. . . . At my last interview with the Dauphine she deigned to confide in me a very interesting interview she had had with the Dauphin. They had discussed the approaching arrival of the bride, the future Comtesse d'Artois, and what a sensation it would cause, in Court and in public, if the Comtesse d'Artois should be able to present an heir to the throne before the Dauphine. The Dauphin had appeared to reflect, and had then embraced his wife and asked, "But you do love me ?" And on her assurances of affection, he had said he "hoped all would be well."

Paris, 12 November, 1773.

CHAPTER XXI

Despatches—Open Secrets—Sanctioned Treasons and
Counterfeit Castigation—Arrival of the Comtesse
d'Artois—Her portrait—Splendour of the Wedding
Banquet and of the Chief Guest—Corn Riots at
Bordeaux—Expenses of Establishments—Thieves
at the Masked Ball—Death of de Chauvelin—
Madame du Barry's Banking Account—Joseph II.
Plans to visit France—Resignation of Kaunitz

THE year 1773 closed for Marie Thérèse without
any lifting of her heavy troubles. Grandchildren
had been born to her, but they had not settled the
question of succession to the various thrones : the
Queen of Naples had only girls ; the Infanta of Parma
had a son (who became King of Etruria in after life
as Louis I.), but with " such a fool of a husband " as
the Empress called her son-in-law, there was every
prospect that his heir would follow his nature. But
the tottering dynasty of France has as yet no heir ; and
the anxiety of Marie Thérèse grows year by year
greater as hope diminishes.

The internal condition of Austria, her difficulties
with her neighbouring enemies, the dread of treachery
from France and from Russia, the open enmity of
Prussia, all strained the wariness of the Empress and

her ministers to the utmost ; and their ceaseless struggle is shown in the letters. The despatches of these Courts, revealing a policy entirely different from that openly carried on by their accredited ministers, are entertainingly public ; for each nation played the ostrich of politics, and imagined its own " secret " cipher to be intact, while reading all the intercepted correspond- ence of the others. There had been a game in progress for some time past in which Louis XV. and the Comte de Broglie had taken a hand, and played their cards with the profoundest dissimulation, unaware that Mercy was seeing all up their sleeve as well as those on the table ; and in a letter of the Empress to Mercy she writes :

" You will receive through the ordinary channel directions upon the affair of de Broglie. By the deciphering of his correspondence with Durand and Vergennes we have just become possessed of a new proof that he has always continued his secret correspondence with the ministers in the foreign Courts, by order of the King. He informs Durand and Vergennes that this correspond- ence is to continue, even after his exile to Ruffec, and that they have nothing to fear in carrying out the orders of the King. In addition he sends to Vergennes the letter he had written to d'Aiguillon, which gave rise to his pretended disgrace, together with the order of the King to retire to Ruffec."

Vienna, 1 December, 1773.

The curious part of this game of diplomacy was that the Duc d'Aiguillon, minister as he was, had no more than suspicion of the moves that checked him, suspicion that naturally occurred to every one who considered the post as a vehicle for the diffusion, rather than the conveyance, of information.

Therefore in France there were, at one time, the Duc d'Aiguillon (the apparent representative of Louis), and the Comte de Broglie (the real agent of his will). By diligent endeavour d'Aiguillon had made a half discovery ; he had found out that de Broglie was intriguing, but not that the intrigues were directly inspired by the King. Consequently when he went with his tale of discovered treachery and told Louis of the acts Louis had himself planned, there was the necessity of counterfeit punishment. De Broglie was exiled to his estate at Ruffec, whence he despatched more " secret " correspondence (copies of which were immediately in the hands of Mercy and of Marie Thérèse) ; and the other agents, detected of treasonable correspondence, were consigned to the Bastille, with the fullest assurances of protection from Louis. Thus every one was satisfied except the Duc d'Aiguillon, who had contrived to include his enemy the Marquis de Monteynard, one of the ministers, in these treasons and plots, and was much irritated to find that he left the Court without a stain upon his character.

Another political point upon which the secret correspondence of Princes shed light was the resignation of the Maréchal Comte de Lacy, who had served in the Austrian army, been President of the Council of War, and been through the Seven

Years' War.   Owing to ill health the Maréchal had
resigned and gone to live in the south of France.
In Paris this was construed, with delight, into the
dismissal of an officer with too much leaning towards
Prussia and distrust of France ; and Marie Thérèse
quotes casually, from an intercepted letter from the
King of Prussia to his Ambassador in Vienna, that
he believes France is trying to engage the friendly
Maréchal in its service, and would do so if it were
possible without embroilment with Austria.

Marie Thérèse ends by saying : " I have just
heard that the Prince de Rohan intends to leave
for Paris in a few days, with the idea of exculpating
himself, and then of returning here, that his recall may
be effected in a manner more worthy of his reputation.   As his relations in France are numerous and
of considerable power, there are some persons here
who fear that they will avenge upon my daughter
the wrongs they pretend have been done him at my
instigation."

The revenge was slow in reaping, but it came in
1785, with the nine months' trial and the eternal
memory of the diamond necklace.

The necessity of securing the succession to the
throne of France had resulted in the hasty selection
of another Savoy Princess, to be the wife of the
Comte d'Artois, who was now sixteen.   The event
was naturally of the highest interest, for various reasons
both present and future ; and Mercy gives an account
of the reception of the bride, who represented to him

THE COMTESSE D'ARTOIS.

(From an engraving.)

[Page 317.

a formidable strengthening of the Savoy party, already powerful enough with the Comtesse de Provence and her followers ; and, still more, an accession to the number of du Barry intriguers. This reception of the third young Princess was accompanied with the invariable ceremony. The King and the Royal family went out to the distance of two leagues from Fontainebleau to meet her. "But there was nothing extraordinary, except the extreme eagerness of the Comte d'Artois and the admiration he showed for the figure of his newly arrived wife ; for this is by no means the best point of this young Princess," says Mercy ; and he goes on to describe the lady : "Very small, of very commonplace figure, although one cannot justly say that its defects are shocking ; her skin is white enough, the face thin, the nose much too long and badly finished, the eyes not well shaped, a big mouth—altogether an irregular physiognomy, unattractive and most vulgar."

This picture is probably drawn to enhance the Empress's maternal pride in Marie Antoinette, for Madame Campan says the bride's face was very interesting, and her skin beautifully white, and gives no hint of vulgarity ; but she too adds that the remarkable length of her nose was the chief point in her face. So it is evident that the Comtesse d'Artois had not even the "passably good eyes under bushy eyebrows" of her sister the Comtesse de Provence. Nor had she the "sweet, insinuating, Italian manner" (The Duc d'Aiguillon's opinion) of that sister.

The Comtesse d'Artois was " ungraceful in bearing, timid and awkward, cannot speak a word, no matter what pains her lady-in-waiting takes to prompt her, dances badly, and, in fact, there is nothing in her that does not point either to faults in her disposition or to an excessively neglected education." Which, as Mercy says, is very sad for this Princess. But she was a year younger even than her boy husband, so that some awkwardness might be pardoned.

The marriage ceremony took place in the Chapel of Versailles ; and the banquet given afterwards was of surpassing splendour, the most splendid of all present being Madame du Barry. The whole of the Royal family was at table ; all the Princes of the Blood, all that the Court could produce that was most beautiful in person and in dress, and most illustrious in name. And in the place of honour, facing his Majesty, sat Madame du Barry, "glittering like the sun," and wearing 5,000,000 francs worth of diamonds [£200,000], "made by her earnings and economies," to quote from her own wonderfully untruthful marriage contract.

One of the most admired features of the banquet was the table centre, which had taken all the skill of the chief Court engineer. Down the centre of the table ran a stream that flowed throughout the dinner ; and upon it floated numbers of boats, bearing little moving automata of great ingenuity ; trees shaded the banks of this little river and charming landscapes stretched on each side.

At this same hour in France, thousands were starving on boiled grass, and bread mixed with dust and sand. The corn riots at Bordeaux, at Montauban, and elsewhere, were raging ; famine was in the length and breadth of France ; but corn was a monopoly and Madame du Barry had a commission on the deal, and the farmers (of the revenues) were reaping heavy crops (of profit) and paying well for the privilege.

But the famine had to be stamped out by the military, who effectually stayed the hunger by executing the hungry.

The Dauphine was not unobservant of all the defects of her sister-in-law, the supposed rival, but no thought of petty jealousy was ever found in Marie Antoinette ; and Mercy says that she spoke " with kindness and indulgence of the young Princess," who was not welcomed at all by the Comtesse de Provence. Mercy was assured that even in their childhood the sisters were bound by no ties of affection, and that the new rivalry of their marriages will only add to their " reciprocal tepidness." Besides, all they have to hope for will come from friendship with the Dauphine, " who eclipses them as much by her personal attractions as by the superiority of her rank."

In the evening of the marriage day there was a grand reception by the King, and his Majesty played lansquenet with the Royal family—and Madame du Barry. The Dauphine was the third player, and in one round she won over 1,200 louis [£1,152], and was as much embarrassed as vexed at her win. She "did the impossible" to lose it again, but, in spite of all her efforts, she was left at the close of play with 700 louis [£672] as her winnings. "The next morning, on her own initiative, she sent 50 louis [£48] to each of the two parishes of Versailles, for the poor ; and declared she would keep none of the remainder. I proposed to the Dauphine to make presents of it to the poor and deserving servants in her employment, to whom eighteen months' wages is still owing ; and her Royal Highness adopted this plan and carried it out instantly. This generosity gave me the greater pleasure because the Dauphine has rarely shown any disposition towards generosity."

The wages of the unfortunate Royal servants were in chronic arrears, even the footmen of the King being reduced to imploring charity from the priest of the parish. The only establishment that was on a business footing, where the wages were paid regularly, was the Parc-aux-cerfs ; in this the servants' wages amounted to 150,000 livres a year [£6,000], the "recruiting service," indemnities to families, dowries, presents, and expenses of the children, cost 2,000,000 livres per annum [£80,000] more, and the total annual payments were four to five million livres [about £180,000] ; and as this emporium was maintained for thirty-four years, the exchequer, however empty to national needs, was able to produce in that time well over £6,000,000 for the Parc-aux-cerfs.

The marriage ceremonies of the Comte d'Artois were marred by two unfortunate events; in the evening, at the masked ball, numbers of " richly dressed " thieves entered with the Court guests, and stole innumerable snuff-boxes, watches, purses, and even clocks ; and so great was the pressure and con-fusion, that Madame du Barry herself was nearly knocked down. To the young man who rushed to her assistance, and saved her from a possible bruise, the King gave a pension of 6,000 livres [£240] from his privy purse.

The retiring pension (as was noted at the time) of a Colonel, after thirty years' service, was 2,000 livres [£80].

The other occurrence of ill-omen was the sudden death of the Marquis de Chauvelin in the King's presence. He had played whist with his Majesty, and was just laughing at some joke of the Maréchale de Mirepoix, when he fell dead upon the ground. M. de Chauvelin was an old and intimate friend of Louis XV., and his sudden death so touched his Majesty that he remembered the occurrence for quite a week ; and when, on a drive to Choisy, the coach stopped, as one of the horses had fallen dead, the King remarked : " How odd ! Just like poor Chauvelin ! "

Mercy relates the increasing credit of the Dauphine, especially with that barometer of the King's favour, the Abbé Terray, Comptroller-General. Terray had come to Mercy and expressed his intention of fulfilling

to the utmost any demands for " pecuniary graces "
that her Royal Highness might desire ; and this, to
the vigilant Mercy, was proof that the time-serving
Terray recognised in the Dauphine the counter-balance
to Madame du Barry, as well as his future Queen.
Mercy remarked that the offer of unlimited drafts upon
the Royal exchequer showed that Terray believed the
opportunity would be exercised by Marie Antoinette
with discretion ; as it was matter of common knowledge
that the *daily* demands from the Comte de Provence
and the Comte d'Artois (the Dauphin never drew an
order), and still more from Mesdames, were constantly
refused, " which establishes and manifests the total
discredit of these Princes and Princesses."

Of course, there was no limit to the demands of
Madame du Barry ; and of her carelessness in money
matters and the way her signature was exploited there
are many stories.   One is said greatly to have amused
Louis and the du Barry herself.   A Jew jeweller, with
a long overdue account, prepared a very small and very
charming piece of jewellery and brought it to Madame
du Barry ; who gave him audience in bed (she usually
received her callers, wrapped in lace, and upon her
gilt bed).   As he foresaw, Madame du Barry, delighted
with the little trifle, told him to draw out the bill
for it and she would sign a draft on M. Beaujon,
the Court banker.   When M. Beaujon met her,
he reproached her with extravagance.   " Such a
fuss about a trifle," said she ; and then found that
she had signed the draft made out with great acumen

by the jeweller for 66,000 francs [£2,640], the whole amount of the overdue bill.

Her own chief extravagances, however, were upon the arts ; and she was a generous patron of painters and artistic workers at a Court where, from Louis downwards, no one had either taste or perception in the fine arts. Whenever she saw an admirable picture she bought it, even if it had been a commission for some one else ; and once, in Vernet's studio, she seized two sea-pieces, made the Duc de Cossé-Brissac and de Vaudreuil carry them off to her carriage, and finding the stump of a pen and a scrap of paper, hastily left in their stead an order for 50,000 livres [£2,000] payable at sight, upon the Court banker.

In Mercy's secret despatch he tells the Empress that her son Joseph II. had written to consult 18 December, him about his proposed journey to France ;   1773. which, as inspired by de Rohan, was considered by her a direct effort of malevolence. Mercy writes that the Emperor's views were in no wise of the Rohan spirit ; that his intentions were to see and study everything interesting in a great monarchy— resources, administration, agriculture, finances, commerce, police, navy, and army ; to avoid society, to go to no dinner, supper, or other entertainment. But, above all, his desire was to see the Dauphine, to make the personal acquaintance of the King, and to judge for himself the present situation and future prospects of the Court, remaining, as far as possible, in the strictest simplicity of incognito. Mercy reminds the

Empress that as long ago as 1770, the year of the marriage, the Emperor had already planned a tour in France; and he gives his whole weight in favour of the proposed journey (which did not, however, take place until 1777).

Mercy says : " The whole subject of this Court and of this monarchy is one full of varied possibilities, for good and for ill, but very interesting to investigate, especially when this investigation is carried on without bias, without prejudices, and with an open mind, which would be the case with the Emperor." And he gives, incidentally, an instance of the administration that Joseph II. is to study. The Empress had sent two letters and a packet of money to Mercy, to be sent to the Maréchal de Lacy. Mercy says that a mere letter, he found, could be sent by a trustworthy man on horseback ; but that this commission, of doubtless important papers, could only be despatched safely to the south of France by a responsible man, in a coach, with all things necessary for such a journey ; and that he had obtained the messenger and equipment from the Prince de Starhemberg.

He adds that the Maréchal de Lacy is living a very retired life in Montpellier, that he has seen no one, and has refused the visit of the officers of the garrison ; that his face shows signs of great illness, that his servants are few, and his living unassuming ; and he dismisses Frederick of Prussia's suspicion, that Lacy is being enticed into the service of the King of France, as " unseemly and absurd."

The last days of 1773 bring a very heavy blow to Marie Thérèse, of which she writes to Mercy. This was the resignation from office of the Prince de Kaunitz (whose signature is so familiar upon documents of the period), the faithful and able minister of the Austrian Royal family for thirty-three years. The position in the Austrian Empire was one of much domestic difficulty. When the husband of Marie Thérèse died, she associated her son Joseph II. with her in the Government; and from 1765 until the date of her death in 1780 the differences of policy between mother and son produced incessant and most painful discords, the political effects of which are seen in the resignation, first of Lacy and now of Kaunitz.

Marie Thérèse writes to Mercy : " I am sending you, by a safe channel, a letter that will give you as much pain as it gave me. I send it in the utmost secrecy, and you will burn it with this letter. Unhappily, the same causes have influenced Kaunitz that drove away Lacy and made Starhemberg go to Brussels. Imagine my position ; it is such that my one hope is that it is impossible to last. There can never be any chance for Starhemberg to take this post. The Emperor has neither regard nor affection for him. He would be miserable, which he does not deserve ; but they all think of you. Tell me sincerely, not as your Sovereign but as your friend, can I count upon you to take it ? And in that case, who could replace you ? I confess that my poor daughter enters into all these considerations ; but the welfare of the State bids this sentiment be silent.   I have patched up, or rather plastered over, things, as I will make no changes until peace is signed, but that may happen at any moment ; and Kaunitz, who is really ageing, may fail me altogether, so that I can remain no longer in this uncertainty."

The letter of Kaunitz places his resignation on the ground of the fatigues of age, which oblige him to vacate his post ; and he says that it would be in the interests of the Empress herself to find some more active successor, as he was now sixty-two, and feeble.

But this was a pretext only, for he remained in office for nineteen years longer, retaining the ministry until 1792.

CHAPTER XXII

Office of Austrian Minister declined by Mercy—De
Rohan, his Excesses and Excuses—*Ecrasez l'Infâme*
—Household of the Comte d'Artois—Diamond
Earrings for the Dauphine, from Madame du
Barry—The Dauphin's Sense of Humour—The
Princes of the Blood—Princesse Marie Christine
de Saxe—Opera Balls—Louis' Conscience and his
Confessor.

THE compliment paid by the Empress in inviting
Mercy to take the highest office in the Austrian
Ministry was weighed by him with every consideration ; but against ambition was set health, for,
although Mercy was only fifty-two years old at this
time, his life had been passed in diplomacy in many
countries, and he writes that he is unwilling to place
further strain upon his strength.

" I have always thought the political administration
of a great monarchy the most difficult of
all employments. It demands a mind so
wide and so just that it can seize and unite
all interests ; it demands the knowledge, gathered in
detail, that shapes the subject to which it is given ; it
demands unceasing work to retain touch with every-

Paris,
9 January,
1774.

thing, to gather up the threads and weave them into action, to decide the measures to be adopted, and to guide subordinates. I am not cloaking myself in false modesty when I tell your Majesty that I certainly have not the quality of mind necessary to combine so many different points of view. Enclosed up to now in the circle defined by your Majesty's interests : armed against only one Court at a time ; and guided by instructions upon the path to be pursued, I feel that my mind would but meander over general combinations. . . . I doubt whether at my age I could acquire the new and necessary learning, even after the longest study. The study of it, added to other work, would wear me out ; and I should fail beneath the weight of my office before I had rendered myself useful in it. My health has suffered since my residence in Russia and Poland, and I can only sustain it by the adoption of a strict regimen of exercise. . . . In addition, it would be an inexpressible grief to me to leave the Dauphine. This Princess, who found me here in the first moments of her arrival, when all was new to her and much was full of fear, has honoured me with her confidence, knowing my uprightness, my zeal and my respectful devotion to her. The Dauphin, too, from the same reasons, shows me a favour that is given to few. In short, I feel that here I serve, with usefulness, both the Dauphine and your Majesty. The King has broken through his custom, and speaks openly to me, so that I am in a position to speak directly to him ; and this could not be done by any successor to my post. If, therefore, I listened to my ambition, I should be leaving a post where I am of real service to take up one in which I should be certain to fail."

The interminable de Rohan difficulty continues; Mercy assures the Empress that both the Prince de Soubise and the Comtesse de Marsan are acting in good faith to try and obtain his recall, but the Duc d'Aiguillon is the obstacle; as he believes that if he can delay the recall until the Empress's patience finally gives out, de Rohan will be packed off in open disgrace, which would suit d'Aiguillon much better than to see the scandal hidden and de Rohan recalled without public degradation.

A letter from de Rohan to a friend of his finds itself (as do so many others) in the hands of Mercy. It had been written in December 1773; and reads like an outburst from a hysterical woman: "They have tried all sorts of rascality against me, even to finding faults in my accounts. But on that point I have been immovable. I proved their falseness. I wrote a terrible letter to the Bureau, with all the haughtiness that such details inspire me and all the contempt such roguery deserves."

(The errors in the accounts referred to the gross smuggling that de Rohan had carried on in defiance of all diplomatic conventions, until the loss to the revenue obliged the Austrian Government to remove all customs privileges from the ministers of every foreign Court.)

" These scoundrels have even attacked my reputation in the priesthood. This would have succeeded, but that I awoke in time. I wrote to the King, and said that I have various disagreeables to endure here and that enemies had been trying to arouse the scruples of the Empress."

This champion of the priesthood gives point to the description of Dom Bequet, the Benedictine, who defined the steps to sanctity, as " *Moinaille, prêtraille, puis la mitraille, et enfin la réligion* " as if grapeshot were the only fruit of such forerunners.

And this opinion of the French Church was endorsed by Catherine of Prussia and Frederick the Great, in their correspondence with Voltaire, who ended all his letters with the mystic abbreviation " *écr. l'Inf.*" All these letters were opened by the French police, who were puzzled for years by the incomprehensible sign, which, to those who knew, meant " *Ecrasez l'Infâme* " —Crush this Iniquity !

Mercy says that the household of the Comte and 19 January, Comtesse d'Artois is turning out as was 1774. expected. " The Comte d'Artois is now emancipated (at sixteen) from even the very light control of his governors ; and is revealing daily proofs of a character, unbalanced, impulsive, and haughty. He has already drawn upon himself severe lectures from the Dauphin, to whom he has shown lack of respect." The irreverent d'Artois had hissed the clumsy dancing of the Dauphin, who, in return, had kicked, fraternally the Prince, now Colonel of the Suisses regiment ; and the Dauphine had been obliged to interpose between the brothers.

Marie Antoinette's method was to chaff the absurd assumptions of d'Artois, whom ridicule galled, who therefore feared her wit ; and she was the only person who had any control over him. He defied the favourite and the whole of the ruling party ; forbade his wife to speak to Madame du Barry and to any of the ladies of her society ; and announced loudly that they had composed his household of such an " assembly of specimens " (selected by Madame du Barry, with one exception), that he should get rid of them all upon the first opportunity ; which was reported to the King, and made his Majesty extremely frigid.

The Comtesse d'Artois remained an absolute nullity, in spite of the Dauphine's efforts to thaw her out of her constraint. " She shows her complete lack of agreeable qualities ; she never speaks, she takes no interest in anything, and her air of timidity and indifference is that which, above all others, displeases in this country."

Mercy gives a curious proof of the endeavours of the favourite to obtain a favourable regard from the Dauphine. " A Paris jeweller possesses a pair of diamond earrings, formed of four brilliants of extraordinary size and beauty ; they are estimated to be worth 700,000 livres [£28,000]. The Comtesse du Barry, knowing that the Dauphine loves precious stones, persuaded the Comte de Noailles to show her these diamonds; and to tell her that if her Royal Highness found them to her taste and would like to keep them, she need not trouble herself about either price or payment, as means would be found whereby they would be presented to her as a gift from the King."

These incessant endeavours to win toleration by the Comtesse du Barry seem rather pathetic in their entire inappropriateness to the Dauphine, probably the only woman at Court who, in face of so delicately arranged an offering, would have replied, she "had quite enough diamonds and did not intend increasing their number."

Even Mercy thinks that the favourite is showing herself in a generous light in adverse circumstances. "For it is certain that this plan was entirely her own. If it had been due to the advice of her counsellors I should have been the first to be asked. And I observe further that this attitude of respectful desire to please is not encouraged by any change that might have taken place in the Dauphine. It is true that for a long time her Royal Highness has ceased from making mortifying remarks, and even from any sign of either aversion or hate ; but this better treatment is only negative, and it necessitates my being continually on the watch to lay stress upon the improvement, and to read a meaning into it of which it is not always susceptible. . . .

"With regard to the Dauphin, he gives his wife all his esteem and friendship, and adds thereto as much tenderness as his character permits ; and beyond that, a docility without limits.   The Dauphine has the improvement of her husband greatly at heart ; she thinks sometimes that she is not succeeding and grows very downcast.   On these occasions I dilate on how much the Dauphin improves and is changing daily ; and encourage her to hope that with sweetness and reasoning she will succeed. . . .

" The Monday balls given by the Dauphine and the Wednesday fêtes at the house of the Comtesse de Noailles are of use to the Dauphin ; they accustom him to see people and to speak."

The extraordinary behaviour of the Dauphin, at all times, gave rise to curious incidents.   He would often advance directly upon a courtier, driving him up against a wall, stand in front of him, and if nothing occurred to him to say (which was nearly always the case), he would burst into a roar of coarse, open-mouthed laughter ; and go.   He insisted upon wrestling with some of the chief men at Court— M. de Conflans or M. de Coigny, for instance—and, without any malicious intention, injured them severely. Upon one occasion he nearly strangled the Prince de Ligne.   But it was not ruffianism, only his method of taking exercise.

Whenever any one spoke to him on any interest-ing subject, it was mere waste of breath, for the Duc de Lauzun writes :   " The only answers he ever gave were those of an idiot or a sporting man."

The Dauphine studies for nearly two hours every day, in spite of amusements, of sledge drives, of theatres and balls ; gives as much time to her music as to her dancing, and has become so perfect in this latter accomplishment that she " has very little left to learn " as Mercy notes.

The prospect of the Emperor Joseph's visit to France, then believed to be in the immediate future, forms a great subject of correspondence ; as Mercy is desirous of presenting the best side of the French nation to a monarch decidedly hostile to the French, of Radical views, and the desire for furious and universal reform.   Mercy says :   " We must expect that the Emperor will be struck at first with a sort of pity and contempt for the individuals who are members of the actual Government of France. . . . One of my first endeavours must be to prepare his Majesty for this, and to induce him to suspend judgment. He has so much wit and luminous knowledge that I shall find no difficulty in showing him that beneath these infinite annoyances and miseries, there are great and good qualities in the national character ; that this kingdom has astonishing natural resources ; and that France deserves much attention from all Powers that are in a position to make her enter into an alliance. . . . As to the idea of his Majesty, to go and see Voltaire, Tissot, and Haller, I think it will come to naught. . . . I shall have that to say of Voltaire which will remove any wish to see him.   Tissot is a doctor and Haller a poet, neither eminent enough to merit the notice of the Emperor. . . and they give examples in their private lives, their works, and their detestable principles, of everything that is calculated to overthrow society and foment disorder. . ."

The one point upon which Mercy asks for full instructions is the view the Emperor Joseph takes of Madame du Barry and her position. When the King of Sweden was in Paris he had supper with the favourite, and gave her many marks of favour ; and Mercy foresaw that the arrival of the next Royal visitor would certainly be taken by the favourite as a tribute to herself ; and she would assuredly found all manner of hopes upon it. Fortunately for the uneasy Mercy, this tax upon his diplomatic powers did not arrive ; when Joseph II. came to France, Louis XVI. was King and the favourite lived sequestered in Louveciennes. So it was Joseph's determination to see the favourite, not Madame du Barry's insistence upon her recognition as *maîtresse en titre*, that brought about a meeting.

The diamond earring episode called forth approving comments from Marie Thérèse. " My daughter was quite right to refuse these jewels at the hands of the favourite. It is a point upon which I am fastidious," (Marie Thérèse *gave* jewels to Madame de Pompadour, she did not *take* them from her), " and I cannot pardon the weakness of the Empress of Russia in taking a present from her subject, Orloff, who gave her a superb diamond ; which she accepted and even made a parade of the acceptance."

Vienna, 3 February, 1774.

But the Semiramis of the North had other reasons for this acceptance than a love of stones.

"There is a new proof of the impertinence and indiscretion of Rohan. He is spreading everywhere here that I wrote a letter to my daughter, the Queen of Naples, a memorandum on the subject of Poland . . . in which, Rohan pretends, I complained, in no measured terms, of the Emperor . . . and this fell into the hands of the Marquis de Tanucci, and by him was given to the Ambassador from France to Naples. Imagine my astonishment ; and this is the second time. Once before he quoted from a letter purporting to be from me to the Dauphine, and now he dares quote me a second time. I have never written anything to my daughter about Poland ; but the most malicious touch is the mention of the Emperor, with whom, as I have already told you, Rohan is too much mixed up. He amuses the Emperor, but he is spiteful and does much harm. . . . I wish the Emperor would accept your views upon France ; because he is always being set against the French nation. All the world here is at present English, adopting even their opinions, ways, fashions, and language ; but I think there should be higher ambition for the greater number of our young nobles than to degenerate into grooms."

In a short while the English modes conquered France also ; and the intimacy of the Duc de Chartres (*Egalité* to be) with the Prince of Wales was productive of many importations, including hunting equipage, top boots, saddles, and "jokeis."

" The suite of the Emperor will not predispose him towards France : the General Comte de Nostitz, who is selected, is a sworn foe to the French ; the Maréchal de Lacy [the supposed ally of France] is the same. . . . I shall tell the Emperor that it is indispensable for you to accompany him if he makes a tour in the provinces. . . . I have no doubt there will be scheming to get the Emperor to have supper with the favourite. . . . I have nothing against it.   I believe the Emperor will go out of curiosity . . . but if my son Maximilian goes to Paris I think he is too young to take part in these entertainments of the favourite. . . . He goes to Paris at the New Year ; he will not sparkle after his brother. . . . With regard to Kaunitz, I have patched up matters for the present. . . . Your own decision I approve ; your health and your happiness interest me, and my own yield place to those of my friends to whom I owe as much gratitude as I do to you."

One of the first signs of the jealousy of the Orléans family against Marie Antoinette (afterwards developed into the mad ambition that **19 February, 1774.** signed the death warrant of Louis XVI. with the *Egalité* signature), arose over a mere trifle, the social demands of a lady called Madame de Blot. She wished to have the privilege of the grand entry at Court, as she was lady-in-waiting to the Duchesse de Chartres.   There was the usual instant kindling of intrigue, burning the more fiercely because Marie Antoinette declined to meddle in the matter.   This was taken as a deadly insult by—the Duc de Chartres, who was much interested in Madame de Blot ; and the suggestion by Marie Antoinette to the Duchesse de Chartres that her lady-in-waiting should be more circumspect when she mentioned the Dauphine's name, did not lessen the grudge that was borne against her.

The pretentious claims of the Princes of the Blood served Mercy for many homilies ; for there was no disguising the fact that they were popular with the people, owing to their resistance to the King's authority.   Their banishment from Court had lowered the King's prestige, not their own ; and made his Majesty unpopular, " or, what is synonymous in that country, *unfashionable*," said Walpole.   Mercy was on his guard against these assumptions, recognising that the King was determined to repress them ; but the schemes of the Duc de Chartres, who was playing for a crown, did not become dangerous until the birth of an heir to the throne rendered them desperate.

Chief among the Princes of the Blood was the Prince de Conti, known as " The last of the Princes," from his personal graces and grand air.   He had attained his greatest power when favoured by Madame de Châteauroux ; was disgraced by the wish of Madame de Pompadour ; and carried with him into exile the affection of the people (he is said to be the only member of the Bourbon family who retained it), together with the consolation granted him by Louis XV., of his appointment as chief of the "secret" correspondence that De Broglie was now exploiting.

The head of the house of Condé, who had supported the cause of "the people" against the King in the question of the Parliaments, was now extremely anxious to be reconciled ; as no patriotism could be expected to stand against the Prince's desire for the post of Director of Artillery. But with all wish to grasp again the benefits of the system of despotism that he had so ostentatiously withstood, the Prince de Condé had not sufficient self-control to mask his irritation at the failure of his scheme for the aggrandisement of the Princes at the cost of the Crown ; and even in begging this favour he sent with his request so "abusive" a letter, as Mercy calls it, that it was ill calculated to win a grace.

Mercy tells a little detail that shows the kind thought of the Dauphine, and, incidentally, the curious lacunae in the etiquette of the French Court. After the death of Marie Josèphe de Saxe (the late Dauphine), her sister, Marie Christine de Saxe, came to live in Paris. She was joint Abbess of Remiremont with the Princesse Charlotte de Lorraine, that near relation of the Empress Marie Thérèse, to whom the Dauphine was constantly sending charitable gifts. But although she was the aunt of the Dauphin, and his brothers and sisters, and thus very closely connected with the Royal family, she had been permitted to take up her abode in a hôtel. "By a sort of forgetfulness that it is difficult to explain, no one had thought of the impropriety of the aunt of the Dauphin lodging in an inn."

There were immense suites of empty apartments in the numerous Royal palaces ; and such surplus of Royal residences in the country that they crumbled from lack of living in, as well as from the impossibility of finding enough money to repair them. The Louvre stood empty, " they are not attempting any repairs in it ; and the project of economy, formed by the Comptroller-General (Terray) of abandoning some of the superfluous Royal houses, met with so much opposition from those persons at Court who drew revenues for looking after them, that it has naturally fallen through."

When, in the natural course of events, the Princesse Christine de Saxe was reduced to begging for the arrears of her pension, the fact of the forgotten aunt in an inn came to the knowledge of the Dauphine ; who intimated that if there were no rooms in Versailles, she would lodge the Princesse in her own apartments. Whereupon a suitable suite was at once discovered at Versailles.

The balls at the Opera continued, and on 30 January and on 9 February the three Princes and three Princesses had gone to them. On the first occasion they retained their incognito almost completely, as they did not unmask ; the second time the public discovered their identity, although they were still masked, and applauded loudly. Much comment of an approving kind was made (in Paris) upon the fact that the Dauphin had spoken to all alike, no matter whom he met, without distinction of persons, and had given several examples of "that kind of humorous jest suited to the locality."

This graceful humour of the Dauphin found vent nightly at the ceremony of the Royal "*coucher*." It was the duty of one great noble to remove his Royal Highness's shirt, and of another to put the night-shirt over his head; and the Duc de Lauzun records that "he believed it funny to make grimaces at the personage who handed it, to bob aside, to avoid the garment, to let himself be pursued with it, laughing all the time '*à gorge déployée*.'" And this, while half-naked, in the presence of the whole Court and often of strangers of distinction.

In his secret report Mercy reveals a curious state of things in the inmost circle of the Court. The whole of the bubble of du Barry-dom may burst at any moment. Balanced on the see-saw between Louis' conscience and his constitution, the "*Aiguillonistes*" and "*Barrins*" watched the decline of his physical health with the certain knowledge that it would imply, as it had always implied, the increase of activity of conscience. They remembered the scene at Metz, when the beautiful Duchesse de Châteauroux (so indispensable that at every halting stage of the vast army "a wooden gallery must be run up between their lodgings") had to fly, ignominiously driven from the side of a Louis whose conscience had been fever-stimulated.

They watched the mind and body fail; and knew

Paris, 19 February, 1774.

that this indicated a phase of virtue that would make its peace with Heaven by discarding its out-worn vices.

And Mercy watched their growing uneasiness, their dread of the time when the King's feebleness would reach the point of overbalance ; and the rise of conscience sweep them away, with all their chances gone.

This fear was growing active, for the signs of a shattered senility were obvious now in Louis. He spoke often of his age, a subject usually tabooed. He said to la Martinière, his doctor : " I have been going too fast ; I must put on the drag." " Sire, you had better *unharness* ! " said the doctor.

He now spoke of his failing health, which it would ill-beseem a courtier to notice first. He was dis-agreeably shocked by the deaths, from exhausted age, of men of his own years. Three persons of his familiar acquaintance—the Marquis de Chauvelin, the Maréchal d'Armentières, and the Abbé de la Ville—had been so ill-advised as to fall dead in his very presence. He had been heard to say that he feared he should have to give a terrible account to the Creator of his misspent time on earth. And in token of repentance of sin, he went so far as to countermand a new coach that he had intended to offer to Madame du Barry. For a whole fort-night in January he had abstained from ascending, even once, the little staircase that led to the rooms of the favourite. The whole forces of du

Barry-dom were arrayed to smother this little germ of repentance.

It was beyond their power to recuperate the vitality of a man whose life was being worn out by exhaustion ; so they directed their attention towards the prevention of any mental stimulus of the uneasy conscience. Unfortunately the King's confessor, the Abbé Maudoux, was a man of unblemished character, virtuous, honourable, truthful, the last man to prophesy deceits to his Majesty or to soothe the guilty soul by smooth suggestions of easy pardon. Further, he was also the confessor of the Dauphine, who greatly respected him, so that the task of removing him from his office was delicate ; although urgently necessary in view of the continuance of the King's feebleness and consequent religious tendency.

The first step was to insinuate to the King that the eyesight of the Abbé Maudoux had become so weak that he intended to retire from the Court altogether ; and but for Mercy this plan would have succeeded, as Louise (of the Carmelites) had been induced to lend her not unwilling self to the intrigue. By explaining the matter to the Dauphine, she was induced to act, and a direct appeal from her to the King not to remove the confessor in whom she had confidence, brought the reply that he would never take from the Dauphine the spiritual adviser of her choice ; and, in fact, he himself considered the Abbé Maudoux the best person possible as a confessor.

So ended this attempt ; the others, to make sure

a footing in the next reign, in view of the imminent passing of this one, commenced upon a paving of diamond earrings.

Well could Marie Thérèse exclaim in her reply :

Vienna, 8 March, 1774 "This intrigue hatched against the confessor of the King and of my daughter fills me with horror. How I pity this good Prince, fettered in a prison-house of his own unworthy favourites. The only ‚hope is in the compassion of God, who in pity for the good (but wavering) feelings of this unhappy Sovereign, may, at the last, open his eyes to the danger in which he lies, of being dragged to eternal perdition."

CHAPTER XXIII

The Comtesse de Mailly—Family Spites—The Comte
d'Artois—Visit of the Maréchal de Lacy—"*Le
Bien-aimé de l'Almanach*"—The *Œil de Bœuf*—
Exit Madame du Barry—Death of Louis XV.—
The Chase to St. Denis

IT is long since Mercy had occasion to complain of
Mesdames as active enemies of the career of
Marie Antoinette ; and in the belief that their
spite was nullified by the growing independence of
the Dauphine, he had simply dismissed their brooding
and sulks as unworthy of notice. However he now
became aware that these ladies, at first angry at loss
of power, then annoyed at their failure to regain
influence by flattery and pleasures, had now taken
to a line of conduct that showed a systematic scheme
to be-little the Dauphine.

He writes : "These aunts make a study of pre-
venting occasions upon which the Dauphine 22 March,
might do some good action, and so win 1774
further admiration and applause from the public.
They try to check the belief in her goodness and
benevolence, sometimes by little mis-placed criticisms,
sometimes by engineering small embarrassments of
etiquette, or similar obstacles of which it is easy to

345

see the aim. . . . Among the ladies connected with the household of the Dauphine is a Comtesse de Mailly, to whom she is, with good reason, attached. She is young, gentle, intelligent, sincere, quiet, and far removed from intrigue. This lady had an only son, whose loss has thrown her into the bitterest grief. The Dauphine, touched with her sorrow, announced that she intended to call upon the Comtesse de Mailly in her own home in Paris.

Every one was delighted with this kind feeling, but Mesdames raised all possible objections and said it had never been the usage of the Princesses of the Royal family to call upon any one outside the Court ; and they backed up this objection by every possible bad reason.

The Dauphine, by now, was a match for these aunts. She wrote direct to the King, telling him of her desire to go and give to the Comtesse de Mailly comfort, although it was not customary ; and the reply was : "My dear daughter, although we are not accustomed to pay outside visits, you are the mistress of your own good heart, and can do whatever it dictates to you for this poor woman."

So the Dauphine went and called upon the Comtesse de Mailly ; and the little act of sympathy had all the effect possible upon a public to whom such acts of compassion from the Princes and Princesses of the Royal family were unknown.

The two sisters, the Comtesses de Provence and d'Artois, were filled even more than Mesdames with the petty jealousy that admiration of the Dauphine induced—the disagreeable, stiff, cross little Madame d'Artois raising quite an angry voice because the Dauphine's supper one night was served before her own ; the sly Madame de Provence, under guise of soft friendship, going to the Dauphin to obtain from him some proof of disapproval of his wife's love of balls, "for she seems only to take pleasure in these frivolities."

The dull Dauphin was not so stupid, however, as to miss the malice; and he came to Marie Antoinette and told her, adding that it would save all trouble if he announced comprehensively that he approved of everything she did, and would never stop her amusements.

"Upon which," says Mercy "the conversation became very tender and amicable."

The chaos of the Court and its incredible confusion, disorder, and desperate jealousies have reached a pitch that taxes all Mercy's wits, to keep in touch himself and yet shield the Dauphine entirely from them. He even writes with joy that the weather has been so bad she has been obliged to stay in her rooms, and thus spend the whole day in innocent employments ; and he is thankful for even stress of bad weather that may save an outbreak for a few days. He says he has glimmerings of a plot against Madame du Barry, "but I cannot get at it in this fog of deceit"; that the Duc d'Aiguillon (her creature) is displeased with her, because she is "inconsiderate and grasping and tactless." He had taken all the six years of her power to discover these qualities, and the end of it was now very near.

In his letter of 19 April, Mercy details still further the development of the sisters of Savoy "with the well-marked Piedmontese character," as Marie Thérèse describes them. At least the Comte and Comtesse de Provence maintain an outward appearance of sleek decorum, although the Prince is meddling in politics above his age, and is well followed in intrigue by the Princesse ; but as long as no trust is placed in them, or their words or their actions, no harm will come. But it is different with the Comte and Comtesse d'Artois. "They are adopting so disagreeable and unsuitable a tone that the whole Court is repelled by it. The young Prince treats the ministers badly, and gives his orders to them in a violent and imperious manner. He has no regard for any one. In every arrangement of his household there is the utmost disorder ; he affronts every one attached to his suite, and all, in consequence, serve him with dislike and without the slightest willingness. On several occasions he has been intemperate in drinking ; he is much addicted to gambling, and plays for, and insists upon, very high stakes in his own house. This last impropriety will have very serious results in this Court. . . . I have begged the Dauphine to discountenance any such disorders. . . .

"Up to now she has been able to influence the

(marginal note:) Paris, 19 April, 1774.

Comte d'Artois by gentle ridicule, but it seems that even that check upon him has lost its power; and it will be the more difficult to restrain or control this young Prince, as the King will not exercise any authority over him. . . . The Comtesse d'Artois has no quality that could supplement the defects of her husband. One cannot make out whether her disdainful and repellant air arises from a haughty spirit or lack of wit; but whichever it be it has the same effect, which is highly disadvantageous to this Princess, and makes her more and more disliked. . . . In comparison with his brothers the Dauphin shines. Under a rough exterior he has frankness of character, regularity of habits, and a desire to do the best in his power."

The three brothers are described by M. de Créquy as: " *Un gros serrurier ; un bel esprit de café de province ; un faraud des boulevards.*" (A fat locksmith ; the wit of a country bar ; a boulevard fribble). The most worthy was the dull, half-alive Dauphin.

It had been decided that the Court should spend the spring at Marly. "The favourite, who plans this sort of thing, imagines that by this arrangement she will procure for herself more kindly treatment from the Royal family ; and in this hope the journey has been fixed for the month of May. But I do not believe it will take place, and am relieved to think so, because these visits to Marly involve the Royal family in spending the evenings in the chosen society of the King; from this result endless disputes, quarrels, remarks, and annoyances which only embitter all minds." This journey, the last planned by the favourite, never took place.

At this time the much-discussed Maréchal de Lacy made a visit to Paris, where Mercy organised him a most flattering reception by all the persons of importance—including Madame du Barry. The Dauphine was overjoyed to see him again; and was so charming and so attractive that after his interview of three quarters of an hour with her, the Maréchal left, quite speechless with enchantment. Marie Antoinette had talked to him of her mother, her eyes filling with tears as she said that the pleasure of one day seeing her again was the only thing lacking to her happiness. She showed him the diamond ornament her mother had sent her, and the porcelain vase, with its paintings of Schönbrunn and Laxenbourg. She spoke of her love of the Emperor, and all her family; and in mentioning her husband, showed the present that the Dauphin had made her the evening before, of a very fine pink diamond in the form of a heart, surmounted by another large green diamond, forming a jewel to wear at her neck, which Mercy estimated to be worth 50 or 60,000 francs [£2,400]; and she had finally made so many pretty speeches to the Maréchal himself that nothing could exceed her gaciousness.

There are no more gay, casual notes upon trifles. The horror of impending death is upon Versailles

and the Court.   Not upon the country nor in Louis'
own Paris is the horror ; rather impatience,   May,
and irritation, and much disgust.   1774.

> " *Le Bien-Aimé de l'almanach*
> *N'est pas le bien-aimé de France . . .*
> *Il met tout dans le même sac,*
> *Et la justice et la finance ;*
> *Le Bien-Aimé de l'almanach*
> *N'est pas le bien-aimé de France.*"

The crowd in Paris is far too much occupied with
preparing epitaphs, to trouble to find out if they
are yet required.   Upon the statue of Louis XV,
is found one morning written :

> " *Grotesque monument, infâme piédestal,*
> *Les vertus sont à pied, le vice est à cheval.*"

First comes a bulletin from Versailles to announce
that " the King has been seized with a
violent fever," on his return from the Petit   28 April.
Trianon on Thursday.   Rumours gather and thicken,
but nothing is thought of the ailment ; least of all in
Paris.   Even in the Court the Doctor Senac had said
that unless the King took violent exercise he risked
falling into the " *affaiblissement d'esprit*," the weakening
of the mind that has threatened him for so long.
(One of Louis XVI.'s first acts of sovereignty was
to disgrace the doctors for omitting to cure his grand-
father).   Besides, the Dauphin always took to his bed
after eating pastry.

But the next day the King is worse.   Still the
doctors are not alarmed, as the King had had smallpox ;

certainly it had been some time ago—in October 1728

29 April. (forty-six years ago)—and it was possible to have it two or three times. But rumours are strengthened by the development of smallpox amongst persons who had been—temporarily—connected with the Court. An official version then was published, that the King had been out riding; and had, with his customary compassion and interest in things morbid, approached a funeral procession, and learned upon inquiry that they buried a young girl, dead from smallpox; and that his Majesty was then struck with the disease.

But the unofficial version gained ground, and it

30 April. was said that both cases were of the malignant form—" very dangerous, although they try to hide it," writes Mercy.

On 1 May he writes again, for confluent smallpox

1 May. had developed in its fullest: the King is doomed; and already the parties of d'Aiguillon and du Barry, their "spies, intriguers, servile satellites, titled or not," are filled with wildest apprehensions, and commence preparations for flight. Mercy says: " In these first moments of so grave and critical a time, it was necessary to decide whether the Dauphine should ask permission to stay with the King, or to remain with the Dauphin. Each alternative has its merits and demerits. I have suggested that the Dauphin should decide; and at the moment I write I do not know what is resolved. . . . The Dauphine will no doubt tell your Majesty, but in the meantime

LOUIS XV.

(From the miniature at the Château d'Argenteau.)

[*Page* 351.

it is certain that her Royal Highness has offered to shut herself up with the King ; and she has at least the merit of having made the offer of sacrifice."

The decision was made by the King who refused to see either the Dauphin or Marie Antoinette. He sent his love to them and bade them, with an unselfishness that should be credited to him, to keep from the infection.

" I have foreseen that the favourite, in her present panic, may take upon herself to address the Dauphin or the Dauphine personally, to know their intentions ; that is to say, whether she is to leave the Court or to stay. And in prevision of such a possibility I have persuaded the Dauphine to make no reply ; and to content herself with saying that neither she nor her husband can have any decision as to the King's choice of society. This circumspection seems to me necessary ; for if the King confesses, it is for the ecclesiastics to drive out the favourite ; and if the monarch recovers from his sickness, it would be very dangerous that any one could attribute to the Dauphin the desire, in such a moment, to expel the Comtesse du Barry."

The dread of all is lest they fall between the two stools of sovereignity. If Louis die, they have run in vain the risk of the loathsome infection that tainted the whole Palace till through merely crossing the gallery at Versailles over fifty sicken and ten die : if he recovers, and they be found to have paid Court to the wrong party, their future may lie in a *lettre de cachet.* Some adroitly wait on both, turning their coats with the skill of supple practice ; though not so successfully but that their liveries are marked. Their coaches drive hereafter to Rueil, as well as to the Dauphine's door ; and for six years, it was remembered against them as a false move, and said of them : " There goes one of the fifteen carriages of Rueil."

Mercy coutinues : " Immediately after I despatch this express messenger I leave for Versailles, where I will remain whatever happens. . . . The Dauphine is revealing herself in the most touching light ; the Dauphin also is behaving quite suitably. . . . I am making preparation for all possible contingencies, that I may be of most service to the Dauphine. The moment is conclusive of the future of my career. . . . I trust that nothing may escape my vigilance."

The King seems better, and renewed hope springs in the hearts of the du Barry partisans. Report said that the improvement was due to the diplomacy of Madame du Barry, who had soothed the King's nerves with an adjusted medical bulletin ; and bribed two doctors to reassure his Majesty by a lie as to the nature of his disease. But they reckoned without the crass veracity—or maybe professional jealousy—of La Martinière, the King's Physician-in-Ordinary, who, bluntly explaining the King's symptoms, told him he had smallpox, of a virulent kind, and that at his age it was grave.

2 May.

To Louis' mind rushes the text of the last sermon

to which he had listened with such obvious disquiet :
" Yet forty days and Nineveh shall be 3 May.
destroyed." His conscience awakes with the
truth of disease : he sends for Madame du Barry.
The favourite, with courage not altogether unheroic
(Balzac says of smallpox : *La bataille de Waterloo
des femmes, le lendemain elles connaissent ceux qui les
aiment*), has faced the awful sick room daily, to cheer
up Louis with bright, light talk and gay stories ; and
she learns now that she is to be discarded. Louis
tells her that he has to remember he is " The Most
Christian King and the Eldest Son of the Church ; "
that he does not wish a recurrence of the scandal of
Metz ; that she had better go, and at once. Then,
with the forethought so markedly reflected in his
Court, he dilutes his sacrifice by saying : " You can
come back if you hear I am better."

And in the coach of the Duchesse d'Aiguillon, the
favourite drives off, with her support and 4 May.
that of Mademoiselle du Barry and of
Madame du Sure, to remain at Rueil until it is
decided whether her office, now vacant by stress of
circumstances, is to be again filled or not. As the
coach rolls away, Louis asks for her again, is told that
she has gone ; and sighs to find himself obeyed and
his spiritual welfare thus, perforce, advanced.

The next three days, the 5th, 6th, and 7th of May
pass ; and Louis' own therapeutics seem as ineffective
as the powdered elm-bark and other remedies of his
doctors. He sprinkles holy water with his own hand

on the bed, to exorcise the demons ; he sends money
to St. Sulpice, to Nôtre Dame, to the Capuchins,
that masses may be said ; he commands that the shrine
of St. Geneviève shall be opened on his behalf.   For
if one of his own ancestors and namesakes, Louis XIII.,
could solemnly ensure, by an enactment that placed
France under the protection of the Virgin Mary, that
"all his loyal subjects might be received into Paradise,
such being his goodwill and pleasure," then must
Louis XV. be able to make certain of the entrance
of one ; and that one—himself.

On Sunday, at midday, Mercy writes again, sending
the Empress a letter from Marie Antoinette,

8 May.

describing the condition of the King, and
saying that he has at last received the sacraments.
For by the night of the 7th, Louis felt his own efforts
were unavailing to procure for him the certainty
of Heaven ; and that other help must be obtained,
and that speedily.   "I am awaiting the news of last
night," writes Mercy ; "it was a critical time.   Up
to now there has been no accident . . . the disease
is following its usual course. . . . It appears it was
the King's own wish, without any suggestion given,
that his confessor (Abbé Maudoux) should be sent
for.   At half-past two in the morning, this desire was
expressed.   The Princes had their watches in hand and
counted sixteen minutes during which the confessor
was alone with the King, who, in the time from this
confession till the taking of the sacraments, called
him back three times."

The Duc d'Orléans, the Prince de Condé, are waiting, watch in hand, "*que cela finisse !* " The Duc de Richelieu ("that old piece of tawdry, worn-out, but endeavouring to brush itself up," as Walpole says), Duc de la Vrillière (corrupt vendor of desolation), his nephew, Duc d'Aiguillon ("a fine gentleman, of mean abilities ")—all three are in that ante-chamber endeavouring to persuade the willing Archbishop de Beaumont that a cardinal's hat would be a suitable reward for a man who did *not* "renew the scandal of Metz ; " and the Archbishop realises that upon Madame du Barry (member of the Order of Jesuits since 1772, and in receipt of the sacred scapulary) hang all the hopes of that Order.

"After confession (absolution had followed immediately), at five o'clock in the morning, the King sent for the Duc d'Aiguillon and whispered to him. They say it was to order him to remove the Comtesse du Barry further away ; but in these last days it is seen that the King is more devoted to the favourite than was imagined, and if his Majesty recovers from his illness it is to be believed, and yet more to be feared, that this woman will be recalled to the Court."

Though not while Mesdames guard the bedside of their father, expiating by this pious duty much, and expecting more ; nor while Abbé Maudoux holds the conscience of the King ; nor while La Martinière (still professionally resentful) can tell the King with his usual bluntness to "finish what your Majesty has begun."

"In so critical and delicate a conjunction the Dauphine has behaved like an angel ; and I cannot forbear expressing my admiration for her piety, prudence, and intelligence. The public [vigilant Mercy !] is delighted with her conduct, and with just cause. Her Royal Highness has remained in strictest privacy, seeing, beside the members of the Royal family, no one save the Abbé de Vermond and myself. I have done what I could to prepare the Dauphine for everything, both in the present and the future.

"If the King loses his life it would be of great benefit to the State if your Majesty would write to the Dauphine that she should ' be watchful and listen well to what he (Mercy) has to say on the great subjects that concern the alliance and the system of the two Courts.' This warning from your Majesty, by giving all the weight necessary to what I shall have to say, will fix the attention of the Dauphine, which has always been a little inclined to stray from serious things. It is necessary, for the safeguarding of her own happiness, that she should at once assume the authority that the Dauphin will never exercise except with vacillation ; and considering the nature of the people who form this Court, considering also the spirit that moves and guides them, it would be the greatest danger to the State, and also to the whole system of government, if the power were assumed by the Dauphin or if he were led by any one but the Dauphine. At this moment I receive the news from Versailles. The night passed fairly well, but at five this morning there was delirium . . . in any case the life of the King is in most imminent danger."

It had become known on the evening of the 9th that it was doubtful whether the King would live through the night, certain he could not **10 May.** live through the next day ; and from early morning, "by order of the Dauphin," all are dressed and in readiness for instant flight from the pestiferous Palace.   All the world gathers and waits—soldiers of the guard ready to march, pages holding horses, equerries in readiness, the great coach, to hold the six members of the Royal family, the Dauphin and Dauphine, the Comte and Comtesse de Provence, and the Comte and Comtesse d'Artois, stands harnessed ; the special coach is stationed apart, prepared to take Mesdames from the infected sick-room to their retreat prepared for the certainty of disease ; and every noble of the Court stays waiting for the signal to fly from the house of death, whether the signal be or not the candle extinguished by Madame Campan, and yet more extinguished by Carlyle.

Mercy writes from Versailles : "The King has been in the death agony since yesterday, he died this afternoon between three and four o'clock. His mind was clear, and at the last minute he gave signs of repentance and truly Christian piety." (His words, as given by the Cardinal de la Roche-Aymon, were that he declared he "repented of any scandal he might have given to his subjects, and that his only reason for wishing to live longer was the support of religion and the happiness of his people.")

"Everything here is in the greatest confusion. The Royal family goes to Choisy ; Mesdames will be in a separate house. I have taken her commands from the Queen who is well ; but her grief and the impossibility of leaving the King, her husband, prevent her from writing to your Majesty in this first moment. . . . Yesterday, when the catastrophe was assured, I had a long audience with the Queen ; and repeated all that seemed to me of use in the circumstances. Her Majesty understood me very well ; and I trust that I have convinced her. We must find out before anything if, and how much, the Queen will be consulted by the King. It would be dangerous for her to appear to wish to meddle in affairs before she is requested. . . . If the Queen is consulted I have advised her to induce the King to promise to change nothing in the Ministry until they have taken time to examine into affairs.

" I have also advised that measures shall be taken to reduce the price of bread in Paris within forty-eight hours. The people say aloud that they look for this favour from the Queen, who is adored."

It was after three when the King died ; by four the last of the Court has left the Palace of Versailles, so poisoned by the infection and by the multitude of perfumes that they had used to try and make them serve the function of disinfectants for ten days, that it stood empty and open for a week before the boldest would again enter it.

Quite gaily Louis XVI. and Queen Marie Antoinette drive away, crying a few tears, till the Comtesse d'Artois' strange mispronunciation in Savoy-French makes them laugh. Only the Duc d'Ayen has to stay, as Captain of the Scottish Guards, and the Duc d'Aumont as First Gentleman of the Chamber—and two scavengers from the Versailles gutters to place the body of Louis XV. in three coffins, and they died of that duty within twenty-four hours.

The funeral procession drove post-haste to St. Denis ; nothing but the urgency of this duty forcing the fulfilment of it upon its unwilling agents. On a hunting carriage ; followed by galloping men with torches ; no sign of mourning dress, not even the coach draped ; rattling through a double row of howling, cursing, malignant rioters, past the taverns full of drunken, rejoicing men—all alike hurling truths at the flying cavalcade in the darkness of night—to St. Denis ; where with shouts of " Tally Ho ! Tally Ho ! " the hunting carriage stops, and Louis XV. is *sealed* within his vault. " *Le Roi ne fera rien.*"

Lines of Condé and Conti.

1530. LOUIS I. DE BOURBON, uncle of Henri IV.

b. 1553, d. 1588. HENRI I., Prince de Condé.

b. 1588, d. 1646. HENRI II.

Condé line:

b. 1621, d. 1686. LOUIS II., Prince de Condé, "Grand Condé," Duc d'Enghien.

b. 1643, d. 1709. HENRI JULES.

b. 1668, d. 1710. LOUIS III. = Mlle. de Nantes in 1685.

b. 1692, d. 1740. LOUIS HENRI, Prime Minister to Louis XV.

b. 1736, d. 1818. LOUIS JOSEPH = Charlotte G. Eliz. de Rohan Soubise.

b. 1755, d. 1830. LOUIS HENRI JOSEPH = Louise Mar. Ther. Bath. d'Orléans in 1770.

b. 1772, shot 1804. LOUIS A. HENRI, Duc d'Enghien.

Conti line:

b. 1629, d. 1666. ARMAND DE BOURBON, Prince de Conti.

b. 1664, d. 1709. FRANÇOIS LOUIS.

b. 1695, d. 1727. LOUIS ARMAND.

b. 1717, d. 1776. LOUIS FRANÇOIS = Louise Diane d'Orléans in 1749.

b. 1734, d. 1814. LOUIS FRANÇOIS JOSEPH = Fortunée Mar. d'Este.

Descendants of Louis XIV. and Madame de Montespan.

LOUIS XIV. = MME. DE MONTESPAN.

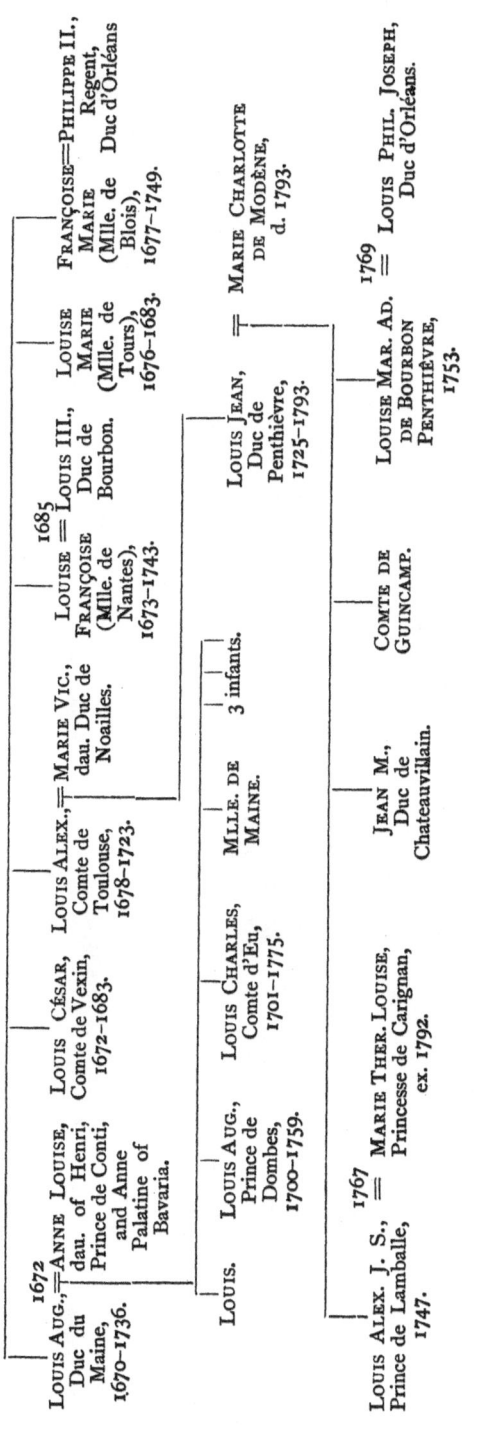

Stewart Descent of Louis XVI.

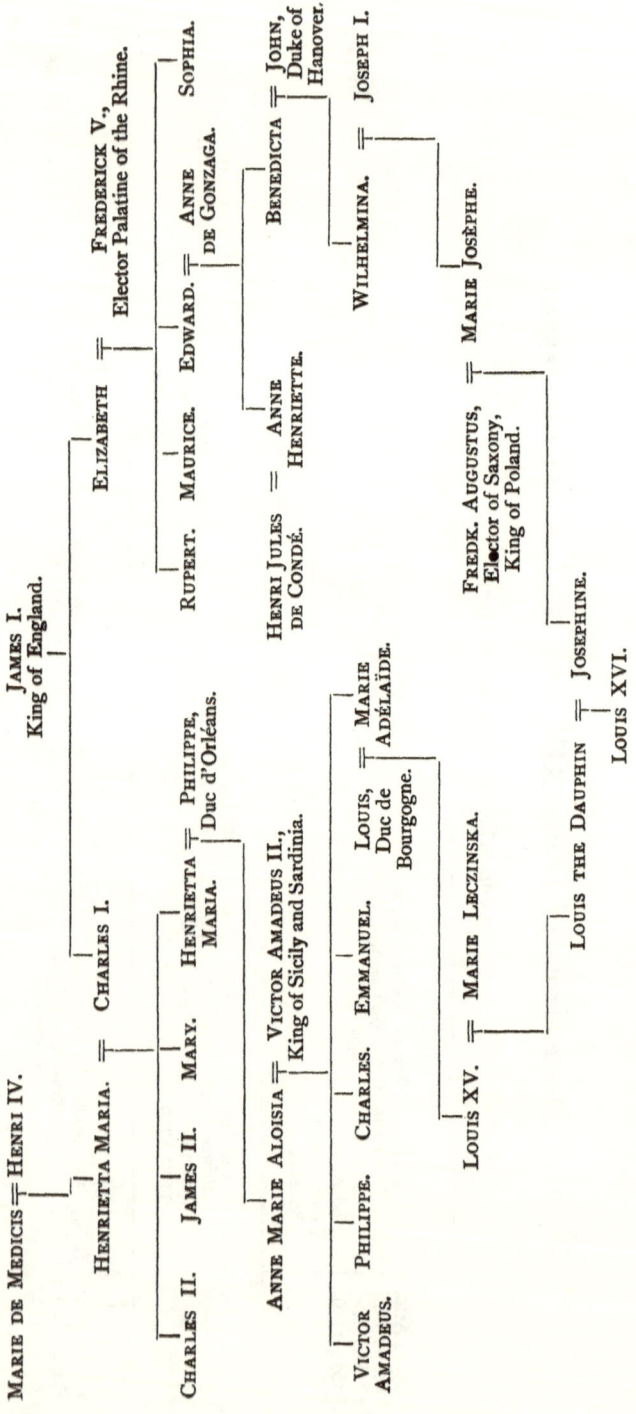

www.ingramcontent.com/pod-product-compliance
Lightning Source LLC
Chambersburg PA
CBHW020835030726
47496CB00001B/241